Praise for The Eastport

"A new voice in Christian fiction, Marilyn K Blair's *The Eastport Series* characters are so real you'll find yourself praying for them and you'll be unable to put down this gripping novel."

Marlene Bagnull
Author, Director of Write His Answer Ministries

"As a born and brought up multigenerational Eastporter, I wondered if this series would be true to life. It didn't disappoint! It was a wonderful reflection of our community."

Tessa Ftorek
Eastport Area Chamber of Commerce, Eastport, Maine

"Marilyn K Blair's characters, with their struggles and vulnerability, grabbed hold of my heart at the start. The mystery of ten-year-old Dev intrigued me, and the struggles he faced had me sometimes holding my breath, and sometimes in tears. Marilyn has an uncanny knack for writing characters and their relationships that get right to the reader's heart . . . I'm certain *A Good Place to Turn Around* will remain on my list of Top Ten All-Time Favorite Reads for a long time, and I eagerly await Ms. Blair's next book."

Kelly F. Barr
Author of Love by Pony Express, Editor,
Former reviewer for Clean Fiction Magazine

"What a lovely new read from Marilyn K Blair! *A Good Place to Turn Around* tells Ben's story–a sheriff from Eastport, Maine, who retires and journeys to Philadelphia . . . Marilyn's gentle narrative is cozy and sweet and just-right for smiling in the evening. I loved it!"

Amy Deardon
Author, Story Coach, Publisher

"A beautiful story full of fun, friendship, family, and faith. A great read for Eastporters and Philadelphians alike!"

Shannon Collins
Librarian, Upper Dublin Public Library

In the Eastport Series

Iris and Mo

A Good Place to Turn Around

Before I Go – Coming in 2025

A Good Place to Turn Around

Marilyn K Blair

KID SPIT PUBLISHING
Life is hard, but God is Good.

All rights reserved. No part of this publication may be reproduced, stored, or transmitted in any form or by any means, electronic, mechanical photocopying, recording, scanning, or otherwise without written permission from the publisher. It is illegal to copy this book, post it to a website, or distribute it by any other means without permission.

This novel is entirely a work of fiction. The names, characters, and incidents portrayed in it are the work of the author's imagination. Any resemblance to actual persons, living or dead, is entirely coincidental.

First Edition
Kid Spit Publishing 2024
Copyright © 2024 by Marilyn K Blair

ISBN: 979-8-9895924-2-5 (Paperback)

ISBN: 979-8-9895924-3-2 (e-book)

Printed in the United States of America

Scripture Translations:

Jeremiah 29:11-14, New International Version, 2011

All remaining scriptures:

English Standard Version, 2016

Dedication

For my father, John the Cop

Acknowledgements

Writing a novel does not happen in a vacuum, so I'd like to take a moment to thank a few folks who inspired, assisted, motivated, and prayed for me as this novel went from idea to book.

To my family, Jim, Holly, Kimberly, and Dylan. You all have kept me grounded, been a source of inspiration, cheered me on, and have supported me in innumerable ways. Love you!

To my father, John Joseph Essaf, to whom this book is dedicated. Among many things, my dad was a Philadelphia police officer, an imaginative storyteller, and a skilled prankster, qualities I instilled in the character, JJ Mongelli. My father passed away before *A Good Place to Turn Around* was completed, but I'm certain he's pleased, and may even wonder why I didn't include some of his tall tales in the book. Thanks, Dad. Miss you.

To my friends, (in alphabetical order), Maura Fisher, Anne Morris, Sue Rossiter, Lynn Stewart, and my "Oldies" family group Sharan McCue, Darlene Pannucci, and Marsha Smith. Your texts, phone calls, conversations, and hysterical memes buoyed me as I sat alone in my office, staring at the computer screen, wondering how to solve the next writing puzzle. Special shout out to Sharan McCue, my awesome roadie, who was the first to suggest Ben should be a sheriff and Anne Morris, who was my first beta reader, publicist, and location scout in Philly. Love you all and thanks.

To my church family at Delaware Valley Christian Church, and the DVCC staff, Scott Fisher, Tammy Calvanese, Bob Alek, and Paul Rule. Thanks for the prayers and wise words. I particularly want to thank Pastor Scott Fisher for ensuring I was on track theologically.

To the Delight in the Lord Women's Bible Study, and the WoW Group. I cherish the prayers you have said on my behalf and the encouragement I receive from you whenever we meet. Thank you.

To Marlene Bagnull's Write His Answer Critique Group and the Lancaster Christian Writers Group. I am honored to be a part of these two organizations who graciously offered critiques and advice in a kind, thoughtful, and helpful way. Thank you, ladies and gents. A special thank you to Marlene who has been a wonderful mentor and model of a Christ-following writer.

To LCW2: Kelly Barr, Megan Ellenberger, and Dawn Haines, my critique partners. Your insights have challenged me and have helped me hone my craft. You are models of support, and I'm blessed to be a part of such a talented group. And thanks, Kelly, for sharing your editing prowess with me. You are amazing at what you do.

To Anita Cellucci, who was the primary inspiration for the character, Angela. Just thinking about you brings a smile to my face. You have such a caring heart. Thank you for sharing it with me.

To Amy Deardon, who helped me navigate through the world of deep POV. Thank you for your guidance and encouragement.

To Pastor Kelly Kopp. Thank you for being a great example of Galatians 6:8-9.

A quick thank you to my newest beta readers, Jennifer Tinubu and Shannon Collins, and the New Holland Coffee Co. for providing a great meeting space for LCW2.

A hearty Downeastern thank you to the wonderful people of Eastport, Maine. Nancy Asante, Matt Boyle, Natasha Dana, Bob

DelPapa, Dale and John Devonshire, Sally Mahoney, Penney Rahm, Karen Raye, and of course, the unofficial mayor of Eastport, Tessa Ftorek, along with many others, welcomed me into the Eastport community with overwhelming kindness. Thank you to William Edward Skinner, the amazing 12-year-old who chatted with me over a spaghetti dinner about what it was like to be a student and a new-arrival in Eastport. Thank you Sally for opening your beautiful home to me, allowing me to experience Old Home Week and the Fourth of July up close and personal. Thank you to Dana Chevalier and Patricia Gardner from the Peavey Library for help with research and the book launch. Thank you all for creating memories with me of "Little Jesus", sunrises, meals at the WaCo Diner, parades, codfish relay races, red snappers, storm cookies, and fireworks. I look forward to creating more memories with you in the future.

I am eternally grateful to Jesus Christ, the author and finisher of my faith. Thank you for continuing to lay out those breadcrumbs.

Finally, I'd like to thank those of you who stopped me on the street, in the grocery store, at Target, in church, and a myriad of other places to share how *Iris and Mo* blessed you. I appreciate you, and I hope you'll be just as blessed with *A Good Place to Turn Around*.

Table of Contents

Dedication .... *ix*

A Glossary of Maine Slang .... *xix*

A Glossary of Philly Slang .... *xxi*

CHAPTER 1   The End *1*

CHAPTER 2   The Beginning *9*

CHAPTER 3   The City of Brotherly Love *23*

CHAPTER 4   Welcome to the Neighborhood *33*

CHAPTER 5   Chase *41*

CHAPTER 6   Mr. Zappone *51*

CHAPTER 7   Dev *57*

CHAPTER 8   Welcome, America *63*

CHAPTER 9   Independence Day *75*

CHAPTER 10   Down the Shore *83*

CHAPTER 11   The Aftermath *97*

CHAPTER 12   Choices *103*

CHAPTER 13   Stakeout *115*

CHAPTER 14   Truth be Told *131*

CHAPTER 15   It Hits the Fan *149*

CHAPTER 16	What's Next	159
CHAPTER 17	Puzzle Pieces	163
CHAPTER 18	Portraits and Poetry	177
CHAPTER 19	Oliver	185
CHAPTER 20	A Lesson in Lobster	193
CHAPTER 21	Kayaks and Eagles	203
CHAPTER 22	The Sunrise Inn	217
CHAPTER 23	Writer to Writer	229
CHAPTER 24	It's a Date	239
CHAPTER 25	Answers	251
CHAPTER 26	Time to Say Goodbye	263
CHAPTER 27	Father Time	273
CHAPTER 28	The Harvest Festival	285
CHAPTER 29	Best Birthday Ever	301
CHAPTER 30	Thanksgiving	315
CHAPTER 31	I am His and He is Mine	329
CHAPTER 32	Tea for Two	347
CHAPTER 33	Merry Christmas	353
CHAPTER 34	Spring Break	369
CHAPTER 35	The Green-Eyed Monster	377

CHAPTER 36	Forgiven	387
CHAPTER 37	Easter	393
CHAPTER 38	Firestorm	405
CHAPTER 39	Up from the Ashes	417
CHAPTER 40	Return to Eastport	423
CHAPTER 41	Summertime	437
CHAPTER 42	Moonlight and Mayhem	447
CHAPTER 43	A Good Place to Turn Around	455
About the Author		469

A Glossary of Maine Slang

A-piece – A measure of distance. How much distance? Hard tellin' not knowin'.

Ayuh – A simple yes

Chupta – What are you up to?

Cunnin' – Cute, mostly reserved for young ones

Dubber – One who is none too smart

Finest kind – The best or excellent

Flatlander – Tourists or anyone not from Maine

From away or PFA (Person From Away) – A non-Mainer, very much like a flatlander. If you don't go back more than three generations of Mainers, you're still from away.

Gawmy – Clumsy

Hard tellin' not knowin' – I have no idea. No, really, that's what it means.

Lobstah – Don't be a lunkhead. Say it out loud and you'll get it. Singular or plural, it's pronounced the same.

Lunkhead – Someone who is dull-witted or foolish, similar to a dubber.

Red snapper – A fire engine red beef and pork hotdog

Right out straight – Busy, busy, busy

Stove up – To damage

Waggy – *Tired*

Wicked – An emphatic "very" or "extremely", as in this is wicked good lobstah, or it's wicked awful weather.

Yessuh – Said in agreement. "He's a good one, yessuh."

A Glossary of Philly Slang

Ah-ite – All right, okay, I'm good. A general expression of positivity or agreement.

Birds – The Philadelphia Eagles football team, aka The Iggles.

Bruh – A modernized version of bro (brother).

Cheesesteak – An iconic meal. A cheesesteak (and yes, it's one word) in its basic form is made of thinly sliced rib-eye beef, melted cheese (could be Whiz, American or provolone), served on a long soft-but-crusty roll. Toppings can include grilled onions, ketchup, sweet and/or hot peppers. Hungry yet?

Down the shore – Going to the beach in southern New Jersey, a must for every Philadelphian in the summer.

Go Birds – Much like "yo", this is an all-purpose phrase. It could mean anything from hello to goodbye to nice talking to you to that cheesesteak was awesome.

Go to market – Go to the grocery store or the corner deli, basically anywhere you can buy groceries. Also known as going to the Acme, (pronounced Ah-ka-me), regardless of the name of the grocery store.

Gravy – Spaghetti sauce with meat. In some neighborhoods of Philly, it's just spaghetti sauce, but we don't talk about that.

Hoagie – You'd better not call it a sub or a hero. A hoagie is a sandwich of cheeses, a little tomato and lettuce, maybe a little onion, some seasonings, and various deli meats you've probably never heard of if you're not from the Philly area, but trust me, it's delicious.

Jawn – Noun. A person, place, or thing of excellence.

Newsy – Nosey. A newsy person can either be a dispenser or a gatherer of neighborhood gossip, usually both.

PA – Pronounced P-A. Pennsylvania's state abbreviation.

Pockabook – Purse

Wawa or *make a Wawa Run* – Wawa is a local convenience store. (Wawa means 'wild goose' in the native Lenni Lenape language.) If you're making a Wawa run, most often it's for coffee.

Wood-er – Water

Wood-er Ice – Water Ice or Italian Ice. If you're unfamiliar with the concept, it's a favorite summer dessert that falls somewhere between a snowcone and gelato.

Yo – A general all-purpose word or phrase. Could mean hello, goodbye, how are you, nice outfit, what are you doing, you're annoying me, don't touch my car, get lost . . .

Youse - The plural of you, the equivalent of *y'all*. In Philly, the proper spelling has an "e" on the end.

"I am with you and will watch over you wherever you go, and I will bring you back to this land. I will not leave you until I have done what I have promised you."

-Genesis 28:15

CHAPTER 1

The End

Sheriff Ben Hudson arrived at the judge's chambers well before the appointed time and paced the hall. He stopped in front of the Missing Persons poster and stared.

My photo should be there. This is a day I've always wanted, but now that it's here–this is the worst. Friday, May thirteenth. Why did we pick Friday the thirteenth?

He checked his phone, then put it back in his pocket. Maybe I'll get called out for an emergency. Or a convict will kidnap me at gunpoint. Something. Anything.

Out of the corner of his eye, he spotted Iris. His heart leapt from his chest to his throat as she approached him with the confidence of a bride-to-be. Her long, auburn curls flowed freely down her back, just the way he liked them. As she caught a glimpse of him, Iris smiled that smile that melted his heart like butter on blueberry pancakes. Beads of sweat formed on his forehead. He swiped them off with his handkerchief.

"Good morning, fiancé. Perfect day for a wedding, don't you think?" Iris kissed him on the cheek.

His insides curled like autumn leaves baking in the sun.

"Iris, we need to talk."

"Is something wrong?"

"We need to talk." Ben took Iris by the hand, led her into a side conference room, and closed the door. The afternoon sun streamed through the upper windows casting an assembly of shadowy witnesses surrounding him. He took a step away from her and raked his fingers through his hair.

Iris asked, "Has something happened? Is everyone all right? Is it your parents?"

"No. No, no. I'm sorry, Iris. Everyone is fine. They're fine, I promise." He took her hand.

"Oh, good." She peered into his eyes. "What is it then? I can tell something's wrong."

God, what do I say? Do I really have to do this? If I do, give me the words.

"Ben?"

He took a breath. "I know you're prepared to go into the judge's chambers and say your marriage vows to me, and I know you'll mean them, and will keep them." He paused, trying not to choke on the words he needed to say. "But I can't have you do that."

"What?" Iris searched his eyes. "Why not?"

"Because Iris, you don't love me." Those words clanged against his heart as harshly as a buoy bell in a summer storm.

Iris stared at him for a moment, then placed her hand on his arm. "We've talked about this. Numerous times. I care for you. I care deeply. And you said you loved me, and you hoped over time I would come to love you in the same way. You said that. That's what I want too. That's why I agreed to marry you."

"I know I said that, but I was wrong." He lifted her hand from his arm. *I wish she wouldn't touch me. This is hard enough.* He took a step away from her.

"But Ben, I am ready to marry you."

"See, that's just it. You're ready to marry me. Not you can't wait to marry me, or you want to marry me, or you're excited to marry me. You're ready. You had to *prepare* yourself to marry me. Even I know that's no way to start a marriage." He turned away from her.

"I don't understand. What made you change your mind like this? Are you angry with me? Did I do something?"

He kept his back to her. "You didn't do a thing. At least, not intentionally."

"What do you mean?" Iris turned him around. "Whatever it is you're trying to say, just say it. Please."

She's right. Spit it out, Ben.

His eyes met Iris's. "What I'm saying is . . . generally, it's not a good idea to marry someone when you're in love with someone else. And Iris, *you* are in love with Frank."

Iris took a step back. "No. I've told you before, Frank and I are just friends." She shook her head. "I haven't been unfaithful to you, Ben. I wouldn't do that to you."

"I know. I know you wouldn't, and I'm not accusing you of anything. I'm just finally facing the truth I've known for months. You'll never feel about me the way I feel about you because you're already in love with someone else."

"No, no. I don't accept that."

"Think about it. When we found Frank passed out in his greenhouse and got him to the hospital, when it looked like he wouldn't make it, I swear, if you could have, you would have taken his place."

Iris closed her eyes.

"I'm sure, if the roles were reversed, if I was the one in the hospital, you would have stayed by my side. You would have made sure I got proper care, and you would have worried, and prayed—"

"Yes, I would have."

"Yes, but I don't believe you would have wanted to switch places with me. That's the difference.

"When you lost your son, Frank stepped up. He knew what to do, and he did it. And he never once asked for credit.

After we got back from Arlington, he stayed with you every night and slept on your couch to make sure you were okay. I wanted to do it, but I couldn't. I stayed the first night, but I knew eventually, I'd be called away on some emergency and have to leave you alone. I couldn't do that to you, so I asked Frank to fill in for me. He agreed, as long as I never told you it was him. He wanted you to think it was me because he knew you'd be more comfortable that way.

"He could have told you, but he didn't. He could have used that time to come between us, but he didn't. All he did was take care of you in ways I couldn't. I hated it was true, but it was. Even a blind man could see it. He loves you, Iris."

"No. I'm not listening to this. You need time to think it over. So why don't we postpone? We weren't supposed to get married until next month anyway. Let's wait and do it then. I will marry you, Ben."

"But I won't marry you, Iris." He paced to the other side of the room. "I'm leaving."

"Leaving? What do you mean, leaving?"

He stayed silent.

"Are you saying you're leaving Eastport?"

"Yes. I'm leaving Eastport. I handed in my resignation this morning, effective immediately. As soon as we're done here, I'm heading to my brother's house to get my feet under me and decide where to go next. I'll be back in a week or so to tie up some loose ends, then I'm hitting the road. I'm gonna take a page out of your book and go exploring." He gave Iris a feeble smile.

"You can't. Eastport is your home. You can't leave here." Iris trembled, clenching and unclenching her hands.

The hands. That's her tell. I know I'm hurting her, but this is for the best. She'll see.

"Fine." Iris patted down her dress. "If you don't want to marry me, fine. I'll go. You don't have to. I'll go. I'll pack my bags and leave tonight. You never have to see me again. I promise."

"You don't want to do that. You said it yourself, Eastport is the first time you've felt like you've belonged, like you're home. I won't take that away from you. You stay here. This is *your* home now. I'm going. I've decided. I've wanted to do this for a long time but couldn't seem to break away. You've given me the push I needed."

"Sounds more like I'm pushing you away from the people you love, the people you care about." Iris's voice broke.

"You're not. I'm not leaving my family and friends."

"No, just me." Iris looked down at the floor and shook her head. She looked back at Ben. "This isn't right. It isn't right."

"*It is.* And if you'll be honest with yourself, you know it is."

Tears filled Iris's eyes. She stared at him for a moment,

then whispered, "I am so sorry."

"It's okay. It's okay." He went to her and held her. "I know you tried. I know it. We can't help how we feel. I love you and that means I want the best for you. Unfortunately, I know that's not me." He stepped back, rested his hands on her shoulders, and looked into her eyes. "Here's what I want you to do. You go find Frank now. Talk to him, tell him how you feel. Tell him the truth. Then I want you to have a good life . . . with him."

"No. No, I won't do it." Iris pulled away from him. "I will not do that to you. I won't."

"You will. And you'll do it with my blessing. You once told me Frank said I was a good man, and he respected me. Well, I never thought I'd ever say this about him, but he's a good man, too. And he's shown me he deserves my respect as well. I wouldn't do this if I didn't believe Frank was worthy of you.

"I'm leaving now. You stay here as long as you want, as long as you need, then you go find Frank. Goodbye, Iris."

He kissed her on the forehead, and left the room, his heart broken once again. He closed the door behind him, exhaled, then left the courthouse, and Eastport.

CHAPTER 2

The Beginning

After saying goodbye to a woman he loved for the second time in his life, Ben sought solace with his younger brother, Oliver. Oliver and his wife, Vanessa, lived in Bangor, Maine, a few hours west of Eastport. Ben made the trip to his brother's house in silence.

Oliver showed him to the guest room, and left Ben to himself, giving him time to process what happened. Ben dropped his duffle bag on the floor and peered out the window. Like confetti after a parade, crocuses and daffodils blossomed along the perimeter of the woods announcing the new life of spring.

"I thought I'd be starting a new life too. This feels anything but new."

Ben stretched out on the bed and stared at the ceiling, his mind empty of thought and his heart full of pain. Twilight crept upon the day and rested on the windowsill as he lay still and sullen. Not one muscle moved in his body and, as the last light dissolved into darkness, he drifted off to an uneasy sleep.

The next morning, he came downstairs and found Oliver in the kitchen, coffee mug in hand, cooking up a breakfast of blueberry pancakes.

"You didn't come down for dinner. Figured you'd be starving. Vanessa's got some women's thing this morning, and she's already gone, so you're stuck with me as chief cook and bottle washer."

Ben gave Oliver a half-hearted smile, then poured himself a cup of coffee. He sat down at the breakfast bar, propped his head on his hand, and watched his brother flip pancakes. Oliver filled a plate for each of them, then took a seat beside Ben.

"Well, big brother, you know what Pop would say."

"Pray on it," the two men said in unison and clinked their coffee mugs together.

"Yeah, I have been praying. That's why I broke up with her." Ben took a long drink of coffee. "I felt God leaning on me to do that a while ago, but . . ."

"It's not always easy to go where we're led."

"Tell me about it." Ben stared into his coffee mug and let out a heavy sigh. "At least I think I'm on the right track now. Just not crazy about the track."

"Well, let's see where it goes. The destination might surprise you." Oliver got up and refreshed his coffee. "Have you thought about what you might like to do next?"

"Thought about it all night. I think I'm gonna sell my house. Go exploring somewhere. What do you think about Greenland?"

"Cold. Icy." Oliver smiled at his brother. "How about this? Instead of selling your home, why don't you keep it and use it as a rental property? It'll give you some additional retirement income and if you ever change your mind about Eastport, you'll have a place to go back to. You can always sell it later." Oliver topped off his brother's mug. "And you have friends all over the country. Why not start your new life by visiting them? That way, you'll have a contact wherever you go."

"Not a bad idea." Ben bobbed his head. "A friendship tour. Wow, brains and good-looking. No wonder people say you take after your big brother."

"Yeah, people always say I take after Jacob." Oliver grinned. Ben flicked a blueberry at him.

That night, Ben retreated to the guest room and got on his knees. He folded his hands and looked toward heaven. "God, I don't know what's going on here. All I know is You don't want me to marry Iris. I'm sure of that, but I can't say I like it. Between You and me . . . it hurts." Ben's throat tightened. He bowed his head. "Can't I have someone to love, and someone who'll love me? Is that too much to ask?" Ben gripped his hands tighter. "Maybe it is. Maybe that's not what you want for me." He sat in silence, taking in the possibility.

"I haven't always understood what You're doing. It hasn't always made sense to me. But, I trust You. You've never let me down. So, I'm gonna trust You again. I'm going to believe You have a plan, just like You say You do. Your plans have always been better than mine, so show me what to do and I'll do it. Thanks. Amen." Ben stood for a moment, then returned to his knees. "And God, please bless Iris."

Ben spent the rest of the night alternating between staring at the ceiling and conversing with God, and at last getting some much-needed sleep. When he woke in the morning, he took Oliver's advice. He made a few phone calls to arrange his next steps and a week later, he was back in Eastport.

Eastport proudly wears the moniker "the easternmost city in the U.S.", though in reality it is more small town than urban mecca. The Downeasters who live there are a sturdy, loyal bunch who look after one another and their city with staunch devotion.

Ben's Eastport roots ran deep. As a nine-year-old boy, he visited the city for the first time with his family and they continued to return each summer. At twenty-nine, he took up residence there, serving faithfully as sheriff for more than thirty years. Eastport is where he first fell in love, where he had his heart broken, and where he repeated the process decades later.

As he approached the city limits, Ben's stomach tightened. "All right, here's the plan. In and out. Take care of business with the realtor, pack up, then leave for the friendship tour. No need to see anyone. Keep to yourself and this will all be over soon."

Before he left Oliver's, Ben hired a realtor in Eastport to be his property manager. He stopped by her office to sign the necessary paperwork, then set off for his house.

Has it only been a week since I left here for my wedding? Ben stood in his living room, duffle in hand. The place seemed unfamiliar. If I didn't know better, I'd say this was another man's house. Someone with purpose who knows what he's doing . . . and where he's going.

"Time to move on, Hudson. Let's get to it. Pack the essentials, store or trash the rest. Figure out what you really need later."

For the next several days Ben worked from early morning to well past midnight. By the end of the week, he sorted, boxed, and stored the last thirty-two years of his life. There remained but one last task to complete.

Earlier in the week, Ben let the police chief know he

would be in town. The chief reminded him of the paperwork he needed to complete for his retirement. Ben agreed to take care of it on Friday. Friday had arrived. He showered, shaved, then stared at himself in the mirror.

"Has there ever been a day when I didn't want to go to the station? Today's a first."

He had a slow breakfast then meandered his way to the station house.

"Bob Rhodes, is that you?" Ben asked, seeing a former colleague standing in the lobby as he entered the station.

A large man with a mammoth smile and aggressive eyebrows extended his hand. "Ben! Good to see you. I hear you're finally packing it in."

"Thought it was time, Bob. What are you doing in—"

"Well, look what the cat dragged in. How you doin', Ben?" Another familiar face walked out of the hallway.

"Hey, Larry. Haven't seen you since you retired. Thought you moved down south," Ben said.

"Yeah, we did. We're up here for a visit."

"Family doing well? How's Marjorie?" Ben shook Larry's hand.

"She's great. She's loving the warmer weather."

"Sheriff Hudson?" A voice called from the reception counter.

"Hi there, Betty. How are you?" Ben smiled at the older

woman behind the counter as he walked toward her. "You're looking as gorgeous as ever."

"Oh, go on with you, flatterer." Betty blushed. "We've missed you round here. You doin' all right? You look a little waggy."

"I'm hanging in there. Sleep hasn't been a top priority lately. I've been getting ready for a road trip."

"Hope it won't be a long one and you'll get yourself back here soon. You can't leave me here alone with these lunkheads." Betty handed Ben a folder. "I need your signature on these, and the chief is waiting for you. You can go on back whenever you're ready." Ben took the folder and Betty took his hand. She whispered, "I'm sorry, Ben. You're in my prayers."

Ben smiled and patted her hand. "I can always count on you for that. Thanks, Betty."

Ben turned to his friends. "Good seeing you guys. I gotta go meet with the chief. If you can hang out for a few minutes, we can grab a cup of coffee when I'm done."

"That'd be fine, Ben. We'll wait for you," Larry said, then he winked at Bob.

Ben walked into the chief's office and found him deep in thought, surrounded by stacks of paper. "Afternoon, Chief." Ben extended his hand.

"Sheriff Hudson." The chief looked up. "Good to see you. Have a seat." The chief shook Ben's hand, then gestured to the chair in front of his desk. "Would you like some coffee or tea?"

"No, I'm good. Thanks."

"How are things going, Ben?"

"They're going. I've got a plan, so that's something. Betty gave me the paperwork, so I'll get it signed, then I'm good to go."

"About that, there may be a delay in your departure."

Ben sat up straight. "What do you mean? I thought everything was in order." The chief looked down at his paperwork. "Chief, what's going on?"

"I know you didn't want to make a big thing out of this, but we couldn't let over thirty years of service end without a proper thank you. A luncheon's been planned for you over at the Sunrise Inn. I promise, it's not a huge deal, but the guys wanted to give you a good send-off. It'll mean a lot to them."

Ben sat back. "That's why Bob and Larry are here."

The chief nodded.

Ben shifted in his chair and stared at the chief. "At the inn?"

"Yes. Emma's taken care of everything."

"Well, if Emma's involved, I guess I don't have a choice. Can't let her down."

The chief smiled. "Wouldn't be advisable. Let's go, retiree."

Ben followed the chief out of the office, then they, along

with Larry and Bob, made their way to the Sunrise Inn.

The little woman behind the front desk squinted her eyes at Ben as he entered the lobby. "Sheriff."

Ben narrowed his gaze. "Mary."

"Afternoon, Chief." Mary turned her attention to Chief Reynolds and gave him a semblance of a smile.

"Afternoon, Mary."

"She's comin' now." Mary went back to squinting her eyes at Ben.

"Ben!" Emma smiled as she came around the corner. "It's good to see you." She wrapped him in a warm embrace.

"Good to be here, Em, even if it's just for a little while."

"Good afternoon, Chief Reynolds." Emma smiled at the chief and shook his hand.

"Afternoon, Emma. Thanks for pulling this together."

"My pleasure. Well, not really, but you know what I mean."

The chief nodded.

"Wish I could change your mind, Ben, but we'll put that thought on hold for now. Come with me." Emma took Ben's arm and ushered him into the banquet room.

Ben's fellow officers filled the room, some current, and

some recently retired, as well as a few city officials, shopkeepers, and a reporter from The Quoddy Tides. Much laughter followed at Ben's expense as his comrades roasted him with their favorite Ben stories and presented him gifts of a golden walker, compression socks, and hemorrhoid cream.

Margaret Robinson, the City Council president, arrived as the last gift had been offered. She quieted the room, and once she had everyone's attention, she called Ben to stand beside her.

"Sheriff Hudson, the city of Eastport thanks you for your years of dedicated service. You have been the embodiment of what it means to be a peace officer, fulfilling your duties with integrity, trustworthiness, and care. Your work with the youth of our city is notable, and in recognition of your support, and encouragement as demonstrated by the numerous games of basketball played with them, your work as a coach for them, and as a mentor to them, I am pleased to represent the City of Eastport, the City Council, and the Eastport Public School District, in proclaiming the gymnasium in Eastport High School will now and forever be known as the 'Benjamin Hudson Gymnasium'. This plaque will be installed today to mark the occasion. Thank you, Sheriff Hudson, and may God bless you."

A standing ovation followed the Council president's pronouncement. The chief called the officers to attention. Ben clenched his jaw, barricading the emotions that gripped his heart. He saluted the chief, turned to the council president, shook her hand, and continued to shake hands and thank friends as he left the room. Upon exiting the banquet hall, he went to the lobby in search of Emma.

The Sunrise Inn had been Ben's second home since the day he arrived in Eastport. Harry and Emma, the innkeepers, became his closest friends. Now, as he walked through the lobby, memories swept through his mind like an unexpected summer storm on the bay.

Ben smiled at the portrait perched above the fireplace. "Hey, Harry." He tapped the back of the chairs near the hearth. *You and me sitting right here, swapping stories while we played chess. Feels like yesterday.* He turned toward the curved staircase on the other side of the room. *There, watching the kids line up to have their chance to sit on Santa's knee. How many years did I do 'ho-ho-ho' duty?*

Ben moved toward one of the tables and touched the petals of the hydrangea blossoms decorating it. *Emma loves these hydrangeas. Still picks on herself for not having flower arranging skills. She's a lot better than she thinks. I'm gonna miss her.* He swallowed hard. He turned toward the front desk. Mary eyed him.

"Sheriff." Mary sneered her usual greeting.

"Mary." Ben sneered in return.

"Office."

Ben kept a squinted eye on Mary as he walked around

the front desk toward Emma's office.

Emma was a pleasant woman who overflowed with the gift of hospitality. Her ever-present smile never dimmed as she took care of her guests as if they were family. Emma eschewed vanity, but she made a promise to herself she would not permit her chestnut-colored hair to turn gray. "Salt and pepper are for the dining table, not your head," she would say. She wore her well-coiffed locks in a low braided bun during working hours, but when off the clock, she allowed her tresses to roam free. Never one to wear much make-up, she chose to wear just a touch of lipstick and mascara to highlight her winsome features.

"Well, Emma, looks like I'll be hitting the road in the morning," Ben said as he poked his head around her door.

"So, you're really going?" Emma stood and came out from behind her desk.

"I'm really going." Ben forced a smile as he entered her office.

"I find that hard to believe, Ben. I've known you forever it seems. Eastport's not going to be the same without you."

"You know, I think you and Harry were the first friends I made here. I don't remember if I ever thanked you for that. You both welcomed me in, made me feel like family." Ben picked up a picture of Emma's husband from her desk. "I miss him. He was a good man, the finest kind."

"He was. And no need for thanks. You've been a great friend, especially after Harry . . ." Emma took the picture from Ben, smiled at it, and placed it back on her desk. "I'm gonna miss you, and it costs me nothing to say so." Emma hesitated for a moment. "Ben, I'm sorry things didn't work out between you—"

"Emma, it's okay. It wasn't meant to be. I see that. And I want you to know, there are no hard feelings between me and Iris. I know you two are best friends, and I don't want you to think you have to choose sides in this. She's a good woman. She just wasn't the right woman for me, or at least, I wasn't the right man for her." That's a familiar feeling.

"Ben Hudson, I'm proud to know you. I'm gonna miss that face of yours popping in here." She shed a tear and took her old friend's hand. "Don't be a stranger, all right? Promise me this, when the time's right, you'll come back. And if you ever need anything, even just to talk, you'll call me."

"I'll do that. I promise." Ben gave Emma a hug. "I love you, Em."

"Love you too." Emma patted him on the back. "Let me know when you're settled, please. Otherwise, I'll worry."

"Well, we can't have that. I'll call. I promise."

"Okay. You take care of yourself. Now, get outta here before I make a scene." She smiled through her tears as Ben gave her one more squeeze. He left before she could see the tears in his own eyes.

The following morning, Ben brought the last of his things to his storage unit and placed them inside. He pulled down the rolling door and locked it into place, wishing he could lock up the pain in his heart as easily.

He climbed into his truck and made his way out of Eastport. When he came to the city limits of his adopted home, he pulled over and got out for one last look.

"Eastport, I'm sorry to leave you, but it's time. Thanks. For everything." He returned to the driver's seat. "On to Philadelphia."

CHAPTER 3

The City of Brotherly Love

"Ben Hudson, you son-of-a-gun! Good to see you! 'Bout time you made it down here. What's it been since we've seen each other in person, ten years?" JJ asked as he tapped Ben's truck.

Ben shook JJ's hand, then patted his friend on the back as they hugged. "Sounds about right. How you doin', JJ?"

"Never had a bad day in my life."

Ben and JJ's friendship went back almost forty years, ever since their days as roommates at the University of Massachusetts. They were enrolled in the Criminal Justice program, and spent many hours studying, playing sports, and experiencing life together. Following graduation, Ben returned to his roots in Boston, and JJ made the trek back to his hometown of Philadelphia, but the two friends kept in touch with occasional visits and frequent phone calls.

JJ picked up Ben's duffle bag and walked toward his house. An affable man, JJ stood about six feet tall, with a ring of grey hair around a smooth topped head. A pair of light brown eyes that disappeared when he smiled, and a mischievous grin were as disarming as they were playful.

"Leg giving you trouble?" Ben asked, noticing JJ's limp was more pronounced than the last time they'd met.

"You mean the old war wound? It's fine. I only feel it when it 'comes on to rain', to quote John Wayne." JJ laughed and opened his front door. "Angie's dying to see you. She's been cleaning and cooking all week. Maybe now you're here, she'll stop sending me on errands."

JJ and his family lived in a typical row home in South Philadelphia. Two stairs led from the sidewalk to a small stoop and a solid oak door entrance. Like an aging dragon, a green metal awning hung over the picture window to the right of the door. A café table and three matching chairs claimed the sidewalk space underneath.

The two men went inside, and JJ yelled toward the kitchen. "Ang, looks like the trashmen left some stuff behind today. I picked it up though."

"Ugh, again? Well, thanks, honey," Angela said from behind the kitchen wall. "Keep an eye out for Ben, will you?"

Ben popped his head around the corner of the kitchen. "Wish that husband of yours would stop referring to me as trash."

"Ben! Oh my, you are a sight for sore eyes. JJ, what's the matter with you? Never mind, that list is way too long." Angela set aside the vegetables she'd been chopping, wiped her hands on her apron, and went to Ben. Two tiny terriers circled her in a frenzy of yapping and jumping. Ignoring them, she stood on her tiptoes to give Ben a warm Italian hug. "You hungry? Thirsty? What can I get you?"

"I don't need a thing, Angela. I'm good, thanks." Ben said. "It's great to see you."

"Well, come in, come in. Whitey, Harry, get outta here." Angela scooted the terriers out of the way with her foot. She took Ben's arm and walked him toward the living room. "Chase! Chase! Where is that boy, JJ? Go find him please and make him come and get Ben's bags."

"Yes, ma'am. Be right back, Ben. Don't steal my wife while I'm gone," JJ said with a wink and a smile.

Angela was a vibrant woman and though she stood just five feet, one inch tall, JJ swore he'd be worried about the attacker if one tried to take her on. An attractive woman, she decided years ago to allow her hair to age with her. She wore her snow-white locks in a bob which framed her Rubenesque face and drew attention to her ebony eyes.

"Oh, ignore him," Angela said, with a wave of her hand toward her husband. "Now, have a seat and I'll be right back." She escorted Ben to the couch, then returned to the kitchen.

The inside of the Mongelli home reflected the woman of the house. Light and airy living and dining rooms were joined as one, and a separate kitchen no one dared enter without permission secured itself at the back of the house.

"You must be starving after that long drive. Have a bite." Angela set a plate of Entenmann's crumb cake and a small bowl of fruit on the coffee table in front of Ben. "And here's a glass of iced tea for you. You like lemon, right?"

"I do. Nice of you to remember." Ben accepted the drink. "So, how have you been? How are the kids?" He popped a grape into his mouth.

Angela took a seat on the chair across from Ben. "Kids are great. Theresa's expecting our first grandchild. Can you believe it? JJ's going to be a grandfather!"

"Amazing."

"Vincent's finishing his grad program at Temple. And Chase, well, Chase is Chase. His father named him right. He's into every sport under the sun. And speak of the devil." Angela stood up as JJ and Chase returned. "Where have you been, young man? You're a mess."

Angela put her hands on her hips and surveyed her disheveled son. Chase's rumpled baseball shirt was caked in dirt and pulled out on one side. He looked as if he'd slid into home plate face first, taking half the infield with him. A swipe of mud across his freckled forehead kept company with his brown hair matted down with sweat. Tall for a boy of ten, when standing next to his mother, the two could almost see eye-to-eye.

"Dev and I were playin' ball." Chase added to the dirt on his brow as he wiped his hand across it.

"Say hi to Ben," Angela prompted her son.

"Hi." Chase gave Ben a quick glance.

"You probably don't remember me. Last time I saw you was when your parents came to Maine for a visit. You were only about three or four years old. You've grown a bit since then." Ben gave Chase a smile.

"Just turned eleven, and as fast as he grows, I can't seem to keep him in pants," Angela said.

"Ma-a!" Chase made a face at his mother.

"Oh, go wash up, and change your clothes." Angela scooted Chase up the stairs. "And don't just let the water run. Use soap!"

"JJ, looks like you've got your hands full," Ben said.

"You speak the truth. Chase is a good kid, though." JJ took a seat. "Lots of energy, so I'm glad he likes sports. He's a bit of a prankster, too."

"Wonder where he got that from?" Ben eyed his friend.

The dining room curtains swayed, caressed by a light spring breeze as Ben, JJ, and Angela spent the next few hours catching up with each other over dinner. Angela kept the conversation going with a myriad of questions, wanting specifics about Ben's life since their last reunion.

While the homemade lasagna held Chase's attention at first, the reminiscing about his parents' and Ben's younger days had him drawing stick figures on his plate with tomato sauce and bread.

"Ma, can I go hang out with Dev?"

Angela eyed her son. "Good conversation not enough for you?"

"Please . . ."

"Oh, all right, go, but be back in an hour. Don't make me send your father out to look for you." Chase jumped up from the table, kissed his mother on the cheek, then ran out the door.

"Kids." Angela said. "Why don't you two go out front while I clean up. I'll join you in a few minutes."

JJ and Ben helped Angela clear the table, then went out front.

"Well, you survived A.I.," JJ said, sitting down in one of the café chairs.

"A.I.?"

"Angela's Inquisition. You know, I think my wife missed her career calling. She should have been a reporter or a lawyer, or maybe she's really an international spy." JJ peered in Angela's direction.

"I heard that," Angela yelled from the dining room.

"See what I mean?" JJ laughed and gave a nod toward his wife.

"Dessert?" Angela asked the men as she came out the front door with two cups of coffee.

"None for me, thanks," Ben said.

"Me, neither, but thanks, honey," JJ stood and kissed his wife on the cheek. "Dinner was great."

"Oh, trying to make up for calling me a spy, are you, hmmm?" Angela raised one eyebrow. JJ flashed his best smile. "You're impossible." She stood on her toes, gave him a quick kiss, and went back inside.

A few blocks away, the traffic on Broad Street provided a low hum and bass beat to the activity outside. Neighborhood children squeezed in their last bit of playtime at the park across from JJ's home, and the streetlights flickered on as the sun tucked itself in below the cityscape for the night.

"I think this is my favorite time of day." JJ let out a relaxed sigh. "So, you miss being a cop yet?"

"It's only been a few weeks," Ben said.

"And?"

Ben gave a small laugh. "Yeah, I miss it. I don't miss breaking up bar fights or the paperwork, but I miss being around the guys in the station and," Ben looked at the children, "I miss the kids."

"I heard they named a basketball court after you."

"Word travels fast. And it was a *gymnasium*."

"A whole gym, huh? Well, 'scuse me." JJ smiled. "I always thought you'd stay in Eastport and run for mayor or something. Everybody loves you there."

"Almost everybody." Wish that knot in my stomach would go away whenever somebody mentions Eastport.

JJ paused for a few moments. "Sorry things didn't work out with your girl. Seriously, you doin' okay?"

"I'll admit it, it stinks. I'd like to be mad at Iris, might make things easier, but I can't be. She's a heck of a woman. And she was honest with me, right from the start. The first time I told her I loved her, she admitted she didn't love me. I just didn't want to hear it. I hoped things would change, and she'd come around. Seemed she wanted too, but . . ."

Ben caught sight of the first evening stars. A memory of the times he and Iris watched the moon rise over the bay pushed its way from his heart to his throat. With a cough, he forced the memory aside. "Iris tried to talk me into postponing, but I knew that wouldn't change a thing. So, I let her go. It was the right thing to do for her. And for me."

"I'm sorry you had to go through all that, buddy. Wish it would have worked out for you."

"Me, too. But hey, if it did, I wouldn't be here talking to you, so that's something." Ben patted his friend on the back.

"Well, I might not be a beautiful redhead, but I am charming."

"If you do say so yourself."

JJ grinned. "So how long you thinking of sticking around?"

"Not sure. I thought I should give it at least six months before moving on. I appreciate you putting me up while I look for a place."

"Happy to have you, and I have news on that front. I've been talking to the guys at work and Maria, well, she's not a guy, but her brother, Lou, has a row home he's looking to rent. It's small, two bedrooms, but it's only a couple of blocks from here, so we'd be neighbors. If you're interested, I'll get in touch with him and maybe we can take a walk over there tomorrow after church."

"Sounds perfect. Thanks, Jay."

JJ raised his cup of coffee to Ben. "To new beginnings."

"To new beginnings."

CHAPTER 4

Welcome to the Neighborhood

The morning sun peeked through the cotton ball clouds and made pop art shadows on the sidewalk as Ben and JJ walked to meet Lou at the rental house the next day.

Lou was there waiting for them, along with two of his young sons. A plump little man, Lou barely reached Ben's shoulders.

"Nice to meet ya, Ben." Lou extended his hand. "Don't mind the kids. The wife needed to run some errands, so I said I'd take 'em." He turned to the boys who were smacking each other on the head. "Yo! Youse guys knock it off. Go play on the playground while I talk here. Go!"

The boys scurried off to the playground across the street, pushing and shoving each other along the way. Lou turned his attention back to Ben and swept his arm toward the row home. "This is a great little house. We just did some renos to it. Come on in. Have a look." Lou unlocked the front door, then allowed Ben and JJ to enter first.

In Maine, Ben enjoyed a small, rustic home. This home, while small as well, had a more modern feel and Ben would come to call it "efficient". A trinity style home, common in Philadelphia, its makeup comprised three levels: a finished room and storage area on the street level, public rooms on the second level, and private rooms on the third.

Ben stepped into a small foyer which opened into the family room. In the back of the room, stairs led to the second floor. He took the stairs and reaching the landing, he made a right turn into the living room.

Not too interesting, just a rectangular box, but I like the hardwood floors, and this huge picture window is great. The sunshine warmed his face as he looked out the window to the park across the street.

"Looks like those boys are giving Lou a run for his money." Ben laughed as he watched Lou's sons fencing with sticks while standing on top of a bench as Lou pointed at them to get down.

"Hey, JJ, is that a community garden in the park?"

JJ came beside Ben and looked out the picture window. "Oh, yeah. It's great. We had a plot there when Vincent and Theresa were growing up. We planted tomatoes, of course, and onions, some peppers, and Angela loved growing fresh herbs."

Without warning, Ben was transported back to Eastport, and Iris's salsa garden, reliving the hours they spent planting, weeding, and harvesting together.

"They loved it—growing their own vegetables," JJ said. "Chase wasn't into it though, not enough action, so we gave it up . . . Ben?"

"Sorry, what'd you say?"

"You okay there, pal? You seem a little distracted. Don't like the house?"

"No, no, it's great. Let's check out the rest." Get it together, Hudson.

Ben and JJ moved toward the back of the house. A small dining room was on their right, and a set of stairs on their left led to the third floor. Ben climbed the stairs and inspected the large master bedroom and bath, a smaller second bedroom and a hall bath. Coming back downstairs to the second floor, he went into the galley kitchen. The kitchen had all new stainless-steel appliances and an exit to a small deck.

"So, what do you think?" Lou asked when Ben finished exploring the house.

"Reminds me of my growing-up years in Boston. Lou, I'll take it. I'd like a six-month lease, if that's possible, and then we'll see after that. If Philly and I get along, you may have a long-term lease coming."

"Sounds great!" Lou clapped his hands together. "Since

tomorrow's Memorial Day, I'll get everything drawn up today. Once you sign and give me your security deposit, you can move in whenever you're ready."

Lou brought the paperwork by JJ's that afternoon, and on Tuesday morning, Ben arranged to have his things moved in the following Monday. Angela convinced Ben to allow her to go to the house the day before the move to clean, even though Lou promised the home would be spotless.

"Ben, no one cleans like a mother cleans. I will do it, then you'll know it's done right and more importantly, I'll know it's done right," Angela said. So, Ben conceded, and Angela scrubbed, mopped, and vacuumed.

On moving day, JJ, by command of Angela, took off work so he could be of assistance. Ben tried to convince her it wasn't necessary, but Angela wouldn't hear of it.

While they waited for the movers, Ben went to the kitchen for a drink. He found a bottle of wine, a vase full of flowers, and a box of Entenmann's coffee cake on the counter. JJ came in behind him and leaned over his shoulder. Spying the display, he said, "She does this for everyone. It's like a ritual. Welcome to the family, bud." He patted Ben's shoulder. "It's official. You have been Entemized."

Ben opened the refrigerator and found it full of individual meals, stacked and labeled with reheating instructions. "Angela?" Ben pointed to the meals.

"Angela. What kind of Italian mother would she be if she let you starve? She said these should last you a week."

"I think a month is more like it." Ben closed the refrigerator door. "You have an amazing wife."

"That I do."

The movers arrived late morning, delayed traffic detours in the city. As they emptied the truck, neighbors came by to welcome Ben. His next-door neighbor to the right, Mrs. Brasko, brought Ben a tray of assorted cheeses from DiBruno Brothers, a fresh loaf of Italian bread, and a bottle of homemade seasoned olive oil.

"This is a little something to get you started. Welcome to the neighborhood."

"Thanks, Mrs. Brasko. This is very kind of you."

"Now, where can I help?"

"Oh, that's not–"

"Gia! Good to see you, my friend," Angela said as she came downstairs.

"Angela! Good morning." Mrs. Brasko patted Ben on the arm. "I'll give Angela a hand." She walked to the kitchen with Angela and started emptying boxes. Ben could hear the two women discussing the condition of his cookware, and their resolution to take care of that "problem". He smiled, then went outside to check on the progress of the movers.

"Good morning. I'm Giovanni Zappone," an elderly man said as he approached Ben. "We're neighbors. I'm here on your left."

"Nice to meet you, Mr. Zappone. I'm Ben Hudson." Ben shook his hand.

"I'd offer to help, but I think my days of moving furniture are behind me."

"That's okay. I've got plenty of help today. I appreciate the sentiment though."

"I know you're busy, but I wanted to say hello. I promise to stop by later when things settle down and we can get to know each other then."

"I look forward to it."

"By any chance, do you play chess or dominoes?"

"Not much of a domino player, but I do like a good game of chess."

"Well then, we should get along fine. I'll let you get back to your work. Welcome home."

Welcome *home*? Is this my home now?

Other neighbors, the Hernikos, the Amicones, and the Trigglias, stopped by throughout the day, all either staying to help with unpacking, or bringing a meal, or inviting Ben over for dinner.

By the end of Monday evening, not only were Ben's furniture and belongings moved in, but the women of his neighborhood made sure he was unpacked, his bed made, and his refrigerator stocked.

I'm not sure if I should feel grateful or overwhelmed. Maybe both. Ben crawled into his crisply made bed and sighed. *Nah, grateful it is.*

CHAPTER 5

Chase

When he lived in Eastport, Ben made it a habit to take a brisk walk every morning. In the early days, he'd stop by the Sunrise Inn to have breakfast with Emma and Harry. Later, it was just he and Emma. On this, his first day on his own in Philadelphia, he thought it was time to establish a similar routine. He laced up his sneakers, put in his ear buds, and headed out the door.

The Italian Market is a few blocks away. I should put on the *Rocky* theme song and run my way down the street. Maybe someone will toss me an orange. Ben laughed at himself as he dodged a bicyclist. Forget that. I think my time would be better spent getting to know my new neighborhood.

Capitolo Playground, an extensive park, spanned the entire city block across from Ben's home on Federal Street. Enclosed by a chain link fence, the park was only accessible by an entrance on Ninth Street. Ben crossed Federal Street, then made a right on Ninth and entered the park.

Murals representing community members adorned the rec center to his left. To his right a painted river on the rubber safety surface twisted and turned its way through various playground equipment.

Nicely laid out. Looks like they've got the right safety considerations.

Moving past the playground, and what he thought could be a junior soccer field, he came to the community garden. *Reminds me of Eastport.* His stomach did a flip. He turned his back on the gardens and looked across the park.

Ah, baseball. Wonder if that's where Chase picked up all that dirt. He took an easy jog diagonally across the park toward the rec center. As he came around to the rear of the building, he smiled.

Look at that—two basketball courts. Looks well maintained. Maybe I could get in some pick-up games. Wonder if they have a league or need any volunteer coaches. I'll have to check that out.

Ben made his way out of the park onto Ninth Street again and smack dab into the middle of Philly's infamous cheesesteak rivalry JJ told him had been going on for decades: Geno's versus Pat's. Overhead, each restaurant proclaimed their superiority in large volumes of garish neon.

"That's gotta be enough neon to be visible from outer space!" Ben said.

He continued down the block, watching as one by one, businesses woke from their evening slumber, rolling up their gates like so many eyes opening to greet the day. After walking several more blocks, he stopped inside a café to pick up breakfast, then headed home. Just as he turned the last corner, Ben caught the sight of a single figure in the park near the rec center, a child or a teenager, maybe. That's odd for this time of day. A bicyclist blew by him. Ben looked again in the park, but the figure had disappeared.

That afternoon, JJ called and invited Ben to dinner. "You gotta come, Ben. Angie insists."

"That's right, Ben." Angela yelled in the background. "Dinner's at six and you'd better be here."

"Yes, ma'am. I'll be there. Did she hear that, Jay?"

"I heard you. See you at six," Angela said.

When he arrived at JJ's house, Angela greeted him. "So, come in and tell me all about it." She put her arm through his and walked him inside. "How do you like the house? Is it too hot? Too cold? Did you sleep well? How are your neighbors? I met a few, they didn't seem too *newsy*. Do you need anything?

Do you have enough to eat? I forget, do you have air conditioning or a whole house fan? You'll need one or the other come July."

"Angela, give the man a chance." JJ said. "Follow me." He put his hand on Ben's shoulder and shuttled him out the front door to the café chairs. "Sorry about that. You know Angie, she needs to be sure everyone and everything is fine."

"Oh, I don't mind. Angie's great."

"Thank you, Ben," Angela yelled from the dining room. A moment later, she joined the men on the porch with two glasses of iced tea in her hands. "Dinner will be ready in about ten minutes. Don't talk about anything important while I'm gone," she said with a wink.

Chase came running over from the neighborhood park.

"Go and wash up, young man," Angela said.

Chase panted, then wiped his brow. "Ma, can Dev stay for dinner?"

"Chase, we have company. Ben's here."

"Ben's not company. He's *Ben*." Chase made a face.

Ben laughed. Glad he's comfortable around me now.

"Fine, Dev can come." Angela narrowed her eyes at her son. "Good thing I like that kid."

"Dev!" Chase rushed back to the park.

Angela stiffened at the sound of Chase's voice. "That boy is not good for my blood pressure." She brushed her hair back from her forehead. "Better go put more gravy on." She went back into the house to perform her version of "loaves and fishes".

"Gravy? I thought you said Angela was making spaghetti for dinner."

"She is. She's making pasta with gravy."

"You have gravy with spaghetti? Okay, I'm willing to give it a shot, but I have to say . . . that's a little different."

JJ laughed. "I'm sorry, Ben. I keep forgetting you're not from around here. *Gravy* is what we call red sauce, that's tomato sauce with meat. And just so you know, pasta is any type of macaroni: spaghetti, linguini, ziti, fettuccine. It's all pasta."

"I see. So, gravy goes on pasta. Then what do you put on your mashed potatoes?"

"That would be . . . gravy." JJ smiled. "*Brown* gravy."

Ten minutes later, Angela called everyone into dinner. As usual, Chase was nowhere to be found.

"JJ?" Angela eyed her husband.

"I'm on it." JJ headed toward the park while Angela and Ben went inside and chatted in the living room. Moments later, JJ returned with Chase and his friend, Dev.

"Hi, Mrs. Mongelli. Thanks for letting me stay for dinner," Dev said as he entered the house.

Dev was a few months younger than Chase, and four inches shorter with a much slighter build. A shock of sandy blonde hair reached below his ears and windswept bangs tumbled over his sapphire eyes.

"Glad to have you, Dev. You know you're welcome anytime. You boys go upstairs and get washed up now. And use soap!"

Dev smiled at Angela and ran up the stairs behind Chase.

Angela leaned toward Ben and said, "There are times when Dev reminds me of one of those street urchins in a Dickens' novel."

A few minutes later, the boys returned, hands and faces scrubbed clean, and ready for dinner. JJ gestured to Ben. "Dev, this is Ben, my college roommate. He just moved into the neighborhood."

"Nice to meet you, sir," Dev said softly.

"He's not a *sir*, he's *Ben*." Chase elbowed Dev.

"Chase Mongelli, you could learn some manners from Dev," Angela said.

"Well, Chase is right." Ben grinned. "Dev, you can call me Ben. It's nice to meet you." He held out his hand. Dev took it and gave Ben a solid handshake. "So, are you and Chase in the same grade?"

"Yeah! Dev's my *jawn*! I've known him since kindergarten," Chase said.

"John? I'm sorry, I thought your name was Dev."

"His name *is* Dev," Chase said, giving Ben a look.

"But you just called him John." Ben turned to Dev. "Is that your last name?"

The boys laughed.

"Let me explain, Ben," JJ said. "*Jawn*, J-A-W-N, noun, referring to a person, a place, or a thing. A term used, by the younger set, to refer to something special, or preferred, or in Dev's case, exceptional." JJ gave a smile and a nod toward Dev.

"I see. So, *Dev* is your name, but you're Chase's *jawn*?"

"I guess so," Dev said with a little nod. "And he's mine." Dev smiled at his friend, then the two shared a special handshake involving slaps, claps, and pats on the back.

These two are a riot.

"We do everything together. We're not in the same class this year, but we're hopin' to be in some next year. Middle school! Wha-what!" Chase said.

"Okay, dinner's ready. Let's go to the dining room," Angela said, scooting the boys along.

"I know Chase loves baseball. You into sports, Dev?" Ben asked, as everyone sat at the table.

"I like basketball and track." Dev took a seat near Chase.

"Well, I'm not much good at track anymore, but if you boys are ever up for a pickup game of basketball, I'm in," Ben said.

"You can still play?" Chase gave Ben a skeptical look.

"Yes, I can still play. I'm not decrepit yet." Ben feigned

insult.

"*Yet.*" Chase laughed and elbowed Dev.

"Oh, I see how it is. So, you think you can take this old man, do you? How 'bout we go for a little game of one-on-one some afternoon?"

Chase narrowed his eyes at Ben. "You're on." He turned toward his mother holding his stomach, "Ma, I'm starving. Can we eat now?"

Angela took a deep breath. "Grace first. Ben, would you do the honors tonight?"

"Absolutely. Let's pray." He bowed his head. "Lord, we thank you for this terrific smelling . . . *pasta and gravy* and we thank you for the hands that prepared it. I thank you for bringing me to this city and for all those who have welcomed me so warmly. And God, thank you especially for this family, for their hospitality, their friendship, and for the kindness they've all shown this almost decrepit old man. Amen." Ben looked over at the boys and winked.

"Ma, you crying again?" Chase looked at his mother, who was dabbing her eyes with her napkin.

"Leave her alone, Chase. You know she cries at everything," JJ said.

"Yeah, she even cried when I sang 'Old MacDonald' in the first grade." Chase laughed and Dev smiled at his friend.

"That was a beautiful prayer, Ben. Thank you." She

pointed at Chase and Dev. "As for you two little hoodlums, you can dig in now. And after dinner, you're both on KP." The boys looked at each other, shrugged their shoulders, then dove into the spaghetti and meatballs.

After dinner, the three adults retired to the back patio while the boys cleaned up the dishes. JJ brought out a bottle of wine for them to share. "This is from a new vineyard I discovered. It's in Michigan of all places, but the owners are Italian, so naturally, it's great wine. This one is Simplicissimus. It's hard to say, but it's a great dessert wine."

"Thanks, honey. Exactly what I needed to end the day," Angela said with a smile as JJ passed her a glass.

"Yeah, thanks, honey." Ben grinned at JJ as he accepted a filled glass from him.

"Go ahead, make fun, but those boys exhaust me," Angela said.

"Ah, I'm just teasing. You've done a great job, Ang. I'm not sure I could have taken on what you and JJ did, with Chase I mean."

"What other choice was there?" Angela took a sip of her wine and sat back in her chair. "When my sister Geena passed away, who else could have taken him in? Chase's dad, Mark, died serving in Afghanistan before she gave birth and Mark didn't have any siblings. Our parents were too old to take on an infant, and so were Mark's. It had to be me . . . us." Angela looked at JJ. "I wouldn't let him go anywhere else."

Angela took a long breath, then stood. "I think I'll check on Thing One and Thing Two, then call it a night. You two take your time out here."

Ben and JJ stood, said their goodnights to her, then returned to their seats and their wine.

"I'm sorry if I upset her, Jay."

"Ah, you didn't. Those memories are still fresh for her. I think they always will be. It was tough for her to lose Geena at such a young age. Still hard to believe someone could die in childbirth these days, but there it is. The doctors warned her it was dangerous with her condition, but she wanted a child so badly, and she was sure she could make it work." JJ took a sip of wine. "It's odd. I know it's been almost eleven years since we adopted Chase, but it feels like yesterday at times."

"Was it hard? Making that decision?"

"You mean adopting him?"

Ben nodded.

"Nah, not really. Angela's right, what else could we do? We couldn't let him go into the system or be put up for adoption and then end up who knows where. Chase is family. He may not be my blood, but he's my family. Always has been, always will be. I knew that from the first day I held him."

"He's a lucky boy," Ben said.

"No, we're the lucky ones."

CHAPTER 6

Mr. Zappone

"Mr. Zappone, you ready to get beat?" Ben joked with his next-door neighbor as he set up the chess board on a table in the park.

"I like your optimism, but I feel it's a bit misplaced." Mr. Zappone took his usual seat across from Ben.

Like most of Ben's neighbors, Mr. Zappone lived in Philadelphia his entire life. A spry man, even at eighty-five years old, he knew his limits and made sure he didn't overdo. Age cost him a few inches in height, and he walked with a cane, but almost every day Ben saw him out for a late morning stroll in the park.

A former business executive, Mr. Zappone had his own stylish uniform—loose fitting trousers with a cuff, never jeans or khakis, a white button-down shirt, and a flat cap to adorn his head. As he walked through the park, he swung and tapped his cane to the rhythm of a tune only he could hear. He would stop by the community garden and lean over the plants as if he were whispering a secret to them, and before he left, he would sing them a song of love in Italian.

Over a game of chess, he'd tell Ben stories of the city he knew as a boy—of the sights and sounds in the Italian market and playing stickball in the streets. An intense sports fan, as most Philadelphians are, he gave Ben a history lesson of the Phillies and what it was like to be swept up in a sea of red when the team won the World Series in 1980 and again in 2008.

They talked football only once, when Mr. Zappone shared what it was like to watch quarterback Norm Van Brocklin lead the Eagles to an NFL championship in 1960, then having to wait fifty-eight years before they won their first Super Bowl against Tom Brady and the New England Patriots. Being from Boston originally, Ben grew up a Patriots fan, so the two knew it would be best to avoid football as a topic, but every so often, especially if he was losing in a game of chess, Mr. Zappone would scoff under his breath, "Brady . . ." and shake his head at Ben.

Ben enjoyed Mr. Zappone's company. He found him to be an excellent chess player and friend, and a model of a successful retiree.

"Looks like you've got a workout routine going in the

morning, Ben," Mr. Zappone said, their game of chess heating up. "Good for you to be staying in shape, that's important. Can't do much when your body doesn't cooperate."

Though Ben's brown hair was graying in the temples, and the smile lines around his eyes were growing deeper, his tall frame and sturdily built body resembled a man closer to his early fifties than one just over sixty. "Used to be part of my job," he said. "I wanted to be in shape in case I needed to chase down a suspect. Now that I'm retired, I thought I'd better keep it up. I joined the YMCA a few weeks ago."

"That's a good thing," Mr. Zappone said.

"I thought so. I take a brisk walk over there, do some laps in the pool, and spend time in the weight room."

"Excellent. That takes care of your body, but you need to keep your mind active too."

"Agreed. I've gotten to know a few of the police officers who patrol the area. I check in with them about the latest events, and we talk shop for a while. Makes me feel like I'm still in the game. Then I come home. I spend the rest of the day exploring the city or playing chess with one of my favorite people."

Mr. Zappone smiled. "Sounds like you're doing all the right things." He moved his king's pawn forward two spaces.

"I'm doing my best. It's a little harder in the city. The Y is great, but I miss kayaking." Ben moved his king's pawn to meet Mr. Zappone's.

"You should check out Boathouse Row. I used to be a member of one of the sculling clubs. Rowing's a wonderful way to stay in shape and you meet a lot of interesting people there." Mr. Zappone winked at Ben and moved his queen out to threaten Ben's pawn.

"People?" Ben tipped his chin at Mr. Zappone. He brought out his knight to defend the pawn.

"Yes, people. I once met a person there that made my heart beat so fast I thought they'd be calling an ambulance for me. Her name was Fiona. She had blue eyes the color of cornflowers and raven black hair. Pale skin, like ivory." He sighed at her memory. "She was Irish, but I didn't hold that against her," he said with a grin. "She had been a competitive rower, but by the time I met her, she'd given that up and was teaching adult rowing classes. I signed up right away." Mr. Zappone moved his bishop.

Ben squinted at him. "But I thought you told me you were a rower in college." He moved his knight out to attack the queen.

"*She* didn't know that." Mr. Zappone chuckled.

"I see. And whatever happened to Fiona?"

"I married her."

"Well, good for you. I think I'm getting too old for that though. Don't think marriage was meant for me."

"You're never too old for love, son. I was sixty-seven when we married. She was sixty-three. We had eighteen wonderful years together before she went home to the Lord. Keep an open mind, and an open heart. Who knows what God has in store for you." Mr. Zappone smiled at Ben. He moved his queen into position. "Check . . . and mate."

CHAPTER 7

Dev

"You know, you're not bad, for an old guy," Chase teased. Three weeks remained in the school year. Chase and Dev made it a habit to visit Ben on their way home almost every school day. Their elementary school was a few blocks from his house, and they were walkers, so it was an easy stopping point for them. They'd finish their homework at his dining room table, then coax Ben into a game of basketball in the park. It rarely took much coaxing.

"Well, you're not bad either, for a knucklehead," Ben teased in return, passing the basketball to Chase. After additional trash talk, and shots at the hoop, the boys shared the latest happenings in school and things they looked forward to doing over the summer.

"Me, I can't wait to go down the shore," Chase said.

"Down the shore?" Ben asked.

"Yeah, you know–go to the ocean. Don't they have that in Maine?"

"Yes, but we call it going to the beach."

"That's weird."

"If you say so. How long do you stay there?"

"Two weeks. We go in July. It's a lot of fun. We go swimmin' in the ocean almost every day. I like to body surf the waves. And we ride bikes on the boards or play mini golf."

"The boards?"

"Don't you know anything?" Chase shook his head at Ben. "The boards . . . *the boardwalk*. We go to Ocean City, and they have a boardwalk next to the beach. It has a pier with rides, and there's places to eat and all kindsa other stuff."

"Sounds like fun. How 'bout you, Dev? Your family go anywhere over the summer?"

"No. My mom, she works a lot. We don't usually go anywhere. I don't mind. I like it here." Dev kicked a stone into the street.

"Well, there's a lot to like."

At that, Chase punched Dev in the arm and said, "Race ya!" The two ran off, leaving Ben smiling as he watched them go.

Ben promised the boys when the school year ended, he'd take them out for ice cream to celebrate. On their last day, they took a short walk to Chase's favorite ice cream shop in the Italian Market.

The shop bustled with students and parents all having the same celebratory idea. After Ben, Chase, and Dev got their ice cream, they found a table and took a seat.

Chase chattered away about all the field day activities that had taken place this last day of school, but Dev didn't say a word. Instead, he continuously scanned the shop with a noticeable frown.

What's he looking for? Why's he keep eyeing the door? "You feelin' okay, Dev? Something bothering you?" Ben asked.

"Nah, I'm *ah-ite*." He shrugged his shoulder.

"You're *ite*?"

"Sorry. I—am—all—right." Dev enunciated his words as if he were a robot.

Chase laughed at Ben. "Bruh, you gotta catch on faster."

"Well, I would if you boys would speak English. *Bruh, jawn, ah-ite, down the shore.* How's a person supposed to make sense of all that?"

"Oh, like 'I need to *pahk* my *cah he-ah*' makes sense." Chase rolled his eyes, mocking Ben's Boston accent.

Dev chimed in. "Did you hear him the other day when he asked where the water fountain was? '*Dev, you know whe-ahs*

59

the bub-lah?'"

The two boys burst out laughing.

"Oh, we're going there, are we? And the word is *wah-tah*, not *wood-er*. What the heck is that?"

"It's called Philly-speak, you foreigner. Better learn it if you're gonna live here."

"*Nev-ah!*" Ben laughed.

The bell over the door rang out. Dev whipped his head toward the sound, and his body tensed, but when a young mother and daughter walked in, he relaxed again.

"I gotta go." He got up and popped the last of his ice cream cone in his mouth.

"Everything okay?" Ben asked.

"Yeah, I told my mom I'd be home early today. I gotta go. Thanks for the ice cream."

Chase stood, and the two boys did their special handshake, then Dev left the shop and disappeared before Ben could see which direction he went.

"Everything okay with him?" Ben turned to Chase. "He's not in trouble, is he?"

"Nah, he's ah-ite. Don't worry about Dev, he never gets into trouble."

Ben walked Chase home and Angela insisted he stay for dinner. Afterward, he and JJ took up residence on the back patio.

"So, JJ, what's Dev's story?" Ben asked as they settled into their chairs.

"What do you mean?"

"There's something off with that kid. You haven't noticed it? Where's he from? What's his family like?"

"Off? No, I haven't noticed anything. Dev's from Philly, like the rest of us. He lives with his mother in an apartment around the corner from you. She's a single mom, and he's an only child. We've known him since kindergarten. He and Chase were in the same class. They got into a fight during recess one day, and they've been best friends ever since."

"Hmmm. Well, there's something going on. I'm sure of it."

"What makes you say that?" JJ sat up in his chair.

"Today I took the boys out for ice cream. I told them we'd have a little celebration for the end of the school year. Dev seemed a bit on edge. Every time someone came into the shop, his eyes would go straight to the door and his body would tense. We barely finished eating, and he said he had to go. He said he told his mom he'd be home early, and he left like a shot. It was very strange."

"That doesn't sound too odd. Maybe his mom wanted him home, and he was afraid she'd come looking for him."

"That's not all. He's got this way of looking at people. Haven't you noticed? He studies them. He's sizing them up. He did that with me the first time we met. He's sized you up . . . you and Angela, for sure."

"Ah, you're imagining things. I think you're missing being on the force. Get a hobby. How about dominoes?"

"Maybe, but I don't think so. I've seen that look before. I'm going to keep an eye on him."

"Do what you want, but Dev, he's a good kid. Chase says he's a straight-A student, and he's a great little basketball player. I've seen him. He's small, but he's fast. Never been in any trouble that I know of."

"Hmmmm. Till now."

CHAPTER 8

Welcome, America

It had been decades since Ben celebrated Independence Day. On most holidays, he worked crowd control in Eastport and took whatever shifts necessary to ensure the safety of the town's citizens and visitors. This year, he planned to join in Philadelphia's weeklong celebration called *Welcome America*. He looked forward to sharing the week with one of his siblings from Maine, his youngest sister, Jennifer, and her husband, Bill.

"Thanks for the invite, Ben. I can't wait to get there and explore all that history! Bill's excited too. It's hard to believe we've never visited the city before," Jennifer said.

"Looking forward to you being here, Jen. So, you think you can stay two weeks?"

"Absolutely. We'll be there the last week of June and stay

through the first week of July. You'll probably want to be rid of us by the end."

"I doubt that. See you when you get here. Love you."

"Okay, Ben, I've got the perfect agenda for your sister and brother-in-law when they come," Angela said, while they sat together on her back patio.

"Thanks for doing this, Angie. I know Jen and Bill will appreciate being shown around by somebody who really knows the city."

"Oh, you know me, I love playing tour guide." Angela waved her hand at Ben. "I think we should start with all the historical sites in Olde City. When we're done with that, we can move on to things like Fort Mifflin, and maybe the Barnes Museum, and the Japanese gardens. Do you think your brother-in-law would like to run up the steps of the Art Museum?"

"Not sure Bill would be up for that, but I'd like to see him try! You sure we can get all this in?"

"If Jefferson could write the Declaration of Independence in seventeen days, we can certainly visit these venues in half that time. Just be sure to wear good walking shoes."

Bill and Jennifer arrived late on a Friday afternoon, parking just down the street from Ben's home. As Bill removed their luggage from the trunk, Jennifer spied her brother.

"Ben!" Jennifer ran and wrapped her arms around him. "Oh, I've missed you."

"Missed you too, little sister," Ben said, returning her hug. He extended his hand to his brother-in-law. "Hi, Bill. Good to see you. Saw you two drive by and thought I'd give you a hand." He helped with the luggage and brought the travelers to his home.

To Ben, Jennifer and Bill were the perfect example of opposites attract. Diminutive in stature, but not in personality, Jennifer had a smile that could melt ice in a blizzard. She liked to pile her hair on top of her head in a way that reminded Ben of a robin's nest. Her chocolate brown eyes sparkled when she spoke, especially if she spoke about something she loved, like literature, or history, or Bill. And she had a way about her when meeting new people that left them feeling like they were her closest friend.

Bill, on the other hand, stretched almost to Ben's six-foot, three-inch height. In his younger days, a mop of curly black hair topped his head, but the hair, merely a memory now, had been replaced by a smooth surface generally donned by a ball cap. His eyes, a serene blue, matched his easy-going personality.

Ben welcomed them into his home and after they settled their things, they relaxed in the living room. "JJ's wife, Angela, has a great sight-seeing plan for us. It's all laid out. A little ambitious I think, but she's confident we can get it all in."

"This'll be awesome. I love the idea of a home-grown Philadelphian escorting us around. I'm sure she has some great stories," Jennifer said.

"Well, she's married to JJ, so that's almost a guarantee."

The next morning, Ben, Jennifer, and Bill ate a hearty breakfast, put on their walking shoes, then made their way to the Mongellis. Once introductions were made, they hopped on public bus to the historic district, Olde City Philadelphia.

First stop–Independence Hall. As they stood on the lawn and admired the iconic Georgian building, Jennifer's eyes grew wide. When it was time, they lined up for their tour of the Hall with the National Park ranger. Ben laughed at his sister, who bounced like a three-year-old waiting to see Santa.

"You gonna be okay, Jen? I've never seen you so jumpy."

"I'm excited. We're about to go into the 'room where it happened'. Can you imagine?"

Ben smiled and gave his sister a quick hug. "Glad you're happy."

The doors opened at last, and the park ranger welcomed the tour guests inside. The group moved from history to history as they passed through the first-floor courtroom, then into the second floor gathering spaces.

"You would have loved this, Jen. I can see you now—fancy gown and giant white wig on your head, doing the minuet with the governor," Bill said.

"Yes, and I can see you over there at the buffet," Jennifer teased.

Descending the staircase from the second floor, they came to the most famous space in the Hall, the Assembly Room. Green tablecloths covered small tables where delegates sat. Each table was fitted with a single silver candle holder, a quill pen or two with an inkwell, books, and writing papers. Looming over the room in the front, a much larger table held sway. Placed behind it, the famous "rising sun" chair.

Seeing the room where fifty-six men pledged their "lives, their fortunes, and their sacred honor" for the sake of freedom brought a tear to Jennifer's eye. She squeezed her brother's hand. "'Life, liberty, and the pursuit of happiness' . . ." she said, looking up at him.

Ben nodded and a chill ran down his back. The quartet lingered behind for a moment as the park ranger continued the tour.

Ben whispered, "You were right, Ang. This is the perfect

beginning for Jen's time in Philly."

Angela gave him a satisfied grin.

"Okay, we've seen a lot of history over the past three days. I think we should switch things up a bit and get a look at life in current day Philadelphia. Let's go to the Reading Terminal Market," Angela said to her tour group on the fourth day of their visit.

Once again, they hopped on public transportation. They made their way to the market which is housed next door to the Philadelphia Convention Center. The group exited the SEPTA bus at Arch Street. An ocean of people rippled along the sidewalk, and Jennifer held a firm grip on Bill's hand as they dove into the crowd. A short walk brought them to the entrance of the Reading Terminal Market and once inside they were met with a kaleidoscope of colors, sounds, aromas, and people.

"Wow! This is amazing," Jennifer said, letting go of Bill's hand.

"What is that awesome smell?" Bill asked.

Angela sniffed the air. "That's DiNic's roast pork . . . or it could be cheesesteaks."

"Ben, we need to make this a food tour. You in?" Bill patted his brother-in-law on the back.

"Absolutely."

While Jennifer and Angela admired the crafts at the stalls scattered throughout the market, Bill and Ben sampled as many edible delights as their stomachs allowed. When they got to dessert, the men quoted from *The Godfather* as they each enjoyed a cannoli from Termini Brothers while Angela and Jennifer enjoyed a scoop from Bassett's Ice Cream. As Ben took a final bite, he saw a small boy duck out a delivery door by the bakery. "Hey, isn't that–? Angela, did you see that?"

"See what?"

"That boy." Ben pointed to the delivery door. "Kinda looked like Dev."

"I think the cannolis are affecting your vision. There's no one there, Ben. Besides, what would Dev be doing here?"

"I don't know. Sure looked a lot like him though."

Bill approached Angela and Ben, rubbing his stomach. "I think you're going to have to roll me home. This was awesome."

"The market's only about a half-hour walk back to my place. How 'bout we walk some of this off?" Ben said.

"And leave these two lovely ladies to fend for themselves on a public bus? I think not."

Jennifer laughed. "I think we all could use the extra steps. Let's go."

As they left the market, Ben took one last glance over his shoulder. Sure did look a lot like the kid.

Following their market excursion, Angela declared a day of rest was in order. "It's important to pace yourself, and with the Fourth just a couple days away, I believe Jennifer and I need a spa day. You gents are welcome to join us, but I don't see either of you lying still long enough to have a cucumber facial."

"Got that right, Ang. Bill, how about you and I take in the Navy Independence Day Regatta in the morning, then go to a Phillies game?"

"Sounds great! Love to." Bill paused. "What's a regatta?"

Ben laughed. "It's a rowing event. It's kinda like a track competition, but on water. There are several heats throughout the day. The preliminaries are early in the morning, with the finals at the end of the day."

"Did you know Philadelphia held the first competitive regatta in the U.S. right here on the Schuylkill River?" Angela asked her guests.

"The tour continues." Ben winked at Angela. "I've been wanting to see one of these races in-person for years, so how 'bout it, Bill?"

"I'll go. Sounds like fun," Bill said.

"I'll see if JJ can join us, and maybe the boys, too. I'm sure they'd have a blast."

The next morning, Angela and Jennifer left for their spa day and Ben and Bill piled into Ben's truck and headed for Boathouse Row. The city's skyscrapers gleamed in the late June sun, and the international flags lining Benjamin Franklin Parkway fluttered in the morning breeze.

"Perfect day for a regatta. I think we should take in the preliminary heats this morning and leave after the first ones in the afternoon. That'll give us plenty of time to get to the Phillies game." Ben pulled onto Kelly Drive. "This is my favorite part of the city. Wait till you see Boathouse Row, Bill. Too bad we won't be around at night when they light up the houses. It's beautiful."

"I can see why you like this. River to your left, lots of trees all around, nature in the city." Bill smiled.

"It's not Maine, but I'd love to put my paddle in the water here. I'll get to that soon, I'm sure."

"So, is JJ going to be able to make it to the game tonight?"

"No, he's on duty. That's the life of a cop. He was disappointed, but I'm sure we'll go another time. The boys are hyped though. I don't know if they're more excited about seeing the Phillies play, staying for the fireworks after the game, or that it's Dollar Dog Night."

"Well, if those two are anything like my Ryan, you'll be glad the hotdogs are only a dollar!"

"Okay, boys, here's the next round. You sure you can

handle this?" Ben said, handing Chase two hotdogs.

"Don't worry, we won't barf on you." Chase laughed as he handed a hotdog to Dev.

Ben leaned over to Bill. "You were right about growing boys being bottomless pits. I'm not surprised at Chase, but I can't believe how much Dev can eat. Where's he putting it all? He's just a little squirt. Good thing those dogs are only a dollar."

Following the game, which the Phillies won, the group stayed to watch their first set of Fourth of July fireworks. They had a perfect view and watched as the exhibition exploded over the city skyline. The finale of the display rocked the stadium and Ben could feel the reverberations in his chest. At last, the "bombs bursting in air" were complete, and Ben looked over at the boys.

"How does that happen?" Ben whispered to Bill and pointed at Dev. The boy sat slumped in his seat, his Phillies ballcap askew on his head. The Phillie Phanatic plush toy Ben purchased for him was tucked under one arm and acted as a pillow for Dev's head as he slept soundly.

"Food coma," Bill said with a grin.

Chase whispered to Ben, "He does that sometimes."

Ben scooped Dev out of his seat as Chase and Bill gathered up the remaining mementos—ice cream dishes shaped like Phillies batting helmets, souvenir soda cups, and Chase's giant foam "We're #1" finger. The slumbering boy's head rested on Ben's shoulder, his right arm draped around Ben's neck. The Phanatic remained nestled in the crook of his left arm. Ben carried Dev to the subway station as Chase walked closely beside them, keeping an eye on his friend. As they entered the subway car, Dev woke. His eyes grew wide as he lifted his head and stared at Ben.

"It's okay, bud. You're fine," he whispered. "You fell asleep at the game, that's all. We're going home now." Ben lowered Dev to a seat and he and Bill stood in front of the two boys as the crowded subway car left the station.

"Hey!" Chase hit Dev on the arm. "How 'bout them Phillies! Wasn't it awesome when Ryan Howard hit that dinger outta the park? I was hopin' we'd catch a ball. Maybe next time. Oh, and my mom said we couldn't stay up all night talkin' like we did last time. Maybe she'll be asleep when we get home, and it won't matter. The fireworks were awesome. I liked the big red ones the best. You know, the ones that look like a giant star?"

Dev turned his attention to Chase as he chattered away about fireworks, the game, and who ate the most hotdogs while Ben kept his eyes fixed on Dev.

CHAPTER 9

Independence Day

As the calendar flipped to July, the *Welcome America* celebration built up to a fever pitch that would culminate with fireworks on the Fourth above the Philadelphia Museum of Art. For Ben, Jennifer, and Bill, the next few days were filled with additional sight-seeing on their own and on the Fourth, they joined the Mongellis for a cookout.

"Ben's told us you were a real prankster in college, JJ," Bill said as they all sat down to a meal of burgers, Italian sausage and peppers, and what seemed to be a thousand side dishes.

"I had my moments back then, but I've given that up."

"Oh, really? Since when?" Angela said.

"You should have him tell you the story of Gung Ho some time, Bill," Ben said. "He got more than one freshman in trouble with that one."

"Still tells it," Angela said, shaking her head.

"And just so you know, that apple didn't fall too far from the tree," Ben said, pointing to Chase and Dev. "Let me tell you what these two knuckleheads did." The boys looked up from their meals with all the innocence of fallen angels.

"I'd only been in my place a few weeks. These two started showing up after school to play basketball, which, of course, I was up for."

"Of course," Jennifer said.

"One Saturday afternoon, we played a great game with some other kids and guys in the neighborhood, lots of fun. And when we were done, I told the boys I'd get us a pizza. I let them in my house, ordered the pizza, then told them to sit tight while I went around the corner to pick it up."

"Well, that was your first mistake," JJ said. "Never leave perpetrators unattended."

"Got that right. I came back, we ate the pizza, and they went on their merry way. Next day, I went on a drive after church. My neighbor, Mr. Zappone, gave me some advice earlier and said I should check out Boathouse Row. So, I hopped in my truck and took off. Now, traffic was heavy in Center City, so I wasn't going too far too fast, but things opened up by the time I got on the Ben Franklin Parkway. That's when I heard it."

"Heard what?" Bill asked.

"This low hum, dooooooooo," Ben said, imitating the sound. "I thought, 'Great, now what?'. The sound stopped every time I came to a red light, so I thought maybe I picked up something in a tire or something got caught in my undercarriage. By the time I got to Kelly Drive, though, whatever made that sound was practically giving me a concert. The pitch changed depending on how fast I went or if I made a turn. I figured I'd better get it checked out, so when I got home, I called Jay to get the name of a mechanic and on Monday morning, I called the shop. They said I could bring it over and they'd take a look, so I did."

"Anthony's Auto, great guys," JJ said.

"Well, I pulled into the garage, explained the problem again, then Anthony put the truck up on a lift. He looked underneath for about twenty seconds, then came to me, and said, 'Found your problem. You're a friend of JJ's, right?'

"I got a familiar feeling in my stomach, one I used to get all the time when JJ and I were roommates. So, I said, 'I guess you could call us friends, but that depends on what you tell me next.'

"He said, 'Come have a look.' I walked with him under the lift and there, zip wired to the undercarriage of the truck, was a harmonica."

"A harmonica?" Jennifer laughed.

"Yes, a harmonica. Anthony said, 'Looks like somebody pranked you.' He called the other mechanics to come have a look see and they all got a good laugh out of it.

"Thankfully, Anthony has a sense of humor, and he didn't charge me for the diagnosis. Just asked that I come see him next time I had a real problem . . . or needed an oil change."

Bill leaned toward Chase and said, "Harmonica, that was genius."

Chase laughed and said, "It wasn't my idea. It was Dev's!"

Everyone turned their attention to Dev. He lowered his chin and smiled, his cheeks matching the red in the American flag behind him.

"You?" Ben said, pointing at Dev with his hotdog.

"Yeah, it was Dev," Chase said. "I wanted to play a prank, and I thought about doing somethin' with a stink bomb, but Dev came up with the harmonica idea."

"I guess I should be grateful." Ben said.

Bill leaned over to Dev and said, "I like your style, kid."

"Yeah, way to go. I'm proud of you, boy!" JJ gave Dev a fist bump.

"Do not encourage him." Ben gave JJ a backhanded swat in the chest. "What's wrong with you people? These two knuckleheads could have set me back a couple hundred bucks or caused an accident."

"Oh relax, big brother. You're fine. And Dev," Jennifer grinned at him. "Way to go. Very creative."

Dev smiled and looked away.

Laughter and groans filled the room for the rest of the evening as JJ took the floor and told his tall tales, including the infamous tale of Gung Ho. Eventually, Angela turned the conversation to other points of interest Jennifer and Bill should visit.

"One thing you should absolutely do is go down the shore for at least a day," Angela said. "It's about an hour's drive from here to Ocean City, and you'll have a fabulous time. It's a family-friendly town, there's a quaint boardwalk, and you'll love the beach. Great place to relax."

"Sounds like something we should definitely do. What do you think, Ben?" Jennifer said.

"You don't have to talk me into spending time outdoors. I'd love to go."

"We're gonna be leaving on Friday for vacation down there, so why don't you all join us for a couple of days? You don't mind, do you, Ang?" JJ said.

"Of course not, we'd love to have you, and we won't take no for an answer."

"Well, that settles that. Angela has spoken." Ben grinned. "You tell us when to be there, and we're there."

Chase and Dev joined other neighborhood kids in

playing soccer after dinner, while the adults worked out the details over dessert. Ben, Jennifer, and Bill would join JJ and his family on Monday, allowing the weekend crowd to disperse.

When at last the boys came in to get ready for the fireworks, they found out about the plans for the shore. Dev looked at the ground for most of the discussion, then retreated to a corner with Chase afterward. Ben watched the boys for a few moments, then got up and joined them.

"So, I was thinking, knuckleheads, why don't the three of us challenge JJ and Bill to a game of b-ball while we're at the beach?"

"I'm not gonna be there," Dev said.

"Well, about that, why don't you come to the beach with us?"

"To the beach?" Chase said. "You mean *down the shore*."

"Sorry, Chase, yes, *down the shore*," Ben said, imitating him. "Dev, you wanna come? You can ride with us on Monday."

"I don't know." Dev glanced at Ben, then turned his eyes toward the floor again.

"You have plans already?"

"Not really. It's just . . ."

"What, bruh, don't make me go with just old Ben," Chase said, eyeing his friend.

"'Scuse me? *Old* Ben?" Ben raised his eyebrows at Chase.

Chase gave an impish grin to Ben. "Sorry." Turning to his friend, he said, "Come on, Dev. Come with us. It'll be fun."

"I'm not sure my mom will let me go."

"Tell you what, why don't you ask her, then let me know. We'll only be there overnight, so maybe she won't mind."

Dev looked at Ben shyly. "Okay, I'll ask her."

The next day, Dev and Chase stopped by Ben's to let him know Dev could join them all for an adventure down the shore. Ben was pleased, but not as pleased as Chase, who insisted Dev help him with all the chores Angela laid out for him to do before they left. As the boys were about to go, Ben grabbed a piece of paper and stopped Dev.

"What's your address, Dev? And can you give me your mom's phone number?"

"Why you want all that?"

"Well, I need to know where to pick you up on Monday and I thought I'd give your mom a call to introduce myself and let her know I'm not kidnapping you."

"Oh, she knows that. She knows you're a cop and a friend of the Mongelli's. That's why she's letting me go. You don't have to call her. Besides, she's at work and she's not allowed to take phone calls."

"Still, I thought she'd like to have my phone number in case she'd like to be in touch."

"She has my number, and I gave her yours already. I got it from Chase. And she has the Mongelli's too."

"Right." Ben eyed Dev. Good at dodging questions, I see.

"Well, I guess that just leaves where to pick you up. What's your address?"

"Come on, Dev. We gotta go! My mom's gonna have a fit if I'm not home in five minutes." Chase grabbed his friend by the elbow.

"I'll come here. Seven o'clock, right?" Dev said, as Chase shoved him toward the door.

"Seven's fine. See you then." Ben furrowed his brow as he watched the boys run down the street.

CHAPTER 10

Down the Shore

"Want me to help pack your truck?" Dev asked. He arrived at Ben's at seven o'clock sharp, bringing a small duffle bag with him.

"Thanks, that'd be helpful. We're not taking my truck though. Bill offered to drive. His SUV can fit everyone, my truck can't. How 'bout you pass me the gear and I'll get it packed away."

"Sure." Dev smiled and went to work. In short order, they had most of the bags and supplies stowed away.

"Dev, I was thinking, I really need to meet your mom before we leave," Ben said, putting the last of the bags into the SUV.

"Why? She said I could go."

"I know, but I'd like to meet her. Let her know who I am and that I'll keep an eye on you."

"She knows that. Besides, you can't meet her right now. She's at work and she's not allowed to have visitors, or she gets in trouble. Don't get her in trouble. Please?"

"All right, you win. But I'd like to meet her when we get back." Ben opened the back door of the SUV. "Hop in."

You're hiding something. Why don't you want me to meet your mom?

"Good morning, Dev," Bill said as he and Jennifer got into the SUV.

"Glad you could join us. This should be a good day," Jennifer said with a smile.

An hour later, they pulled into the driveway of the Mongelli's rental house. Chase ran out to meet them with Angela not far behind.

"Welcome to Ocean City!" Angela shooed away Whitey and Harry, who were barking at her heels. "Boys, help bring in the bags, please."

Angela showed her guests to their rooms. "I'll finish packing up the coolers. While I'm doing that you all can get unpacked and changed into your bathing suits."

"Yeah, then we'll head to the beach! Dev, the waves are great today." Chase grabbed Dev's duffle, and the two boys headed to Chase's room.

The sun shimmered in a clear blue July sky with the wispiest of cotton candy clouds overhead. Even the wind welcomed Ben, Jennifer, and Bill to their first outing at the Jersey shore with a light, cooling breeze.

Ben thought they looked like General Sherman's troops marching toward the sea as they walked the few blocks to the beach. JJ took the lead, pulling a large red and white cooler on wheels with a folded cabana bungeed on top. Chase and Dev came next, struggling to pull a wagon laden with chairs and beach umbrellas. Ben followed the boys, carrying yet another cooler while Angela, Bill, and Jennifer brought up the rear with beach bags, blankets, and towels.

When they reached the beach, everyone pitched in to get things set up. Once the cabana was in place, umbrellas unfolded, coolers set in the shade, books retrieved, and sunscreen applied to everyone, Angela gave the okay. "You are released! Enjoy this beautiful day!"

Chase grabbed Dev by the arm and raced to the shoreline. Ben watched them from his beach chair, and as they approached the ocean, Chase ran in and dove into the first wave he could while Dev stood on the shore and watched. After several minutes, Dev hadn't moved from his spot.

Curious. Why's he not going in?

Ben walked down to the shoreline and stood next to Dev for a few moments. The boy didn't say a word, nor did he move a muscle. Ben watched him staring out at the sea, his eyes moving from wave to wave, cloud to seagull, surfer to sailboat.

"Dev? What is it? You don't like the ocean?"

"I didn't know," Dev said, still staring.

"Didn't know what?"

"I didn't know how big it was. Dang."

"You've never seen the ocean?"

Dev shook his head.

"You've never been to the ocean. You're only an hour away. How's that possible? Didn't your mom ever bring you?"

Dev scraped the sand with his foot. "We don't go many places. My mom works a lot."

"Right, I remember," Ben said with a nod. "Well, it is big and I'm glad you have the chance to see it." They stood together in silence, admiring the immense horizon before them.

"Why's the ocean brown? I thought it'd be blue. Is it from pollution? Bet that's from New York." Dev scrunched his nose.

"No, it's not pollution. It's because of what's underneath. The ocean churns up a lot of stuff, especially with the undertow."

"What's undertow?"

"It's a current that's under the surface. You can't see it, but you can sure feel it. Look at your feet. See how the ocean is pulling the sand away?"

"Yeah, I'm sinking," Dev said with a laugh, staring at his feet and wiggling his toes.

"That's part of the undertow. It pulls at what lies on the bottom and in this part of the country, what's on the bottom is a lot of silt, mud, and clay. See how the color kinda matches the water? All that stuff gets churned up, and that's what makes the water look brown."

"Mud and clay," Dev bobbed his head and continued to look at his feet. "Hey, how'd you know all that?" He glanced up at Ben.

"I'm not as stupid as I look." Ben laughed. "And JJ explained it to me the first time I visited here. I thought the same thing you did."

"Really?"

"Yeah, I did." Ben looked back at the horizon. "I've seen the ocean off the coast of Maine many times, but it looks nothing like this. You can't swim in it because it's too cold, but in some places the water is crystal blue and in other places it's emerald green and in most places, it's so clear you can see right to the bottom. No mud and clay, but lots of granite and other rocks. It's beautiful."

"I'd like to see that someday."

"Dev! C'mon bruh, you're missing the good waves!" Chase ran up to Ben and Dev.

"Go on, get in there, knuckleheads. But stay between the flags and watch the undertow." The boys took off together and Ben smiled as he watched Dev join Chase in diving into the waves.

Ben returned to the cabana and took the chair next to JJ.

"Jay, let me ask you something. Have you ever met Dev's mom?"

"Dev's mom? Yeah, years ago at one of those school functions. Angela knows her better than me. Why do you ask?"

"Because I haven't met her. I've been spending time with her son, and now I've brought him here, and I think it's odd we haven't met. She's never called to check on who I am and every time I ask Dev about her or try to meet her, he puts me off. I mean, here I am, taking her son out of state to the beach, for the first time apparently, and there wasn't even a phone call between us to say it was all right. Something's up."

"Ah, it's nothing. Angela's known his mom since kindergarten. She knew he'd be with us and he's with Chase all the time. He even spends the night with us, a couple of times a month it seems. Those boys are like two peas in a pod. That being the case, I'm sure she wasn't worried."

"I don't know. I still think it's odd."

Chase and Dev came up for air long enough to have lunch and to allow Angela to apply more sunscreen. As they went back to play in the ocean, Ben and the others alternated between swimming, reading, and chatting. Though the temperature was nearing ninety degrees, the wind had shifted, and a strong ocean breeze made it comfortable in the shade.

"How you feeling, big brother?" Jennifer handed Ben a water bottle.

"Relaxed. First time I've felt that in months. The ocean's good for me."

Jennifer patted him on the shoulder. "Glad to hear it. I've been worried about you."

"I'm good, little sis."

Something caught Ben's eye. It was Chase running toward the cabana. He dashed to his parents. Panting, he pointed to the ocean. "Dev—Dev!"

Ben and JJ jumped up and scanned the sea. Without their notice, the waves had changed in character from gentle curls caressing the skyline, to a horizon undulating in a hypnotic staccato of white caps and waterfalls.

Ben spotted Dev off in the distance, swimming at the top of one of those waterfalls, much too far from shore.

"Get the lifeguards, Jay!" Ben raced toward the ocean. He ran as fast and as far as he could into the sea, then dove into the waves.

God, keep him above the water till I can get there. And help me get there.

Even at sixty-one, Ben was an excellent swimmer, but swimming in the ocean is far more treacherous than doing laps at the local YMCA. A dozen feet offshore, the breaking waves buffeted his body. The penetrating cold of the water stung his skin like so many hornets disturbed from their nest. Even so, he ducked under the waves, pulling himself underwater to avoid being pushed back inland.

Once past the breakers, he rose above the surface. A forceful pull tugged his body. Rip current. Dev's gotta be caught in it. Stay with him, Lord.

Ben upped the tempo of his strokes. Use the current. It'll get you there faster. His arms and legs pummeled the water, propelling him forward.

He caught a glimpse of Dev struggling to keep himself afloat, barely managing to doggie paddle.

"I'm coming! Keep swimming, Dev! I'm coming!"

He can't hear me.

Wave after wave after wave crashed over the boy's head. Each one pulling him farther out to sea and away from Ben. The next wave broke, and Dev toppled behind it in the swell.

Where'd he go? Where'd he go? "Dev!" Ben's heart pounded in his chest. Fear is fuel. Use it.

Each stroke, each kick, shot pain through Ben's tiring limbs. "Go!" He willed his body through the onslaught of waves. He spotted Dev. Only a few feet away from him, the boy's head bobbed just about the surface.

"Dev!"

Dev turned toward him. The look of terror in his eyes sent a jolt of adrenaline surging through Ben's body. With a few powerful strokes, he reached him. He grabbed Dev in his arms as a towering wave crashed over their heads. It separated them like a giant cleaver and sent them tumbling under water.

Ben fought his way upward, broke through the surface, and gasped for air. He scanned the horizon.

No sign of the boy.

"God, help me!"

He dove underwater. His hands reached out in the darkness. Saltwater stung his eyes. He came up for air. Scanned the surface again.

Nothing.

He dove. He felt something. In desperation, he grabbed it and swam toward the light. As Ben broke through the surface once again, he held Dev in his arms. He was alive and breathing, but exhausted.

"I've got you, buddy. I've got you," Ben said as he hugged Dev. The boy coughed up water as he held on to Ben. "That's it. Hang onto me. You're gonna be okay. Hang on to me."

Gotta get him back to shore fast. He flipped Dev onto his back and the weary boy wrapped his arms around Ben's neck. "Hold on tight."

Ben turned toward the shore. He could feel Dev's body shaking against his own. He took a few strokes toward land, then stopped. The lifeguards were almost to them rowing out in a rescue boat. "Thank you, Jesus."

The lifeboat pulled up beside the two and Ben lifted Dev up to the lifeguards, then accepted their help getting into the boat himself. Once onboard, Ben sat behind Dev and rubbed his shoulders and arms to warm him. Dev sat in silence, his eyes wide, his lips blue, and his body spent and shaking.

When the boat arrived on shore, JJ kept everyone at a distance as Ben carried Dev back to the cabana. Ben placed him gently in a chair, then accepted a water bottle and beach towel from Angela. He wrapped the towel around Dev.

"Sip this slow now, Dev. No gulping," Ben said.

JJ moved close to Ben and said softly, "A lifeguard contacted Emergency Services, and an EMT is here to examine Dev." JJ nodded to the EMT, a young woman in her twenties, and she approached Dev.

"You're a lucky young man," she said. "What happened out there?"

Dev looked up at her without answering.

"I get it. You're not ready to talk. Can you nod your head to answer some questions?"

Dev barely nodded a yes.

"My name's Amanda." She gave Dev a soft smile. "Does anything hurt?"

Dev shook his head no.

"Do you feel funny in your head? Like fuzzy or you can't think straight?"

Dev shook his head no.

"How about your stomach? Do you feel sick?"

Again, Dev shook his head no.

"I need to get some vitals on you now. Is that okay?"

He nodded yes.

Amanda knelt and checked Dev for any body trauma. She took his temperature, felt his pulse, and listened to his heart and lungs. Wrapping her stethoscope around her neck, she said, "Okay, I think you're gonna be fine. It doesn't look like you have any serious injuries, but I bet you're really tired, huh?"

Dev nodded yes.

"Well, maybe you should go home now and get some rest. You did a fantastic job keeping yourself afloat, but that cost your body a lot of energy. By any chance did you swallow some of the ocean while you were out there?" She tilted her head at him.

He nodded yes.

"I thought so. The ocean level looked a little lower than it was this morning." Amanda smiled, then patted Dev's knee. "This is important. You need to drink a lot of water now and let all that saltwater pass through your system. You should be fine, but if you start feeling funny in any way—dizzy or you get a headache or a stomachache, or your vision gets a little blurry, you tell someone right away. Understand?"

Dev nodded yes.

"Pinky swear?" Amanda held out her pinky. Dev hooked his pinky with hers and the two shook, then pulled apart.

Amanda stood up, then went to Ben, and took him aside. "Are you his dad?"

"Me? No. I'm a friend." Ben looked over at Dev. "His parents aren't here. He came down with us for a couple of days. This is his first time at the ocean."

"That was a rough introduction for him. Well, he seems to be fine, but I am a little concerned about the amount of seawater he may have swallowed. That can dehydrate him. Keep an eye out for any dizziness, or headaches, and if he seems confused or disoriented in any way, get him to the ER." She looked over at Dev. "Is he normally this quiet?"

"No. He is on the quiet side, but this is unusual."

"Keep a watch on that, too. He's not showing any signs of shock. His vitals are good, and everything else seems normal, so he's probably feeling overwhelmed. If he doesn't start speaking in an hour or so, get him checked out."

"Will do," Ben said. "Thanks."

"How are *you* feeling? Do I need to check you out?"

"No, I'm fine. Just worried about the kid."

"Good job by you, going in after him. Not sure if it was smart, but it was brave. You remind me of my dad. That's something he would have done. He was a cop."

"Me, too. I just retired."

"That explains it. Well, officer, job well done." Amanda held out her hand. Ben shook it, then returned to the cabana.

Chase sat close to his friend, watching him with a wrinkled forehead and sympathetic eyes. Ben knelt in front of Dev. "How 'bout we go back to the house? I could use a rest. You too?"

Dev nodded, then stood up, and swayed. Ben caught him.

"Whoa, there partner. Tell you what, you go for a ride instead. Hop on." Ben turned so Dev could climb on his back. Dev wrapped his legs around Ben and clutched onto his neck.

"Hey, it's not polite to choke your horse," Ben said.

Dev whispered, "Sorry," and loosened his grip.

"Don't worry about any of your things," JJ said, handing Ben the key to the house. "We'll get this all packed up and meet you back at the ranch."

"Hey, thank the lifeguards for me, will you?"

"Will do." JJ patted Dev on the arm. "You get some rest, Sport. Glad you're okay."

Dev nodded and laid his head on Ben's shoulder as Ben carried him back home.

CHAPTER 11

The Aftermath

"Is Dev gonna be okay?" Chase asked.

"Yes, I think so. We need to keep an eye on him, make sure he drinks lots of water and gets some rest. Think you can help with that?"

"Absolutely. He's my jawn. I got his back."

"And I've got yours, knucklehead," Ben said with a smile. Chase grinned back. "You did a great job running for help today." Ben held out a fist and Chase tapped it with his.

"Ma, do we have enough water? I can walk to the store and get more."

"I'm sure we're fine—but let's be safe and get some extra. Go grab a ten from my pockabook, take the wagon and go to the Wawa. Thanks, sweetie."

Chase retrieved the money, then left on his mission of mercy.

"Boy needs something to do. He's worried," JJ said.

Angela nodded in agreement.

"Chase told us what happened," JJ said to Ben. "He and Dev were having a race. They weren't paying attention to where they were and before they knew it, they'd passed the safety zone. They turned to come back in, and Chase thought Dev was beside him, but when he got to shore, Dev wasn't around. That's when he saw him heading out to sea."

"He did the right thing coming to get us. I'm sure he was scared," Ben said.

"We all were," Angela said. "What you did today, Ben." Angela wiped a tear from her eyes.

"It's what anyone would do. I'm just glad I was there." Ben paused. "I don't know how I'm going to explain this to his mother."

"Don't tell her," a voice called out from the stairs. "Don't tell her. She doesn't need to know." Dev walked gingerly down the stairs and over to Ben.

"I've got to tell your mom. She *does* need to know. What happened to you today was very serious. I need to explain."

"No, you don't. I'm fine. If you tell her, she'll worry, and she won't let me go anywhere again, ever. Please, Ben." Tears formed in Dev's eyes.

What aren't you telling me?

"Let's go outside." Ben stood and put his arm around

Dev's shoulder. He led him to the back patio and sat him down in the shade.

"Stay here a minute." Ben went back to the kitchen and retrieved a couple of water bottles. He returned to the patio and handed one to Dev.

The afternoon sun eased itself into a hammock of clouds as an ocean breeze flitted through the leaves of the crape myrtle bordering the patio. Laughter and conversation from those still on the beach rolled over them like a gentle wave.

"I understand you're upset. I get it. But if I don't tell your mom, she won't trust me. She'd want to know, I'm sure of it." Ben paused and took a drink of water. "There's something else though, isn't there?"

Dev looked at Ben, then bent his head toward the ground and nodded. Ben waited.

Dev whispered, "I lied."

"You lied? Lied about what?"

Dev looked away from Ben. "My mom doesn't know I'm here."

"What?" Ben sat back in his chair. "Why not? You didn't tell her?"

Dev shook his head no.

Ben leaned toward Dev. "Where does she think you are?"

"She thinks I'm home. She's . . . away."

"Where is she?"

"She's . . . she's um, she's visiting her sister."

"Her sister. Where's her sister live?"

"She lives in," Dev scooted his eyes away from Ben's. "in Alabama, yeah, Alabama."

Right. Alabama. Why are you lying to me? "And your mom went to see her. Without you?"

"Yeah, I've been there before. There's nothin' to do. I told my mom I could stay home, hang out with Chase. I'm old enough. She didn't want to let me at first, but then she said it was okay. And I *was* with Chase, so it wasn't exactly a lie," Dev said, getting quieter.

"Not exactly, but pretty close," Ben said. "So, she thinks you're home." He stood up and walked behind his chair, raking his fingers through his hair. Keep it together, Hudson. Losing your temper won't help. He turned toward Dev. "When is she due back?"

"I don't know exactly. She said Friday, maybe Saturday." Dev fidgeted in his seat, then took another drink of water.

"Hmmm." More lies.

"You can't tell my mom. You can't. Please," Dev said. "You don't understand . . ."

You're worried, that makes sense. But you're not worried about being punished for lying. It's something else. Let me help you.

"You're right. I don't understand. This is serious. I'm not

sure I can do what you're asking. I will not lie to your mother."

"I'm not asking you to lie. I'm asking you not to tell. There's a difference."

"Not much of one in my book." Ben took a deep breath and sat back down. "Why'd you lie? Why'd you feel you had to do that?"

"Because. I wanted to come. I wanted to see the ocean." Dev returned his gaze to the ground. "I'm sorry, Ben."

Ben could see a tear hit the ground by Dev's feet. He rubbed his neck and studied the boy. There's more to this, I know it. You don't trust me yet. Okay, I'll give you some time.

"I'll tell you what, I'll think about it. I'll let you know before we leave for home what I decide to do. Deal?"

Dev nodded.

"Listen, I want you to know something." Then, not taking his eyes off Dev, he said, "You know when we were out in the ocean, and I told you to get on my back and hold on?"

Dev nodded.

"Anytime you need me, you can hop on my back. Anytime. I will carry you. I'll help you, Dev."

Dev looked at Ben, his brow furrowed. "I don't need help. I'm fine and I'll be even more fine if you don't tell my mom." He stood and went back into the house.

Later that evening, while sitting on the patio, Ben told JJ about his conversation with Dev. "You still think there's nothing going on, JJ?" He pointed toward the house. "That boy is lying. He lied about his mother and he's still lying. She's nowhere near Alabama. I'm sure that woman has never left the city. Why would he lie? There's something going on and I swear to you, I'm going to find out what it is."

"Just be careful, Ben. Dev's a good kid and . . ."

"And? And what?"

"And he's getting attached to you."

"Attached?"

"Yes, *attached*. Do you know the only person I've ever seen Dev let touch him is Angela? And that's because she doesn't give him a choice and he knows it, so he tolerates her. Everyone else, me included, has never gotten more than a handshake from him. Yet today, he wrapped his arms around you—twice."

"What are you saying?"

"I'm saying he's just a kid. A kid without a father. I don't want to see him hurt or you hurt. Just be careful. Tread lightly."

"I'll tread however is necessary. And I will get to the bottom of this."

CHAPTER 12

Choices

After a restful night's sleep, Dev recovered well from his ordeal in the ocean. Ben considered returning immediately to Philadelphia, but the boys convinced him to give them one more day. It was against his better judgment, but he couldn't resist the puppy-dog eyes both boys gave him, especially after Dev knocked on his bedroom door first thing in the morning.

"Can I talk to you?" Dev asked.

"Sure, bud, what's up?" Ben pulled on a t-shirt.

Dev looked at the floor, then up at Ben. "Thanks . . . for saving me. I should have said that yesterday." Dev's eyes focused back on the floor.

"No worries. I was happy to do it. Yours is a life worth saving." Ben mussed Dev's hair. "Even if you are a knucklehead."

Dev glanced up at Ben, hugged him around the waist, then ran out of the room. Ben stood still, JJ's words ringing in his ears.

Ben went downstairs and Angela informed him Chase volunteered to get fresh doughnuts for everyone from Brown's Restaurant, a favorite breakfast tradition of the Mongellis while down the shore. When he returned, everyone gathered in the dining room.

Chase rapped his knuckles on the table. "Attention! Attention! I hereby officially nominate myself for the position of Recreation Director for the day. Any objections?" Chase squinted his eyes at the adults in the room. They smiled, but no one made a sound. "Good. It's uni-nanimous. I am hereby officially elected."

Dev giggled.

Chase shot a look at his friend, then smiled. "Here's my official plan. After breakfast, we'll go for a bike ride on the boards, then play a round of mini golf. Dev, you'll love it. They have a huge shark at one hole!"

Dev raised his eyebrows, showing he was uncertain a giant shark would be something he loved.

"After golf, we can have pizza at Manco & Manco's, then go to the Wonderland Pier for some rides."

"And then we collapse in a heap?" Angela said.

"No, Ma, then we get some funnel cake and Kohr

Brothers' frozen custard!"

Bill laughed. "This sounds like another food tour."

"Sounds exhausting," Angela said.

"I dunno, sounds like a good time to me," JJ said, smiling at his son.

"C'mon, Ma, please? It'll be fun."

"Jennifer, Bill, what do you think?" Angela asked.

Jennifer smiled and said, "Chase, it does sound like fun. Bill?"

"You had me at mini golf." Bill took a bite of a cinnamon sugar doughnut.

"Ah-ite! Let's go!" Chase said.

"Sunscreen first," Angela said. She pulled Dev aside and applied lotion to his back. "You be sure to drink extra water today, young man. I'll have plenty on me and I don't want you arguing with me about it. You understand? And you tell me if you start feeling funny. Remember, you pinky promised Amanda yesterday."

"Yes, ma'am."

Angela turned Dev around and pulled him in for a hug. "Let me do this, it'll be over soon, I promise. I'm so glad you're all right, Dev. You had me worried." She released him then held him by the shoulders. With a tear in her eye, she said, "Okay, you're free to go."

Dev looked at Angela with a tear in his own eye, then

turned and ran to find Chase.

Late that afternoon, after bike rides and mini golf, amusement parks, and pizza, the group visited Kohr Brothers for their famous twist cones of orange and cream frozen custard. They found a few benches facing the horizon, sat together, and watched the sun's rays melt into the ocean.

Angela left JJ talking with the boys and walked over to Ben. She slid next to him. "How are you feeling?"

"Sore, tired." Ben smiled. "Think I'm finally feeling my age. Next time I'll leave the rescuing to the younger guys."

"Nonsense. You'd do exactly the same thing again if you had the chance."

Ben nodded.

Angela leaned on his shoulder and while watching the sandpipers scurrying along the shoreline, she whispered, "You're right. There is something going on with Dev. JJ told me what you asked earlier, and I've been thinking about it all day." She looked at Ben. "I realized I haven't been around Dev's mom since the boys were in fourth grade. I've seen her from a distance this year at some of the school functions, but she never says hello anymore. She's just there, then she's gone. Something's not right. You find out what it is." She patted Ben's knee, stood, and went back to JJ and the boys.

Ben stared out at the vast ocean and the limitless sky above with stars appearing as if a lamplighter was setting each ablaze one by one. A mysterious pull tugged at his heart. He closed his eyes.

God, if it's necessary, help me rescue Dev once more.

Ben tossed and turned throughout the night, trying to decide what to do about contacting Dev's mother. At dawn, he was still uncertain.

"God, I don't know what to do here. Trust is at stake with both parties. I want to honor Dev's mom's parental right to know what happened to her son, but I'd also like to honor Dev's request to keep what happened between the two of us. Under normal circumstances, I'd know exactly what to do, but this isn't normal. Something's going on. I know it. And I know You know what it is. Help me figure it out."

He got out of bed, stretched his stiff muscles, got dressed, took two ibuprofens, and headed for the beach. As he walked along the shore, pink and purple swatches of dawn gave way to a milky blue sky. A morning mist reached down from the clouds and kissed the sand, turning the ocean view into a dreamy, watercolor painting. The retreating tide left bits of seaweed, shells, and the occasional horseshoe crab strewn about the beach adding texture to the artwork. Ben walked closer to the shoreline and every so often, a rebellious wave that refused to withdraw with the others slipped its way up higher on the beach and nipped at his heels.

Still unsettled, he continued his conversation with God. He laid out the issues as he saw them and asked for wisdom about how to proceed. After several miles of walking in tandem with His Creator, Ben returned to Angela and JJ's.

As he came through the door, sounds of an awake house greeted him—dogs barking at Angela's heels while she made breakfast, pounding footsteps on the floor above, and laughter pouring in from the back patio.

Ben went to the kitchen. "Morning, Angie."

"You were up early," she said as she scrambled eggs.

"Good day for it. Is that the boys I hear upstairs, or did you rent some elephants while I was out?"

"Haven't seen any elephants, must be them." Angela grinned.

Ben took the stairs by two and went to Chase's bedroom. The boys were together, Chase watching as Dev packed his belongings into his duffle bag. Ben tapped on the open bedroom door.

"Hey, when you're done with that, Dev, meet me out back."

"Want me to come too?" Chase asked.

"No, I can only handle one knucklehead at a time this morning," Ben said with a smile.

A Good Place to Turn Around

Ben went to the kitchen and poured himself a cup of coffee, greeted Jennifer and Bill as they went to their room to pack, then sat outside on the patio waiting for Dev. He arrived not too long afterward, looking very much like a prisoner heading toward the gallows.

"You don't have to look so scared," Ben said. "I'm not gonna hurt you."

"Yeah, but you're gonna tell my mom, aren't you?"

"Actually, no. No, I'm not."

Dev started to smile.

"I'm not going to tell her *yet*, on one condition."

"What's that?" Dev's brow furrowed.

"On the condition you tell me the absolute truth when I ask you one question. If you do that, I give you my word, I won't tell."

Dev bit his lip. "What's the question?"

"No, it's not that easy. You need to swear first you'll answer truthfully, and not just a partial answer, the whole truth or once she gets back, I *will* talk to your mother."

"Doesn't sound like I have a choice." Dev kicked a pebble.

"You do, but I'll admit, it's not a great one. So, will you tell me the truth?"

Dev stared at Ben.

Sizing me up again, I see.

Dev nodded and whispered, "Yes."

Guess I passed the test.

"Have a seat." Ben gestured to the chairs nearby.

The two sat down and Ben pulled his chair around so he could speak to Dev face-to-face. Ben stared into Dev's eyes, leaned toward him, then asked quietly, "Are you being mistreated at home?"

Dev stared at Ben, then sat back in his chair. His eyes grew wide, and his mouth opened. "No . . . No! You think my mom is . . . *abusing me?*"

"I don't want to think that, Dev. I don't. But I can tell, something's bothering you. Something's very wrong and you won't talk about it. I've known lots of kids in situations where their parents, well, let's just say they weren't good parents, and those kids needed help and I helped them. If you need help, I want to help you too."

"Well, I don't. I'm fine. My mom's fine. We're fine." Dev stood and paced around to the back of his chair. "You don't know anything about me or my mom. My mom's great. Don't say anything against her." He shoved the chair.

"Okay, okay, I'm sorry," Ben said, raising his hands toward Dev. "I don't want to be disrespectful to your mom. Okay? I'm sure she's a good woman, but I had to ask."

"I answered your question. Does that mean you won't tell her about what happened? You won't tell?"

"No, I won't. I gave you my word. But Dev, *you* should tell her. You should tell her the whole truth. If she finds out you left without her knowing, it'll be a long time before she trusts you again. Trust is a hard thing to come by, and it's easy to lose. You should tell her."

Dev looked at Ben, then looked around the yard. "Are we done?"

"Yes, we're finished. We'll be leaving as soon as everyone is packed."

Dev turned his back on Ben and went inside.

About an hour later, Jennifer, Bill, Ben, and Dev were on their way back to Philadelphia. As they traveled the highway, Dev remained taciturn, choosing to stare out the window despite Jennifer's attempts to engage him in conversation.

As they neared Ben's neighborhood, Bill asked, "So, where do we drop you off, Dev?"

"You don't have to drop me off. I live close to Ben's so I can walk home."

"I insist. I want to make sure you get home safely."

Dev chewed on his bottom lip. "I live at the Tenth Street Apartments."

Ben asked, "Is that the building before you get to

Ellsworth Street?"

Dev nodded.

"I go by that on my walk in the morning. Just make a right on Tenth after you pass my house, Bill."

Bill made the proper turns and pulled up to the apartment building. He found a parking spot on the corner.

"Well, we'll be going back to Maine the day after tomorrow, so we won't see you again, Dev," Jennifer said. "I'm glad we met and I'm really glad you're okay."

"Glad to meet you, too." He turned to Bill and said, "Thanks for bringing me down the shore."

"Happy to do it. Enjoy the rest of your summer."

"Let's get you inside," Ben said. He opened the car door and Dev slid out of the back seat. Ben handed him his duffle bag from the trunk.

"I'm sorry I upset you earlier. I just wanted to be sure you're okay. Do you understand? I meant no disrespect."

Dev nodded.

"I've been thinking. Why don't you stay with me till your mom gets back? I don't like the idea of you being all alone."

"I'm not alone. I have neighbors. I'm fine."

"Well, if you need anything, you let me know, even if you're just bored. I may not be as entertaining as Chase, but I can keep you company. Why don't you stop over tomorrow, and we can play a little one-on-one?"

Dev looked toward the ground, then said, "Thanks again. You know, for . . ."

"Don't mention it," Ben said. "Want me to walk you in?"

"Nah, I'm not a baby." Then, with a slight smile, he looked at Ben and said, "Night, ol' man."

"Night, knucklehead."

He watched Dev walk toward the front door. Dev stared at the entrance, then looked back at Ben and, for a moment, Ben thought he may change his mind and not go in. Just then, a man emerged from the apartment building. Dev greeted him, and the two chatted, then Dev went inside.

There's more to your story, Dev, and I'm gonna find out what it is.

CHAPTER 13

Stakeout

"What's bugging you, big brother?" Jennifer asked as she gathered some things to pack. "You've had a frown on your face all day."

"Missing you already, that's all."

"Nice try. You're worried about something."

"I'm not worried, just . . . concerned. I was wondering about Dev. I thought he would have stopped by today."

"Well, the fact that he didn't should tell you something. He was probably too busy having fun with his friends. If you're concerned, why not give his mom a call and see how he's doing?"

"Yeah, maybe."

Not a chance. Definitely better to wait and let him come to me in his own time.

"Enough about little knuckleheads. What can I do to help

you get ready?" Ben said.

"Grab a suitcase and follow me."

"This has been the best vacation I've had in a long time," Jennifer said as she put a suitcase into Bill's trunk the next morning. "Thanks for having us."

"Glad you could come, Jen. It's been nice having family around."

"It's good to see you happy. And I have to say, it's pretty amazing to have a hero for a brother. Glad I got to see you in action."

"Ah, I'm no hero. Just doing what I was trained to do."

"Yeah, you keep telling yourself that." Jennifer patted Ben on the chest, then gave him a hug. "I'm gonna miss you. You're coming back home for the Harvest Festival, right?"

"Wouldn't miss it."

"Maybe you should invite the Mongellis as a return favor for them taking us to the beach."

"You mean *down the shore*," he said. "I might just do that. Maybe I could convince Dev to come, too. That boy needs to widen his horizons."

Jennifer tilted her head at her brother.

"What? What are you thinking, oh sister of mine?"

"Dev, he's a special kid."

"Why do you say that?"

"He doesn't miss a trick that one. He's shy, but he takes in everything that's going on. Very observant. I've taught kids like him. Smart, inquisitive, but oh so quiet. They're like a duck on water, everything's smooth on the surface, but underneath, they're paddling like crazy."

Jennifer lowered her voice and took a step closer to Ben. "I don't know what's going on, but I know there's something and you're right in the middle of it. I can see it in you. And I know you won't let it go, whatever it is. So, please be careful. I don't want anybody getting hurt, especially you."

Ben kissed his sister on the forehead and said, "Thanks for the concern, but I'll be fine. And you're right, I will not let this go. But, I am going to let you go, sorry as I am to see the back of you."

"What's wrong with my back?" Jennifer said, turning her head and looking over her shoulder.

"Nothing as far as I can tell," Bill said, coming up to her.

"Charmer," she said, smiling at Bill.

Bill laughed and put his arm around his wife, then he extended his other hand to Ben. "Thanks, Ben. This has been great. Now, you get yourself back up to Maine soon. The entire Hudson clan has been in mourning since the day you left. I think they have a petition in to the governor to lower the flags for the next month."

"Oh stop. Just because we love our brother," Jennifer said, giving Bill a playful slap on the shoulder. "But he's right. You get yourself back up to Maine. Don't wait till Harvest. I'm glad you're having a good time here, but you belong there."

"Yes, ma'am," Ben said with a two-finger salute. "All right, you two have a safe trip and let me know when you get home. Give Ma and Pop a hug from me and I'll be talking to you." Ben gave them each one last hug, then watched them get into the car and waved as they drove off. Standing on the sidewalk for a moment, he thought he saw a person out of the corner of his eye. He turned toward the park and scanned the area.

Not a soul. Musta been shadows.

Ben spent the evening mulling over ways to help Dev, and after a night's sleep, he still hadn't come up with any solutions.

"Vacation's over, Hudson. Time to get back to work. You think better outside, let's go." He got dressed, laced up his sneakers, put in his ear buds, and headed out the door by five-thirty.

He went west on Federal Street to begin his trek to the YMCA. He walked past Capitolo Playground, crossed Tenth Street, then after crossing Eleventh, he picked up his pace. Midway down Eleventh Street, Ben thought he spotted a familiar silhouette ahead.

That looks to be the size and shape of Dev. Can't be. Maybe... Either way, it's awfully early for a kid to be out on his own.

A hint of daylight emerged over the cityscape, but not enough to make out who owned the silhouette in front of him. Ben kept his distance but maintained his focus on the dark form. The figure came to Twelfth Street and stepped under a streetlight.

It is him. What are you up to, Dev?

Ben shifted into full law enforcement mode, tracking his suspect. He hung back and allowed Dev more distance, but kept his eyes trained on the boy. Dev wore shorts and a red t-shirt, and he walked at a steady pace, his thumbs resting in the straps of a backpack flung over his shoulders.

Dev crossed Thirteenth Street, then Clarion, and Juniper, and when he came to Broad Street, he made a right. Ben hurried to the corner, then paused a moment before turning. He inched his way around, wanting to keep the distance between him and Dev. When he turned the corner, Dev had disappeared.

Where'd he go? Did he know I was following him? Nah, he couldn't have seen me. Where'd he go?

Ben walked down the block, searching left and right for any sign of Dev. The street held an assortment of office buildings, apartments, storefronts, and spaces for lease. The singular business open at this hour was the Broad Street Diner. Ben went inside and gave a quick scan of the patrons. He stopped by the cashier.

"Have you seen a boy, about ten years old? Blond, has a backpack."

"Yeah . . . every day at noon after summer school lets out."

Ben gave a sarcastic, "Thanks." He went out the door to continue his search.

"It doesn't make sense. Why would he come here?"

Ben took inventory as he walked down the block to Ellsworth Street. "Chinese restaurant, bar, dancewear shop, church, thrift store."

He came to the corner and stopped, then turned, and studied each store front as he walked the two blocks back to Federal Street once more. He stopped at one of the office building's doors. "Wait, I thought this was a second entrance. This is a separate building." The indistinct glass door had the letters "IC" painted on it, along with the numbered address.

Ben sat on a bench outside of a nearby restaurant. Could Dev be visiting someone in the apartment building? Why would he be visiting this time of the morning? What's with the backpack? And what's behind the IC door? What does "IC" mean anyway? Law office, maybe?

A Good Place to Turn Around

A few minutes passed, and Ben watched as an unkempt man walked by, opened the IC door, and went in.

What's that all about?

Ben kept his eyes focused on the door. Fifteen minutes later, Dev walked out. Ben jumped to his feet and moved inside the doorway of the restaurant, blocking himself from view, but keeping a watchful eye on his suspect.

Dev walked down Broad Street without a sign he was aware of Ben's surveillance. The boy made a left on Federal Street and as he did, Ben stepped away from the restaurant and followed him again. Dev retraced his steps as he crossed Juniper and Clarion streets, then the numbered streets. Ben was sure Dev would turn left at Tenth to go to his apartment building, but instead, he kept going straight.

"Odd." Ben picked up his pace. *What if he's coming to see me? We're almost to my house. Maybe I should cross the street and run ahead, like I'm out for my morning workout.*

Instead, he fell back. *Let's see where he's really intending to go.*

Dev walked toward Capitolo Playground. Just when Ben thought he would turn and knock on his front door, the boy continued walking to Ninth Street and made a right.

"Now where's he going?"

Ben hurried down the street, staying in the shadows. Reaching the corner, he saw Dev walking into the park. Ben followed and entered through the gate on Ninth.

He passed the rec center on his left, and expected to spy Dev as he reached the front of the building, but the boy was nowhere in sight.

Where'd he go? I know I saw him come in this way. He checked the playground, the soccer field, and even the community garden.

Where is this kid? Who is he? Houdini?

Ben went back toward the rec center and took in the view of the entire area. Nothing. He walked to Passyunk Avenue, at the Ninth Street entrance. "There's only one way in or out and this is it." He looked at the gate in the fence. "How could I have missed him?" He shook his head. "Good thing I retired. I'm losing my touch."

His suspect having escaped, Ben returned home to formulate his next plan.

He poured himself a cup of coffee, went to the living room, and stared out the window overlooking the park.

"All right, let's figure this out. Dev, walking down the street. Backpack, shorts, red t-shirt. Goes into the IC building, whatever that is. Fifteen minutes later comes out. Backpack, shorts, blue t-shirt–wait, blue t-shirt! He had different clothes on . . . and his hair was wet. What was he doing in there?" Ben checked the time—ten minutes after seven. He picked up the phone and called JJ.

"Hey, man. Got a question for you. There's a building on Broad Street, between Federal and Ellsworth, and it has IC on the door. Do you know what it is?"

"Kinda early for this, don't you think, Ben? I'm still on vacation," JJ said with a yawn. "I need my beauty sleep."

"Seriously, do you know what it is?"

"Sure. It's an 'In Community' building. It's a homeless shelter." JJ yawned again.

"Homeless shelter?"

"Yeah, the city has them scattered around, sorta inconspicuous, but they're there. Why do you want to know? You behind on your rent?"

"Funny. I saw it on my walk this morning and was curious."

"Next time you want to satisfy your curiosity, could you at least wait until after nine o'clock?"

"Sure. Sorry about that. I just needed to know."

"You okay?"

"Yeah, I'm fine. I'll talk to you later. Sorry to wake you." Ben hung up the phone and stared out the window again. "Huh, homeless shelter."

A few hours later, there was a knock on Ben's front door. He opened it, and there stood the street urchin, blue t-shirt and all.

"Hey, knucklehead. What are you up to?"

"Nothin' much. Thought you might wanna play a game of one-on-one," Dev said, a hopeful look in his eye.

"Can't think of anything I'd rather do on a beautiful day like this. Come on in while I grab my sneakers." Ben brought Dev upstairs and showed him to the living room. "You feeling all right? Want some water?" Ben made his way to the kitchen.

"Nah, I'm good," Dev looked around the room. He picked up a magazine that had fallen on the floor and laid it on a pile on the end table, then straightened up the pile. "Your sister leave yesterday?"

"Yeah, she and Bill should make it back home today. It's a long drive." Ben came back into the room with his sneakers and a water bottle.

"Miss Jennifer, she's nice. I like her." Dev picked up a newspaper strewn on the couch, folded it neatly, placed it on the pile of magazines, then sat down.

"I'll tell her you said so. She liked you too. She thought you were a smart kid, but she doesn't know you well." Ben grinned as he tied his shoes. Dev rolled his eyes.

"All right, let's go before the sun makes it too hot to play."

"Want me to recycle those? It's trash day, you know." Dev pointed to several empty water bottles left on an end table.

"Uh, right. Guess I forgot, vacation and all. Might as well take it all out on the way." Ben gathered up the rest of the trash and recycling and set the bins on the curb as they went to the park.

A father and son were on the basketball court shooting free throws, and a few kids sat on the sidelines. Ben talked to everyone to see if they'd like to form two teams, and they happily agreed.

The players were divided into the Shirts and the Skins. For the next forty-five minutes a rollicking competition ensued, with the result being Shirts, Dev's team, sixty-five and Skins, Ben's Team, sixty-four. The Shirts went into a wild celebration, while Ben did his best to buck up the Skins. In the end, a handshake line formed and the phrase "Good game," echoed a dozen times as the teams dispersed.

"You hungry, champ?" Ben asked Dev as they walked off the court.

"A little. I guess I should go home."

"Why don't you stick around? We can go grab a pizza from the shop around the corner."

Dev stared up at Ben for a moment.

"C'mon, you'll keep me company. I hate eating alone."

Dev nodded then walked with Ben to the pizza shop.

When they settled into a booth, Ben cleared his throat. "I have a question for you and it's pretty important."

Dev shifted in his seat.

"I want you to tell me the truth, okay?"

Dev stared at Ben and gave him a slow nod.

Ben leaned in. "Plain . . . or pepperoni?"

Dev grinned and said, "Mushroom and sausage."

"Wasn't an option, but I like how you think." Ben placed their order when the waitress came. As they waited, he said, "Your lay-up's improving. You been practicing?"

"Yeah. Sometimes I go over to the dog park and practice there. I like seeing the dogs."

"You like dogs? You ever have one?"

"I like 'em, but my mom doesn't think we could take care of one. She doesn't like the idea of having a dog in the apartment. She says it's too small for an animal."

"She's probably right. I had a dog, and they're a lot of work."

"You had a dog? What kind? What was his name?"

"He was a bloodhound, and his name was Arnold."

"Arnold!" Dev laughed. "Who names their dog Arnold?"

"Arnold's a fine name. How dare you laugh!" *This is the first time I've heard him laugh in a while. That's a good step.* "I named him after one of the greatest golfers of all time."

"And you call me a knucklehead. Arnold . . ." Dev said, still laughing. "Was he a good dog?"

"The best. He stunk as a bloodhound, though. He had allergies, and was always congested, so he couldn't track a thing."

"Your dog had allergies?" Dev laughed all the harder.

"Yes, it happens. Arnold had allergies." This sent Dev falling onto the seat of the booth howling.

"Sounds like you and your son are having a good time," the waitress said as she brought over the pizza. "Here you go. Let me know if you need anything else." She set the pizza on the table, then walked away. Dev stopped laughing, sat up, and gave the waitress an uneasy look as she went to serve other customers.

Well, that was awkward. Could the boy look any more uncomfortable? Bring him back to the dog.

"Arnold wasn't a good tracker, but he was a great watchdog. Believe it or not, once there was a small herd of wild pigs that came through Eastport."

"Wild pigs?" Dev turned his attention back to Ben. "Wait." He lifted his chin and narrowed his eyes. "Is this like one of Mr. Mongelli's stories? There's not some guy named Gung Ho in it, is there?"

Ben laughed. "No, this is not a Mongelli special, and yes, there really were wild pigs, boars actually. It seems someone back in the day thought it would be a good idea to raise them, but somehow, they got loose. They got most of them back, but a few were still in the wild. Those few had babies and before you knew it, there was a small herd of about ten boars living in the forest.

"I'd only been in Eastport for a couple years, and I knew

nothing about them. But one morning, Arnold had a fit. He kept barking at the door, as if someone was outside. I looked out the window, but couldn't see a thing. I was just about to open the door when Arnold blocked me. He didn't want me to leave, so he put his body up against the door. I got mad at him, but then I thought, 'He's never done anything like this before. There must be something going on.' So, I went to the window and looked out again, and this time—I saw it."

Dev leaned into the table. "Saw what? What'd you see?"

"I saw a full-grown, ugly, 300-pound male boar rooting around in my vegetable garden." Ben spread his arms to show the boar's size.

"What! Three hundred pounds? What did you do?" Dev pulled himself to the edge of his seat.

"Nothing. I stayed inside. Those things are dangerous. That bad boy could have had me for lunch if I'd gone outside unarmed. I called the station and let them know what was going on. They called the game warden, then he and a few officers came, and took care of the invaders."

"Took care?" Dev wrinkled his forehead. "Did they shoot them?"

"Yes. With tranquilizer guns. There ended up being five boars all together, and they'd been terrorizing the neighborhood all morning. The game warden trucked them to a rescue center where they lived a happy, "boarish" life for the rest of their days."

"Then what did you do?"

"I got everyone together for a pork barbeque to celebrate and as a warning to the other pigs in case they were nearby," Ben said with a laugh and Dev joined him.

"Let's say grace." Ben smiled at Dev, then bowed his head. "Lord, thanks for sunshine and fresh air. Thanks for basketball and pizza. And thanks for good friends, like Dev. Amen." Dev kept his chin tucked to his chest and smiled at Ben.

"Dig in." Ben handed Dev a slice of pizza and before Ben had even taken a few bites of his own slice, Dev finished his. He gave Dev another, then another. As he gave him a fourth slice, he asked, "Are you holding out on me?"

With a full mouth Dev said, "What d'ya mean?"

"You have a hollow leg or something? Didn't think you could put away this much pizza at once."

"Sorry. I'm hungry. I didn't have much breakfast this morning. Wasn't hungry then."

I doubt that.

"Well, you can take whatever's left home with you to snack on later, if you'd like."

"No, I'm good," Dev said with a hesitant smile. "Thanks."

"You doing okay by yourself?"

"I'm ah-ite."

"And your mom, have you heard from her?"

"Not yet. They don't have good cell service where she is. And it's only Thursday. 'Member, she said she wasn't coming back till Friday or Saturday?"

"Right, I forgot."

Still lying.

"I should get goin'. Thanks for lunch. It was good." Dev slid out of the booth.

"Okay, you take care of yourself. Stop by tomorrow. Maybe those kids will be out again, and we can have another game. I need revenge," Ben said, squinting his eyes.

"Ah-ite. See ya . . . old man." Dev grinned.

"See ya . . . knucklehead."

Ben watched Dev leave the pizza shop, then he jumped up and went to the window. He watched as Dev turned toward the park instead of toward the apartment complex. He tilted his head. "Nah, that can't be it."

CHAPTER 14

Truth be Told

The alarm sounded at five a.m. Ben fumbled around for the clock, slapped it off, and hauled himself to an upright position. He stretched, rubbed his hair, then remembered why he wanted to wake so early. He got a quick shower, dressed, and made himself a cup of coffee.

"Coffee, binoculars, let's go." Ben went upstairs to the guest room and sat by the window facing the park. From this vantage point, he had a panoramic view of Capitolo Playground from the swing sets to the community garden.

Ben had been on many a stakeout in his life and while this one was more comfortable because he was in his own home, it was just as tense. Maybe even more so due to the suspect he hoped to observe.

A half-hour later, Ben saw movement from the side of the rec center. He squinted. "Looks like a kid." Through the binoculars, Ben confirmed his thought from the day before.

It *is* Dev.

He watched the boy move onto the street, then head in the same direction down Federal as he had the previous day. Ben put the binoculars down and picked up a flashlight. He moved without a sound through the house, even though it wasn't necessary, and went outside. He made a beeline to the park and started his search at the rec center. He was certain he'd find a piece of Dev's puzzle there.

The rec center was a typical brick and mortar one-story building. Ben began his search at the front. As he walked around the center, he examined every window and door for any signs of a break-in.

All secure.

When he got to the back of the building, all looked well. He turned toward the side facing Federal Street. Several trees formed a triangle on the back corner of the building, and those trees were surrounded by large bushes Ben guessed were azaleas.

"No way I'm getting through that. Those azaleas are too overgrown."

He went back to the front of the building. "None of this makes sense, but I know the answer's here." Ben moved closer to the building and searched again. As he walked, he examined every brick, branch, and twig.

"Nothing new on the front, nothing new on the side. The back looks the same. The only thing left is the side of the building with those bushes."

Ben walked closer to the azaleas and shined his flashlight from top to bottom of the shrubs. Hmmm, what's that? He fixed his flashlight on a hole at the bottom of the bush. It was about a foot in diameter between two azaleas. He knelt and turned his flashlight into the tunnel-like space.

There's something in there. What *is* that? Fabric, plastic maybe? Can't believe I'm gonna do this.

He got on his knees and pushed himself through the hole. "I'm too old for this."

Once he got through, he found himself standing in a triangular clearing between the bushes, the trees, and the building. Tucked inside this small area, was a two-person pup tent.

Please God, let it be empty. With one swift motion, Ben threw open the flap. He let out a sigh of relief. Nobody's home. Thank you, God.

Ben crawled inside and sat in the middle of the tent, his head touching the top. He scanned the interior with his flashlight.

"What do we have here?" Ben looked to his right. "Shirts, pants, underwear, socks, shoes. All in columns. Very neat. Very organized."

He turned to his left. "Looks like library books. That's quite a stack. Notebooks, a case of pens and pencils, flashlight, Tupperware container—looks like cash and some other papers." He saw another container with peanut butter and a box of crackers. "The boy knows how to protect his food."

Ben turned himself around to the back of the tent.

"Basketball, duffle, sleeping bag, a pillow and hey, Phanatic. I know you. Good to see ya again."

Ben sat still, looking at what surrounded him.

"What is going on here? Why are you living in a tent, Dev? Why aren't you with your mother? And where exactly is your mom?"

He lost track of time and lingered in the tent far longer than he intended. A rustling noise startled him out of his thoughts, and in a flash, the tent flap lifted. There stood Dev. He took one look at Ben, turned, and bolted.

"Nuts!" Ben jumped up, pulling the stakes of the tent out of the ground and scattering its contents. He pushed himself through the bushes and ran after Dev. The boy almost reached the top of the exit to the park. He turned to look back at Ben, tripped, and fell face down. Ben rushed over and grabbed him from behind before he could get up and run again.

"Let me go! Let me go!" Dev squirmed to get free from Ben's grip.

"No, I'm not going to let you go. You're gonna talk to

me." Ben wrapped his arms around Dev.

"I'm not going! You can't make me! I'm not going!" Dev continued to flail his arms and legs. Ben tightened his grip on the boy, picking him off the ground.

"I'm not taking you anywhere. Calm down. I promise, I'm not taking you anywhere you don't want to go."

Dev stopped yelling, but he continued to squirm.

Ben placed him back on the ground. "Look at me." He turned Dev around, then got down on his level. Still holding him by the shoulders with a firm grip, he looked him full in the face.

Dev stood still. He lowered his chin, his hair tumbled over his eyes. He glared at Ben.

"I promise. I won't take you anywhere you don't want to go."

Dev continued to stare at Ben, his eyebrows knitted together in an angry knot, and his teeth clenched. Ben locked his eyes on Dev. "You have my word." Ben won the staring contest as Dev looked away.

Ben pointed to Dev's leg. "Will you come home with me so I can patch you up?"

Dev looked down at the blood dripping from his knee. He stared at Ben again for a moment. Still frowning, he pursed his lips and nodded his assent.

"Okay, I'm going to let go, but before I do, will you give me your word you won't run?"

Dev closed his eyes, then looked back at Ben, and nodded

once more. Ben released his grip on Dev but continued to look him in the eye. He waited for a second to be sure he wouldn't run, then he stood and, with his hand on Dev's shoulder, he led him back to his home.

Ben sat Dev down in his living room. He went to the kitchen and got the first aid kit. Neither spoke a word as Ben cleaned Dev's wound, applied ointment, then bandaged it. When he was through, Ben sat in the chair on the other side of the room and waited.

Give him time.

The only sound was the ticking of the clock, which kept pace with Ben's heartbeat. "Whenever you're ready, Dev. There's no rush."

Dev sat for several more minutes, staring at his feet.

He's trying to work out what to say. Hopefully, it'll be the truth this time.

At last, Dev spoke. "How'd you find it?"

"I saw you leave there this morning. At least, I saw you leaving from the rec center. I thought I'd seen you a couple other times in the park. Today I decided to investigate."

"Investigate? Am I going to jail?"

"No, you're not going to jail. Why would you think that?"

"Well, you're a cop. You said you investigated me."

"Former cop, and it wasn't much of an investigation. It was more of a stakeout. I was watching for you, that's all."

The two fell back into silence.

After another minute of the ticking clock, Ben asked, "Why are you living in the park, Dev?"

Dev took a few moments, then whispered, "Because . . . I don't have anywhere else to go."

Ben pulled himself closer. "What do you mean? What about your apartment?"

"I couldn't stay there anymore. I couldn't pay the rent."

"*You* couldn't pay the rent?" Ben sat back. He watched Dev clench his hands together, then he asked the question he'd been dreading. "Where's your mom, Dev?"

Dev hesitated, then said, "I . . . I don't know. I don't know." His voice trembled. "She's gone. I got up one morning like normal and when I went to get my breakfast, my mom wasn't there. I don't know what happened. I don't know where she is." Dev wiped away a tear.

"When was that?"

Dev whispered, "Four months, one week, two days ago."

"You've been home alone for over four months?" Catching himself, Ben took a breath. "You better tell me the whole story."

Dev wiped away another tear with the palm of his hand. "When I figured out my mom wasn't there, I went to school like normal. She's done this before. She'd go away for a day or two. Once she was gone for three days."

"And she doesn't tell you when she's going? Or where?"

Dev shook his head no.

"Or even when she'll be back?"

"No. But she always comes back. I thought this was like the other times."

"Why didn't you call the police?"

"'Cause, I was scared. I didn't want to get her in trouble, and I didn't want to leave the apartment for when she came home. I knew the police would take me away and she wouldn't know where to find me."

"But how did you manage? How could you stay in the apartment without your mom all that time?"

"I'm used to being alone there. I wasn't lying when I said my mom works a lot. She does. And she works lots of nights and weekends, so I know how to be by myself." Dev started bouncing his knee. "My mom wasn't so good with money or with paying bills, so she gave me that job. I knew I'd be okay for a while."

"You paid the bills? How? You're just a kid." Is he lying again? This is unbelievable.

"My mom let me set up online bill pay. She wasn't good with computers either, and I had one from school. So, I set up the accounts, and I paid them," Dev said with a shrug.

"What's your mom's job? Do you know where she works?"

"She's a waitress. She started at a new restaurant a while ago. I forget the name. My mom mostly got paid cash, so I learned how to make deposits and I'd do that sometimes, too. She gave me an allowance from that. She said it was my fee," Dev said with a little smile.

"I see." Maybe he is telling the truth. "So, what happened? How'd you end up in the park?"

"I knew I had enough money in the bank to pay rent for two months, so I stayed in the apartment and waited for my mom to come home. When the money ran out, I knew they wouldn't let me stay. But I thought I could stay another month before they found out I couldn't pay. One of our neighbors, they stayed for months and months without paying and the landlord, Mr. Versace, he had to call the police. I like Mr. Versace, and I didn't want him to have to do that, so I started looking for another place to live.

"The weather was getting nice, and I had a tent from Boy Scouts, so I just needed a place to put it. I checked out the dog park, but it was too open. Someone would see me. When I looked in Capitolo, I saw the bushes and the trees on the side of the rec center. I thought maybe I could put my tent in there and no one would notice.

"I started going over late in the afternoon, after the center closed, and I brought some scissors and a penknife with me. There was a dead spot near the bottom of one bush, so I broke off all the dead stuff, and crawled through. When I got to the other side, it was like a private little space. Well, you saw it."

"It was the perfect hiding spot."

"That's what I thought, so I cut off more of the bush from that side so the tent would fit better, and I made the hole bigger. Then I stuck that stuff into bare spots in the bush. I guess they'll be mad about all that."

"Maybe. You're very resourceful. You did a good job. I missed it completely the first time around."

Dev walked over to the window and looked out at the park. "Once I knew the tent would fit, I brought it over and left something in it to see if anybody would take it. They didn't. So, I left some more stuff, and nobody took that either."

"How did you keep anyone from seeing you?"

"Did you know they lock the park at night? I liked that. I thought I'd be safe. I put stuff in my backpack or my duffle bag, then walk over every night right before they locked it up. I'd hide and wouldn't come out till way after dark. Nobody noticed. Then I left what I brought in the tent, hopped the fence, and went home. I did that for a few weeks."

Resourceful *and* brave.

"When did you move in?"

"Rent was due on the first, so I figured I had a couple weeks till somebody said somethin'. I moved in on May thirteenth."

Ben's stomach dropped. *How could it be the day I walked away from Iris and my home is the same day Dev left his?*

"So, you've been living in the tent the entire time I've known you."

Dev looked at Ben for a moment, then answered, "Yes, sir."

"When we were at the Terminal Market, that was you. I saw someone duck out a delivery door. That was you?"

"Yes, sir. I saw you, so I left. I started going there because some of the stores would pay me to run an errand, like if they ran out of onions or something. It was only a couple dollars, but it helped. And the bakery, they would always give me food."

"Did they know? Did they know how you were living?"

"No. I lied. I told them I was saving for a bike. I know that was wrong. My mom says you shouldn't lie."

"Dev, you're ten years old. You were trying to survive. Your mom's right, you shouldn't lie. But in this case, it's understandable. But why didn't you tell me? Why didn't you tell the Mongellis? They love you. They would have helped."

"I don't know," Dev diverted his eyes to the floor. "I was scared."

"Scared? Of what? What did you think we would do?"

Dev looked up at Ben, his breathing becoming more rapid. "Mr. Mongelli, he's a cop. So are you. I thought you'd put me in the system when you found out. I'm not going in that. I'm not. I was there once and I'm not doin' it again." Dev's body trembled. "If you put me there, I'll run away, I swear. And you'll never find me. I know stuff now."

"The system? You mean Child Protective Services?"

Dev nodded.

Ben joined Dev at the window and put a hand on his shoulder. "I'm gonna make you a promise. I won't do anything without your consent. You've earned the right to have a say in what happens to you. You've done a fantastic job taking care of yourself all this time. You have my respect and my loyalty. And now, you're gonna have my help." Ben knelt in front of Dev. "Look at me."

Dev slowly lifted his eyes to meet Ben's.

"We're going to figure this out. Together. You and me." Ben paused, his heart sinking in sympathy. "I'm sorry this happened to you."

A tear rolled down Dev's cheek. Ben pulled him in for a hug. Dev wrapped his arms around Ben's neck and clung to him as if he were back in the ocean. Ben held the boy close and whispered, "It's gonna be all right. I've got you. You're gonna be all right now."

Ben could feel the tension in Dev's body relax. Dev released his hold and said, "I'm sorry for lying to you."

"I get it. I'm glad I know the truth now. Thanks for telling me."

Dev nodded and wiped his tears on his sleeve.

Ben stood. "You hungry? I know I am. How 'bout some breakfast?"

Ben led Dev into the dining room and sat him down at the table. He pulled a box of Entenmann's coffee cake from the freezer and placed it in the microwave to warm it. He brought a glass of milk for Dev and made another cup of coffee for himself. When the microwave beeped, Ben took the cake out of the oven and grabbed a couple of forks. "Angela said I should have this on hand for company. Guess that's you."

Dev smiled. "Want me to get some plates?"

"Plates are for chumps," Ben said, sitting down. "Dig in, dude." He handed Dev a fork, then picked up his own and took a bite of cake. Dev smiled at Ben, then dug in.

A million questions raced through Ben's mind while Dev filled his empty belly. How did he know about the IC building? Why didn't anybody turn him in? How did he manage to eat every day? Did he eat every day? How did he get himself to school? How was he able to keep up with all his schoolwork? Why didn't anyone ask questions there? Where does he think his mom went and what about his dad?

When they finished the coffee cake, Ben put his fork down and said, "Okay, buddy, let's figure out what we've got to do next. There are a couple of things I know have to happen. One, you can't stay in the park anymore."

"But—"

"No buts. You can't stay there. You keep calling me an old man, well, this old man won't get a wink of sleep knowing you're across the street in a tent. So, have some mercy on me. Plus, it's illegal."

Dev sat up straight. "Where will I go? I'm not goin' in the system."

"I didn't say anything about the system. You can stay here."

"Here?" Dev said, raising his eyebrows and looking around.

"Well, don't say it like that. What's wrong with here?"

"Well . . ."

"Well, what?"

"Well, you're a slob," Dev said, making a face at Ben.

"I see, suddenly you're picky about your surroundings. Tell you what, you can help keep this place straightened up. That can be your rent."

Dev looked around at the disheveled home, "Rent's pretty high."

"All right, wise guy, next thing. We're gonna have to tell the Mongellis."

"What? Why? Can't this be between me and you?"

"No. It can't. Dev, I don't understand. You've known the Mongellis practically your whole life. Why don't you want them to know? I'm sure they'll want to help you."

"That's why. I don't want them to feel sorry for me and I don't want them to be," Dev looked at the floor and whispered, "ashamed of me."

"Ashamed of you? They have no reason to be ashamed of you. This wasn't your fault. You've been doing the best you can. You've been incredible. Ashamed of you? No way. They'll be proud of you.

"And what about Chase? He's your best friend. Shouldn't he know? Why didn't you tell him? He wouldn't judge you. Heck, he probably would have helped you set up the tent."

"That's why. I didn't tell him 'cause I didn't want to get him in trouble."

"How would he get in trouble?"

"Chase would've helped me, and he wouldn't have told. I know him. He would've brought me food and whatever I needed. And if somebody found out, he'd get in trouble. I didn't want that."

"You were protecting him."

Dev nodded.

"Well, now *I know*, so they have to know, too. It wouldn't be right keeping something like this from them. They won't be home for a few more days, so that'll give us time to work out how we're gonna tell them."

"We? You mean you'll go with me?"

"Absolutely. We're in this together now. I meant it when

I said you could climb on my back, and I would carry you. This is one of those times. As long as you want me, I'll be here for you."

Dev got up from his chair and stood next to Ben. His eyes flooded with tears. He leaned over and hugged Ben. Ben held the boy as he cried.

"It's gonna be okay, buddy. It's gonna be okay. I promise."

Ben prayed often, but rarely on his knees, especially after turning sixty. At the end of the day, he was there for the second time in the past several months, this time praying for Dev.

"Well, God, this is a mess, isn't it? A ten-year-old boy living by himself . . . in a tent. Thanks for watching over him and keeping him safe. Help him to sleep easy tonight. I'm sure that will be a change for him.

"What about his mom, Lord? What happened to her? Help me to figure that one out. And the Mongellis . . ." Ben exhaled. "I know they love Dev, help them to take all this in, then give Dev the support he's gonna need.

"I'm gonna need help too. Please give me wisdom to deal with what's ahead. These could be hard days coming. I know you'll work it all out . . . somehow. I pray all this in Jesus's name.

Amen."

He got into bed and tried to sleep. Instead, he tossed and turned as he played out various scenarios in his mind. He sat up, turned on the light, and picked up the Bible on his nightstand. His bookmark was in the twenty-ninth chapter of Jeremiah. He began reading and when he got to verse eleven, he nodded and read the passage out loud.

"For I know the plans I have for you," declares the Lord, "plans to prosper you and not to harm you, plans to give you hope and a future. Then you will call on me and come and pray to me, and I will listen to you. You will seek me and find me when you seek me with all your heart. I will be found by you," declares the Lord, "and I will bring you back from captivity. I will gather you from all the nations and places where I have banished you," declares the Lord, "and will bring you back to the place from which I carried you into exile."

CHAPTER 15

It Hits the Fan

Ben answered his phone. "Hey, JJ, welcome back. Hope the rest of your vacation went well."

"It did. It always feels good to get away, but it always feels good to get back home, too. Anything new with you?"

"Actually, yes. Could I stop by tomorrow afternoon, and can I bring a friend?"

"A friend, huh? Well, I'm sure that would be fine."

"Come on over, Ben, but you have to stay for dinner. And your *friend,* too!" Angela called from the background.

"I don't know how she does that," JJ said.

"Tell her I said thanks, and I'll see you tomorrow."

"You're welcome!" Angela said.

Sunday morning, Ben quietly opened the door of his guest room. Dev was sound asleep, laying on his side, the Phanatic tucked under one arm.

How could anyone in their right mind ever leave him?

Ben sat at the bottom of the bed. "Hey, buddy," he whispered and gave Dev's leg a gentle pat.

Dev rolled onto his back, blinked a few times, then opened his eyes slowly.

"Good morning. Sorry to wake you," Ben said softly.

"Did something happen? Am I in trouble?" Dev bolted upright.

"No, you're not in trouble. Everything's fine. Sorry I scared you." Ben patted Dev's leg again. "I only thought maybe we could go to church together this morning. Ever been?"

"Oh." Dev rubbed his eyes then stretched his arms and yawned. "Yeah, me and my mom always go at Christmas."

"Well, it's not Christmas, but it's a regular thing for me. I was thinking, since you're here, maybe you'd want to come too, especially today."

"You think it could help with the Mongellis?"

"Couldn't hurt." Ben stood up.

Dev nodded and got out of bed.

"See ya downstairs. I'll make us some breakfast."

Dev was silent through breakfast. The silence continued as he walked down the street with Ben to the church, and through the service, and back to Ben's home. Ben allowed the boy to be lost in his thoughts, knowing what was to come would be difficult for him.

When the clock struck two, Ben looked at Dev and said, "Time to go."

"You sure about this?" Dev asked, his forehead crinkled and his eyes pleading.

"Yes, I'm absolutely sure. The Mongellis won't disappoint you. It's gonna be okay."

Dev sighed, then walked with Ben out of the house and to the Mongellis.

"There you are!" Angela said, opening the door to her home. "Come in, come in! Can't believe it's only been a week or so since we saw you, Ben. Seems longer. And Dev? This is a nice surprise. Is this the friend you were talking about?"

Ben smiled. "Yes, didn't think you'd mind, Ang."

"Of course not." She opened her arms to Dev. "Come here, *amorino*, and give me a hug. I've missed you." Dev went to her and clasped his arms around her tightly, laying his head on her shoulder. She looked up at Ben with a question in her eyes. She patted Dev on the back, then released him. "Chase is upstairs in his room. Why don't you go get him and bring him down?" She watched him leave the room, then whispered to Ben, "What's going on?"

"Where's JJ? We need to speak to you all. Together."

"I'll get him. He's out back." She hurried out of the room and returned with JJ as Chase and Dev came down the stairs.

Once they were all together, Ben said, "Dev has

something he'd like to tell you all. It's important."

"Why don't we go sit in the living room? We'll be more comfortable there," Angela said with a smile toward Dev. With his chin tucked to his chest, Dev trailed behind everyone into the room. They sat and waited for him to speak. He remained silent on the sofa next to Ben, staring at the floor.

"C'mon, bruh. What's goin' on? Can't be that bad," Chase said.

Dev looked up at him and in a voice just above a whisper he said, "It is." He glanced at Ben, then returned his gaze to the floor. "I've been lying to you . . . to you all."

"Lyin'. About what?" Chase asked, frowning.

Dev looked at Ben again then at each of the Mongellis. He swallowed hard. "When I went down the shore with you, my mom didn't know. I, um, I didn't tell her."

"What?" Angela said. "You came without your mother's permission?"

Dev nodded.

"Why? Why would you do that? That's not like you, Dev."

"Because. I, um," Dev twisted the bottom of his t-shirt around his index finger, then whispered, his eyes watering, "I don't know where my mom is."

Ben put his hand on Dev's shoulder. "Dev's mother is missing. She left . . . a while ago. He doesn't know where she's gone."

"Oh, my," Angela said, catching her breath.

"How long has she been away?" JJ asked.

Ben patted Dev's back. "A little over four months."

Angela cried out, "Four months! Dev, why didn't you—" JJ put his hand on his wife's knee. Angela turned to him, and he gave her a quick shake of his head. She nodded and shifted in her seat.

"You've been in your apartment on your own for four months?" JJ asked.

"Not exactly," Dev said, clenching his hands together, his shoulders hunched. He looked at Ben again and trembled. Ben patted his back then took over the conversation.

"Dev stayed in the apartment as long as he could. When he ran out of money and thought he'd be evicted, he set up a tent in the park. That's where he's been living the past couple months."

"In the park. What park?" Angela asked, her eyes filling with tears.

"Capitolo Playground," Ben said. "The park across the street from my house."

"You've been living in the park," Angela said. "Dev . . ." She put her hand over her mouth.

"I'm sorry to hear what's happened," JJ said. "We're all sorry and we want to help."

With that, Chase stood and glared at his friend. He

turned his back on him, stomped up the staircase, and slammed the door to his bedroom.

"He's upset. I'll go," Angela said, getting up.

"No, I'll go." JJ patted Angela on the shoulder. "I'll be right back." He smiled at her then pointed to Dev. "You stay put."

Dev nodded. "Yes, sir."

JJ walked up to Chase's room and pushed open the door. He watched as Chase went to his dresser, opened drawers, and rooted through the clothing inside. T-shirts and socks cascaded from one open drawer to the next and onto the floor. Chase gave up on the dresser and went to the closet. He got on his knees, plunged his head inside, and threw clothing and shoes over his shoulder into the middle of his room, digging for something with as much energy as a dog digging for a bone.

"Chase, what are you doing?"

"I'm looking for somethin'."

"Chase."

He ignored his father.

"Chase, stop."

The boy froze. He sat back on his heels, his face hardened, and his eyes fixed on the closet.

"Come here, son." JJ sat on Chase's bed. Chase rose slowly. With hot tears rolling down his cheeks, and his jaw jutted forward, he went to his father.

"I know you're upset. We all are."

Chase's voice trembled. "He lied to me. My best friend lied to me for months!"

"I know. I know. But think about what it's been like for Dev. He wakes up one morning and his mom is gone. Can you imagine what that felt like? He's been through something traumatic. He's still going through it. We shouldn't be angry with him."

"Angry at *him*? I'm not angry at him." Chase stepped back. "I know why he did it, why he didn't tell me. He does stuff like that all the time. He probably figured I'd wanna help him and I'd get in trouble somehow. Dev's always trying to keep me out of trouble. That's why he didn't tell."

"Well, if you're not angry at him? Who are you angry with?" JJ pointed to the disarray around Chase's room. "And what are you trying to accomplish here?"

"I'm angry . . . I'm angry at his mom," Chase's voice cracked. "How could she do that? Just *leave*. Doesn't she know a kid needs his mom?"

JJ shook his head. "I don't understand either. I'm sure she had a reason."

"Not a good one. No one should do that to a kid, 'specially a mom." Chase scanned his room, then stared at his desk for a moment. He walked over to it and opened a drawer.

"There it is." he sighed. "I knew I had it. I forgot I put it here to keep it safe."

"What's that?"

Chase reached into the drawer and pulled out a baseball housed in a plastic case. He held it up to his father. "This, my autographed Chase Utley ball. Remember when we got this? When we were at the game, and he hit that homer right at us?"

JJ smiled and said, "Yes, and you nabbed it. Couldn't believe you caught it. You were amazing, but why are you looking for it now?"

"I thought I could sell it."

JJ tilted his head. "Sell it? Why? I thought you loved that ball."

"Dev needs help. I thought I'd sell it and give him the money."

JJ stood and said, "Come here." Chase trudged his way back to his father. JJ rested his hands on his son's shoulders. "That's about the kindest thing I've ever heard. You're a fine man, Chase Mongelli. I'm proud of you."

JJ stooped and hugged his son. Chase buried his head in his father's chest, wrapping his arms around his waist. JJ kissed him on the head, then knelt to look him in the eye. With his own eyes glistening, he said, "You're right, Dev needs help. And we're going to give it to him, all of us. Don't you worry, we'll figure this out." He tapped Chase's chest. "You keep that ball safe for now. I'll let you know if we need it."

"Dad, you cryin' too?"

"Yeah, well, don't tell your mother." JJ grinned and wiped his eyes. Chase nodded and wiped his own eyes and nose on the bottom of his t-shirt.

"All right, can we go back down now? Dev needs us." Chase nodded. Father and son walked downstairs together and back to the living room.

The room was silent as Chase approached Dev. Dev stood. "I'm sorry, Chase."

"It's okay. But Dev, you ever lie to me again, I'm gonna punch you in the face." A slow smile crossed Chase's face. Dev smiled back as Chase held out his hand for their special handshake. Ben breathed a sigh of relief, JJ smiled, and Angela went in search of more tissues.

CHAPTER 16

What's Next

Angela brought out a tray of fruit and cookies and set it on the coffee table. "I thought we could use some food."

"Thanks, babe," JJ said, smiling at his wife speaking her love language again.

"Okay, so what's next?" Angela sat next to JJ.

"What's next is we make sure Dev has a safe place to stay. I assume you're not still in the park," JJ said.

"No, I'm staying with Ben." Dev looked toward Ben and dipped his head. "He found my tent."

"We moved him out of the park and into my house right after I found him. He's been there the past few days."

"Glad to hear it, but now, we need to get you settled somewhere while we find out what happened to your mom, and that may take a while." Then turning toward his wife, he said,

"What do you think, Ang?"

Angela smiled. "Vincent will be working down the shore till the end of summer then he'll be going right back to Temple. You could stay here and have his room. We'd love to have you, Dev."

Dev smiled at her, then looked down at his lap and squeezed his hands together.

"What is it? You don't want to stay here?" Angela asked.

Dev looked up at Ben. "Could I stay with you?"

"Uh, me? You want to stay with me?"

Dev nodded.

"With *Ben*?" Angela asked incredulously.

"Well, don't say it like that," Ben said, making a face at Angela.

"I'm sorry, Ben, but . . . you're a slob. No offense."

Dev smiled. "Yeah, he is. He needs me." He turned to Ben, "You said I could have a say about what happens to me."

"That I did." Probably wasn't a good idea to say that.

"So, can I stay with you?"

"Of course you can." Ben looked at Angela. "And I'll work on my housekeeping skills."

Angela smiled a worried smile.

"All right, that's settled," JJ said. "Now, I have to tell you, Dev, as a sworn officer of the law, when I hear something like this, like what happened to you, I'm obligated to report it. Do you understand?"

"Yes, sir." Tears travelled down the well-worn path from Dev's eyes to his cheeks.

JJ leaned forward. "Hear me on this. You will not spend one day in Child Services. There's no way on God's green earth Angela will let that happen, not while she has breath in her lungs. And neither will I, and neither will Ben."

"And me neither," Chase chimed in.

"We're going to take care of you. All of us. Believe that."

Dev nodded, wiped his eyes on his sleeve. "Yes, sir."

"I do have to report what's happened. But I don't have to do it right away," JJ said with a wink and a smile. "I'm going to work tomorrow, and I'll check in with some friends, get their advice on what to do, how to handle this in the best way for you. Then I'll let you know. Okay?"

"Okay."

"And I think tomorrow Dev and I will pay his landlord a visit," Ben said.

"Mr. Versace? Why do you wanna see him?" Dev asked.

"I was thinking, it hasn't been that long since you left the apartment. Maybe he hasn't done anything with it yet, and there may be a clue or two there about where your mom went. Think you can handle going back?"

"I'll go with you," Chase said, volunteering. Dev smiled and nodded quickly at his friend.

"All right, sounds like we have a plan," Ben said. Then, turning and looking at everyone in the room, he asked, "So, does everyone think I'm a slob?"

They all smiled and in unison said, "Yes!"

CHAPTER 17

Puzzle Pieces

In the morning, Ben, Dev, and Chase went to the Tenth Street Apartments and met with Mr. Versace, the landlord. Ben explained what happened.

"*Che tragicità!* So sorry to hear this," Mr. Versace said. "I wondered what was going on. It was odd the rent was late, usually she pays a few days in advance. I sent a notice and called, but I didn't hear back. After a few more weeks, I thought I should check, so I got the master key and went into the apartment. Everything looked neat, like they'd left and planned to return. I thought maybe there was an emergency. I had no idea . . .

"I've never had any trouble from them, so I thought I'd give it a little time. If I didn't hear from her by the end of this month, I was going to start eviction proceedings." He put his hand on Dev's shoulder. "I'm so sorry to hear your troubles,

Dev. I'd like to help."

Ben said, "That's very kind of you. What we'd like to do is get back in the apartment and check for any clues of where Dev's mother may have gone. And I'd like to pay the back rent."

"No. No, that won't be necessary. This young man," he tapped Dev on the shoulder. "He's a good kid. He takes care of his mom, and he helps other people around here too. A little while back, my wife was very sick. Dev stopped by every day after school to read to her while she was in bed. He even went to market for me so I wouldn't have to leave her."

He squeezed Dev's shoulder. "You helped me, now I'm gonna help you. That's how it works." He looked at Ben. "I'll take the back rent out of their security deposit. Anything over that, I'll forgive. If you want to keep the apartment, you can start paying rent on the first, no security necessary."

"That's awfully nice of you, Mr. Versace. It'll be a big help. I think we'd like to keep the apartment for a month, and hopefully by then, we'll have some answers."

"Very good. Dev, you still have your key?"

"Yes, sir."

"Feel free to use it any time. And let me know if there's anything else I can do for you." Mr. Versace tapped him on the shoulder again. "You're a good boy. I'll say a prayer and light a candle for your mother."

"Thank you, Mr. Versace."

Following their conversation, the trio went to Dev's apartment. While Dev and Chase packed up some of Dev's belongings, Ben searched for clues. Several hours passed when Ben received a phone call.

"Ben, can you meet me at the station house?"

"Sure, JJ, we're wrapping up here. We can pop by after that."

"Not we. I think you should leave the boys at home. Have them go back to my place and hang out there for a while with Angela."

"Okay, sounds serious."

"Yeah, it is. See you soon."

Ben dropped Dev and Chase off with Angela then drove to the station house. JJ met him, escorted him to his office, then closed the door. He poured Ben a cup of coffee.

"All right, we need to talk. Dev doesn't need to hear this, at least not yet. You and I, we've been around long enough to know odds are this will not end well. I'm sure we have the same suspicions."

"Drugs are involved," Ben said as he sat on the chair in front of JJ's desk. "When Dev told me his mom has done this before, I thought that may be the case. I didn't want to push him about it, though. It took him a while to tell me about living in the park. I thought we'd get to his mom another time."

"How'd it go with the landlord?" JJ asked as he poured

himself a cup of coffee.

"Really well. Long story short, he was surprised to hear about what happened and he was concerned for Dev. I offered to pay the overdue rent, but he refused. He said he'd take it out of the security deposit and anything else owed, he'd forgive. He said if we want to keep the apartment, we can. Just start paying rent on the first."

"Wow, that's something," JJ said, moving to his desk chair.

"Yeah, it was pretty kind. I thanked him, said we'd like to keep it for a month, and by then hopefully, we'd know more. Now we can take our time and get some answers before we make any permanent decisions."

"Good. We're gonna need it."

There was a knock on the office door. "Enter," JJ called out.

"Here's the printouts you asked for, Captain," an officer said, handing JJ a folder.

"Thanks, Rodriguez." JJ put the folder on the corner of his desk as the officer exited. "Were you able to find anything helpful in the apartment?"

"No. I went through the entire place. I didn't see anything that could have pulled her away from home. No notes, no extraordinary bills, nothing. And there wasn't even any evidence of drug use. She must have been careful not to bring

A Good Place to Turn Around

anything home. Speaks well of her. And it doesn't seem she took much with her at all when she left. Dev said the only things missing were her keys and her phone. She even left her purse behind. Maybe we're wrong about drugs. It really did look like she was going out for a walk or something and then vanished." Ben took a sip of his coffee.

"She wasn't going for a walk." JJ took the file folder the officer dropped off and slid it in front of Ben. "Take a look. I had a few things printed out for you." The file was labeled "Anna Murphy".

Ben opened the folder. "Anna Murphy, that's Dev's mom?"

"That's her. Arrested once for shoplifting. That's when Dev went into the system. That's why he doesn't want to go back. He was only there for a couple of months when he was in second grade, but it was enough."

"She's twenty-seven? Seems young to have a ten-year-old," Ben said, looking at her statistics.

"It is young. She was seventeen when she had him. Keep reading." JJ pointed to the file.

Ben turned the page, read it, then looked up at JJ. "She was raped?"

JJ nodded. "Coming home from a high school football game. She was attacked. They caught the guy a few months later. Anna was his third victim. He was trying for a fourth when he was nabbed. Only two of the women pressed charges—the last girl and Anna. She's a brave girl."

Ben stared at the folder, absorbing what JJ revealed. "Yes, she is. And she kept him. Dev, she kept him. At seventeen."

JJ nodded. "Yes. She dropped out of school, no wonder. She didn't have much of a home life herself. Dad was a drunk. Killed himself in a one-vehicle car crash years before Dev was born. Mom wasn't much better. She was a drug addict. OD'd a few years ago."

"Man . . ." Ben continued to turn file pages. "Looks like she was in and out of rehab several times."

"Yeah, just didn't stick. Addiction's rough."

"I wonder how much of this Dev knows."

"Good question. I've never heard him speak of any family besides his mom. And he's never said anything about rehab. Hopefully, he's been spared some of this." JJ took the folder back and placed it on the corner of his desk. He tapped it. "This is tough stuff."

Ben nodded. "I checked in with a few of the neighbors, and no one saw her or anything unusual. I found a picture of her in the apartment and thought I'd start canvasing the neighborhood. I doubt it'll amount to anything, but it'll give me something positive to do."

"Good idea. I've put in a request for Anna's phone

records. We may turn up something there." JJ took a deep breath. "You sure you're okay keeping Dev? Kids can be a lot of work, and you know Angela, she'd love to have him."

"I'm sure, for now. It's what he wants, and I promised he'd have a say in what happens to him. I'd like to keep that promise." Ben took another sip of coffee. "We took more of his belongings over to my place, so at least he has most of his clothes and some of his things to make him feel comfortable. Who knows? Maybe we'll have a family reunion between him and his mom in a little while. That's my hope anyway."

"Yeah," JJ said with a sigh that showed he didn't have the same hope. "The next thing is, I'm going to report this at the end of the day. If you want Dev to stay with you, you'll have to get appointed as his temporary guardian. I talked to a friend in the law department, and she said she could pull a few strings and get you in front of a sympathetic judge. You haven't been a PA resident long, so they may want to appoint someone else, but considering you saved his life, and you're a former police officer, they may be willing to forego that detail. If they don't, Ang and I will do it."

"All right, I'll let Dev know what's happening and then you tell me when and where to show up and I'll be there," Ben said, standing. "Thanks, JJ."

JJ filed his report at the end of the day, and the next morning Ben filed the necessary paperwork to obtain temporary guardianship of Dev. A hearing was set for Thursday morning and Ben and Dev appeared before the judge. After a review of the petition and some questioning, the judge agreed to Ben's request and his temporary guardianship was granted.

Following the hearing, the two went back to Ben's house. Rain murmured like white noise against the windows as they had a quiet lunch together. When lunch was over, Dev cleared the table, then disappeared to the guest room.

Ben sat in the living room, reviewing notes from his investigation. He closed his eyes. *God, please help me with what I'm about to do. Give me the right words and give me the insight I need to help Dev.*

Ben went upstairs and knocked on the guest room door. He popped his head in. "Can I talk to you?"

Dev was sitting on the bed writing in a spiral notebook. He put the notebook aside. "Sure."

"I need to ask you some questions, some personal stuff. I'm sorry to do it, but it may help us find your mom."

"Okay." Dev sat up and gave Ben his full attention.

Ben sat on the foot of the bed, rubbed his hands together, tapped them on his knees a few times, then said, "Do you know, did you ever see . . . Ah, I hate to ask this, Dev. I mean no disrespect, and I pass no judgment, but I have to know. Do you know if your mom ever did drugs?"

Dev looked at his notebook, his forehead wrinkled. He

nodded.

"Did you ever see her with them?"

"No. I only know because that's why I was in the system. My mom told me about it later, that she did a bad thing. She stole something from a store to get money to buy drugs. She felt real bad about it, 'specially 'cause they took me away from her. That's when she went to rehab for the first time. I didn't see her for months."

Well, that's a relief. He doesn't know his mom was in jail during that time.

"Drugs are a hard thing. They change people. Your mom, she was trying, though. JJ said she was in rehab a few times."

"Yeah, she was."

"What happened to you when she was there? Where did you go?"

"I stayed with her mom the next time. She wasn't very nice," Dev said with a troubled look. "The last time, Mom asked Mrs. DeSantas if she would look after me. And she did. I like her."

"She seems like a kind lady," Ben said, remembering the conversation he had with Dev's neighbor when he canvased the apartment building.

"Do you know anything about your grandfather?"

"No. He died before I was born. My mom never talks about him. I think she was afraid of him."

"What makes you say that?"

"A look she'd get. My grandma would say something about him, and my mom would get that look. I didn't like it."

Anna, how bad was your past?

"And what about your father? Do you know anything about him?"

Dev's face tensed.

Yes, you do know something, don't you?

"He was not a nice man," Dev whispered.

"No, he wasn't."

"Do you know about him?" Dev asked, his chin trembling.

"A little. Why don't you tell me what you know."

Dev shifted in the bed. "You sure you wanna know?"

"I'm sure." He patted Dev on the leg. "I know this is hard, and I wouldn't ask if I didn't think it could help. Whatever you say, it'll be between you, me, and JJ, all right?"

Dev nodded. He picked up a pillow and put it on his lap. "Last year, Chase and me, we found out you can google people and see what the internet says about them. So, we googled his dad, and we saw an article about when he got shot by a robber. Did you know that?"

Ben nodded.

"We didn't know. Mr. Mongelli always said it was a war wound. I don't know why he said that," Dev said, shaking his head. "When I got home, I googled my mom, and that's when I saw it."

"What did you see?"

"An article about her. Some group that helps women interviewed her, and she talked about what happened. My mom came in the room and when she saw what I was reading, she closed the computer. She wasn't mad at me. She was sad. She asked if I wanted to know what happened, and I said yes."

Dev held the pillow up to his stomach and squeezed it. He spoke softly, as if he thought someone may overhear. "After one of the football games, she walked home by herself. Some guy came out of the alley, and grabbed her, and pulled her back there. She fought real hard, but he was too strong." Dev's eyes welled with tears.

"I'm sorry, Dev." I hate having to ask these questions. It's tough enough for him without having to relive the past.

Dev wiped his eyes on his sleeve. "Mom said that man thought he took something from her, but he didn't. She said he gave her something instead."

Ben smiled. "You."

"Yeah. She said I was her present. She never got much for Christmas, so I was the gift she waited for."

"Best present ever."

"I asked her why she did the interview. She said she wanted to help other women. Sometimes they're afraid to tell what happened to them. She wanted them to know if she could do it, they could do it, too."

"Your mom is something else," Ben said, feeling a tightness in his throat. "You okay answering a few more questions? We can stop if you want."

"I'm okay." Dev gripped the pillow harder. "What else do you want to know?"

"Do you know what happened to that man?"

"Mom said he's in prison. She said I never have to worry about him." Dev clutched the pillow, his breath quickening. "Is he out? Is that why you're asking questions? Is he gonna try and get me? To take me away?"

"No. No, he's not. You don't have to be afraid. I'm asking you these questions because I need to know all I can about your mom. You never know what little detail can help find her."

Should I tell him the rest?

"You know something."

Ben sat back.

"Tell me." Dev put the pillow down. "Please."

Ben sighed. "Your mom was right. You never have to worry about that man. He's gone. He got in a fight in prison and well, he's gone." Ben could see Dev's body relax with the news.

"I'm sorry for him."

What kind of kid are you that you can show compassion to a man like that? You're something else.

"Thanks for telling me all this, bud. I appreciate it. That was very brave of you."

"Just find my mom."

"I'm trying." He patted Dev on the leg and left the room.

CHAPTER 18

Portraits and Poetry

Over the next week, Ben scoured a four-block radius in the neighborhood using Dev's apartment building as the center. Few people recognized Anna, and those who did, had little to say about her. Like Dev she was quiet, unassuming, and kept mostly to herself.

Ben did discover one interesting puzzle piece. One of the local police officers knew Anna and, more importantly, he knew where she worked. She was a waitress at a local pub, about five blocks away from her apartment building. When Ben visited the pub, the owner told him Anna had been laid off. Business was slow, and she had been the last waitress hired, so she was the first to go. He called JJ with the news.

"She lost her job?" JJ asked over the phone. "That could do it, that could have sent her over the edge."

"That's what I was thinking," Ben said. "It happened the

day before she disappeared."

"I've got some other news, and it's not good. I got the phone records back from the phone company. It looks like the last time she texted Dev, she was in Kensington and from what you just told me, that was the day she was let go."

"Kensington? Where's that?"

"It's a neighborhood of Philly, about five miles north of here. The locals call it 'Zombie Town'. If you want to find drugs or do drugs, that's where you go."

"Oh, man."

"At least we know where to focus our attention now, and we have a reason for her being there," JJ said. "I'll get in touch with that precinct. We'll keep up the search."

"I think I'll wait to tell Dev any of this until we know more."

"Good idea."

"I could use your advice about something, Jay. I've been thinking about heading back to Maine for a bit. Thought it might do Dev some good to take a break from all this. He's been pretty tense. He's putting on a good face, but if he cleans my bathroom one more time . . ."

JJ laughed. "Sounds like that would be a good idea for you both. Go. School's gonna start in a few weeks, so it would be good for him to get out and get some fresh air. Maine might be just the thing. Give his mind a rest, if that's possible."

"All right, I'll see what I can arrange. Thanks again, Jay."

Ben returned home to find Dev lying on the living room floor, surrounded by papers and spiral notebooks. "Hey, I'm back. Anything happening?" Ben looked at the heap of papers. "What's all this?"

Dev closed his notebook and collected the papers. "It's nothing. Chase called. He wants to know if I can come over and play video games. Supposed to rain again today, so no basketball. Can I go?"

He waited to ask permission. That's a surprise.

"Sure, that's fine. You go have a good time. I've got some things to do around here. Just be back for dinner, okay?"

"Okay." Dev stacked his papers and notebooks in a neat pile on the coffee table, then ran down the stairs and out the door. Ben watched him from the window, then turned back to sit on the couch. As he did, he knocked over Dev's papers, scattering them across the floor.

"Great." He took a deep breath. "Okay, Benjamin, let us not be a slob." He picked up the pages. "What's this?" He held a drawing of a young woman. It was Anna. He looked at each page, and each displayed a drawing, sometimes of Anna, sometimes a car, or a dog, or a building. There was even a pencil sketch Ben thought looked a lot like him. Along with the sketches, each page contained writing. Ben sat down on the couch and began to read.

Poetry filled each sheet. Poems about friendship, and nature, and as Ben read a poem he assumed was about Anna, a voice startled him.

"What are you doing?"

Ben looked up to see Dev staring at him.

"You're back. What happened?"

"I forgot my phone. Thought I should keep it with me just in case. What are you doing with my papers?" Dev asked again, staring at the papers in Ben's hands.

"Uh, nothing. I was gonna sit on the couch and I knocked them over by accident. I was just picking them up. You know, trying to be less of a slob." Ben smiled.

Dev frowned in return and took the papers out of Ben's hands. "These are private. You shouldn't be looking at them."

"I'm sorry. It was an accident."

"Knocking them over was, but not reading them." Dev bit his lip.

"You're right. I'm sorry. I should have waited and asked you, but I saw the pictures and Dev, these are fantastic. You did all this?" Ben pointed to the drawings.

Dev nodded.

"You're some kinda artist, dude. I can't even draw stick figures." Dev gave Ben a small smile.

"And the poetry. You like to write poetry?"

"Yeah," Dev said with a shrug of his shoulder. "I know

it's not cool, but I like it."

"Well, I think it's cool, and it looks like you're good at it too. I liked the one about the ocean, about how big it is. Reminded me of when we were at the—*down the shore*," Ben said, correcting himself.

"I like that one too." Dev looked at the floor. "But you shouldn't have read 'em. I don't like people reading them."

"Why? These are really good. Why don't you want anyone to see them?"

"I just don't." Dev's eyes pooled with tears.

"I'm sorry, buddy. You're right. They're yours and no one should see them unless you want them to. I know they're private now and I swear, I won't look at any of it again unless you give me permission. Okay?"

Dev nodded. "I'm gonna get my phone now." He grabbed it off the table, then left the house once more and ran toward the Mongelli's.

"Ben? I'm back. Where are you?" Dev said.

"In the kitchen. Come on in."

"What's that?" Dev pointed to the pot on the stove and took a whiff.

"Chili. It's my mom's recipe."

"Smells good. That's for dinner?"

"Yep. I may be a slob, but my mom made sure I knew how to cook before I left home. 'It's a skill every man should have,' she used to tell me and my brothers."

"Maybe I should learn too."

"Good idea, knucklehead. Why don't you give me a hand finishing this?"

Dev helped Ben stir, add ingredients, then stir some more. When it was finished, with his head held high, he marched two steaming bowls of chili to the dining room table. Ben said grace, then picked up his spoon and raised his eyebrows at Dev. Dev picked up his spoon as well and they tapped their spoons together in a toast to chili. They each took a taste.

"Well?" Ben asked.

Dev smiled. "Good. I like it!"

"My mom would be happy to hear that." Ben took a bite. "I was thinking. I haven't seen my mom and dad in months, and I'd like to. I thought I'd pay them a visit . . . *in Maine*. Would you like to go?"

Dev's eyes lit up. "Can we see the ocean? Like you said, with the granite and the other rocks?"

"Absolutely." Ben smiled. "I'll see if we can stay with my sister, and we can go visit some of my friends in Eastport, too. Eastport's right on the bay, so you can get a good view of the

Maine coastline from there."

"Awesome! When do we leave? What should I pack?" Dev stood up.

"Hang on there, partner. I need to check in with Jen first and make a few other phone calls, make sure it's all right to take you out of the state. If all goes well, we can leave on Friday."

"Okay. Can I go to the library?"

"Now? I don't think they're open. Why do you want to go there?"

"Research. I had to turn in my computer at the end of the school year, but I can use the one at the library. I want to know some things before I get there."

"I see. Tell you what, you can use my laptop."

"Yours? Really? You don't mind?"

"I don't mind at all. We're partners, we can share. It's up on my desk in the bedroom. Why don't you go get it and bring it down here."

Dev started to leave, then stopped. He went to Ben and hugged him. He whispered, "Thanks," then turned and ran up the stairs.

Once again, Ben was left with a lump in his throat and worry on his mind.

CHAPTER 19

Oliver

Dev bounced his way into Ben's truck and as they pulled onto the highway, his knee continued to bounce at a speed that matched the flow of traffic. Once out of the boundaries of the city, the thoughts he'd been holding tumbled out in a freefall of questions.

"Do you think we'll see a moose? Or seals? Or whales?"

"Mebbe," Ben answered with a sly smile and raise of the eyebrows.

"What's lobster taste like? Chase says it's rubbery. Is it like a Gummi Bear?"

"Don't believe everything Chase tells you."

"What about the kids? Do they play basketball?"

"Sure they do. They're kids, just like you."

"It snows a lot in Maine, right?"

"Yes, Maine can get a wicked amount of snow."

"Do kids get off school every time it snows?"

"Not every time."

"What was it like to be sheriff? Did you have to shoot anybody?"

Ben gave Dev a sideways glance. "Is this what you're really like?"

"Huh? What'd you mean?"

"I don't think I've heard you string this many words together at once since I've known you. Is this what you're like when Chase isn't around?"

"Don't pick on Chase. He's my best friend."

"I know, he's your *jawn*. I'm not picking on him. I'm just saying his spotlight can be a little bright and sometimes I think you get lost in his shadow."

"I don't mind. I don't like the spotlight." Dev looked out the passenger window. "He can have it."

That evening they stayed at a hotel in Portsmouth, New Hampshire, and they were back on the road early in the morning. As they crossed the Piscataqua River Bridge, Ben announced, "Welcome to Maine!"

"We're here?" Dev asked. He looked out his window. "Kinda looks the same."

"We're just over the border and we're still on the highway. It's gonna look like this for a while, but believe me, we're in Maine now."

"Awesome." Dev grinned.

Three hours later, they pulled into Oliver's driveway. Ben got out of the truck and removed his and Dev's duffle bags.

"Hey, there, brother!" Oliver said, coming out of the house.

"Ollie. Good to see you." Ben gave his brother a hug.

"Thought you were bringing someone with you," Oliver said.

"I did. Dev?" Ben looked around and spied Dev still in the car. He opened the door. "You okay, buddy?"

Dev nodded.

"Listen, you don't have to be nervous. Oliver's great. Besides, if he gives you a hard time, I can still beat him up."

"Don't believe it! This guy's ancient now. I can take him," Oliver said, coming behind Ben. "You must be Dev. Nice to meet you." He reached out his hand.

Dev smiled and shook Oliver's hand. "Nice to meet you too, sir."

"Sir? I like this kid already. I think *you* should call me sir." Oliver elbowed Ben.

"In your dreams, Sparky. All right, Dev, let's get our stuff inside."

Dev slid out of the car and laughed at the brothers as they continued to poke fun at each other. Vanessa, Oliver's wife, met them at the door.

"Ben, good to see you. And Dev?" she held out her hand. "I'm Vanessa. Welcome to Maine."

"Thanks," Dev said, shaking her hand, then looking at the ground.

"Ben, go ahead and put your things up in the guest room, Dev can have Peter's room. Come down soon, dinner's about ready."

"It's tacos tonight!" Oliver said.

Dev whispered to Ben on the way up the stairs. "Is he your twin?"

Ben laughed. "No, but a lot of people think so. I guess we do look alike."

"Must be nice to have a brother."

Over dinner, Oliver shared stories about his and Ben's childhood days when they would go traipsing through the Maine woods.

"There was one time, Dev, when we were on vacation in Eastport. We were about your age. The family was spending the day over by Boyden Lake and Ben and I decided to take a hike. We hadn't been hiking through the woods long, maybe a half hour, when I saw something rustling in the bushes ahead. I motioned for Ben to hold still. I was afraid it was a moose. Ben wasn't one for holding still, so he marched ahead and instead of a moose, out of the bush came a skunk. It took one look at Ben, lifted his tail and–" Oliver waved his hands in front of his nose.

"It sprayed you?" Dev asked, bouncing in his seat.

"Yes, sir, it did. And it didn't miss! Got us both, but good," Oliver said with a laugh. "We took off running, headed straight to the lake and jumped in. Didn't help much. It was in our hair, on our skin, in our eyes. That stuff stings!"

Ben laughed and said, "We stopped at the IGA on the way back and Ma emptied the tomato juice shelf. She made us both bathe in it—outdoors, of course. No way she was letting us in the house. Ma made us sleep out under the stars that night!"

"Tomato juice?" Dev asked. "Are you making this up?"

"No, we really bathed in tomato juice," Oliver said. "That was an old school remedy for skunk, but Ben stunk too much. They had to bring out the big guns for him—hydrogen peroxide and baking soda. We called him *Peppe le PeeYou* for a while after that." Oliver held his nose and waved his hands at Ben. "We even had to burn his clothes!"

"Thanks for sharing, bro," Ben said.

"*Peppe le PeeYou*." Dev laughed.

"I think that's enough out of you, knucklehead. Why don't you go get ready for bed while I beat up my brother for telling secrets on me?"

Dev continued to giggle as he made his way to the bedroom.

"Nice kid," Oliver said.

"Yeah, he is. Got a rough road ahead of him, I'm afraid."

"Well, with you in his corner, he'll be fine."

"Hope so. Guess I'll hit the sack too. It's been a long day. See you in the morning."

"'Night . . . *Peppe*."

The following afternoon, Ben and Dev said goodbye to Oliver and Vanessa, then Ben pointed his truck toward their next destination, Perry, Maine.

Dev looked out the passenger window. "You said yesterday Eastport is the easternmost city in the U.S. What about Perry? Is there anything special about it?"

"Well, aside from Jen living there, what makes Perry special is it sits on the 45th parallel. It's halfway between the North Pole and the equator. There's no real town, but there's a working waterfront, and farmland, and it's home to the easternmost lake in the United States, Boyden Lake."

"Halfway to the north pole? That's cool."

"Yeah, when I was a kid, Oliver and I used to believe Perry was Santa's midway stopping point on his Christmas Eve run. We always wanted to come up here for Christmas and see if we could spot him."

Dev laughed. "And there's a lake?"

"Yes, a huge one. It covers about fifteen-hundred acres.

The lake is only about ten miles or so from the Canadian border and there's lots of wildlife–kingfishers, bald eagles, loons . . . and skunks."

Dev laughed. "What's a kingfisher? What's a loon?"

"They're types of birds."

"Did you go to the lake when you lived here?"

"Yeah, I'd be there as much as I could. I like to kayak and the lake's only about fifteen minutes from Eastport, so whenever I got the chance, I'd go kayaking or sometimes I'd go sailing with Bill and Jen."

Dev stared out the window.

"Dev? You okay?"

"I'm ah-ite. I'm just watching for it. I've never seen a lake before."

"Well, we've got a couple of hours before we get there, but you will definitely see a lake today!"

CHAPTER 20

A Lesson in Lobster

Jennifer and Bill lived in a two-story home on a quiet street in Perry. Several years ago, they added an in-law suite to their home to accommodate Jennifer and Ben's parents. While the house was charming, the setting was what kept Bill and Jennifer in their home for decades. They owned a prime lot on Boyden Lake.

"You made it!" Jennifer said as she stood up from weeding her flower bed. "Thought I'd get a few chores done before you got here."

"Looks good, little sister," Ben said, getting out of his truck and giving Jennifer a hug.

"Long trip from Philadelphia, right?" Jen smiled at Dev.

"Yes, ma'am, it was."

"I'm so glad you could come. You're gonna love it here. Let's get you two inside and settled." Jennifer put her arm around Dev's shoulders and led him into the house as Ben followed with their bags.

Look at that. Guess he's comfortable with Jen. Of course, she makes everybody comfortable.

"This will be your room, Dev," Jennifer said, leading him and Ben to the first room down the hallway. "It was my son Ryan's. He's been promising to clear away his things since he moved out, but that's been about five years now. Guess I'll have to get around to it someday."

"I think it's great!" Dev circled the room, admiring the trophies and sports memorabilia. "He did all this stuff?"

"Yes, he was into almost every sport. Mostly he liked track and archery," Jennifer said, pointing to one of Ryan's awards.

"I like track," Dev said staring at the hurdling trophy. "I like how the sun feels warm on your face. And how on a windy day, it's like the wind picks you up and wants to help you run, like it's part of the team and is cheering you to the finish."

"That's very poetic," Jennifer said with a smile. "I think Ryan felt the same way about it." Exiting the room, and pointing, she said, "Ben, you'll take Jessica's room."

"I'm sleeping with NSYNC again?" Ben made a face.

"Well, you could go *Bye, Bye, Bye*, and stay somewhere

else," Jennifer said, singing the NSYNC hit, complete with hand motions. Dev giggled at the two siblings.

"Keep laughing, knucklehead, and we'll be switching rooms." Ben said with a twinkle in his eye.

"All right, you two get settled in and then come out back. Bill's manned the grill tonight. Dev, you're going to get your first taste of Maine lobster!"

Once they unpacked, Ben and Dev joined Bill and Jennifer on the back deck. The senior members of the Hudson clan were there as well.

"Pop, Ma, this is Dev, my friend from Philly," Ben said.

"Nice to meet you, Dev," Ben's father, Phil, said. "First time in Maine for you, I understand."

"Yes, sir, it is." Dev shook Phil's hand.

"Well, I hope you're liking it so far," Ben's mother, Elsie, said.

"Yes, ma'am. It's so green. And there's so many trees!"

"That's true, on both counts. Come with me, let me show you the lake," Elsie said, walking Dev to the edge of the deck.

Dev held on to the railing, looking at the lake as if he were trying to swallow it whole. From this vantage point, he had a panoramic view from the marsh reeds in the foreground, to the Iron Works Mountain in the distance. A mild breeze wafted through the reeds, and a mallard, disturbed from his slumber, took flight. Dev jumped. A flash of blue and white zipped through the air, just over the shoreline.

"What was that!"

"That was a kingfisher," Elsie said. "Keep your eyes open, he'll be back in a minute. They fly up and down the shoreline looking for small fish. Once they spot one, they'll dive down, take it right out of the water, then be on their way."

"Cool," Dev said, scanning the shoreline. "This is a lake? It's huge!"

"It is huge, but it's a lake," Elsie said.

Phil walked over and stood beside Dev. "It's not even one of the biggest lakes in Maine. It's a baby pool compared to some others."

Bill called over from the grill. "If you and Ben have time this visit, we'll take you up to Moosehead Lake. That's the largest lake in Maine."

"Bigger than this?" Dev asked, his eyes wide open.

"Much bigger. About three times the size. Moosehead Lake is almost as big as Philadelphia," Bill said.

"Are there moose there? Is that why they call it Moosehead? I'd like to see a moose."

"Yes, there are lots of moose. Fun fact—moose outnumber people three to one in that area. Put that one away for trivia night," Bill said with a laugh.

"Even though there's a great deal of moose, it's called Moosehead Lake because it's shaped like a moose's head," Phil said.

"I'll show it to you on a map later." Bill closed the grill.

"Awesome!"

Jennifer called everyone to the table. She dished out the meal in small individual aluminum baking pans and served everyone. She set a pan in front of Dev that held a whole lobster, grilled corn on the cob, boiled potatoes, and a slice of watermelon.

"Now, I know you've never eaten lobster before, but are you up for trying it?" Jennifer asked.

Dev nodded. He stared at the lobster. "He looks angry."

Bill closed the grill, then looked over Dev's shoulder. "Yeah, he does look a little *steamed*."

Jennifer groaned, "Oh, don't get him started. He'll be at this all night."

"I don't know what you're talking about, Jen. It's not like I'm *fishing* for a compliment," Bill said with a chuckle.

"See what I mean?" Jen whispered to Dev.

"Hey, Dev, what do you call an annoyed lobster?" Ben asked.

Dev shrugged his shoulders.

"A *frustacean*!" Ben laughed.

"That's a good one!" Bill said. "What do you call a lobster that's afraid of tight spaces?" He looked at Dev.

"I dunno," Dev said, looking very confused.

"*Claw-strophobic!*"

Jennifer rolled her eyes and shook her head at the two men, who clearly were entertaining themselves.

"Why don't lobsters like to share, Dev?" Ben asked.

Dev looked at Ben, then a slow grin curled his lips. "Because they're *shellfish!*"

"Oh no, we've got another one. All right, that's enough of that, all of you. Dinner's getting cold. Let's say grace. Bill?"

"Okay, let's pray." Bill smiled, then bowed his head. "Lord, thank you for laughter, and for family and friends. Thank you that we can gather here together on this beautiful night and enjoy your creation. We ask you to bless this food and our time together. And I ask for a special blessing on Dev. Thank you that he can be with us tonight. In Jesus's name, Amen."

The rest of the family said their "Amen" and smiled at Dev.

The boy looks uncomfortable with all this attention. He does not like the spotlight, for sure.

Ben picked up his lobster and using it as a pointer he pointed it at Dev. "Okay, lobster eating—it's a messy job, but somebody's got to do it. Just follow me . . . and use lots of butter," he said with a wink.

He held the lobster with two hands and grabbed it where the tail and body met. Dev's eyes were glued to Ben's hands as he twisted and pulled the tail to separate it from the body. Dev tried to perform the same action himself with his lobster but struggled.

"I've got you, little man," Ben said. With a quick twist and pull, Dev's lobster was in two pieces.

"Okay, next are the claws." Ben detached each of his lobster's claws by pulling them with a slight twist. Dev accomplished this on his own, which brought a broad smile to his face.

After they separated the parts, Ben pointed to the tail and said, "This is the prized part of the lobster. It's where most of the meat is, and here's where you'll find out whether you can be a *Downeaster*."

"What's that?" Dev asked.

"A Downeaster is someone from this area, and every Downeaster *loves* lobster. We eat them for breakfast, lunch, dinner, and dessert!"

"Oh, don't listen to him," Jennifer said, "Not everyone likes lobster. It's kinda like country music—you either love it or you don't. There's usually not much in between." She eyed Ben. "And I can't think of one time when I've had it for dessert. You have a taste, and if you don't like it, Bill will cook you up a hotdog."

"Sacrilege!" Ben exclaimed.

Jennifer whispered to Dev, "Just ignore him. I always do." Dev shared a laugh with Jen.

"All right, you ready?" Ben asked. Dev nodded yes. Ben took a large knife and cracked the tail in two, revealing the meat inside. He showed Dev how to remove it, and which nasty bits to avoid, then he placed a small bowl of drawn butter in front of him.

Dev looked at the lobster, then at Ben, then back at the lobster. He picked up his fork.

"Ah-ah-ah," Ben said. "Fingers are the required utensil here. Watch and learn." Ben picked up a piece of his lobster, dipped it in butter, put his head back and popped the bite in his mouth.

Dev picked up a small piece of lobster and dipped it into the butter. Then, he closed his eyes, put his head back, and popped the lobster bite into his mouth.

"Well?" Ben asked.

Dev smiled, picked up another piece of lobster, dipped it in butter, and popped it into his mouth.

"Atta boy!" Ben laughed, patting Dev on the back. Everyone else clapped their hands in approval. Dev smiled, his cheeks blushing, then he made short order of the rest of the lobster tail.

After additional lessons on how to remove the meat from the claws and the body of the lobster, and gobbling it all down, Dev dug into the more familiar food items in his pan. As he did, Bill and Jennifer told stories of what it was like to live on the lake, and about all the various kinds of animals and birds that make it their home. They also shared about going sailing and kayaking, how peaceful and quiet it could be.

"How would you like to go kayaking tomorrow, Dev?" Ben asked.

"Kayaking? I've never been kayaking. I don't know how."

"Would you like to learn?"

Dev smiled and nodded his head quickly, his eyes shining.

"All right, let's hit the sack early, then tomorrow—we attack the lake!"

CHAPTER 21

Kayaks and Eagles

Dev woke before sunrise the next morning, eager for his kayaking adventure. He lay in bed, waiting to hear footsteps or chatting, something that would let him know others were awake. Silence was his only companion. He closed his eyes, and tried to go back to sleep when he heard a cry coming from the lake. His eyes opened wide and listened, not moving a muscle. The cry came again, but this time, he didn't believe the sound was human. He got out of bed and went to the window.

A dark blanket of mist covered the lake as it slept. Dev watched as a small fist of light from the east unfurled itself into illuminated fingers. The fingers reached out and delicately touched the water, rousing it from its slumber with a warm golden shimmer that extended from one shore to the other. Dev was mesmerized. As the shimmer grew, he imagined a flock of woodland sprites flying low across the lake, much as he'd seen the kingfisher do, spreading golden glitter as they flew. His thoughts were interrupted by another cry.

He peered at the water. He could see two small, dark shapes resting near the reeds. As the waterscape grew brighter, he could see the shapes were a type of bird and the sound seemed to come from them. As he listened to them cry to each other, he found himself crying, too.

He wiped the tears from his eyes, then got himself dressed. He sat on the edge of the bed and waited.

Wonder what Chase is doing? Can't wait to tell him lobster isn't chewy. It's soft and buttery and melts in your mouth like an M&M on a hot day.

The cry from the birds on the lake came again. Mom, I wish you were here. You'd love Maine. He went to the window and looked out. I miss you.

He wiped away another tear then went to his duffle bag and pulled out a spiral notebook. He sat at Ryan's desk and turned on the lamp. Picking up a pencil, he tapped his cheek with it a few times, then began to write.

Dev jumped when there was a knock on the door. He got up from the desk and answered it.

"Wow, you're dressed already? Good man," Ben said.

"But you're going to want to have your bathing suit on today. There's a pretty good chance you'll be getting wet. Go ahead and get changed. I'll meet you in the kitchen."

Dev nodded, then shut the door. He had no idea how long he'd been writing, but when he went back to his journal, pages had been filled. He closed his book, put it back in the duffle, then got changed.

Ben kayaked most of his life. For him, kayaking was as easy as riding a bike and as necessary as breathing. He cherished the time he spent on the lake, and being near it now reminded him how much he loved it and how much he missed it.

Dev joined Ben in the kitchen. The two ate a quick breakfast, grabbed a few water bottles, and headed out. Bill and Jennifer owned a dock, and by it was a large shed that housed their kayaks and other lake equipment. Ben's own kayak was stored there, so he pulled it out, along with a smaller kayak Jennifer kept since her children were small.

"Good thing my sister has a hard time getting rid of things," Ben said as he laid the kayaks on the ground. He went back in the shed and pulled out two lifejackets. "Okay, little man, this is the most important piece of equipment to have while kayaking," Ben said as he helped Dev put on the lifejacket.

"But I know how to swim. Why do I need this?" Dev asked, wiggling in the jacket.

"Aside from it being the law, it'll keep you safe. The lake isn't like a pool. It's bigger, deeper, and colder. And anything can happen when you're kayaking. You could tip and fall in, you could hit yourself by accident with the paddle, I could hit you with a paddle . . ." Ben said with a grin. "It'll keep you safe, so it's not up for debate. Sorry, knucklehead."

"Ah-ite." Dev clicked the last clip on his jacket.

Ben took Dev over to the kayaks and had him get in the smaller one while it was still on land. He showed him the proper way to sit, how to paddle, and he gave him a few tips to ensure he had a fun experience while staying safe.

"All right, I think you're ready!" Ben said. "Let's get these to the water."

They carried the kayaks to the lake, then Ben held Dev's kayak while he climbed inside. He gave him a solid push and Dev glided out and away from the dock. Ben hopped into his kayak, and with a few strokes, he was beside Dev.

The two explorers kayaked close to shore for most of the morning, weaving in and out of the reeds. Dev was a natural and followed Ben wherever he led. The boy was doing so well by late morning, Ben ventured out toward the middle of the lake. There they took a break and drank from their water bottles. Ben watched as Dev turned his kayak in a circle so he could take in the full view of his surroundings.

I wonder what poetry he'll write after this experience. A tightness in his chest worked its way to his throat and stung the back of his eyes.

You're getting to be an old softie, Hudson.

He pulled his paddle through the water and resumed the tour of the lake with Dev staying close behind. As they turned back toward the shore, a large shadow floated over Dev's kayak. A bald eagle, talons extended, dove toward Dev. He ducked as the eagle flew over his head, then swooped in the water three feet in front of his kayak, grabbed a large bass, then flew to the top of a nearby tree.

"Did you see that? Did you see that?" Dev yelled to Ben. "He..." Dev motioned with his hand to demonstrate the eagle's dive, "then he..." He mimed the eagle snatching the fish from the water. "Then...!" and he finished with the upward flight of the eagle. "That was ah-mazing!"

"Yeah, it was," Ben said, laughing. "Look up in the tree." Ben pointed to a nearby cedar tree. Dev looked up and watched as the eagle devoured his lunch.

"Well now, that was something for your first day on the water. I think it's time for us to head back." Just then, the eagle took flight. Dev wanted to follow him, but he jerked his body around too quickly, flipped the kayak, and dumped himself in the water. He bobbed to the surface, holding on to his lifejacket.

Ben extended a paddle to him and pulled him to the kayak.

"It's freezing!" Dev said with a shudder. After a bit of maneuvering, Ben had Dev back in the smaller kayak, and they headed toward the dock.

"Guess that lifejacket wasn't such a bad idea after all," Ben said, not able to resist a version of "I told you so."

"I guess not." Dev pulled his kayak onto shore. Ben smiled and mussed Dev's hair.

Once they showered and changed, they joined the others for lunch. The grown-ups marveled at Dev as he told the story of the morning's adventure.

Ben watched him carefully. *I've never seen him this animated. Good decision to bring him here.*

After lunch, Ben and Dev cleared the table. "Hey, buddy, I've got some things I need to take care of in town. Would you mind hanging out here with Jen while I do that? I shouldn't be too long, an hour or so maybe."

"Would you like to visit with us for a while?" Elsie asked. "Phil can show you some of his navy collection."

"You were in the navy?" Dev asked. Then turning to Ben, he said, "Can I?"

"Absolutely," Ben said, then mouthed, "Thanks, Mom."

Ben drove into Eastport, down the familiar streets, and

parked his truck a few doors past the Sunrise Inn. He turned the truck off and sat for a moment, holding on to the steering wheel.

"I knew this day would come. I just didn't think it'd come so soon." He took a deep breath. "This isn't about you. It's for the kid."

He got out of the truck, walked to the front door of a small, gray cottage, knocked and waited.

"Ben?" a familiar voice said, as she opened the door.

"Hi, Iris."

"This is a surprise," she said with a catch in her breath. "It's good to see you. Are you well? Oh, what am I thinking? Can you come in?"

"Sure, if that's all right."

"Of course, of course. Come in, please." Iris stood aside to let Ben enter. He walked into her home, as he had done many times before only this time he did so with an unfamiliar awkwardness. Everything looked the same, except for a few items placed here and there indicating she no longer lived alone.

Wonder if he's home.

"What can I get you to drink? Iced tea, lemonade . . . shot of whiskey?" Iris gave Ben a nervous smile.

"Iced tea would be great, thanks."

She's as nervous as I am.

"Please, have a seat." Iris went to the kitchen to get the drinks. Ben sat on the sofa and a white bundle of fur jumped into his lap.

"Well, hello. Who is this?" Ben petted the kitten.

"Oh, that's Mosey. We got her about a month ago. For someone who doesn't like cats, I can't seem to stay away from them."

"I can see why. She's a cute one." Ben admired the newest addition to Iris's family.

Iris brought the drinks in and set them on the coffee table. She sat beside Ben, clenching and unclenching her fists.

She *is* nervous. Me, too.

Mosey moved to her lap, but Iris petted her so stiffly she jumped off and repositioned herself at the opposite end of the sofa.

Iris looked up at Ben and gave him an uneasy smile. "So, are you visiting . . . or are you back?"

"Iris," Ben said, furrowing his brow.

"Oh, Ben," Iris burst into tears. "I am so sorry. I am so sorry. I hope you've forgiven me."

"Forgiven you?" He took her hand. "That's not why I'm here. I'm not angry with you and I'm not looking for an apology. No forgiveness is needed."

"But you left. You left your home. I'm responsible for that. I am so sorry."

"You weren't responsible. It was my choice. It was what I wanted to do. You and I, we weren't meant to be, that's all. It's nobody's fault." He reached over to the tissue box and handed her a tissue.

"Let's not rehash the past. It's done and we're both where we should be. And we're both happy. You're happy, right? With Frank?"

Iris dabbed her eyes. "Yes, I am. You were right. I'm just sorry I put you through all that."

"You didn't put me through anything. I was where I wanted to be, and I loved every minute I was with you, every single one. I have no regrets."

"I don't either, except for the hurt I've caused you." Iris dabbed her eyes again.

"We can't help who we love. I know I caused you pain as well. I am sorry about that."

"You don't need to be sorry about anything. You helped me. You helped me see I *could* have a relationship. You gave me a wonderful gift. I'll always be grateful to you."

The two allowed silence to take over as they drank their tea and absorbed the ebb and flow of emotions.

"You know, I think we're both pretty awesome people."

Iris laughed at Ben's observation.

"I mean, here we are, two adults who almost got married, and we're sitting together, having an honest conversation over what I must say is excellent iced tea. So, how about we put this behind us? Do you think we can just be friends now?"

"Oh, I would like that very much." Mosey returned to Iris's lap, nuzzled her hand, and received a much gentler petting. After a few more quiet tears, and consolation from Mosey, Iris looked at Ben with a smile. "I'm so happy to see you, Ben. I've been worried about you. How are you doing? Are you happy? Truly?"

"I am. I'm doing well. Philadelphia has been an adventure. It's been good for me."

"Ah, Philadelphia. I lived there for a couple years a long time ago. The thing I remember most is the people. And the cheesesteaks." Iris grinned. "The people, they're hard workers, passionate about their sports, and they'd give you the shirt off their back if you needed it. How's the city treating you?"

"I'm finding it the same. It's treating me well. And the cheesesteaks? They're great."

"So, you're staying there for a while?"

"Yes. I stayed with JJ, my college roommate, when I first got there until I found my own place. I'm committed for at least six months."

"JJ? Is he the one who used to tell the Gung Ho story?"

"That's the one. He and his family took me in like one of their own. JJ has a son, Chase, and Chase has a friend. And that's why I'm here to see you."

"His son's friend brings you to my door? I'll have to thank him."

"Well, you may get the chance, if you're willing. You see, his friend, his name is Dev. He's ten, and he's going through a rough time right now, family stuff. I brought him here to give him a break from it. I found out accidentally he's a writer. I read some of his work, and it's pretty good. At least I think it's good, but I'm no writer. I'm not sure how to help him, or if I should even encourage him. Would you mind meeting him, maybe reading some of what he's written, and giving him some advice?"

"I would love to! I'd be happy to help. I'm always up for encouraging a fellow writer, especially a young one. Would tomorrow work for you?"

"It would, if it wouldn't interfere with any plans you and Frank have."

"Frank's out of town. He will be for a few more days. His daughter-in-law, Violet, is only about a month or so away from giving birth, so David thought he'd like to get some father/son time in with Frank before he became a dad himself. They're out camping at Moosehead Lake. So, I'm totally free. Any time you want to come will work for me."

"And Frank, he's well?"

"He is. He'll be sorry he missed you."

Probably will have to bury the hatchet with him some

time . . . but not today.

"How about tomorrow afternoon then? We'll be checking into the Inn in the morning and that'll give me time to spend with Emma and catch up with her."

"That'll be fine," Iris said. "She's missed you too. We all have."

Ben stood. Iris stood with him, and they walked to the door. "Thanks for the tea, and for being willing to see Dev."

"Anything I can do." She hugged Ben and the two shared an embrace that spoke all the words they couldn't say. They looked at each other and Iris wiped tears from her eyes and took Ben's hand. "I promise, this will be the last time you see me cry like this. From this moment on, whenever I see you, I will greet you happily . . . my good friend."

Ben wiped a tear from her cheek, then kissed her on the forehead. "My good friend," he whispered. They stood for another moment, then Iris smiled, and opened the door. Ben turned, got in his truck, and took several deep breaths before turning the key and returning to Jennifer's house.

"Ben! Did you know your dad was in World War II?" Dev shouted as Ben came through the door.

Ben smiled. "Yes, I knew that."

Dev jumped up and ran next to him. "Well, did you know he had to peel fifty pounds of potatoes once and he did it in an hour to win a bet?"

"Fifty pounds? Hmmmm, that pile of potatoes keeps getting bigger."

"And you should see his stuff! He still has his uniform. He let me try on his hat," Dev said lifting his chin. "Thanks for letting me stay."

"I'm glad you had a good time, bud."

Dev watched Ben for a moment. "You have a good time in town?"

"It was okay. No, it was good. Listen, there's something I'd like to talk to you about. Let's go outside."

"Okay." Dev followed Ben out onto the deck.

"Remember when I knocked over your journals?" Ben asked as they sat down.

"Yeah."

"Well, I've been thinking. Seems to me you're a pretty good writer. I don't know much about writing though, but I know someone who does. She's a writer, and she lives in Eastport, just a few houses down from where we'll be staying. I was wondering if you'd like to meet her. Maybe she can give you some advice. You could share some of what you've written with her."

"I don't know. It's kinda private." Dev shifted in his seat.

"I know, I know. This isn't something you have to do. I only thought it might be a good opportunity for you. Here's an idea. Why don't you meet her, then decide if you want to share anything with her."

"She's your friend?"

"Yes, a very good friend."

"Okay, I'll meet her."

"All right. I talked to her today and we can go see her tomorrow afternoon."

The rising moon sent the afternoon sun on its way and the exchange of colors between the two left an orange glow hovering over the lake.

"Would it be all right if I took a walk around the lake?" Dev asked.

"That sounds like a great idea. Mind if I join you?"

Dev smiled and shook his head. The two walked down to the lake. As they walked along the shoreline they spoke of kayaks, and lobsters, and eagles.

CHAPTER 22

The Sunrise Inn

The next morning, Dev rose early again. He packed his things, then waited for Ben and the others to wake. He pulled out a spiral notebook from his backpack and sat by the window to watch the sunrise. As the light broke over the lake, he began to sketch.

A black and white bird skimmed the water and landed with a light splash. "Hey, that kinda looks like a penquin." He laughed to himself then did a quick drawing of the fowl.

I wonder if we'll see a moose today. Wish Chase could be here and see all this stuff. He would've loved that eagle. Dev retraced the flight of the eagle with his hand.

Mom, I wish you were here too. Please come home soon. He gripped his pencil until his hand shook. What was it you used to tell me? Oh, I remember, "Be strong and courageous." I'm trying, Mom . . . but it's hard.

He went back to his sketching, and he didn't have to wait much past sunrise before hearing sounds of adults waking. Soon the others were up, and breakfast served. Following the meal, Dev and Ben said their goodbyes, and drove the twelve miles to Eastport. As they pulled into town, Dev hung on every word of Ben's as he pointed out some of his favorite places.

"There's the Police Station, Dev. Spent a lot of years there."

"How many?"

"How many years? Over thirty. Doesn't feel that long though." Ben made a left on Water Street. "Over there, by the dock, that's the Eastport Port Authority and the Coast Guard. And there's Eastport Windjammers on your left. They do whale watching tours that leave right from the Breakwater Pier."

"Whale watching! You can see whales here?"

"Yes, and porpoises, and seals. Maybe we can squeeze that in." Ben made a U-turn. "See that little yellow building? That's Rosie's Hotdogs. You'll have to try one of their red snappers."

"A snapper? You mean like a turtle? I don't think I wanna try that," Dev said with a wrinkled nose.

Ben laughed. "No, it's not a turtle, it's a hotdog. They're called red snappers 'cause they're bright red and they snap when you bite into them. You'll have to see how they compare to the hotdogs at the Phillies' ballpark." They continued down

Water Street.

"Whoa! That statue is huge!" Dev said.

"Yeah, he is. The fisherman statue is pretty popular with tourists. Believe it or not, he's a leftover prop from a TV show."

"TV? That's cool."

"And that building right there–one of my favorite places to eat, the WaCo Diner."

"The *Whack-o* Diner? You're making that up."

"Nope, that's what it's called."

"I like it." Dev turned his head and perched on the corner of Water and Key Streets, he spied a large Romanesque building with an antique canon out front standing guard. The deep red brick exterior and curved wing seemed to call to him. "Peavey Library," he read from the archway over the door. "Is that really a library?"

"Yes, that's the library. I thought you'd like that. We can visit it later. They have a great kid's section. All right, that's the end of downtown. A few more blocks and we'll be at the inn."

"That's the end? This is a city? It's so small."

"Smallest one in Maine, but yeah, it's a city. And here's the inn. This is where I stayed when I first moved to Eastport. Met two of my best friends at this place."

Ben parked the truck and Dev watched as Ben sat, staring ahead at the inn.

"Must feel weird, huh?" Dev asked.

"What do you mean?"

"I mean, the last time you were here, you were sheriff, and you lived here. Now . . . it's different," Dev said with a shrug of his shoulders.

"Different can be good." Ben started to get out of the truck, then stopped. "I know I call you a knucklehead, but you're a pretty smart knucklehead."

"I know," Dev said with a grin.

Ben gave him a friendly push. "Go get your bags."

They entered the lobby of the inn, duffle bags thrown over their shoulders. Mary, Emma's assistant, sat behind the front desk, hunched over the computer keyboard entering information at a frenetic pace. She raised her head toward the two visitors as they approached the desk.

"Sheriff." Mary said, sneering over her reading glasses.

"Mary." Ben squinted his eyes at her.

"Down the hall."

Mary eyed Dev like a predator eyes its prey. Dev shuddered. Looks like she wants to turn me into tonight's dinner special—boy stew. He took a step behind Ben.

"You have a tagalong," Mary said, continuing to eye Dev.

"Dev. Friend of mine."

"Hmph." Mary went back to her typing.

"Ben Hudson, as I live and breathe," Emma said coming in from the hall. "It's about time you got back up here."

A Good Place to Turn Around

Ben tapped on the front desk and with his eyes still squinted, he said, "Nice talkin' to you too, Mary."

He turned to Emma with a smile. "Em, it's only been four months. Hardly enough time to miss me."

"I missed you the day you left," Emma said with the warmest of smiles. She welcomed him with a hug. She started to say something, then noticed Dev. "And *you* must be Dev. I'm Emma. I'm so happy to meet you. Ben's told me a lot about you."

Dev smiled and tucked his chin to his chest. He glanced up at Emma. She's pretty. I like her eyes. Kinda like my mom's. As he shook her hand, Dev caught a sweet and delicate scent. She smells good. Not like those ladies on the city bus. Their perfume stinks. And her hand is so soft.

"So, how are you liking Maine so far?"

"It's great. I love it here," Dev said, beaming.

"I'm glad to hear it. And I'm happy you two will be staying here for a few days. It'll give us time to get to know one another, and time for you and I," she said, looking at Ben, "to catch up and—" A booming crash came from the banquet hall.

"Uh-oh, Eddie." Emma turned, hurried toward the sound and Ben followed.

Dev looked over at Mary, who was still entering information into her computer at a feverish pace. She's looking for a recipe for boy stew, I know it.

Mary lowered her reading glasses again and peered over them at Dev. He turned and ran to catch up with Ben.

"Eddie!" Emma cried, as she entered the room. The young man was sprawled on the floor surrounded by overturned chairs.

"Sorry, Miss Emma. Thought I could handle all these chairs. Musta tripped over my own feet. Lunkhead."

"You okay?" she asked as she helped him up.

"Oh, I'm fine." He brushed himself off. "Sheriff Ben!"

"Hey, Eddie, good to see you, my man," Ben said, as he walked over to give Eddie a hug.

"I've missed you! *Chupta*? You back now?"

"No, we're just visiting. You sure you're all right?"

"Yeah, I'm just gawmy today, that's all." Eddie pointed to Dev who hid himself behind Ben. "Who's this?"

"Eddie, there's someone I'd like you to meet." He pulled Dev from behind him and said, "This is Dev. He's a friend of mine from Philadelphia."

"Hi, Dev. I'm Eddie. Nice to meet ya." Eddie pumped Dev's hand up and down. "Sheriff Ben and I are pals. Known him all my life."

"Really?" Dev asked, looking up at Ben.

"That's true. I was there the day Eddie was born," Ben said with a smile toward Eddie. "He's one of my favorite people."

Eddie gave Ben a broad smile. "Well, I'd better get back to work." He started to stack up the chairs. "Good to see you, Sheriff Ben."

"What's going on here, Emma? Must be at least a hundred chairs."

"We've got a big dinner party tomorrow, fiftieth wedding anniversary. Eddie's been giving me a hand this summer. We've had more business than usual, so I've needed some extra help. Eddie's becoming my right-hand man when it comes to set-up."

"Dev, what say you and I pitch in and give a friend a hand? We can knock these chairs out in no time, Em." Dev nodded in agreement.

Emma frowned. "No, you're my guests. I can't have you working."

"No, we're your friends, and friends help."

"People helping people, huh?"

"Absolutely. Don't rob us of a blessing now."

"Pulling that line, are you?" Emma smiled. "Okay, I give in. While you're doing that, I'll have Joseph take your bags up to your room."

"Joseph? Who's Joseph?"

"Joey Harper from down the street. He graduated from

college this spring and he wants to get into the hotel business. He told me he wanted to 'start from the bottom' and asked if I'd be willing to hire him as a bellhop. I was looking to hire someone anyway, so I took him on. He wants to be called *Joseph*, thinks it gives him an air of dignity. I'll call him the Sheik of Araby if it means I'll have a steady worker," Emma laughed.

Ben laughed with her, then he and Dev joined Eddie in setting up chairs and tables. In little under an hour, they had the entire space ready.

Emma rejoined them. "This is perfect! Thank you so much. Can you all stay for lunch?" Emma asked.

Eddie blushed. "Sorry, I can't stay Miss Emma. I have a lunch date with Mandy and then more lawns to cut. Hope you don't mind."

"Not at all. You go have fun."

As Eddie left Ben said, "That boy amazes me. He's going to make something of himself."

"Already has Ben, he already has." Emma escorted Ben and Dev to the outside patio where she laid out sandwiches and cold drinks for them.

"Can you join us?" Ben asked.

"I'd love to. Mary's got the front desk covered, so I have time." Dev watched as Ben pulled a chair out for Emma. "So, Dev, tell me about Philadelphia. I've never been. What do you like best about living there?"

"I like the people," Dev said with a small smile.

"That's what I like best about Eastport, too. What about the people do you like?"

"I live in an apartment building and the people there are really nice. Mr. Versace, he's the landlord, he used to be a concert pia . . . I forget how you say it, but he plays the piano. He's awesome and sometimes he gives a concert in the lobby for everybody in the building. Mrs. Versace, she's nice too. She makes the best pizzelles."

"What's a pizzelle?"

"The best cookie ever! You make them with this little waffle maker thing. Mrs. Versace lets me help her. I roll the dough into little balls and then she puts the ball on the waffle thing and squishes it into a cookie then it cooks it. It's a lot of fun and I get to eat the broken ones. She sends me home with a bag of whole ones too."

"Sounds like they are very nice people," Emma said. "And Ben told me about your best friend, Chase. Where'd he get his nickname? Does he run a lot?"

"He does," Dev laughed. "But that's his real name. His dad's favorite baseball player is Chase Utley. He used to play for the Phillies. Chase is named after him."

"Oh, I see, and is Chase a good ballplayer?"

"Which one?"

Emma laughed. "Never mind, I bet they both are."

"Yes, ma'am, they are," Dev said with an enthusiastic nod.

Dev asked Emma questions about the inn and about Ben for the rest of the meal. Emma told him about the retirement luncheon and about the Ben Hudson gymnasium.

"They named a gym after you?"

"Yeah, well, I guess they had to call it something." Then changing the subject, Ben said, "Dev, remember what we talked about last night before you went to bed?"

"Yeah."

"Well, we should wrap up here. It's about time for us to go."

"Sounds mysterious," Emma said, with a tilt of her head.

"Ben knows a writer, and he's gonna introduce me to her. I like to write."

Emma looked at Ben with a cautious eye. He looked down and folded his napkin.

"Why don't you go wash up, grab your things, and then meet me in the lobby?" Dev got up and walked away from the table. He turned back and went to Emma.

"It was nice meeting you, Miss Emma. Thanks for lunch. It was really good. And next time me and Mrs. Versace make pizzelles, I'll send you some."

"That would be very kind, thank you."

Ben and Emma watched as Dev walked into the inn, then Emma turned her attention to Ben. She raised her eyebrows at him and waited.

Ben shrugged his shoulders and said, "The kid likes to write. He does it all the time. I found some of his stuff by accident, and it's good. At least, I think it's good. Iris is the only writer I know, and I hoped she'd take a look, and give me some ideas about how I could support him. That's all."

"I'm sure she'll be happy to see you."

"Actually, I saw her yesterday. I thought it'd be best for us to meet on our own first. You know break the ice, get rid of the awkwardness."

"Well, if I tell the truth, Iris called me last night and told me all about it. She seemed relieved and genuinely happy to see you. We've all been worried about you." Emma stared at Ben. "Are you okay? With what happened yesterday, are you okay with seeing her again so soon?"

"I'm fine. It was good to see her. You don't have to worry."

"What, me worry? About you? Why would I do that?" She stood, and Ben stood with her. "I need to get back to work. I'm glad you're back, Ben. I'll catch up with you later."

Emma walked away as Ben watched, noting her face reflected anything but the lack of worry.

CHAPTER 23

Writer to Writer

Iris smiled as she opened the door. "Hello, my good friend. Nice to see you."

"Hi, Iris. Nice to see you too," Ben said. Their eyes met for a moment, then Ben pointed to the boy beside him. "This is Dev, my friend I told you about."

"Dev, nice to meet you. Come in. Would you two like something to drink?"

"Nothing for me, thanks. Dev?" Ben looked Dev's way. He shook his head no. "And nothing for Dev either. We just had lunch with Emma."

"I see. Well, that explains it."

"Explains what?"

"The contented look on your faces. Emma's lunches do that every time." Then, looking at Dev, she asked, "Did you get to eat on the patio?"

Dev nodded yes.

"And did you see the seals?"

"Seals? On the patio?"

Iris laughed. "No, although that could be fun. I meant the seals in the bay. You can see them from the patio."

"No, I didn't see them," Dev said with a sad shake of the head.

"Well, we're going to have to fix that at once. Come with me." She walked toward the back door. Dev looked at Ben and he nodded, so Dev followed her outside and Ben trailed behind. They went to the back of her property and Iris had them sit on a bench overlooking the bay. "There they are." Iris pointed to a large rock in the bay covered with seals.

Dev looked at the seals, dropped his jaw, looked at Ben, then back at the seals.

"That's about how I looked the first time I saw them. Pretty cool, huh?" Iris said.

Dev nodded.

"Oh, I forgot something. May I ask you a favor, Dev? Would you mind running to the house and bringing back the binoculars on the coffee table? You'll get a much better view if you use them."

"Sure!" Dev scampered back to the house.

"Thanks for doing this, Iris. We talked about it last night and Dev was fine with meeting you, but he's reluctant to share anything he's written. He said, 'It's private.'" Ben imitated the solemn look Dev gave him.

"I get it. Sharing your writing can be pretty scary. Don't worry, I've got this."

Dev ran back with the binoculars and held them out to Iris, "Are these the ones?"

"Yep, those are them. All right, stand here in front of me, and I'll introduce you."

"Introduce me?" Dev asked, looking at Iris side-eyed.

"Yes, these seals are just like people with their own personalities. I've named a few of them. I'll show you." Iris put her hands on Dev's shoulders, turning him toward the rock. "Point the binoculars toward the edge of the rock, on the left-hand side. See the huge seal lying on his back?"

"Um . . . yeah, I see him!"

"He's a grey seal. They're humungous. I call that one George. He reminds me of my dad on his day off. My dad's name was George. Like my father, this George likes to lie around for most of the day. Occasionally, he'll slip into the water, grab a few fish, then he's back on his spot, snoozing away."

"Hi, George." Dev smiled.

"Now, go to the right of George and see how the rock gets taller? On the top of the rock, you'll see a brown seal, just a little lighter than the other seals around her." Dev scanned the rock for the seal. "Find her yet?"

"Yes, I got her," Dev said with a jump.

"Her name is *Becca*." Iris frowned.

"Becca?" Dev looked at Iris. "You don't like her?"

"Well, Becca is a mean girl, and I'm not fond of mean girls. I try to make an exception for Becca, though. She acts like the queen of all the seals. She sits atop that rock every day and it's like she expects the other seals to come and pay tribute to her—and sometimes, they do."

"What's *pay tribute*?"

"It's what peasants used to do for royalty back in olden times. They would bring gifts to the queen as a way of saying, 'Thank you, oh queen, for being a most lovely queen and not chopping off my head.'"

Dev laughed at Iris's fake British accent.

"Sometimes the other seals will bring Becca fish and leave them for her. She doesn't even say thank you. She's quite the prima donna."

Ben smiled as he watched the two interact. "Iris, would you mind if I stepped into the house for a minute? I need to make a phone call." He winked.

"Fine with me. Take your time. We'll keep getting to know the seals. That good with you, Dev?"

"Yeah, this is awesome." Dev went back to the binoculars. Ben nodded and excused himself.

"Okay, now for one of my favorites. Look for the guy on

the end, all the way to the right. See how he's sitting up, watching the bay?"

"I found him," Dev said. "He's staring like he's a look-out or something."

"That's exactly what I think," Iris said. "He sits there every day and watches. Sometimes he moves to the top of the rock next to Becca to get a better view, but most of the time, he hangs out right there. If there's any trouble, he's the first to spot it and he lets the others know. He even breaks up fights between the other seals. He's a pretty good guy. Guess what I named him?"

"I'd name him Ben."

"We think alike. I named him Sheriff."

"Sheriff Ben," Dev said as he smiled through the binoculars.

With a bark and a splash, two seal pups began racing around the rock. One pup swam near Sheriff Ben, flipped his flipper, spraying him with water. Sheriff Ben barked at the pup, then went back to his sentry duty.

"What about him?" Dev laughed and pointed at the pup.

"That's a harbor seal. They're on the smaller size and that one? I named him Birch."

"Birch? You mean like the tree? Why'd you name him that?"

"Birch is my son. He couldn't sit still for beans. He was

always jumping and playing like this pup. Birch was a lot of fun."

"Does Birch live with you?"

"No," Iris said with a sigh. "Birch lives in heaven now."

"Oh," Dev's smile turned to a frown. "I'm sorry." Then, waiting a moment and watching Iris, he asked, "Did I make you sad?"

"No, it's okay. I like to think of Birch, and I know I'll see him again someday, so remembering him in the meantime makes me feel better."

Dev nodded. They both sat and watched the seals for a few more moments. One seal sat off on a rock alone.

"How about him?" Dev pointed to the singular pup. "Why isn't he with the others? Why's he all alone?"

"That one? Well, I don't know about him. He showed up about a week ago all by himself. That's unusual for a seal, especially one that young. He's just a pup. I'd guess he's about your age in seal years. The other seals seem to have accepted him and they let him up on the rock when he wants to come. He likes to stay by himself though, and he looks out at the bay a lot." The pup opened his mouth and let out a low groan, as if he were calling someone.

"He's looking for his family." Dev took in a slow breath as he focused on the pup.

"That may be the case. He sure acts like he's looking for

someone. I haven't named him yet."

"Dev. I'd name him Dev," Ben said as he returned from the house.

"Dev . . ." Iris said. "What do you say? Can I name him after you?"

The boy looked out at the seal pup, then nodded.

"Dev it is," Iris said. Ben sat next to Dev then the threesome continued to watch the seals at play. After some time, Iris looked at Dev and said, "I was wondering if I could ask you another favor."

"Sure."

"Ben told me you're a writer. I'm a writer too and recently, I started writing poetry. Poetry is new for me, but I wanted to give it a try. I've been working on a poem about these seals, and I'm stuck. Just can't find the right word. Would you mind listening to it, and maybe you could give me an idea?"

"Me?"

"Sure, one writer to another. Would you mind?"

Dev shook his head no. "I can listen."

"Great. It's in the house. I'll go get it and be right back." Iris stood and Ben stood up with her. She walked back into the house.

"I only told her you liked to write. I didn't tell her anything more," Ben said, sitting back down. "Just in case you're wondering."

Iris returned with her own spiral notebook. She opened it, rifled through several pages, then flipped the book open. "Okay, this is just a rough draft, so . . ."

Dev nodded. He sat up straight and turned himself more toward Iris.

Playful pups dancing in the sun,
Their bronze skin gleaming.
Sliding, slipping, barking, sleeping,
Plunging downward in the emerald darkness.

Alone, one pup sits in wait,
He searches the horizon in vain.
His ...

"Ugh, that's where I'm stuck. I've been trying to think of a word or phrase to describe the sound the pup makes, but nothing seems right. Moaning, groaning, growling, sniffling, they're all terrible."

Dev nodded and furrowed his brow. He closed his eyes, and after a moment he said, "Plaintive." He opened his eyes and looked at Iris. "He makes a plaintive cry."

Iris looked at Dev, then up at Ben, who matched her look of surprise. "Dev, that's an excellent word choice. It's exactly what it sounds like. *Plaintive.* How do you know that word?"

"Miss Jen, Ben's sister, taught it to me. We were talking

about the loons on the lake. I heard them one morning and I thought they sounded like they were sad, like they were really lonely. She said they sounded plaintive to her. She said plaintive was the feeling you get when you miss somebody a lot. I think the pup misses his family. That's why he makes that sound. He's worried he's never gonna see them again." A hint of a tear in Dev's eyes brought more than a hint to Iris's.

"Do you mind if I use *plaintive* in my poem?"

"No, I don't mind." Dev watched the seals for a few moments. "Miss Iris, would you like to read something I wrote?"

"Really? I'd love to!"

"Can we come back again?" Dev asked Ben.

"Well, I told the guys at the station I'd stop in tomorrow. Iris, if it's convenient, could Dev come by while I'm there? It would be after lunch."

"I don't have any plans, so that would be terrific. Here's an idea. Why don't you drop Dev off a little earlier and the two of us can have lunch and a joint writing session. When we're through, we can go to the inn and visit with Emma for a while. She's been working too hard, so maybe Dev and I can persuade her to take some time off and we'll do something together. What do you think?" Iris asked, looking at Dev.

"Yeah, that'd be great. I like Miss Emma."

"I like her too. She's my best friend. Okay, it's a date!"

"A date?" Dev raised his eyebrows. "But aren't you married?"

Iris laughed and said, "Yes, I am. But I don't think my husband will mind . . . this one time."

"Okay, it's a date," Dev said, with a grin.

Ben stood. "Well, I think we've taken up enough of your time today, Iris. Thanks."

"It was my pleasure. It was good to meet you, Dev."

"Good to meet you too. See ya tomorrow."

CHAPTER 24

It's a Date

"Time to go yet?" Dev asked, his knee bouncing up and down.

"Yep, I think we can head over now. You have everything you need? Sharpened pencils? Notebooks? Genius ideas."

Dev smiled. "I have it all." He tapped his backpack.

"I'm sure you're going to have a good time with Iris today, but if you need me, you call. Okay?"

"Okay."

A quick walk a few doors down the street, brought Ben and Dev to Iris's door.

"Well, look who it is. My favorite ex-sheriff and my favorite co-writer. Come on in."

"I'm gonna leave you two to it and head over to the police station. They're expecting me. Thanks for this, Iris."

"You're very welcome. You go have a good time, Ben."

"All right, knucklehead, I'll see you later. Happy writing."

Dev and Iris began their time together sitting at the breakfast bar. Iris brought out sandwiches, then she and Dev got to work. He listened as Iris read him her updated version of the seal poem. He offered more suggestions, and the two added additional stanzas to the piece.

Afterward, Iris brought out some cookies and milk. Setting them on the breakfast bar, she said, "Reinforcements. I find cookies and milk are the best fuel for writing."

Dev smiled and took a cookie. He took one bite, set it down, then bit his lip.

"You okay?" Iris asked.

Dev nodded, then opened the spiral notebook he brought. "I'd like you to read one of my poems." He turned the pages. When he found the right page, he paused for a moment, then he slid the notebook slowly over to Iris.

"Are you sure you want me to read this? I won't hold it against you if you change your mind."

"No, it's okay. Writer to writer?"

"Right," Iris nodded. "Would you rather read it to me?"

Dev shook his head no.

"Okay, then." Iris smiled at Dev and began to read. A few lines in, she covered her mouth with her hand, then her eyes teared. As she continued to read, she wept, and when she finished the poem, she sat with her eyes closed. Dev watched her every move.

She retrieved a tissue, dabbed her eyes, then sat and patted the book. She took a deep breath and whispered, "Do not change one word of this." Turning to Dev and regaining her voice, she said, "Not one word. Do you hear me? This is perfection."

"I didn't mean to make you sad."

"Oh, you didn't. I get like this whenever I read good writing, and this? This is excellent writing. You have a writer's heart.

"Few people can do what you've done here. They're not brave enough. I know I wasn't when I started writing. To bare your soul like this . . ." Iris dabbed her eyes, then took a breath and sat up straight. "You should pursue this—writing. You are very talented. When you get back to Philadelphia, if you ever want to talk about writing, call me. I'd like to help you any way I can."

"I knew you'd understand, Miss Iris, my poem. I knew you'd get it 'cause of Birch."

"Thank you for sharing this with me. It's very special and I feel honored. I'll remember this day when you become a famous author."

Dev blushed as he put his spiral notebook back in his backpack.

"Enough tears." Iris wiped her eyes with her hands. "I think we should go see Emma now. Maybe we can talk her into getting some ice cream. I know I could use some."

Dev helped Iris clear off the breakfast bar, then the two made the short walk to see Emma.

"Good afternoon, Mary!" Iris sang as she and Dev entered the Inn.

"Afternoon yourself," Mary grunted in reply. "See you've got the tagalong." Dev tucked himself behind Iris.

"Dev? He's one of my favorite people." She retrieved Dev from behind her and placed her hands on his shoulders. "Mary, I don't believe you've met this young man properly. *This is Dev Murphy.* He's a kindred spirit of mine, and a wonderful writer. I'm sure you'll be reading some of his work in the future."

"You don't say."

"I do say. Dev, this is Mary Giroux. She's Emma's assistant, been with her for years. She's lived all her life in Eastport, but her ancestry goes back to France." Then, whispering in his ear, she said, "Which explains some of the attitude." Dev smiled at Iris. "Now, Mary, don't go scaring this young man or you'll have me to deal with."

"Oh, go on with you. I don't scare nobody, don't cha

know. Boy, you scared a me?" Mary asked, peering over her glasses.

Dev cleared his throat, and said softly, "No, ma'am."

"Ha! Don't sound too convincing. C'mere." Mary crooked her finger at Dev. He looked up at Iris, hoping she would place him behind her again.

Mary chuckled, "C'mon over. I don't bite . . . hard."

"*Mary*," Iris said, tilting her head at the woman.

"Come 'round yonder," Mary said, pointing to the opening in the desk. Dev took his time making his way to Mary. He stood in front of her and swallowed hard. She hopped down off her stool and stood beside him, looking him over from toe to cowlick.

She's only a little bigger than me.

Mary walked around him, eyeing him up and down.

Measuring me for a pot of boy stew. I know she is.

"You're a cunnin' boy. I can see you're not a dubber. Must have a fine mama. I'd know for sure if I could get a look at your eyes, but with all that hair . . ." Mary made a tsk-tsk sound between her teeth.

"Mary? What's going on?" Emma said, coming out of her office.

"Mary's sizing up Dev," Iris said.

"I knew it," Dev mumbled.

"I see. And what's the verdict?" Emma asked with a smile.

"He'll do. He's a good'n. Just need to do somethin' with that hair. Boy's got nice eyes, but he's hidin' 'em. Just like he hides behind every soul who brings him in here."

"Well now, Dev, that's high praise. I know it doesn't sound like it, but you just got the Mary stamp of approval and that doesn't happen often. She's got an excellent eye for people. We can do something about your hair, but it's good to know we don't have to do a thing about your character."

Dev smiled and stood up straight.

"Good t' meet you, Dev Murphy." Mary held out her hand.

"Good to meet you." The two shook hands.

"So, what are you two doing here?" Emma asked Dev.

"We wanted to take you out for ice cream, Miss Emma. Can you come?"

"Ice cream? Well, that's a hard thing to pass up. I'd love to."

"Miss Mary, would you like to come too?" Dev asked.

Mary was already back at the computer. She stopped her typing and, with a look of surprise, said, "Ah, no. But I thank you for the invite. Someone has to mind the store and Emma here, she could use some ice cream." Mary muttered as she went back to her typing, "Yessuh, he's a good'n."

Emma smiled at Dev, then tilted her head and took a little walk around him. With a twinkle in her eye, she said, "Before we go, Iris, how 'bout you and I give Dev a little trim?"

Iris clapped. "Love the idea! Let's do it!"

Emma and Iris whisked Dev back to Emma's office and sat him in a chair. They tilted their heads this way and that, and discussed what style would look best, then went to work. Emma doing the cutting, and Iris doing the critiquing. Dev sat stock still, afraid to move or speak. When Emma was through, she and Iris stood back and looked at Dev as if they were admiring a rare work of art.

"Oh, my," Iris said. "Those eyes . . ."

Emma smiled and nodded. "Dev, you have got to be the most handsome young man I've ever seen. Mary was right."

Dev smiled, stood up, then took Emma and Iris's hands, and said, "Ice cream?"

They laughed and said, "Ice cream!"

Sitting on the back deck of the WaCo Diner, Emma and Iris shared story after story with Dev about how they became friends and what life was like in Eastport. Iris even told him a few stories about her former cat, Mo. They asked Dev question after question about Philadelphia and how Ben was really doing there.

When their time was over, and the check came, Dev picked it up. Iris said, "Oh, no, I'll take care of it, sweetie."

"Nope, I'll do it. You said this was a date and Ben says

the guy should always pay. Ben gave me money for helping around his house, so I'm payin'. For you too, Miss Emma. Your husband wouldn't mind either, would he?"

Emma smiled and said, "No, he wouldn't mind either. He'd be very proud of you." Emma and Iris watched Dev as he went to the counter and paid the bill. He returned, calculated the proper tip, and tucked it neatly by his empty ice cream bowl.

"Thank you, Dev. That was kind of you, and I'm glad we could spend time together today," Iris said.

"Me, too. Would you like me to walk you home?"

Iris raised her eyebrows and shared a look with Emma. "No, I'll be fine, but thanks for the offer. You go back with Emma and make sure she doesn't work too hard the rest of the afternoon."

"Okay," Dev said. Then standing behind Emma's chair, he pulled it out for her as he had seen Ben do. Emma eyed Iris, and the two smiled at the little gentleman before them.

"Dev, you're going to be a heartbreaker someday," Emma said.

"What d'ya mean?"

"You'll find out when you're older."

Back at the inn, Dev began exploring the lobby while

Emma relieved Mary from behind the front desk. He checked out the books on the bookcase then went up the curved staircase at the east end of the lobby. He felt the smooth oak finish of the handrail.

This would make a great slide. Should I? Chase would. He sneaked a look at Emma. Nah, she might not like it.

He walked down the stairs instead and sat in one of the overstuffed chairs. He took out his notebook, pulled his legs under himself, and began to write. He filled several pages, then looked up at the fireplace. Hanging above the mantle was a portrait of a man. He walked over to it and stared at the painting.

"Miss Emma, who's this?" he asked, pointing to the portrait.

"Oh, him?" Emma smiled. "That's my Harry, my husband."

"He's got a friendly face," Dev said, studying the portrait.

"Yes, he was a friendly guy," Emma said. "He would have liked you. And I think you would have liked him."

"What happened to him?"

"He got sick. Harry had ALS."

"He got sick from sign language?"

Emma grinned and said, "No, that's A-S-L. Harry had A-L-S."

"A-L-S? What's that?"

"Have you ever heard of a baseball player named Lou

Gehrig?"

"Is he an old-timey player? Chase talks about him sometimes. Him and some guy named Joe the Maggio."

"Yes, he was an old-timey player. He used to play for the Yankees, and he was a really, really good ballplayer, but then he got very sick. People didn't know what his disease was, so they called it 'Lou Gehrig's Disease', but now they call it ALS. It's a disease that affects the muscles in your body."

"So, your husband, he died? From ALS?"

"Yes, he did, some time ago."

"Was it hard?"

"You mean losing him?" Emma asked.

Dev nodded.

She came around the front desk to where Dev was standing. She put her arm around his shoulder as she looked up at the portrait.

"Harry was a wonderful husband. A good friend. He was a fine man. But that disease, it took a lot away from him. It was painful–for him and for me. As much as I wanted to help him get better, there wasn't anything I could do. So yes, it was hard."

"I wanna help my mom. She has a disease too. I wanna help her get better, but I don't know how. I keep trying, but nothing seems to work."

Emma went to the loveseat by the fireplace and sat down. Dev followed her and sat beside her. "Dev, may I ask you something? Something personal?"

Dev nodded yes.

"Do you believe in God?"

"I think so," Dev answered.

"Harry, he believed in God and so do I. So, I know as difficult as it was to say goodbye, he's now someplace so much better than here. Harry's in heaven and he's not in pain anymore. He's got a new body, one that works. He's happy again. Knowing that makes it easier.

"Your mom, I don't know what her disease is, but I'm sure you're doing all you can for her. I can see that in you. Things like this, they're out of our control. There's nothing we can do, nothing but hope and pray God will take care of those we love."

"Hey, two of my favorite people! How convenient," Ben said as he came into the lobby and spotted Dev and Emma. "Emma, when was the last time you had dinner somewhere other than the inn?"

"Couldn't tell you, Ben."

"Well, I think we should fix that, don't you, Dev?"

Dev smiled. He took Emma's hand. "Miss Emma, would you have dinner with us? Please?"

"Well, how can I turn that down?" She smiled at Dev. "I'd love to."

"Great," Ben said. "Well, Dev—wait. Are you Dev? You

look different." Ben took a closer look at the new Dev.

"Miss Emma and Miss Iris gave me a haircut."

"Yeah, they did. You look very sharp. I like it."

"Me, too." Dev grinned.

Ben turned to Emma. "Thanks, Em. That was very nice of you."

"Actually, Mary was the one to give me the idea."

Ben's eyes narrowed at Mary's name.

"I don't know what it is with you two," Emma said with a laugh.

"And you probably never will." Ben patted Dev on the back. "Okay, let's you and I go get washed up, and meet back here in say, an hour? Would that work for you, Emma?

"That'd be fine. Thank you. This will be very nice," Emma said as she and Dev shared an understanding look.

CHAPTER 25

Answers

An outing to Machias to see the waterfalls with Ben's parents, sailing with Jennifer and Bill on the lake, a whale watching excursion, and dinners with Emma at the inn filled Ben and Dev's next few days. At the end of each evening, the two would sit on the patio. From there, they'd watch the lobster boats and trawlers come in from their day of fishing and Dev would check on his new friends, the seals, with the binoculars Iris lent him.

After one relaxing meal with Emma, Dev and Ben took their place on a patio bench. "So, are you having a good time?" Ben asked.

"The best." Dev put the binoculars down. "Can I ask you somethin'?"

"Sure, anything, bud."

"Why'd you leave here? This place is great."

Ben let out a long sigh. "Ah, it's a long story."

"I got time."

"Yeah, well, it's complicated." Ben shifted in his seat.

"You ask me stuff all the time, personal stuff." Dev raised his eyebrows at Ben and shrugged his shoulder.

"Fine." Ben sat up straight. "You know Miss Iris . . ."

Dev nodded.

"Well, she and I . . . She and I . . . We were kind of a thing. We were gonna get married. And then we didn't. And then I moved away. The end."

"That's not a very long story."

"Like I said, it's complicated."

Dev stared at Ben, watching him watch the seals. "So, you and Miss Iris were gonna get married."

"Uh-huh."

"Then she dumped you, and then you ran away."

Ben turned toward Dev. "She did not dump me. As a matter of fact, if you must know, I broke it off with her."

"And *then* you ran away."

"I did not run away. I moved. There's a difference."

"Not much of one in my book," Dev said, cocking his head and shrugging his shoulder again.

Ben narrowed his eyes at Dev. "Don't go using my words against me."

Dev grinned a cheeky grin. He looked through the

binoculars. "Miss Iris is nice."

"Yes, she is."

"I like her."

"I like her, too."

"But she's not right for you."

"Well, I know that, especially since she's married to somebody else now."

Dev put the binoculars down. "No, I mean before. She wasn't right for you."

"And what makes you say that? You barely know Miss Iris."

"Because she's . . ." Dev looked out at the bay. "She's an ocean."

"An ocean? What's that supposed to mean?"

"Remember when we went down the shore and you told me about the undertow? You said it pulled stuff from the beach and from underneath the waves and mixes it all up. Miss Iris is like that. She has a lot of stuff underneath."

"How could you know that? You only met her a few times."

"'Cause, my mom's like that." Dev paused. "You need somebody more like a lake."

"A lake, huh. Okay, I'll bite. What's a lake person like?"

"They're like the lake we went kayaking on. The surface was all smooth and even. When I fell in the water, it was smooth underneath too. Nothing pulled or pushed me. It was the same. Calm. Top to bottom. Like you. You need a lake lady."

"And I suppose you have a particular lake lady in mind?"

Dev smiled and nodded.

"And who might that be, pray tell?"

Dev's smile stretched across his face. "Miss Emma. She's a lake."

"Miss Emma? You want me to date Emma, one of my best friends?"

"Uh-huh." Dev nodded his head rapidly.

"And who are you all of a sudden, the Love Guru? And why I am taking dating advice from a ten-year-old?"

"'Cause you're not doing so hot on your own," Dev laughed.

"Boy, you better get up and start running. I'm gonna throw you in that ocean and I'm not coming in after you this time." Dev hopped up, and ran screaming toward the inn, waving his arms in the air.

Ben stood to chase him but stopped to answer his phone. "Yeah, Jay," Ben said laughing. As if smacked in the face, Ben's laughter stopped. His eyes narrowed and his jawline tensed. "Uh-huh . . . uh-huh."

Dev stopped running and turned around. He kept his eyes fixed on Ben and walked back toward him, his steps slow and cautious.

"Okay, I got it." Ben nodded. "Yeah, I'll let you know. Thanks." Ben hung up the phone and stared at it in his hand for a moment. He closed his eyes and exhaled, then looked up at Dev standing in front of him.

"That was JJ. He had some news, about your mom . . . Let's go sit down."

"No. Tell me," Dev said, standing up straight.

How am I going to tell you this? God give me the words. "Let's go sit."

Dev frowned. He stared at Ben for a moment, then whispered, "She's dead, isn't she? My mom. She's dead."

I should have known he'd figure it out. "I'm sorry, Dev." He put his hand on the boy's shoulder. "I'm very sorry. Yes, she is."

"I knew it. I've known for a while." He put his head down.

"How could you know?"

"Because my mom, she was a good mom. I know people think because she did drugs she wasn't, but she was. She took care of me. I know she wasn't good at math, and computers, and stuff like that. But she was good at other things like, like art and poetry. She taught me. We did things together. She wouldn't have left me if something bad hadn't happened. I know it. She wouldn't have done that. She was a good mom," Dev's voice quivered.

"I'm sure she was. I'm sure she was a good mom."

"How do you know? You never met her."

"But I know you. Dev, you are one of the strongest, smartest people I've ever met, adults included. You lived on your own for months, and you did an excellent job taking care of yourself. You went to school, you did well. You kept up with your sports and your friends. You kept a roof over your head. I don't know how you did all you did. If it were ten-year-old me? I would have curled up in a ball in a corner, and I'd probably still be there.

"You are an amazingly responsible young man. You care for other people, and you look out for them. All that doesn't happen by accident. You learned it somewhere, and I believe you learned it from your mom. She may have made a mistake or two, but not with you. She *was* a good mom. And she has my respect."

"What happened to her?"

"It's all done now, buddy. You don't wanna know that."

"Yes. I want to know. She was my mom and I wanna know what happened."

Ben put his arm around Dev's shoulders. "Come with me." He led him back to the bench. They sat down and stared at the bay for a few moments, then Dev looked at Ben.

"Do you know anything about Kensington?" Ben asked.

"You mean Zombie Town?"

"Yes. I guess you know about it."

"Everybody does. Is that where my mom went?"

"As far as we can tell. She probably went there to buy drugs. I looked through your whole apartment, and there weren't any drugs there, nothing she would have used. Your mom was careful. I'm sure she didn't want them around you. So, she had to go somewhere to get them, and that seems to be where she went."

"But what happened? How did she die?"

Should I tell him this? He's only ten.

"Tell me."

"Okay, all right. I'll see if I can explain. The drugs she took were laced with something called fentanyl. It's a really dangerous drug, and if you don't know it's in what you're taking, you can overdose easily. That's what happened to your mom. She wasn't alone when she took it, and whoever she was with must have seen she was in trouble because they called 911, but it was too late. By the time the ambulance got there, she was gone. She didn't have any ID on her, and no one stuck around to talk to the police. That's why it took us so long to find her."

"Where is she now?"

"Ah, Dev," Ben looked away.

"Where? I wanna know."

Ben rubbed his forehead then looked at Dev. "Her body is in the city morgue."

"What's that?"

"It's a place where they keep people's bodies who've died."

"Like on TV? In those refrigerator drawers? My mom is in, my mom is—"

"No, Dev. Your mom's not there."

"But you just said, you said she was in the morgue."

"No, what I said was her *body* is in the morgue. That's just her shell. She's gone, and she's in a much better place."

"I don't understand."

Ben paused. "Think of it this way. Our bodies, they're only temporary housing for the most important part of who we are, our soul."

"Our soul?"

"Yes, our soul. That's the part of us we can't see or touch, but we know it's there. It's the part of us that holds our memories, our hopes, our faith. It's where love lives."

"How can that be separate from your body?"

"Close your eyes."

Dev tilted his head at him.

"Go ahead. Close 'em."

Dev conceded and closed his eyes.

"Can you remember what it was like the first time you saw the ocean? Do you remember how big it looked?"

Dev nodded.

"Do you remember what it felt like? How it felt to have

the waves wash over your feet? Do you remember what it tasted it like?"

"Yeah, super salty, like when you get too much salt on a soft pretzel," Dev said with his eyes still closed.

"Right," Ben said with a smile. "Do you remember what it felt like to ride the breakers with Chase? Or the sound of the waves pounding on the shore? And the seagulls squawking?"

"Yeah, and how they stole my chips from me."

"Dev, are you down the shore now?"

"No." He opened his eyes. "I'm here with you."

"That's right. And all the stuff you remember, that's what's in your soul. That's what we take with us when we're done with our bodies. Your mom, her body's here, but she's not. Who she is, her personality, her memories, who she loves, that part of her, that part has moved on. And where she is now, it's a wonderful place. And I'm sure she's happy, and she's not in pain anymore."

"No more drugs?" Dev asked with tears in his eyes.

"No more drugs."

"Is that heaven? Miss Emma said her husband Harry is there. And Miss Iris's son, Birch, is there too. Is that where my mom is?"

Ben smiled a sad smile remembering his friends. "You told me once every night your mom would say, 'I love you, and Jesus does too.'"

"Yeah, she did."

"Well, to me, that sounds like she believed in Jesus, and if that's the case, yes, your mom's in heaven."

"I wish she was here, but . . ." Dev wiped a tear with his sleeve.

"I know."

Dev stared at his feet. "Thanks for telling me."

A weighty silence pressed in on the two.

God, help me here. What should I do next? What does he need? This is going to be tough on him. Show me how to help.

Dev looked up at Ben, his chin trembling. "What's gonna happen to me now?"

Ben got up from the bench, then knelt in front of the boy. He placed his hands on Dev's knees and looked into his tear-filled eyes. "I'll tell you what's gonna happen. You're gonna keep going. You're gonna go to school, and you're gonna keep learning. You're gonna play basketball and run track and you're gonna keep writing. And you're gonna grow into a fine man, the finest kind. And one day, you'll fall in love. You'll get married and have kids of your own. And you are going to be a fantastic father. You're gonna have a great life. That's what's gonna happen to you. And I'll be standing in your corner, cheering you on. And so will Chase, and JJ, and Angela, and Emma, and Iris. We're all with you in this, Dev.

"I am so sorry this happened, but you are not alone, bud.

I'm here for you. I will carry you."

Dev looked up at Ben, then leapt into his arms. Ben picked him up, held him close, and rocked him. "I'm sorry. I am so sorry." Ben whispered over and over as Dev allowed himself to express the grief he'd been holding in for weeks. When the boy was calm, Ben put him down.

"We should head back tomorrow. On the ride home we can talk about what has to be done. I'll let Emma and Jen know we're leaving." He put his arm around Dev, and Dev leaned his head into Ben. The two walked back to the inn.

Emma saw them coming back and rushed to them. "What's happened?"

Ben shook his head. Emma looked at Dev, tears streaming down his face. She knelt in front of him.

"Your mom?"

Dev nodded.

Emma looked at him with tears in her own eyes and said, "I am so sorry, Dev."

Dev threw his arms around her neck. Emma held him, rubbing his back while he cried. Ben turned away, unable to keep his own tears from flowing.

Dev released his hold on Emma, and she took both his hands in hers and, holding them against her chest, she said, "This is hard. It's the hardest thing, losing someone you love. But remember, you have people who love you all around you.

I'm one of them. We haven't known each other long, but I believe *we know each other.* You know what I mean, right?"

Dev nodded.

"Good. So, you understand then. I'll be right here for you. Anything you need, you tell me. If you want to talk, you call me and we can talk, or if you want to call and be quiet, I'll be quiet with you."

She kissed his hands, then kissed him on the forehead, and hugged him again. She stood, wiped away another tear, and said to Ben, "I guess you two will be leaving then?"

"Yeah. I thought we'd take off before daybreak. I'll drive straight through so we can be back by tomorrow night. That's probably best, for everyone," he said with a glance toward Dev.

"Okay. Well, I'll pack up a basket with meals for you, so you don't have to stop anywhere long. You let me know what time you'll be up, and I'll make you breakfast."

"Em, that's not nec—"

"I'll be up. Let me do this."

Ben nodded. "Thanks, Emma."

Ben led Dev back to their room. He packed while Ben called Jennifer and JJ to let them know the plan. The next morning, they were on the road at four-thirty, back to Philadelphia.

CHAPTER 26

Time to Say Goodbye

A bright azure blue filled in the cloudless dawn. Ben left his home for a morning run and as his feet pounded the pavement, Ben pounded the gates of heaven.

Lord, I've never had to do something like this before. I'm gonna need your help. This kid—how's he supposed to deal with this? Listen, I know you're not into trading, but if you want to take some strength from me and give it to Dev, that's fine with me. Whatever he needs, God, if I have it, give it to him. And please help me get him through today.

The sea was calm, with the gentlest waves forming in the distance. Ben, Dev, JJ, Angela, and Chase walked solemnly to the Ocean City docks and boarded the boat Ben chartered to take them well beyond the shore. Once at sea, the crew dropped anchor, and the service began.

JJ stood and walked to the center of the boat, Bible in hand. He opened the Good Book.

"Romans 8:35,37-39 says, 'Who shall separate us from the love of Christ? Shall tribulation, or distress, or persecution, or famine, or nakedness, or danger, or sword? No, in all these things we are more than conquerors through him who loved us. For I am sure that neither death nor life, nor angels nor rulers, nor things present nor things to come, nor powers, nor height nor depth, nor anything else in all creation, will be able to separate us from the love of God in Christ Jesus our Lord.'

"Let's bow our heads. God, we come to You with heavy hearts. Today we're remembering a very special lady, Anna, Dev's mom. We ask You to be with us, and especially, that You be with Dev. Comfort him with the comfort only You can give. We love him and we know You love him too. Help him to feel Your love, especially now. In Jesus's name, Amen."

JJ went to Angela and helped her stand, then he took a seat beside Chase. Angela went to the center of the boat.

"Anna and I first met after Chase and Dev got into a fight in kindergarten. I knew she was a good mom because she said we should let the boys work it out themselves. And they did." She smiled at Chase and Dev. "Anna wasn't available for things like chaperoning field trips, but she could always be counted on to bake something yummy for class parties or fundraisers. She made the best chocolate chip cookies.

"I wish I knew her better, but I'm glad I knew her at all. She was a beautiful woman with a kind heart. God bless you, Anna." Angela dabbed her eyes as she went back to her seat.

Ben stood. He scanned the ocean for a moment. The sun's rays brushed across the water, painting contrasting shapes of light and dark. A reflection of the juxtaposition of life and death those on the boat were experiencing. Looking back, he smiled softly at Chase who sat by his friend, silent and immovable, as if he were Dev's bodyguard, trying to protect him from the unseen dangers of grief.

"Psalm 34:18 says, 'The LORD is near to the brokenhearted and saves the crushed in spirit.' I think we're all feeling a little crushed today. I'm glad He's near.

"I wish I could have known Anna, but in some ways, I feel like I do know her. She was a woman of quiet compassion. She was thoughtful and caring. Despite the odds against her, she was determined to protect and care for the person she loved most." He nodded toward Dev.

"Above all the things she was, she was a good mom. A very good mom. Her life wasn't easy, but she tried her best to provide a safe and nurturing home for Dev. And she did. Well done, Anna. Now, you can rest in peace. God bless you." He walked over to Dev and put his hand on his shoulder. "And you don't have to worry, we'll look after your son."

Ben took a seat next to Dev. The boy stared at his feet for a few moments, then stood. He walked to the center of the boat holding a spiral notebook. He opened it to a page he marked, and with hands trembling, he read.

Mom
I say that word and I see you.
Your hair as bright as sunshine,
Your eyes as blue as the sea,
Your smiling face gazing at me like I'm your prince.

Mom
I say that word and I can smell you.
The scent of cinnamon and vanilla,
Of chocolate and of peanut butter
The sweetness of who you are.

Mom
I say that word and I can hear you
Calling me your favorite names like
Pookie, and Dev-On, and Mister
And my favorite one—son.

Mom
I say that word and I can feel you.
Your strength, your fear,

A Good Place to Turn Around

The pain you hid behind your eyes,
But most of all, your love.

Mom
I say that word and I need you.
I'm not a prince. I'm not a Mister,
I'm just a kid, a kid who wants his mom.
I miss you. I love you,
Mom.

Dev closed his notebook. His eyes flooded with tears, and he looked to Ben. Ben knelt and hugged him.

Angela leaned into JJ, and wrapped her arm around Chase, pulling him in for a hug. Even the captain and crew had to dry their eyes before weighing anchor.

"It's time. You ready?" Ben asked Dev. He nodded and went with Ben to the side of the boat. Ben handed him a velvet pouch and as the captain moved the vessel at a measured pace through the water, Dev poured its contents overboard. When the pouch was empty, the group watched as the ashes floated, then slipped under the surface.

Dev whispered, "Bye, Mom. I love you." He turned and buried his face in Ben's body, his shoulders heaving under the weight of his grief.

A few days later, Ben visited JJ at the station house. On his way to JJ's office, several officers who worked on the case expressed their condolences and their concern for Dev.

"Come on in, Ben," JJ said. "Coffee?"

"Sure, thanks."

JJ poured them each a cup. The two men sat in silence. JJ put his coffee cup down and said, "Rough day down the shore."

"Yeah, one I don't want to repeat anytime soon." Ben rubbed his thumb around the top of the cardboard cup.

"It was a good thing to do though. How's Dev?"

Ben blew on his coffee, took a sip, then said, "He's holding up. He's writing a lot. Iris said that's a good thing. She said he has a knack for it, a genuine talent, and writing's gonna help him get through this."

"That's good. He's got a rough road ahead, adjusting to a different life." Silence returned between the two men.

"Jay, is there something you want to tell me?"

JJ tapped his fingers on his desk. "Ben, you've done a great job with the kid, but I think it's time to consider what's next for him."

"What'd you mean, *what's next*?"

"Well, I know you have temporary custody, but that's only going to last till what? October?"

"Yeah, right, October 31st."

"What's gonna happen after that?"

"Eh, I don't know." Ben blew out a heavy sigh. "We haven't talked about it. I'm just trying to get him through this part. You know, one day at a time."

"You might want to start thinking about it. First day of school is in a little over a week. A lot goes on with that. I know Angie is already running around like crazy getting Chase ready."

"What are you trying to say, Jay? You worried I can't handle it?" Ben pulled himself up straight in the chair. "Just so you know, I've already been in touch with the school. I have a meeting with the principal on Monday."

"Nah, it's not you I'm worried about, but since you mentioned it, Ben, you've never done this, parent a kid. You sure you want to take it on?"

"Honestly? No. No, I'm not sure. All I'm sure of right now is Dev seems to need me. And he knows he can depend on me. I took an oath a long time ago to protect and to serve. And that's what I'm doing—protecting and serving."

"I know. I know you're doing your best. I'm not questioning that."

"Well, you're questioning something. I can hear it. Just say it. What do *you* think I should do?" Ben furrowed his brow.

JJ stared at his friend, rested his elbows on his desk and rubbed his hands together. "I think you should consider carefully what's gonna happen with Dev long term. Okay, he needs you. And you're right, he is depending on you. He's been through a shock and he's grieving. I'm sure it's best not to make any other changes right now. But what about later? What about when October rolls around? What then?"

JJ took a long sip of coffee. "And what about you? How are you feeling about all this? What do *you* want to happen? Do you want to keep him past temporary custody?"

Ben stared, the muscles in his jaw twitching.

"Do you want to adopt Dev? I'm sure you've asked yourself that question, probably more than once. So let me tell you this, raising a kid, it's the hardest and best job there is. If you want to take it on, you'd better be ready. There are no givebacks, no time-outs, no vacations off. It's a 24/7/365-day-a-year job, and it never ends, not even when they're grown. You ready for that?"

"I suppose you think he'd be better off with you and Angela," Ben said, lifting his chin.

"Ang and I have talked about nothing else since all this started. Dev has practically been a part of our family for years. He and Chase are like brothers. You know Angela, she'd take him in and raise him like one of her own. There'd be no difference to her. And there'd be no difference to me either. I can guarantee it."

Ben swirled his coffee. What am I supposed to say to

that? You think I haven't been losing sleep over this? I have no idea what I should be doing. How'd I get into this anyway? And what about what Dev wants? Doesn't he count?

"I don't know, Jay. I hear what you're saying. I know I have to think about this, and you're right, I have been. I also know I have to include Dev in the decision."

"You sure? I mean, he's not even eleven yet. That's a heck of a decision to make at ten years old."

Ben rubbed his forehead. "The boy took care of himself for four months. He paid the rent. He paid the bills. He got himself to school and to sports and somehow, he did all that with no one knowing his mom was missing. He gets a say."

He finished his coffee, crushed the cup, and tossed it in the trash. "I'll think about what you've said. I will. But I won't do anything without including Dev. That's non-negotiable." Ben stood and turned toward the door. "I'll talk to you later."

Ben started up his truck and turned off the radio. "JJ has a point, Lord. Dev knows the Mongellis, and they know him. Angela would take him in and treat him as if he were her own son. I know that. He'd have a father *and* a mother. And then there's Chase. Chase would do anything for Dev. But Chase throws a big shadow. Dev could get lost. And it's one thing to be best friends, but brothers? That's a different animal. What should I do? What do *You* want me to do?"

By the time he reached his home, Ben still didn't know

the answer. He went inside, sat on the sofa in the living room and an hour later, when Dev walked in, he was still there, staring at a crack in the wall.

"Hey," Dev said.

"Hey." Ben remained still.

Dev looked at him for a moment, then sat beside him. Ben didn't move or speak, so Dev slid closer. Ben reached over and put his arm around him, and the boy brought his feet up on the sofa and nestled into Ben's side. The two sat in silence and watched the evening stars appear through the living room window like miniature beacons in the sky.

CHAPTER 27

Father Time

Ben did his due diligence and met with the principal. Afterward, and with some assistance from Angela, he made sure Dev had all he needed to begin middle school. When the first day of school arrived, it was difficult to tell who was more nervous—Ben or Dev.

In their elementary school years, Chase would meet Dev on the corner of Tenth and Federal near Dev's apartment building and the two boys would walk the rest of the way to school together. On this first day of middle school, Chase came to Ben's home instead.

"Chase, come on in. We're just about ready," Ben said.

"We? Who's we?" Chase asked.

"I thought I'd walk along with you boys today, being the first day of middle school and all."

"Aw, man, you're kiddin' right? You wanna make us a

target before we even get to school?"

"No, I just want to make sure you get there safely, that's all."

"I think we can handle eight blocks." Chase tilted his head at Ben.

"Tell you what. How 'bout I pace you instead. I'll walk behind so no one will know we're together. And I promise I won't yell, 'Make good choices' once we get there.'"

"Fine." Chase said with a shake of his head.

Ben yelled up the stairs. "Dev, you ready?"

"Comin,'" Dev said as he came down the stairs, flinging his backpack over his shoulder.

"All right, you two have a good day. Dev, call me if you need me." Dev nodded.

The trio arrived at the school without incident, and with Ben trailing a tolerable distance behind the boys. Once they came to the building, it was all Ben could do to keep his promise and not yell an encouragement to them.

Ben spent the rest of the day pacing. He paced home, then paced his way to Washington Square Park, paced his way around the park, then paced to Independence Square, through Little Italy, and finally, paced back to the school.

When the school bell rang, Ben was there, waiting for the boys. Dev grinned when he saw him, but Chase grabbed his friend by the elbow and escorted him down the sidewalk. As in the morning, Ben stayed a reasonable distance behind the two. When they got back to the house, Chase put his hands on hips and looked Ben up and down. "You gonna do this every day, ol' man?"

"That's the joy of retirement. I'm available, so yeah, maybe... knucklehead." Chase rolled his eyes, then he and Dev went upstairs and took a seat at the dining room table. Ben watched them as they began their homework.

Funny they didn't ask to do this. They just assumed they could. Like it's supposed to be this way.

After they wrapped up their homework, they played a quick game of HORSE with Ben on the basketball court before Chase ran home for dinner. The next day, the boys went to Chase's house to do homework and Dev was the one running home for dinner. This became the routine for the next few weeks.

By the end of September, Dev seemed to have adjusted to his new reality, although there were times when he would quarantine himself in his room. Ben could hear Dev's pen scratching on paper, and the rustling of pages.

As the weeks counted down to October, the pressure to make a decision mounted inside of Ben. Despite his continual prayers, he had no clarity over what his course of action should be. The Perry Harvest Festival would be coming up soon, and he thought perhaps a change in scenery would clear his head and help him come to a decision.

"Dev, what would you think about going up to Maine again for a long weekend? Remember I told you about the Harvest Festival? Well, it's coming up and I need to be there. My entire family gets together every year for the festival and this year, it's even more special because we're going to celebrate my parents' ninetieth birthdays."

"Ninety? Wow. They were born on the same day?"

"No, but pretty close. My mom's birthday is September twenty-ninth and my dad's is October eleventh. They're only two weeks apart, but Pop likes to tease he married an older woman," Ben said with a laugh. "Listen, I know you have a lot going on with school, so if you don't wanna go, I'm sure you can stay with the Mongellis."

"Not go? I wanna go. Can I?"

"The thing is, you'd have to miss a Friday and a Monday of school. Do you think you could make up the work?"

"Yes, I can do it. I promise! I can talk to my teachers. Maybe they'll give me the work ahead of time and I can do it before we go. Can we see Miss Emma too, and Miss Iris?"

"I'm not sure. We'll be staying at the inn, so we'll at least get to say hello to Emma. I don't think we'll have time to see Iris. We're gonna be on a pretty tight schedule. As it is, we'll have to fly up and back."

"Fly? I've never been on a plane before."

"Plane? Who said anything about a plane?" Ben gave Dev a look. "We're just going to think lovely thoughts, and up we'll go," he said with a laugh, quoting *Peter Pan*.

Dev shook his head and even though the trip was a few weeks away, he went to his room to pack.

Ben checked with Child Protective Services and Dev's school and received permission for Dev to leave. Two weeks later, they were on a flight from Philadelphia to Bangor. From there, Ben rented a car for the drive to Eastport. Along the way, he prepped Dev for the mayhem he was about to encounter. He knew when all the Hudson family gathered, there would be over thirty adults and children, and to an outsider, that could be overwhelming, especially an outsider as shy as Dev.

Once they arrived at the Sunrise Inn, and unpacked their things, they returned to the lobby to find Emma.

"Sheriff," Mary said, sneering over her glasses.

"Mary," Ben said, narrowing his eyes at her.

"West wing."

"Hey, Miss Mary," Dev said, smiling.

"Hey, Tagalong. Good to see ya," Mary said with as much of a smile as she allows. Ben shifted his eyes to Dev, then to Mary, then back to Dev.

"Am I in the Twilight Zone?" he asked, continuing to shift his eyes between the two.

"What's that?" Dev asked.

"Never mind." Ben showed Dev to the west wing of the inn, Emma's living quarters.

"Hello, you two! Come on in." Emma said.

"Emma, why do you keep that old gnome of a woman at the front desk?"

"Old gnome? You mean Mary? That's not very kind."

"Well, neither is she. Why do you keep her around? Can't imagine she makes a good first impression."

"I'll have you know Mary is an excellent assistant. She knows my business before I do. And she's very friendly . . . with most people."

"I guess I'm not most people."

"No, you are not," Emma said with a smile and a look that made Ben's heart skip a beat. She turned her attention to Dev. "So, how's school going? Do you like your teachers?"

"It's going good. Most of my teachers are okay, except for Mr. Dixon. He teaches science. He's bor-ring. How do you make science boring?"

Emma laughed. "That's a good question."

"But I have Mr. Wolfe for English. He's awesome."

"Dev's in the advanced English class," Ben said.

"Really? Well, I guess that's not too much of a surprise. What about Chase? Are you in many classes with him?"

"All but English. Chase doesn't mind, though. He doesn't like English," Dev explained. "He barely speaks it."

Dev told Emma about the sports he was playing, and how he and Chase have challenged Ben to a HORSE tournament. Ben shared about some places he discovered in Philadelphia and that he renewed his lease for another six months, which brought a tight smile to Emma's lips.

Over dessert, Emma caught Ben and Dev up on the latest happenings in the community, especially about how the seals were doing. "Iris wanted me to be sure to tell you about Dev, the seal, that is. His parents showed up!"

"What? How does she know they're his parents?" Dev leaned toward Emma.

"She was out watching them one afternoon, not too long after you'd left, and she noticed two seals approaching the pup. He got very excited and jumped into the water. Then the three of them circled and circled each other, barking and flipping. It was obvious they were a family."

"Have you seen them?"

"Yes. When you get up in the morning, head to the patio. You can see them from there. I know nothing about seals, really, but I think the colony has accepted them. I don't think they'll be leaving anytime soon."

Dev became quiet. He looked up at Emma. "I'm happy for him. He has a family now."

Emma nodded in agreement. She shared a look with Ben.

"Miss Emma, would you mind if I went to my room?

We're supposed to read a couple chapters over the weekend, and I'm trying to get them done before the festival. I thought I'd read tonight."

"I don't mind at all. That's good thinking. You're going to have a great time at the festival, and it'll be nice not to have to worry about homework."

"That good with you too, Ben?"

"More than good. You go ahead. I'll be in later."

Dev cleared his plate, then left for his room.

"Oh, I feel so badly for him," Emma said after Dev left. "I'd just like to scoop him up . . ." She took a deep breath. "Okay, the truth. How's he doing, really?"

"He's doing well, considering. He has his moments. He doesn't like to talk about it. I can see a dark cloud come across his face though. He gets sad, and even more quiet than usual. When he's like that, he goes to his room, and he writes or draws. Iris said it's a good thing, so I let him go. I figure he knows I'm here if he ever wants to talk. I try not to push him. Don't know if that's the right thing to do, but . . ."

"And what about you? How are you doing with all this?"

Ben smiled. "I'm doing fine."

Emma studied Ben as he ran his finger around the rim of his coffee cup. "We've known each other for ages. Now is not the time to start lying to me."

Ben looked down at his cup, swirling it until the coffee

formed a whirlpool, then he looked up at Emma. "Em, there are days when I wonder what in the world am I doing. And whatever it is, am I doing it right? Am I doing the best things for Dev? Am I giving him what he needs? Would he be better off with someone else? What if I screw him up?"

"You're asking the same questions every parent asks."

"But I'm not his parent. I'm only his guardian and that's supposed to end soon. Then what? Do I let it end? Is that the right thing to do? Do I let JJ and Angela take him so he can be with a real family? Or do I try to keep him? I've been thinking about this and praying about it for weeks. I don't know what to do. I mean, I'm almost sixty-two-years old. What am I thinking, trying to raise a kid?"

Emma frowned. "You know, for a smart man sometimes you say the stupidest things."

"Excuse me?" Ben cocked his head at Emma.

"Since when is there an age requirement for loving a child?" Emma folded her arms in front of her and leaned on the table. "Do you think Dev cared how old you were when you pulled him out of the ocean? Or when you brought him into your home and fed and clothed him? Do you think he cared a smidge about your age when he found out about his mom, and *you* were the one he chose to comfort him? Age has nothing to do with this. You know, in the Bible, Abraham was a hundred years old when Sarah gave birth to his son."

"Yeah, but that was miraculous."

"Oh, and you don't think this is? You think it's a coincidence the first person you go to visit when you left Eastport is your college roommate and he just happens to live in a place called the 'city of brotherly *love*'? And you just happen to meet his son's best friend. Who just happens to be living in a tent across the street from the house you just happened to rent? You think that's all accidental? Because I don't."

Emma took a moment, then said gently. "When you left here, when you left Eastport, I thought you were running away from someone, but I was wrong. You were running *to someone.*"

Ben furrowed his brow and pursed his lips as he listened to his friend.

"Love is looking you squarely in the face. Don't turn away from it. You'll regret it the rest of your life."

Ben swirled the remaining coffee in his cup. Then he looked up. "You really think I can do this, Emma?"

"Doesn't matter what I think." She leaned back in her chair. "What do you think God's asking you to do? You know, don't you? It's written all over your face. You just don't want to believe it yet."

"Since when did you get so smart?"

Emma smiled and said, "I've always been this smart. You just never noticed. And for the record, I believe you can do almost anything."

Ben sat for a moment, then pushed his chair away from the table and came behind Emma. He put his hands on her shoulders and kissed her on top of her head, and whispered, "I don't deserve you."

"I know. You're my charity case." Emma patted Ben's hand.

Ben laughed and said, "I'd better go. Gonna be a long day tomorrow. Thanks for dinner. And the truth."

Emma stood and walked Ben to the door. "You're going to be fine. I know you. And you're gonna do the right thing."

"Yeah, as soon as I figure out what that is."

CHAPTER 28

The Harvest Festival

"Keep that up and I'm going to have to tighten every bolt in this truck," Ben said as he looked over at Dev's leg bouncing up and down. "You doing okay, buddy?"

"Yeah, I'm fine."

"Nervous?"

"A little. But I'm excited too. I've never been to a festival. There were some block parties on my street, but they don't sound anything like what you said a festival is like."

"Probably not. Don't worry, you're going to have a good time."

Fifteen minutes later, Ben pulled into Jennifer's driveway, and before getting out of the car, he said, "Remember, my family is loud. Not that they'll let you forget it. If you get overwhelmed, don't feel bad about taking some time by yourself. Just let me know and I'll cover for you. Okay?"

Dev nodded a nervous nod.

"All right, let's go."

They walked to the back deck, where the first half of the family was gathered. Dev smiled when he saw Ben's brother, Oliver, a face he'd already met.

"Hey, Dev. Welcome back to Maine. Oh, yeah, and you too, Ben," Oliver joked.

"Dev! I'm so glad you're here!" Jennifer said, running over and giving him a long hug. "Oh, yeah, and you too, Ben."

"Sibling love, nothing like it." Ben said.

Jennifer escorted Dev around the deck to begin introductions. "Dev, you remember my parents." She walked him over to her mom and dad.

"Come here, young man, and give these old bones a hug," Elsie said with her arms open. Dev smiled and allowed himself to be enveloped in her embrace.

"Good to see you, Dev," Phil said, mussing Dev's hair much like Ben had done many times.

"Good to see you too, sir."

Jennifer wrapped her arm around Dev's shoulder and led him to another group of family members. "This is my oldest brother, Jacob, and his wife, Marissa. Jake, Marissa, this is Dev."

"Nice to meet you." Jacob extended his hand. Dev gave him a firm handshake.

"We've heard a lot about you," Marissa said. "I'm glad you could make it up for the festival." Dev smiled and leaned closer to Jennifer.

Jennifer turned Dev toward the lake. "Jake's kids are down by the shore, although I guess I shouldn't call them kids anymore." She pointed to a group of young adults. "The one in the blue that's Bobby, then next to him is Adam, then . . . hmm, I can't really tell who's next to him," Jennifer said with a laugh. "Oh, let's forget this. I don't remember half these people anyway. You'll learn names as the day goes on. And if you want anyone's attention, just yell, 'Hey you!'. We all answer to that."

Dev grinned.

"Hey, you!" One of the Hudson grandkids who was about Dev's age ran up to him. "Hey, I'm Curtis. Wanna play basketball while we're waiting? We're getting a game up in the driveway."

Dev looked over at Ben, who gave him an encouraging nod. Dev said, "Okay," then ran off with Curtis. Jennifer stood by Ben and watched Dev join the other grandkids, and soon he was laughing with them.

"That's a good thing to see," Jennifer said. "You've done well with him, big brother." She put her arm around his waist and gave him a squeeze.

"From your lips to God's ears."

"What do you mean by that? He giving you a hard time?"

"Nah, he's great. Don't you worry, everything's fine." Ben gave his sister a squeeze in return, then walked away.

At the appointed hour, everyone piled in their cars and made their way to the festival. The grandkids commandeered Dev and insisted he ride in one of their cars, so Ben accepted being ditched and gave a ride to his parents instead.

Once at the festival, Dev walked around wide-eyed, and shadowed his new friend, Curtis. He and Curtis entered the scarecrow building contest and competed against several other grandkids, local children, and tourists. Though their entry of a baseball playing scarecrow was creative, the prize went to a ten-year-old girl from across the bay in Canada. Curtis and Dev redeemed themselves in the blueberry pie-eating contest, coming in first and second.

The Hudson grandkids traveled throughout the festival in a pack, bringing Dev in as one of their own. Ben followed the pack from a distance, keeping an eye on his charge.

"You're hovering," Jennifer said, coming up behind Ben.

"I am not. I'm keeping an eye out."

"Mm-hmm. Your 'keeping an eye out' looks a lot like hovering. He's fine. Relax. Let him enjoy himself with kids his own age."

"You really think he's fine?" Ben's brows formed a narrow V.

"Look at him," Jennifer pointed with her head. "He's

smiling, laughing. How long has it been since you've seen him do that?"

"It's been a while."

"You're doing a fine job, big brother. Let him have some fun, without you. It'll be okay, I promise." Jennifer patted her brother on the back as he stared at Dev and the grandkids. She turned him toward the other adults, and he went back with her, though his mind stayed with Dev.

At the festival's end, everyone gathered back at Bill and Jennifer's to bring the day to a close. The Hudson brothers built a bonfire, while the Hudson sisters prepared hot chocolate for the kids and mulled cider for the adults. Everyone gathered round the fire as the sun went down.

Ben and Oliver brought out their guitars, and their older brother, Jacob, retrieved his concertina. The rest of the clan formed a family choir. As was their tradition, Oliver started the singing with a song for the kids, "There's a Hole in My Bucket", then they went to Ben's favorite hit, "Yellow Submarine". From there it was a sing-along of other tunes, ending with an a cappella version of "Amazing Grace".

As the song fest ended, Phil stood, this lion of the Hudson clan. He bowed his head and prayed.

"Father God, we thank you for one more year. We thank you for your provision and for your care. Elsie and I especially thank you for blessing us with ninety years on this wonderful earth and almost seventy years with each other. Tonight, we are surrounded by those we love the most, the greatest blessing of all. May we all gather once again next year. In Jesus's name."

And everyone said, "Amen."

With the "Amen" came a loud clap of thunder and the first drops of rain.

"Okay, that's it everyone! Grab something and head into the house before we get soaked!" Jennifer said.

The clan went into action. Chairs were folded, dishes, cups, and tablecloths were removed, the fire doused, and within minutes, every last Hudson was safe and dry inside Jennifer's home.

Curtis ran over to Dev, who by now made his way back to Ben. "Dev, come on. We're going to play some video games in the game room."

"Can I?" Dev asked Ben.

"Sure. I think we'll be leaving in about an hour. I'll call you when it's time. Go have fun."

The family scattered throughout the house, with Oliver and Ben finding a quiet space in Bill's office. After Oliver caught Ben up on all the happenings with him and his household, he turned the conversation to what was happening in Ben's world.

"How are things in Eastport? Has much changed since you left?"

"Mostly the same. Hasn't been long, really. I got some

disappointing news today, though. There was a kid I was trying to help. He was a reluctant mentee of mine. He has real potential, but he's stubborn. He prefers to learn things the hard way.

"Well, he's done it this time. He broke into someone's car, took it for a joy ride and totaled it. He got caught, and they held him for trial. He's only fifteen."

"Car theft is serious business. They try him as a juvenile?"

"Yes, thankfully. Much good it'll do him if he doesn't have a change of attitude. Ollie, I tried with this kid, I did. I feel awful, but what else can I do? I hate to say it, but he's going away. It's up to the system now."

The sound of breaking glass shattered Ben's conversation. He and Oliver looked over to see Dev standing in the doorway, his face contorted, and a broken drinking glass scattered at his feet. He started to say something to Ben, but turned and ran instead.

"Dev?" Ben said. He rushed to the hallway, and noise from the foyer drew his attention. The front door banged against the house, flung open by an unforgiving wind that swept rain into the foyer. Ben stepped out into the storm. "Dev! Dev!"

Oliver joined Ben in the foyer. Ben closed the door and wiped the rain from his face. "Dev's bolted. I've gotta find him. He has no idea where he's going. God forbid he heads toward the lake."

"You go. I'll organize the others and we'll join you," Oliver said.

Jennifer came into the foyer. "I heard something break. What happened here?" She looked at the broken glass and water-soaked floor.

"Dev's gone. He ran out. Ben's gonna go look for him," Oliver said as Ben pulled on a borrowed raincoat.

"Gone? Why?" Jennifer asked.

Oliver shrugged. "I don't know. He was standing there, dropped a glass, then ran out the door. Not sure what it was, but by the look on his face something upset him . . . a lot. I'm going to round up the others and join Ben in the search." Oliver left to gather up the adults.

Ben started for the door when Jennifer grabbed him by the arm. "Wait, wait!" She went to the closet and pulled out a flashlight. "Here, take this." She handed it to him then opened the door. Ben turned it on and ran out into the storm.

He rushed straight to the lake. Only the tops of the marsh reeds were visible above the water's surface. Fear slithered down his spine. He went to the shed and opened it.

All the kayaks are still here. Thank God. Where to next? Where are you, Dev?

Ben followed the edge of the lake, sweeping his flashlight across the yard and the water all the while calling out Dev's name. The earth, saturated under his feet, spewed mud up the leg of his jeans with every step. Useless against the deluge pounding his body, his raincoat whipped open and flapped like a banner on a pole.

He came to the edge of the forest bordering the property. He shuddered as he looked up at the conical spires of pine that a few hours ago stood straight and true, but now were bending low in submission to the ruling tempest. He drew his attention to the interior woods.

Lord, did he go in there? On a night like this, smaller animals will be taking cover, but the bear and moose? He has no idea where he's going. What if he gets disoriented? How am I going to find one small, frightened boy in there?

Water streamed from Ben's forehead and ran in tiny rivulets down his neck and back. Ignoring them, he stood still, faced the forest, and closed his eyes.

"God, please. You helped me find this boy when we were in deep waters. I'm in deep water again and I need your help. Show me which way to go. Please."

Ben opened his eyes and shone his flashlight around the area. A clap of thunder quaked the ground under his feet. He looked down and saw a set of small footprints in the mud a few feet away from him leading into the forest.

Like a hound locked on a scent, Ben followed them, not wanting to miss a single step of where the prints led. Pouring down in unmerciful sheets, Ben knew the rain would erase the impressions in moments.

About thirty feet into the woods the footprints stopped. The pine needles on the ground acted as a mat and wiped clean the shoes which created them. Ben scanned the area.

You're nearby. I can feel it. At least, I hope that's what I'm feeling. He shone his flashlight and turned in a circle. "Dev, please, come out. I need to find you, buddy. It's gonna be okay. Whatever you're worried about, we can fix it."

He waited for an answer, but the only one he received was the sound of the rain hammering the forest floor and the growl of thunder in the distance. The trees above him creaked and swayed sending an ominous message of warning to vacate the premises.

"Please, Dev, it's dangerous out here! I don't want anything to happen to you. Everyone's worried—Jen, Oliver, my parents. Dev, please. I need to find you! Where are you?"

"Here. I'm here," came a voice from behind a large boulder twenty feet away. Dev stepped out. His clothes were soaked through and clung to his body.

He looks so small.

Dev glared sideways at Ben, his chin jutted forward, his body shaking, and his hands knotted in fists.

"Oh, thank God." Ben ran toward him. "All right, let's get you back in the house, buddy."

"I'm not going anywhere with you." Dev stepped back. "And I'm not your buddy, or your knucklehead, or your *anything*!"

Ben stopped in his tracks. "What are you talking about?"

"You don't care about me. You're a liar!"

"A liar?"

"Yes, a liar! I heard you. I heard what you said!"

"I don't know what you heard, Dev, but I do care about you."

"No, you don't! You want to send me away. I heard you! You said there wasn't anything else you could do, and it was up to the system now. You promised I wouldn't go there! You promised I'd have a say. You lied to me!" Dev's voice broke.

No wonder he ran.

"I wasn't talking about you. I swear it." Lightning flashed overhead and thunder followed seconds later. Ben shouted over the storm.

"There was another boy, a teenager from Eastport. I've been trying to help him for a long time, but I found out today he did something I can't help him with. He broke the law. And now, he's going into the system, but not the one you're thinking of. He's going into juvenile detention. And I'm sorry. I wish I could have done something more for him. I tried, but he's made his choice, and there's nothing else I can do."

Ben took a step closer to Dev. "I wasn't talking about

you." He took another step, then knelt in the mud and met Dev's eyes. "I would sooner cut off my right arm than to see anything happen to you, much less send you away. *Anywhere.* I gave you my word. And that still stands."

Dev stared at Ben, his tears mixing with rain.

"You and me, we're partners. No. We're family." Ben extended his arms out to Dev. "Please. Come home with me."

Dev stood motionless.

"Please, Dev." Ben kept his arms extended. "I need you to come home."

Dev ran into his arms, his tears giving way to sobs. Ben embraced him and kissed him on top of the head as he shed his own tears. The boy buried his head in Ben's shoulder. "I'm sorry, Ben. I'm sorry."

"It's okay, buddy. It's all right." He closed his eyes for a moment and said a quick prayer of thanks. "How about we go home now before Noah stops by on his ark. Hop on."

Dev jumped on Ben's back and wrapped his arms around his neck. Once more, Ben carried Dev back to safety.

As they entered the house, Jennifer was there with towels. She bundled Dev in one, handed another to Ben then left to notify the rest of the search party who came running back into the house, all wet, but relieved the crisis was over.

Curtis lent Dev some dry clothes, as Oliver did for Ben. By the time they'd changed, and Ben explained to the adults why Dev ran off, the rain slowed down enough to make it safe to travel back to Eastport.

Ben and Dev didn't speak during the ride back to the inn. Once they were showered, and changed, Ben had Dev get into bed. He gave him a few minutes, then sat at the foot of his bed and said, "Okay, let's talk."

"I'm sorry for running away."

"I know."

"I called you a liar. And I ruined the party. I'm sorry for that, too." Dev lowered his head and twisted the blanket.

"I know you are, and you didn't ruin the party. I'm not mad at you."

"You're not?"

"No. I get it. The one thing you've told me from the very beginning is you're not going into the system, you'd run away first. You heard me talking, and it sounded like I betrayed you, so you ran. It was self-preservation. I get it."

"I didn't understand. I didn't know why you'd do that."

"Well, you didn't understand because it wasn't true. What you thought you heard went against everything I've told you. No wonder it didn't make sense.

"Dev, all I want for you, what I've wanted from the very beginning, is for you to be safe and happy. I'll do whatever's necessary to help make that happen."

Ben stood. "Listen, I know I haven't done everything right. I know I've made mistakes with you, but I'm trying, really, I am."

Dev said softly, "I know."

Ben paced the room for a moment. He rubbed the back of his neck.

Lord, Emma's right. I think I do know what You want, but do You really believe I'm ready for this? And how about Dev? Is he *gonna want this?*

He turned back to Dev. "I've been thinking about something for a while now and I'd like to know what you think." He paused. "When we were in the woods, I told you we were partners, that we were family. What would you think . . . if we made it official?"

"Official? What d'ya mean?"

Ben sat back on the bed. "I mean, how would you feel, what would you think if," Ben rubbed his hands together. "What would you say if I, uh, if I wanted to adopt you? What if we became family for real? What would you think about that?"

"You mean, like, you'd be my dad?"

"Yes. I'd be your dad."

"I never had a dad before."

"Well, I've never had a son before. We could figure it out together."

"Yeah, together." Dev got to his knees on the bed and hugged Ben.

Ben held the boy, and whispered, "I love you, Dev."

With his arms wrapped tightly around Ben, Dev whispered back, "I love you, too . . . Dad."

CHAPTER 29

Best Birthday Ever

The following morning, Dev sat on the edge of Ben's bed, waiting for Ben to finish dressing. Ben buttoned up his shirt and noticed the look on Dev's face. "You okay?"

"Yeah, I'm ah-ite."

"You look like something's bothering you. Wanna talk about it?" Ben sat next to Dev.

"Not really."

"You change your mind? About me adopting you?"

Dev shook his head no.

"Well, we can let this go for now, but you know you can talk to me about anything. That's what I'm here for." Ben patted Dev on the knee, then stood to put on a tie.

"Why you getting so dressed up?" Dev stood on the bed watching Ben in the mirror as he tied his tie.

"Ah, my mom, she likes it when I wear a tie, especially to

church. It's her birthday, she doesn't ask for much."

"Can I wear one?"

"She would love that. I didn't bring an extra one though. You know, Emma always has all kinds of things on hand. Maybe she has something that'll work. We'll ask at breakfast. You good to go?"

Dev nodded.

"All right, let's go hit the breakfast bar. Emma said there'd be blueberry pancakes today. She makes *the* best pancakes, second only to her coffee cake." He put his arm on Dev's shoulder and led him out the door.

The Morning Room was humming with activity as guests fueled up for the day. Dev and Ben filled their plates with pancakes and found a table in a corner. Emma came in soon after to check on her guests. She was fresh faced and glowing on this beautiful fall day. Her chestnut-colored waves tapped her shoulders as she walked toward Ben and Dev.

"Good morning, gentlemen." She looked them both over, then smiled. "We're looking very dapper today."

"Morning, Em," Ben said, standing up. He took a second look at her. "You cut your hair. It looks very nice that way. I like it. You look very pretty."

Emma blushed at the compliment. "I thought it was time for a change. Kimberly opened a new salon down the street, so I thought I'd give her some business."

Seeing Emma blush made Ben's heart skip a beat. He grabbed his water glass, took a sip, then nodded toward Dev. "One of us would like to look a little more dapper. Any chance you know where we could get our hands on a tie? Dev would like to wear one to church today. It's Ma and Pop's birthday celebration, so..."

"You know, I think I may have just the thing. Dev, why don't you come with me? And you," she patted Ben on the arm, "You stay here. Sit, finish your breakfast."

Another skip of a heartbeat. *What's with me today? I'm gonna have to call the doctor.*

"We'll be back in a few minutes. Relax, have another cup of coffee." Their eyes met for just a moment, then Emma took Dev by the hand and led him to her wing.

Emma didn't say a word to Dev as they went into the first bedroom. Instead, she started muttering to herself and began rummaging through the bedroom closet. "Hmmm, I know it has to be here. Ah." Emma smiled and pulled out a tie hanger that held eight different ties. "I knew I still had this," she said. "Dev, these were my husband's."

"Harry's?"

"Yes, Harry's. Now, let's have a look at you and see what

would match. Usually, you wear a different type of shirt with a tie, but I think we can make your polo shirt work, at least it has a collar." Emma gave Dev the once over with her eyes, then looked at the ties and pulled one off the hanger.

"I think this one would look nice. Hmmm." She held it up to have a better look. "No." She tossed the tie onto the bed. "I know, this one." She pulled a blue tie off the hanger and held it up to Dev's face. "Yes, this is the one. It matches your eyes. Elsie will love that."

"Ben's wearing a blue tie too, so we'll match. Like father and son," he said with a smile.

Emma took a quick breath.

Dev's eyes grew large. "Miss Emma, can I tell you something? It's not a secret, at least, I don't think it is."

"Okay, if you think it's all right."

"Ben asked me last night if I'd like him to adopt me," Dev whispered.

"Really? And what did you say?"

"I said yes."

"Well, that's wonderful news!"

Dev nodded then looked at the floor.

"At least I think it's wonderful news. What is it? You don't want Ben to adopt you?"

Dev bit his lip and looked away from Emma.

"Dev?"

"Can I ask you a question?" Dev fiddled with the bottom of his shirt.

"Sure."

"You're a mom, right?"

"Yes, four times over." Emma smiled.

"Do you think, do you think my mom would mind?"

"Mind? Mind what?"

Dev stared at Emma.

Taking a breath she said, "Ohhhh. Would she mind Ben adopting you? Is that it? You're worried she wouldn't like it?"

Dev nodded.

"Why do you think that?"

"I dunno. It's just, my mom . . ." Tears made their way down Dev's cheeks. "I don't want her to think I don't want to be her kid anymore. I don't want her to think I forgot about her."

"Oh, Dev, I'm sure she wouldn't think that. And you'll never forget about her. And you shouldn't. She was your mom, and she loved you very much and you loved her. That's how it should be," Emma said, stroking his arm.

"But do you think she'd mind if I became Ben's son, not hers?"

"Honey, you will *always* be her son. Ben adopting you won't change that, not one little bit. Listen, I didn't know your mom, but from everything you've told me, and from what I know of you, I can tell your mom wanted you to live a good and happy life. So let me ask you a few questions and let's figure this out together. Okay?"

Dev nodded.

"Here, sit." Emma sat on the bed and tapped it for Dev to sit next to her. He sat and wiped his tears.

"All right, let's think. If your mom was here, and she got to know Ben, would she have liked him?"

"Yeah, she would have. She would've thought he was funny, especially when he calls me a knucklehead." Dev gave a small laugh.

"Would she have trusted him?"

"I think so. Yes, she would. I know I do."

"Do you think she'd believe Ben would want to do everything he could to keep you safe and give you a happy life?"

Dev nodded. "He saved me in the ocean. She wouldn't have forgotten that. She'd know he'd keep me safe."

"Well, there's your answer. Your mom wanted what every mom wants—for her child to be well cared for, to be safe and happy and loved. I don't think she'd mind at all Ben wants to adopt you." Then wrapping her arm around Dev's shoulders, she said, "And I don't think she'd mind at all you want him to.

"Think of it this way, Ben isn't replacing your mom. She will *always* be your mom. Ben is just going to continue what she started—raising a wonderful young man. That's all. He's picking up where she left off."

"Like a bench player in basketball?"

Emma smiled. "Yes, exactly like that. You don't forget about the first stringer, right? But they can't play the entire game by themselves, they need help. That's what Ben's doing, he's coming off the bench to help your mom, and to help you. But there's one big difference." Emma took Dev's hand. "Ben loves you and he won't care how hard the game is, or how long he has to play, he will not sit back on the bench again until the game, *raising you*, is done. You can relax and so can your mom. Ben is the type of man every mother wants to have raise her son. Of all the things in life there are to worry about, this isn't one of them." Emma patted Dev's hand.

"Now come here, this mom needs a hug," Emma said with tears in her eyes.

Dev leaned into her, and Emma held him close. After a moment, she released him and held his hand. "Feel better now?"

Dev nodded. "You?"

"Yes, me too," Emma said with a smile, and a wipe away of a tear.

"I love you, Miss Emma."

"I love you too, Dev." She kissed him on the forehead.

Emma wiped the remaining tears from her eyes. "And here's me imagining I looked nice today. That's what I get for thinking so well of myself. I'll have to go fix my make-up."

"I think you're beautiful."

"And that comment will earn you extra dessert tonight." Emma gave Dev another hug.

"Now, let me tie that tie. Stand here." Dev stood in front of Emma as she put the necktie around him, then tied it. "There, handsome. Just like your dad."

Together, Dev and Emma returned to Ben in the breakfast room. He stood with a grand smile. "Well, now, aren't you the handsome devil?"

"Good thing we're going to church then, huh," Dev said with a grin.

"Knucklehead," Ben said, mussing Dev's hair. "Emma, thank you. My mom's gonna love this." He smiled down at Dev.

"Yes, she will," Emma said with a shake in her voice.

"Em, you okay?"

"Yes, I'm fine. I'm just . . . really, really happy for you," she said, wiping away a tear that escaped.

"He told you," Ben said with a nod.

Emma nodded, finding it difficult to maintain her composure. "And I'm so proud of you." She leaned up and kissed Ben on the cheek, then patted his arm. "Give your parents my best. I need to get back to work." Emma started back

A Good Place to Turn Around

for the lobby.

"Em."

Emma stopped and looked over her shoulder. "Yes?"

Ben paused. His heart raced from his chest to his throat. "Ah, never mind. Just, uh, thanks. For everything."

Emma nodded, then turned and wiped away another tear. Ben watched as she went back to greeting her guests on her way to the lobby. He looked down at Dev, who was staring at him, eyebrows raised, arms folded, and shaking his head.

"What?"

"She likes you."

"You're imagining things."

Dev shook his head at Ben again.

"Let's go."

Ben's mother, Elsie, told him she loved seeing two of her favorite men wearing ties to church this day, but Ben hoped she love even more what he had to tell her when they returned to Jennifer's house. Ben pulled his parents aside and let them know his plans to adopt Dev.

"May we speak to him?" Elsie asked.

"Of course," Ben grinned. "I'll go round him up." Ben came back to his parents in a few moments, his arm on Dev's shoulder, walking with him into the room. Elsie's tears were already making their way to the surface. Ben's father stood and placed his hand on Dev's shoulder.

"Young man, welcome to the family."

"Thanks, but I'm not family yet. Ben said it's not official till the judge says so," Dev explained.

"It's official for me, and for your grandmother." Phil nodded toward Elsie, who was dabbing her eyes with a handkerchief. "Doesn't matter what a judge says, we know already. You're family, one of us. You belong here and we're thrilled to have you."

"I'm happy too," Dev said glancing at his new grandfather, then looking toward the floor.

"May I pray for you?" Dev looked up and nodded his consent. Phil placed his large right hand, knotted with age, on Dev's head, and cleared his throat.

"Father God, we come to you so thankful today. As we celebrate our birthdays, you have given us the most wonderful gift of all—another grandchild, another person whom we can love and care for. You have brought Dev to this family in a miraculous way, so we know you want him to be here. We ask for your help as we look after him, as we love him, as we bring him up in the knowledge of you. We ask you to clear the way for Dev and Ben to become father and son—officially," Phil said with a wink at Dev, who'd been looking up at him. Then, placing his left hand on Ben's shoulder, he said with voice trembling, "And I thank you, Lord, for my son Benjamin. He has a father's heart and I know he will do all he can for his son. Bless him with wisdom, guide him in what he should do, and bring people alongside to encourage him, help him, and love him as we do. We ask all this in Jesus's name. Amen."

Phil looked at his son, both men with tears in their eyes, and they shared an embrace. Phil whispered in Ben's ear, "I am so proud of you, son. God bless."

"Thanks, Pops," Ben said. "If I can be half the father you are, Dev will be all right."

"And you," Phil said, tapping Dev's shoulder, "Better go give your grandmother a big hug before she sails off in a lake of tears." Dev nodded at his grandfather and stepped toward Elsie. She opened her arms to him, and he gave her a hug as she pulled him close.

"Welcome to the family, Dev. I love you," Elsie said.

"Thanks, grandma. I love you, too."

Jennifer entered the room. "Well, there you are! Everybody's been wondering where you disappeared to, Ma." Then looking at the tear-stained faces of her parents, Ben, and Dev, she asked, "Oh no, what's happened? What is it?"

"Nothing bad, Jen. Sorry to worry you," Ben said, wiping his eyes.

"Well, what is it? Everyone's been crying. Even you!

What's going on?"

"I'll tell you, but it's not official yet, and we probably shouldn't spread the word. I'm going to adopt Dev."

"Well, hallelujah, praise the Lord, and Jesus, don't let the creek rise! About time you got around to that!"

"What?" Ben laughed.

"I've known for months this is exactly what you should do, so good for you to finally do it." Then going to Dev, she smiled and said, "Dev," She continued to smile and nod.

Dev wrapped his arms around her.

"This makes me soooo happy." Jennifer kissed him on both cheeks. "Guess you'll have to call me 'auntie' now."

"Okay, Auntie Jen," Dev said with a grin.

"Ugh, that sounds too old. How about just 'Aunt Jen'?"

Dev nodded in agreement as Bill walked into the room.

"Bill! Ben's going to adopt Dev!"

"Well, it's about time," Bill said, coming over and shaking Ben's hand.

"You too?" Ben asked.

"Writing was on the wall, bro," Bill said with a smile. Over his shoulder, he could hear Jennifer in the next room announcing the impending adoption.

"So much for not spreading the word," Ben said.

Dev walked over and put his arm around Ben's waist and looked up at him.

"You good?" Ben asked.

Dev nodded and settled into Ben as Ben put his arm around him.

Phil leaned into his wife and, admiring his son and new grandson, he whispered to Elsie, "Best birthday ever."

CHAPTER 30

Thanksgiving

Ben dove into the adoption process as soon as he and Dev arrived back in Philadelphia. There were mountains of paperwork to be completed, interviews, appointments with lawyers and social workers, and endless phone calls.

"It's only a matter of time. Time and paperwork," Tina Shaffron, Ben's lawyer said. "If we're lucky, we could have this wrapped up by Christmas. In the meantime, I'll apply for an extension of the guardianship."

While Angela hoped Ben and Dev would join her family for the Thanksgiving holiday, the two traveled to Maine and rejoined the Hudson clan instead, staying at the inn with Emma.

"Ben, there you are." Emma said embracing him. "I expected you about an hour ago. Trouble on the roads?"

"Holiday traffic, I guess. Haven't seen that many cars here since summer."

"And Dev," Emma gave the boy a warm hug. "You look wonderful. Things are going well?"

"Yeah, things are good. Is Miss Mary around? Can I say hi?"

"She's in the office. Go ahead in, I'm sure she'd be happy to see you." Dev ran around the front desk and into Emma's office.

"He looks good, very relaxed. Wish I could say the same about you."

"I'm ah-ite."

"You're what?"

"Sorry, guess Dev's rubbing off on me." He smiled a tired smile. "I'm good. I'm just beat."

"Well, you two should head up to your room and get some rest. Gonna be a busy weekend."

"Right." Ben took a long look at Emma. "It's good to see you, Em."

"It's good to see you too."

Thanksgiving Day was spent at Jennifer's. Her children, Ryan and Jessica, returned for the weekend, each bringing a significant other. Oliver and Vanessa were up from Bangor and Janice and her husband were there for the day as well, along with their grandson, Curtis.

Dev was happy to see Curtis again and the two boys ran off to play a quick game of basketball. Inside, the adults caught up with each other as everyone pitched in to get dinner ready. The main topic of discussion was the adoption progress.

"Don't have much to say about that, unfortunately." Ben frowned as he helped Jennifer put on the tablecloths. "We've got all the paperwork submitted, and we're working our way through the process now. My lawyer thinks there's a chance to have this wrapped up by Christmas, but . . ."

"Have faith, big brother," Jennifer said. "It's gonna happen."

Curtis and Dev returned from their game, laughing with each other. "Looks like you two are having a good time," Jennifer said. "Could you boys bring in some more firewood, please? Curtis, show Dev, okay?"

"Sure, Aunt Jen. Come on, Dev." Curtis and Dev left to perform their duty.

"See, he fits in already. Just a matter of time," Jennifer squeezed Ben's hand.

Once the final preparations were completed, Jennifer called everyone to dinner. A snake of tables extended from the kitchen to the living room. Dev stood next to Ben and stared at the set-up. He pointed to the tablecloth covering the first table, "What's that mean?"

Ben smiled. "What you're looking at Dev, is history. Your soon-to-be grandmother—"

"There is no 'soon-to-be' I'll have you know," Elsie said.

"Right. Your *grandma* started this tradition when she and your granddad first got married. They used this tablecloth on their very first Thanksgiving together and they had everyone sign it at the place where they sat, along with the date. After the holiday, your grandmother embroidered each name and date as a remembrance of who was there. She's kept it up ever since. There's sixty-seven years of memories in this cloth."

"Wow," Dev whispered.

"That's right," Elsie said. "The cloth is a little worn, but the memories of the people who created them are fresh. And this year, you'll get to add your name."

"All right everyone, let's say grace," Phil said as the family gathered around the table, holding hands. "Father God, You are gracious. My heart is full today as I look at this tablecloth and think back on all those who have sat here and shared this meal with us. Some of whom are with You now, praising the God from whom all blessings flow. And this year, we add a new name. We are a blessed clan, and we are a grateful clan. We thank You, we honor You, and we ask You to help us keep You in our hearts and minds throughout this season and beyond. Bless this meal and those who prepared it. In Jesus's name, Amen."

With the 'amen', the feasting began. Dev's eyes were wide through most of the meal, and he spoke not a word. Ben leaned over to him. "You doing okay?"

"Uh-huh," Dev said with a nod. "This is awesome." He looked up at Ben in a way that made Ben's throat tighten. He patted Dev on the back and took a sip of cider.

"How come no one's eating that?" Dev pointed to an untouched bowl of creamed carrots.

"Ma, you want to explain the carrots to Dev?"

Elsie smiled a wistful smile. "Dev, my mother-in-law, your grandfather's mother, her favorite dish on Thanksgiving was creamed carrots. It was his sister's favorite, too. So, every Thanksgiving, I made it for them. Problem was, no one else liked them." She laughed. "And even though no one eats them, I still make them every year as a sign I remember them and love them." Phil patted her hand.

Dev got up from the table and went to Elsie. He whispered in her ear, "My mom liked them too. Can I remember her like that?"

Elsie hugged him and whispered back, "Yes. Of course, you can."

"Hey, Sheriff Ben! Happy Thanksgiving!" Eddie said, giving Ben a hug. Ben and Dev were back at the inn. It was Black Friday and Eddie had come to set up for a large family reunion.

"Same to you Eddie. I see you're keeping yourself busy, as usual. Everything good with you?"

"It's great! Had my best summer ever with my landscaping business, and Miss Emma is keeping me busy here. That'll help till it snows and I can work on snow removal."

"Eddie, my man, I am so proud of you. It does my heart good to see you doing so well."

"Thanks. I'll be graduating in June, so next summer, I can really get my business going. And remember my goal of earning enough for my own truck by the time I'm eighteen?"

"Yes, that was a pretty ambitious goal."

"Well, I did it and I'm not even eighteen yet! Dad and me, we looked over my finances last night and I've got enough. I've got some things to do for Miss Emma this morning and then we're gonna go check out some used trucks."

"Congratulations, Eddie. That's amazing! Way to go, dude." Ben gave him a fist bump. "Next thing you know, you'll have an entire fleet of 'em."

"I like that idea. Well, I gotta get goin'. I'm setting up for a big fancy something or other here tomorrow. Hey, Dev, would you like to make some money? I could use a hand. You could be my assistant."

"Yeah! I could use some extra money for Christmas. Dad, is that all right with you?"

"*Dad?* Something happen I don't know about?" Eddie stared at Ben.

"I'm in the process of adopting Dev. He's not my son officially."

"*Yet*," Eddie added. "He's not official yet, but he's your son. I can tell."

A knot gripped Ben's stomach and traveled to his throat. All he could do was nod his appreciation in response.

"All right, Dev, let's go. You and me, we're gonna be a team. Anytime you're up here and need to earn some money, you give me a call. Okay? I can be like your big brother."

Dev nodded his approval and went with Eddie, shoulders back, and a smile stretching across his face. Ben stood in the lobby and watched the two young men he adored most in this world go off together.

"Ben?" Emma said as she came out of her office. "If you're waiting for the bus, it's best to go outside."

"Huh?" Ben brought himself back to the present. "No, I, uh, I'm just. I don't know what I am, Emma, except thankful."

"Well, it's a good time of year for gratitude."

Ben stood still, staring toward the boys even though they were no longer visible.

"You know what? Let's you and I go have a cup of coffee.

Mary's got everything under control out here."

Ben nodded and followed Emma to the west wing.

"Why don't you build us a fire?"

"Sure." Something I know how to do. That's nice for a change.

In no time, Ben kindled a roaring fire. The crackle of wood and the smokey scent comforted him. He watched the embers fly up the flue like sparklers on the fourth of July. He took a seat in a wingback chair and turned toward Emma as she made the coffee, moving like a dancer through her kitchen. Her movements fascinated him, and he found he couldn't keep his eyes off her. When she handed him a cup, he asked, "How do you do that?"

"Do what? Make coffee? Water, coffee grounds, heat. It's not complicated." She laughed and took a seat in the chair beside him.

"I don't mean that. I mean, how do you make it look . . . Eh, I don't know. I'm being ridiculous."

Emma took a sip of coffee. "Fatherhood looks good on you."

"I'm not a father yet. We don't even have a date for the hearing." Ben's forehead wrinkled, and he clenched his jaw.

"Are you okay? Is everything all right between you and Dev?"

"Oh, yeah. It's great. He's great. Everything's great."

"Sounds... great." Emma sipped her coffee, keeping her eyes on Ben.

He rubbed his forehead. "Maybe it's the holidays. I don't know."

"You say that a lot." Emma put her cup down.

"What?"

"*I don't know.* You say that a lot." She took a moment, then placed her hand on his arm. "It's the truest friend who tells you the things you need to hear, not just the things you want to hear."

Ben rested his elbow on the arm of the chair, then put his hand to his chin. "Emma, you're the truest friend I've got. Go ahead." He sat up straight, preparing himself for the news.

"I think you do know. I think you know exactly what's bothering you." She patted his arm. "You're afraid."

"Afraid? Afraid of what? Of Dev? He just turned eleven. I can take him." Ben tipped his chin up.

"Ha, ha, funny man. He may be eleven, but he has a grip on your heart. And that's what scares you."

Ben stared at the fire, avoiding eye contact with Emma.

"Talk to me, please."

Ben turned toward her. "Emma, what if . . ." His face grew tense.

"What if what?" She took his hand. "Tell me."

"What if it doesn't happen? What if the judge thinks I'm

too old? What if he doesn't like that I'm not from Philadelphia or that I've never had kids? What if he denies the petition? What if I don't get to be Dev's father?

"And what if he *does* grant it? What if I'm not the father Dev needs?"

"That's a lot of what ifs," Emma said.

"That's just the start." Ben stood up and began pacing. "He's a couple of years away from being a teenager. What if I can't manage those years? What if things from his past come to the surface and I don't know how to deal with them? What if I can't protect him? What if I . . .disappoint him? This is a whole new world, Em." Ben stood still and stared at the fire. "I didn't think it was possible." He returned to his pacing.

Emma sat forward in her chair. "Didn't think what was possible?"

"I didn't think. I guess I couldn't imagine." Ben stopped and looked at Emma, his eyes betraying the emotions he was trying so hard to control. "I couldn't imagine I could ever love someone as much as I love him. You're a parent, is this what it's like? Sometimes I'm overwhelmed by the thought I may actually get to be his father. I want that so much I can feel it in my bones."

Emma nodded and smiled. "Yes. It's exactly what it's like. You look at your child and you think, 'God has entrusted me with this wonderful little soul? I don't deserve that.'"

"Right. And I want so much for him. I want to make up for all the bad things that have happened in his life." Ben rubbed his forehead. "No kid should have to live through what he has. Emma, he's only eleven." He pounded his fist on the stone mantle. "He's already lost so much. I don't want to see him hurt again. I'd do whatever I could to prevent that, give up whatever limb necessary, but what if I don't get the chance?"

Emma stood beside Ben. "I have never known you to be a worrier. This child has changed you. He's made you vulnerable."

Ben went back and slumped in the chair. "I hate that feeling."

"Of course you do. You've spent a lifetime in a career that demanded you *not* be vulnerable. But Ben, vulnerability is what makes you human. And it'll be what makes you a good father."

"Ha! How do you figure?" Ben pointed to himself. "I'm supposed to protect him, to look out for him, to be strong for him. I can't afford to be vulnerable."

Emma sat beside him. "You can't afford not to be. Dev doesn't need some comic book superhero for a dad. He needs a real person. He needs someone who'll make mistakes, and then own up to them. He needs someone who doesn't pretend he has all the answers. He needs someone who'll be real with him, so he can be real in return. That's how he'll heal from all that's happened. That's how he'll learn. And that's how he'll become a fine man of integrity, like you. He doesn't need a perfect father. He needs an honest one."

Ben sighed and stared at the fire. "How do you handle it, Em? This whole parenting thing? How do you not go crazy with worry? I'm not used to this—having someone so dependent on me. What if I'm not up for the job?"

"Oh, now I see," Emma said with a nod.

"What do you see?"

"The truth. I knew there was more. You don't think you can do this." Ben's eyes retreated to the fire again. "You don't, do you? You think in some way you're inadequate and that's what's making you afraid."

How does she know me so well?

"Do you remember the story of Jesus walking on the water, and Peter getting out of the boat to meet him?"

"Sure. Peter gets out, sees the waves, gets scared, sinks. Oh, ye of little faith . . ."

Emma smiled. "That's the one. I used to think Jesus meant Peter's faith was small. But it wasn't. He got out of the boat—eleven other men sat there, *but he got out*. He had huge faith! But then, he took his eyes off Jesus and looked at the storm. He was afraid, and he sank. He didn't sink because his faith was small. He didn't sink because he didn't have enough faith. He sank because his faith had no staying power in the storm. He let the waves distract him. That's what Jesus was saying—why doesn't your faith last longer in life's storms? Why are you allowing fear to take over?"

Ben sat up straight. "Are you saying I don't have faith?"

"No. I'm not saying that at all. I'm saying you're in the storm. It has your attention and you're afraid. You're afraid to believe this can happen, that you *can* be Dev's father.

"Here's the thing about fear. Fear wants you to believe something that hasn't happened yet. It's all those waves of 'what ifs'. But faith—it wants you to believe something that hasn't happened yet too, *the possibilities*. Fear and faith, the two can't coexist. You have to choose. Which one are you going to believe?"

Ben sat back in the chair.

"Ben, do you believe God brought you and Dev together?" Emma asked.

"Well, it took me a minute to get there, and I had a little help from a friend, but I see what He did to make it happen."

"So, if God wants the two of you together, doesn't it seem logical He would provide you with whatever you need to raise Dev?"

"I guess so."

"You don't have to guess. God has been preparing you for this your entire life. Think about it, all the kids you've mentored over the years, the time you've spent with troubled youth, all the things you've done to protect and to serve. That's been training for this moment. 'For such a time as this'."

Ben looked down. He nodded, taking in the words Emma spoke to him.

"Now, look at me." Emma took Ben's hands. "I never want to hear 'what if' from you again. If God has ordained this to happen, it will, and all indications are He has. So, go where He's leading you and be confident. God's got your back and so do I. Be the man I know you are—the one who turns 'what ifs' into possibilities."

Emma patted Ben on the knee. "Now, why don't you go make yourself useful and stir up the fire. I'll heat up our coffee."

Ben reached for her hand as she stood. He said softly, "Thanks, Em."

She put her hand on top of his and smiled. "Anytime."

CHAPTER 31

I am His and He is Mine

After their return to Philadelphia, Ben longed to talk to Emma. Something about the sound of her voice calmed him and made him feel everything would be okay, maybe even more than okay, but he hesitated to call her.

A week later, after a full day of Christmas shopping, he mustered up the courage and dialed her number. "Ho, ho, ho, Santa here. Are you being a good girl?"

"I most certainly am, you foolish man. Out Christmas shopping I gather?"

"Yes, this is craziness. I miss Maine. Things were simpler there."

"Then come home, Ben."

Emma's words caught his heart off-guard. *I would love to. I miss Eastport . . . and you.*

Emma broke the silence. "Any word about the adoption

hearing?"

"Not yet. Lawyer's still hoping we'll have something on the docket before Christmas, but I'm not sure that's gonna happen."

"Don't give up hope. And remember, you and Dev, you're already family. This is only a formality. It will happen, maybe not as soon as you'd like, but it *will* happen."

"You're right. You're right, as usual."

"Do you have plans for Christmas yet?" Emma asked.

"I'll be home for Christmas."

"Ben, if you start singing, I'm hanging up."

"I thought you liked my singing."

"I do, but—oh, never mind. I think I'm on Christmas song overload. You know, they started playing them in the stores right after Halloween."

"Em, is everything okay? You don't sound like yourself. You working too hard?"

"No, I'm fine. I probably should go though. It's been a really busy day here, and I've got another full day tomorrow. I am a little tired."

"Emma . . ."

"Yes?"

"Uh, nothing, never mind. You get some rest. Take care of yourself, okay?"

"I'll try. You, too. It was good to hear your voice, Ben.

Thanks for calling."

"I'll call you again, soon. Goodnight." He hung up the phone, knowing very well everything was not fine with Emma.

Three days later, Ben received a call from his lawyer. "Yeah, Tina. I see. That's not much time, but sure, I can make it work. All right, I'll keep an eye out for it."

Ben looked over at Dev. He sat at the dining room table, pencil in his teeth, calculator in his hand, working on his math homework.

"Hey, knucklehead." Ben rubbed his hands together.

Dev looked up from his homework. He frowned, and asked, "What is it? What's wrong?"

"I've got some bad news. Looks like we're going to have to get a later start to Maine."

"Why?"

"The adoption hearing's set for the twenty-second. It's gonna happen." Ben smiled at Dev. The boy leapt from his chair and threw his arms around him. "It's gonna happen, buddy. It's gonna happen." Ben picked him up with a great hug.

Snow was predicted for the twenty-second, a bit early for Philadelphia, but Ben already decided he would commandeer a snowplow to get himself, Dev, and the judge to the courthouse, if necessary. Thankfully, what fell from the sky that day was a light flurry, just enough to turn the city from bleak grey to festive white.

"How you feelin'? You ready for this?" Ben asked Dev as he came down for breakfast.

"I'm nervous. What if the judge says no?" Dev put the tie Emma gave him around his neck.

"Impossible. But if he does, we'll just have to persuade him he's wrong and get him to change his mind."

"How we gonna do that?" Dev stretched his neck out for Ben to tie the tie.

"One word—Angela," Ben said, moving his eyebrows up and down. Dev laughed as Ben finished tying his tie.

"It's gonna be okay. Don't worry, it's gonna happen. Emma said so." Ben tousled Dev's hair, then pulled him in for a hug.

Despite the closeness to Christmas, Jennifer and Bill flew down from Perry, bringing hugs and good wishes from Phil and Elsie, and the rest of the Hudson clan. Angela said she, JJ, and Chase would be there with sleigh bells on. Dev's favorite teacher, Mr. Wolfe, took time off from school to attend. Dev's former neighbor, Mrs. DeSantas, as well as Mr. and Mrs.

Versace were also in attendance. Mr. Zappone, Mrs. Brasko, and a few of Ben's other neighbors filled in the gallery.

Angela, already in tears, greeted Ben and Dev as she, JJ, and Chase entered the courtroom. "I'm so happy for you two," she said, embracing them. "This is a wonderful day, and you look handsome, both of you. *Sono felice!*" She straightened Ben's tie, then did the same for Dev. She gave Dev a kiss on the forehead.

"This is a great day, pal," JJ said. "Glad I'm here to see it."

"Thanks, Jay. You had a lot to do with it."

"And you," JJ pointed to Dev, "I couldn't be happier for you, Dev."

"Thanks, Mr. Mongelli. I'm happy too."

Chase came up to Dev and the two did their special handshake.

"All right, Angie, let's get ready for the show." JJ offered Angela his arm and escorted her to the gallery with Chase.

Jennifer and Bill made their way to Ben. Jennifer gave Dev a long hug, then wrapped her arm around her brother's waist. She had tears in her eyes as well.

"You guys better stop with the crying or you'll have me going too. I don't think that's a good look for the judge," Ben said, teasing his sister.

"Oh, I disagree, but I'll try," Jennifer said.

"All rise," called the bailiff.

Jennifer grabbed Bill's hand and squeezed. "We'd better sit. It's starting." She blew a kiss to Ben, then took a seat with Bill.

Ben and Dev took their place by their lawyer. Dev looked around the room, searching the faces in the gallery.

"You okay?" Ben asked.

"Yeah, just lookin' to see who's here."

The judge entered the courtroom. "You may be seated," Judge Reilly said as he sat behind the bench. He shuffled a few papers, then looked up. "Mr. Hudson, please rise and raise your right hand."

Ben stood and raised his hand.

"Do you swear or affirm the testimony you give in this matter will be the truth, the whole truth, and nothing but the truth?"

"I do."

"State your full name, please."

"Benjamin Philip Hudson."

"Mr. Hudson, I have a petition to adopt in front of me this afternoon. Is it your intention to adopt Devon Murphy?"

"It is, Your Honor."

"Why is it your desire to adopt this young man?" Judge Reilly said with a nod toward Dev.

Ben looked at the boy and tried to maintain his composure. "Because I love him more than my own life . . . sir."

The judge smiled and continued. "You understand if the court grants you the adoption petition today, Devon will legally be your child, and you will be responsible for his welfare, providing him with the necessary physical, financial, and emotional support, as well as the spiritual and moral guidance he will require to grow into a mature and responsible adult?"

"I do."

"Are you ready, willing, and able to accept this responsibility?"

"I am, Your Honor. More than willing." Ben placed his hand on Dev's shoulder.

"You may be seated, Mr. Hudson." Ben sat down, thankful to have the support of the chair for his quaking knees.

"Devon Murphy, please rise." Dev stood, looking very small, but very much the gentleman in his new white shirt and Harry's tie. "You understand you are to tell the truth, young man?"

Dev nodded.

"I'm going to need you to answer 'yes' or 'no', son."

Dev stood up straight, then looked directly at the judge and with a clear voice said, "Yes, sir."

"Mr. Hudson has expressed his desire to adopt you. Are you in favor of this adoption?"

"Yes, sir."

"And why would you like Mr. Hudson to adopt you?"

"Because." Dev looked at Ben, then back at the judge. "He saved me. I was drowning in the ocean, and he swam out to me and when he got to me, he told me to hold on to him. He put me on his back, and he carried me. He saved me."

Dev swallowed. "When he found out my mom was missing, and I was living in a tent, he saved me again. He brought me to his home. And he worked real hard to find out what happened to my mom. When he found out . . . when he found out . . ."

The judge said quietly, "The court is aware of what happened to your mother, and you have our deepest sympathies. I understand Mr. Hudson took you in and became your temporary guardian. Is that what you want to say?"

"Yes, sir." A tear made its way down Dev's cheek and Ben reached for his hand. "I was afraid of what was gonna happen to me, but he told me I could hop on his back again, he'd carry me, and he wouldn't let anything bad happen to me. *He saved me.* That's what he does. I can't think of having a better dad than that."

"Neither can I," said the judge.

"Your Honor, can I ask you somethin'?" Dev said.

"Yes, go ahead."

"I never had a dad, but isn't that what a dad is supposed to do? Take care of his kid, no matter what?"

"Yes, that's exactly what a dad is supposed to do."

Straightening himself to his full four-foot, eight-inch height, Dev said, "Then I think you should grant our petition. Otherwise, Mrs. Mongelli is going to have to have a talk with you."

The judge laughed, as did the rest of the courtroom. He looked out over the gallery and gave Angela a nod. She blushed, but smiled proudly at Dev. "Well now, having encountered Ms. Angela Mongelli in the past, you make a powerful argument, Mr. Murphy."

The judge signed a document, then raised his gavel, and in a booming voice announced, "Based upon the reports and recommendations I have received, the moving words of both Mr. Hudson and Mr. Murphy, and the desire to not upset Mrs. Mongelli, this court finds granting the petition for adoption *is* in the best interest of Devon Murphy. Mr. Hudson in all respects has gone above and beyond to demonstrate his willingness and ability to support, promote, and foster Devon's welfare. The court will therefore enter the order of adoption and Benjamin Philip Hudson will forever be legally the parent of Devon Murphy Hudson." The judge brought his gavel down and a cheer rose up from the gallery.

Friends and family gathered around Ben and Dev, offering congratulations, hugs, and more than a few tears. As he worked his way through the throng, Ben's heart stopped when he saw one special guest.

"Emma? You're here? How—" Emma smiled and went to Ben. They kissed each other on the cheek. Ben took her hand. "How are you here?"

"Well, your son invited me. He called me the night you got the court date. He said he wanted me to be here and asked if I would come. He said something to Angela and well, she's a force of nature, that one."

"Yes, she is," Ben said, trying to calm his now racing heart.

"Miss Emma!" Dev ran to her, tripped, and fell into her arms.

"Dev, it's so good to see you," Emma said as she caught him. "I am so happy for you. Thanks for inviting me. What a wonderful day."

"I didn't think you were coming. I didn't see you here when we came in. I thought maybe you changed your mind."

"Change my mind about something as special as this? Never. My flight was delayed. I was worried I'd miss everything, but I got here just as they were starting. I snuck in the back."

"Thanks for comin'. I'm wearing Harry's tie you gave me."

"I see that. And you look very handsome in it."

Dev smiled. "We're glad you're here. Right, Dad?"

"Very glad," Ben said, resisting the urge to embrace her.

"Come meet everybody!" Dev pulled Emma by the hand toward the Mongellis.

"I'm so happy to meet you! It's nice to put a face with a voice, Emma," Angela said, hugging her. "So glad you made it after all. We were worried."

"I was worried myself, but I'm here now. Even if it's only for a little while."

Angela planned a small celebration in her home, so everyone migrated to the Mongelli residence. When the new father and son arrived, the house was already filled with additional neighbors and friends.

After receiving more congratulations and well wishes, Ben made his way to Emma. "Why didn't you tell me you were coming?"

"I wasn't sure I could pull it off, but I have a wonderful staff. Mary's manning the front desk, and Joseph has volunteered to help in any way he can." Emma laughed, "I never thought of that before—I have Joseph and Mary staying in my inn."

Ben joined her in a laugh.

"Iris is helping, too. She sends her best."

Ben took her hand. "It's good to—"

JJ tapped a spoon on his glass and stood. "Everyone! I'd like to propose a toast." The crowd quieted. "This is a great day. I've known Ben Hudson for well over forty years now. I've seen him make some bone-headed decisions in that time, but this is not one of them. Ben, welcome to fatherhood. Angela and I wish you nothing but happiness as you start this new chapter. So, raise a glass, everyone. *Tanta felicità! Dio vi benedica! Lots of happiness and God bless you!* To Ben and Dev."

"To Ben and Dev!" the crowd answered.

"Can I say somethin'?" a voice asked from the back of the room. All eyes turned to see Chase standing on a chair.

"Go ahead, son," JJ said with a smile.

"Dev is my best friend. I've known him ever since kindergarten when we got in a fight. Me and Dev, we got lots in common. We both like basketball, and mushroom and sausage pizza, and playin' in the fire hydrant on a hot day. And now we have somethin' else in common. I'm adopted too.

"Dev, when you know your parents chose you, that they didn't have to do it, but they wanted to, it's the best feeling. And even though he calls me a knucklehead, I know Ben's gonna be a good dad. But I'm still gonna beat him in HORSE."

Angela dabbed her eyes as the rest of the crowd laughed.

"Maybe we should hear from the new Papa," JJ said with a smile and a pat on Ben's back.

"Yeah! Speech, speech, speech!" the guests chanted.

"All right, all right, already. There is something I'd like to say," Ben said, taking the floor. "First, I'd like to thank all of you for being here and sharing this day with us. You've been a great support system for Dev and for me, and we appreciate you all.

"You never know where God is going to lead you, or what He has in store for you." Looking at Emma, he continued. "Someone very wise told me in the middle of all this, she thought when I left Eastport, I was running away from someone. Once she met Dev, she said she was wrong. She said I was running *to someone*."

Emma smiled.

"I didn't know that was the case at the time. And it seems, there's a lot I didn't know. Dev, *my son*," Ben smiled at the thought. "He's a writer, a poet, really. He's fantastic at it. And today, I'd like to share something I wrote for him. I'm no poet, but in his honor, I thought I'd give it a try."

Ben pulled a sheet of paper from his inside blazer pocket and unfolded it. Angela and Jennifer started to cry and held each other's hands. JJ passed them a box of tissues. Ben cleared his throat, took a deep breath, then began.

I Didn't Know

When I asked you to stay with me
to trust me,
to confide in me,
I didn't know it would lead to this.

I didn't know a person so small could be so brave.
I didn't know what it would mean to see you look at me

Marilyn K Blair

as if I were your hero,
and I didn't know I'd want to be.

I didn't know how it would feel
to have you place your hand in mine
trusting I would take care of you.
I didn't know.

I didn't know I would cherish
sleepless nights of worry,
or extra trips to the grocery store,
or finding a wayward sock clinging
to my shirt in the laundry.

I didn't know a hug around the neck
could leave me breathless,
or that 'good night ol' man' would resonate in my ears
like ocean waves on a summer's day.

I didn't know what it would mean to have a son
to play ball with,
or to walk with,
or to watch the stars with.

I didn't know a little word like Dad
could reach into my soul and turn me inside out.
I didn't know.

I didn't know how much I'd want to protect you,
how much I'd want to teach you
about being a man of integrity and honesty,
and I didn't know how much you were already there.

I didn't know God carved out a place in my heart
just for you.
I didn't know I could feel
this hopeful,
this purposeful,
this thankful.

And I didn't know how much I'd love you,
Dev,
my son.
I didn't know.

Dev went to Ben and hugged him. Angela passed around the box of tissues to the rest of the guests, none of whom could hold back their tears.

JJ hopped up. "Hey, this is a party! What's everybody crying for? Angela?"

"Give me a minute and dessert will be on the table." Angela stood, wiped her tears, and headed for the kitchen. She took a detour and went to Ben. She crooked her finger at him to bend down, then she kissed him on the cheek, and gave his face a pat. She kissed Dev on both cheeks, then finished her journey to the kitchen.

Following dessert, the crowd dispersed. Ben accepted the well wishes and congratulations from every person, shaking hands and giving hugs as they left.

"Bill and I thought we'd head back to your place. We can take Dev. Why don't you catch up with Emma for a bit?" Jennifer nodded toward Emma, who was chatting with Angela.

Ben kissed his sister on the cheek. "Thanks, Jen."

Ben went to Angela and gave her a hug. "Ang, thanks so much for this. You and JJ . . . I don't know what to say."

"The look on your face and on Dev's when that gavel came down is all the thanks I need. This is a wonderful day. I'll remember it always." Angela reached for another tissue.

"You're the best, Ang. And Jay, brother," Ben said, giving JJ a hug and a pat on the back.

"You mean, 'bruh'," JJ said with a laugh. "Ang is right. This has been a great day. So happy for you."

Angela clapped her hands and put a smile on her face. "All right now, JJ and Chase are on clean-up duty, while I take care of leftovers. Ben, why don't you take Emma out for coffee?"

"Tryin' to get rid of me?" Ben said.

"That's about right," Angela said with a smile.

"Em? Coffee?"

"Angela, you sure I can't help? I'd be happy to," Emma said.

"Nonsense. You didn't come all this way to do dishes in my kitchen. I'm sure you get enough of that at the inn. Please, take this one and go." She pointed at Ben. "He's had me crying so much today, I'm borrowing against next year's tears."

"I'm sorry, Ang." Ben said. "Didn't mean to make you cry."

"It's just seeing Dev so happy . . . and you," Angela's eyes started watering again. "See! Get him out of here, Emma, please," she said, sweeping Ben out of the room with her hands.

Emma laughed. "I'll see what I can do. And thank you for taking me in. We won't be late. I won't keep you up."

"Don't give it a second thought. We'll keep the door unlocked. You come in whenever."

CHAPTER 32

Tea for Two

Ben escorted Emma out of the house. Not a word was spoken between them as they strolled to a small café Ben frequented often. The comforting aroma of freshly ground coffee met them at the door.

"It's quiet here for a Friday night," Ben said. Glad there's a booth free and we can have a little privacy. The two sat down. "I'm still kinda in shock you're here, Em."

"Well, Dev wanted me here. I did what I could to make it happen . . . for him."

"He's not the only one who wanted you here."

"Can I get you something to drink?" the waitress asked as she placed menus on the table.

"Emma?"

"Hot tea would be fine, thank you."

"Tea sounds great for me too, thanks." Ben gave the

menus back. "Sorry your flight was delayed, but I'm glad you made it."

"I couldn't miss this. Why a storm in Chicago should affect a flight from Maine is beyond me, but I'm glad I got here in time."

"Me, too. And you're staying with the Mongellis? Angela worked her magic again. Honestly, she and JJ have been the best."

"They are quite a family. And they love you. You're not just a friend to them. I'm happy you have that."

Ben paused and folded his arms on the table. "Emma, I need to know something. I've been worried about you, but with all that's been happening here, I've neglected you. I should have called. Are you all right?"

"You don't need to worry about me. I'm fine. It's just, oh, this time of year I get sentimental."

"I see." Sentimentality probably isn't the full story.

The waitress came with the tea. Ben placed a teabag in the cup of hot water. "You're missing Harry?"

"Harry, my kids. You." Emma sighed as she steeped her tea.

Ben started to reach for her hand. "Em, I—"

"Maine Man! Hey, congratulations." Ben looked up to see one of the district police officers. "It's all around the station. Everybody's happy for you and the kid."

A Good Place to Turn Around

"Thanks, Carlos. It's been a good day."

"I bet. Glad it worked out. You did some great detective work. You might want to think about coming out of retirement." Officer Carlos gave Ben a pat on the back. "So, everything went well at the courthouse?"

"Went perfect. It's all official now."

"That's awesome news. Well, sorry to interrupt. Just wanted to wish you the best and pass on the congratulations. I'll let you get back to your tea. Ma'am." He tipped his cap to Emma and shook Ben's hand. "Have a merry Christmas. I'm sure it won't be hard this year. Go Birds!"

"Merry Christmas to you, too. See you around, Carlos." Ben watched the officer leave, then turned to Emma. "Sorry about that."

"You're a popular guy it seems."

"I met Carlos and his partner the first day I arrived. This is their beat. They picked me out as a cop right away. I guess we give off a scent."

"I'm glad you've made friends."

"Me, too. So, how long are you going to be in town?"

"I leave in the morning."

"The morning? So soon? You sure you can't stay longer? I'd love to show you the city. It's beautiful this time of year. There's even a Christmas village downtown."

"No, I can't. I have to get back. You know what the inn is

like around Christmas. Plus, they're calling for snow and I don't want to get stranded in Bangor." Emma took a sip of her tea. "When are you coming home? For the holidays, I mean. You're flying in soon, right?"

"I know I told you I'd be home for Christmas, but I don't think that's gonna happen."

"Oh?" Emma took another sip of her tea and squeezed the cup.

"The adoption hearing kinda threw things outta whack, and Dev's got some special writer's event for school as soon as they get back from break. If we go and get snowed in . . ." Ben took a sip of his tea. "As much as I'd like to be back in Maine, I have to think of Dev. Looks like we'll be staying here for Christmas."

"Well, that's the life of a parent. Kids first." Emma finished her tea, then placed the cup on the saucer. "You know, I'm kinda tired. Would you mind taking me back to the Mongellis?"

"Already?" Ben looked at Emma and saw the hint of a tear in her eyes. "Emma, you're not okay, are you?"

"I'm fine, just tired."

"You don't want to talk about it."

Emma looked down.

"All right, I won't push. Can I see you in the morning? I can take you to the airport."

"You don't have to do that. I'll call a taxi."

"You will not call a taxi. I will take you. I insist. Besides, you came all this way, it's the least I can do. And I'd like to see you again before you leave."

Emma sighed. "All right, if you insist." Emma rubbed her forehead.

Is that a tear you're brushing away? Why won't you talk to me?

"I need to be at the airport by seven-thirty," Emma said.

"Okay, I'll be by to pick you up at seven, unless I can talk you into having breakfast with me at six."

"Seven will be fine, thanks."

"Emma, have I done something? Are you angry with me?"

"No, of course not." Emma took a breath and looked at their surroundings. "It's just . . . seeing you here, in this place. I couldn't imagine it. And now that I'm here, and I see you with all your friends, and how happy you are." Emma closed her eyes for a moment. "I'm glad you're happy, Ben, truly." Emma brushed away a tear. "We should go."

There was silence again as Ben escorted Emma back to the Mongelli's. She said a quick goodnight and was in the house before Ben could even utter a goodnight in return.

At seven a.m. sharp the next morning, Ben arrived at the Mongelli's front door. He and Emma left for the airport and once more their time together was consumed with awkward silence.

There's so much I want to say to you, Em. I just can't bring myself to say it. Heck, I'm not even sure what it is I want to say exactly. I only know I'm glad you're here and I hate that you're leaving.

They arrived at the terminal, and Ben pulled his truck over. "How about I park, then come in with you and keep you company till your flight?"

"No, that's not necessary. I'll be fine. I don't want to put you out anymore."

"Put me out? Em . . ."

"I should go, they're moving cars along." Emma got out of the car, and Ben retrieved her suitcase from the trunk. "Take care of yourself, Ben. You and Dev have a happy Christmas."

"You too, and I'll call you." Ben went to Emma and hugged her. He could feel her body tense as he did, so he pulled away and looked her in the eyes.

"Bye, Ben." Emma turned and hurried into the airport.

CHAPTER 33

Merry Christmas

At the crack of dawn on Christmas morning, Dev slipped silently out of bed and tiptoed to Ben's bedroom door. He listened to the rhythmic rumbling, snorting, and snuffling emanating from the room. He smiled, then snuck down the stairs and into the kitchen. With his hands on his hips, he surveyed the battlefield, then implemented his Christmas morning tactical plan.

An hour later, Ben woke up to the smell of freshly brewed coffee and something else he couldn't identify, but whatever it was, it reminded him of the Sunrise Inn and Emma. He pulled himself to an upright position, stretched his arms over his head, then went downstairs to investigate.

He heard talking and movement in the kitchen, so he approached with care, not wanting to interfere with any Christmas morning magic. He got close enough to the entry to hear, but stood next to the wall so he would not be seen. Positioning himself at just the right angle, Ben could see a reflection on the refrigerator door of the activity taking place in the room. Apparently, there had been a baking accident which covered Dev in flour from head to toe. His sandy blonde hair exchanged itself for the crystalline white of Santa's beard. Oblivious to his new hair color and with ear buds in his ears, Dev stirred something in a bowl and chatted away.

"I did that. It's all mixed, but it's a little lumpy. Oh, okay, yeah, it looks just like that." Dev went to the oven. "Yup, the green light is on now."

He went back to what he was stirring. "I should put all of it in? You sure it'll fit?" He looked at a pan on the counter. "Okay, I'll try."

Dev picked up the mixing bowl and poured its contents into the baking pan. "It fit!"

He picked up another bowl. "Yeah, I mixed that up already. Put it on top? Won't it sink? Ohhhhh, I get it."

Dev spread the contents of another bowl on top of the mixture in the baking pan. "Cool!"

He picked up the pan and placed it into the oven. "Forty minutes. Got it. Thanks, Miss Emma. Hope I didn't bother you too much. Merry Christmas to you too. Sorry we couldn't see you over the holidays, but maybe Easter, okay? I will. Love you too. Bye."

Ben put his back to the wall when he heard Emma's name. *I haven't called her once since she left. I'm sure she was upset with me, but I have no idea why.*

A loud crash coming from the kitchen shocked Ben out of his thoughts. He took a few steps backward, then called out as if he'd just come downstairs.

"Who's in there? Am I being robbed on Christmas Day?"

"It's me, Dad. Don't come in!"

"What are you up to, knucklehead?"

"You'll see. Go sit in the living room. I'll call you when it's time."

"Yes, sir." Ben smiled and went to the living room as instructed. He sat in his favorite chair, and admired the tree he and Dev decorated the day before. Ben always enjoyed Christmas, but now, seeing it through the eyes of a child, his child, made the day even more meaningful. He closed his eyes and said a prayer of thanks.

"Okay. It's almost ready! Come to the dining room."

Again, Ben did as he was told. Dev came out of the kitchen with a smile that set off his face like ribbon on a giftbox.

"Hey, it's a snowman! Alive, in my house!" Ben grinned at the flour covered Dev.

Dev looked himself over, then scrunched his face. "There was an accident."

"I can see that."

Dev brushed his shirt, sending a cloud of flour into the atmosphere. He giggled, then pointed to the head of the table and said, "Sit here."

"You're kinda bossy today."

"Sorry. Sit down. Please?"

Ben sat and eyed Dev.

"I'll be right back." Dev raced back to the kitchen. He returned in a moment, taking the smallest of steps as he carried a hot mug of coffee with two hands. He placed it in front of Ben, who looked for cream and sugar. Dev said, "Don't worry, it's in there."

Ben raised his eyebrows at Dev, then took a sip. "This is terrific. How'd you know how I like it?"

"I live with you, remember? All right, there's more." Dev disappeared into the kitchen again. "Ow!"

"You okay in there, Frosty?"

"Yes. Don't come in!"

Ben stifled his laughter. Dev emerged once more, carrying a fresh-out-of-the-oven coffee cake. He placed it on the table, then sat beside Ben.

"Wow, that looks good. I'll get us some plates." Ben stood.

"Plates are for chumps. Dig in, dude." Dev handed Ben a fork.

Ben smiled and sat back down. He hovered his fork over the coffee cake, then cut off a bite. "This smells amazing."

Dev's knee began to bounce, and he bit his lip as he watched Ben's every move.

"Okay, here goes." Ben put a morsel in his mouth, and the warmth of the cake came close to the warmth he was feeling for his son over the effort he'd put into making this morning special. Ben closed his eyes and smiled, enjoying every sensation. He opened his eyes and said, "So, what are you going to eat?"

"Huh?"

"Well, this piece of artwork is too delicious for someone your size. I think I'll have to manage all this on my own."

Dev exhaled. "You really like it?"

"Bud, you can make this any time. This is awesome! You know, it tastes like the coffee cake Emma makes for the inn. How'd you know how to do this?"

"I had help. I tried to do it myself, but there was an explosion with the flour." Dev made a face. "Sorry. I'll clean it up. I called Miss Emma. I hoped she could help me, and she did. We FaceTimed."

"She does make great coffee cake. That was nice of her." Ben took a sip of his coffee. With an air of nonchalance, he asked, "So, how is she?"

"What do you mean?"

"I mean, how did she sound? Is she happy? Is she doing okay?"

"I guess so. She was nice on the phone like always."

"Like always?"

"Yeah, I call Miss Emma. I miss her. We talk at least once a week. She says she doesn't mind."

"I'm sure she doesn't." Ben sipped his coffee again, then put his cup down. "So, what do you two talk about?"

"Oh, all kinds of stuff. Things that happened in Eastport, what Eddie's doing, the inn. Sometimes we talk about her kids. I tell her about school, and about Chase . . . and about you." Dev gave Ben a look.

"About me, huh?"

Dev nodded. "She doesn't ask, but I know she wants to know. I can tell."

"I see. The Love Guru is back."

"You should call her. You miss her too."

"I don't think she wants to hear from me. She didn't seem too happy with me when she left."

Dev muttered, "No wonder."

"What's that supposed to mean?"

"Dad . . ." Dev tilted his head at his father.

"I don't think I like your tone, young man, or where this

conversation is going, so—let's have Christmas." Ben stood up as did Dev. "Come with me." Ben picked Dev up and tucked him under one arm, carrying him like a newspaper.

"Dad!" The boy laughed and giggled as he bounced under Ben's arm the rest of the way into the living room. Ben put him down and they sat on the sofa together, gazing at the tree.

"I want you to know, Dev, you are the best Christmas present I've ever gotten. Some days, I have a hard time believing God made us a family, but I'm glad He did. I love you, son."

Dev smiled at Ben, his cheeks blushing, then he gave him a hug.

"Love you too. I never thought I'd have a dad. I always wanted one, and sometimes—" Dev looked away.

"Sometimes?"

"Aw, nothin'."

"No, you can tell me. Sometimes what?"

Dev sighed. "Sometimes, I was jealous of Chase 'cause he had a dad. And Mr. Mongelli, he's pretty cool. But now, I have a dad too. And Chase is right. It's the best feeling ever. Thanks for adopting me."

The two sat back on the couch, Ben's arm around his son, as they admired their Christmas tree.

"Can I give you my present?" Dev asked.

"Presents! Yeah, time for presents!" Ben sat upright and clapped his hands.

Dev went and picked up a gift from underneath the tree. He handed it to Ben and stood in front of him as Ben unwrapped it. Inside was a plain, white box. Ben opened it, revealing a coffee mug.

"A mug? Great. I can always use another mug," Ben said, trying to sound excited.

Dev rolled his eyes. "Take it out, Dad."

Ben smiled and removed the mug from the box. He turned it around and read it aloud, "'*Some people don't believe in heroes, but they haven't met my dad.*'" Ben took a deep breath and tried to swallow the golf ball that lodged itself in his throat.

"You like it?"

"You bet." Ben stared at the mug, clasping it in his hands. One more thing to add to my list of things I didn't know—how a coffee mug could make a grown man want to cry.

Ben composed himself, then said, "My turn." He went to the tree and pulled out a small box, and handed it to Dev.

Dev peeled the wrapping paper from the present and opened the box inside. He pulled out an ornament with a photograph of him and Ben when they were down the shore.

"Remember when we were on the boardwalk, and we all took turns in the photo booth? This is the first photo of us together," Ben said.

"I remember. That's the day you changed my life."

"And you changed mine."

Dev went to the Christmas tree and placed the ornament in a prominent place. He stood back and admired it, then he used his sleeve to wipe away a tear.

Ben came up to his son. "I know we said we were only going to give each other one present, but I broke the rule. And since I'm the dad, I figured it's okay." Ben stooped and picked up another present from underneath the tree and handed it to Dev.

"Now, I want you to know, I had help with this. It's from me, but there were many people involved."

Dev carried the gift back to the couch and sat, tucking his feet under himself. He unwrapped the present, revealing a photo album. Embossed in gold on the cover were the words, "The Devon Hudson Family Album". Dev looked up at Ben, who nodded his head. "Take a look."

Dev opened the book, and on the first page was a photo of his mother, the one Ben used when canvasing the neighborhood. The next page contained a drawing of her Dev sketched, along with the poem he read at her memorial service. Ben sat down next to Dev as the boy scanned the pages. The following were pictures of Dev's childhood, photos Ben found while clearing out Dev's apartment. Then there were pages of the Mongellis and of Dev and Chase as small boys in kindergarten through their last year in elementary school.

These made Dev laugh.

The next pages were of Phil and Elsie, Dev's new grandparents, and of the aunts, uncles, and cousins, each labeled with names, nicknames, or "Hey, You!". There were pictures of Eastport, of Iris, and Eddie, a few of the seals taken from the patio of the inn, and a special one of Emma.

The last pages were filled with images of Ben and Dev together. As Dev reached these, he leaned into Ben and Ben put his arm around him. They looked at the final page together, a copy of the adoption decree and a picture of the new father and son with Judge Reilly. Dev looked up at Ben and said, "I never want another present in my whole life."

Ben squeezed Dev around the shoulders and kissed him on the forehead. "Well, that's too bad, because I believe there's one more."

"But we agreed—one present each. And you already broke the rule."

"This one isn't from me. It's from Iris and Emma. Emma brought it with her when she came, and she said not to give it to you until today." Ben got up and brought the last gift over to Dev.

Dev read the card, "To Dev, our aspiring writer. Let the voice within you be heard. Merry Christmas and much love, Miss Iris and Miss Emma." He pulled at the corner of the wrapping paper, and when he caught a glimpse of the box, he tore the paper away.

"A laptop!" Dev held the box up to Ben.

"Iris said it's next to impossible to be a great writer without a computer nowadays. And Emma, well, you know how she feels about you and your writing. This way you can keep things separate from your schoolwork and you don't have to worry about giving the computer back over the summer."

Dev sat on the couch admiring the computer. Tears pooled in his eyes, then poured down his cheeks.

"Dev, what is it?"

"Is this what it's like to have a real family?"

Ben took his hand. "You had a real family. You and your mom, you made a great family. Now, your family's gotten bigger, that's all. Just more people to love and to love you."

"Can I call them?"

"Who? Everybody? That'll take all day."

"No, Miss Emma, and Miss Iris." Dev wiped away his tears again on his sleeve. "I wanna thank them right away."

"That's a great idea. Better make it snappy though, we're due at the homeless shelter in about an hour. And you need to get a shower, so you don't look like a zombie snowman and scare the kids."

Dev looked at his pajama shirt and pants, having forgotten he'd been covered in flour. He laughed, then ran and got his phone. He curled up in the chair by the window holding his new laptop and he called Iris first, thanking her profusely. Then he dialed Emma.

"Merry Christmas, Miss Emma. Yes, the coffee cake turned out great! Thanks again for helping me. Dad really liked it. He said I could make it any time." Dev looked at Ben and made a guilty face. "No, he hasn't seen the kitchen yet.

"I wanted to call you and say thanks for the computer. It's awesome. I can't wait to use it. I promised Miss Iris I'd write every day." Dev stared at Ben while he listened to Emma. "Uh-huh, yeah, I think so. Would you like to talk to him?"

Ben's stomach turned.

"Sure, he's right here. Just a sec." Dev walked over to Ben and whispered, "Miss Emma wants to talk to you."

Ben stared at Dev.

"*She does.*" Dev tilted his head at him and handed him the phone then walked backward to the chair, his chin down, keeping his eyes fixed on Ben.

Ben took a breath, then held up the phone and said, "Merry Christmas, Emma."

"Merry Christmas, Ben. Sounds like you and Dev had a great morning."

"Best one I can remember. Thanks for giving him the computer. It's an amazing gift."

"Well, Iris and I wanted to do something special for him, and this seemed like the best idea. I hope you don't mind."

"Mind? How could I mind anything you do?"

At that, Dev smiled and ran upstairs to shower.

"Emma, I'm sorry I haven't called you and I'm sorry I didn't spend more time with you when you were here."

"You've had a lot on your plate."

"Don't make excuses for me. I told you I would call, and then I didn't. I'm sorry."

"It's Christmas, I forgive you." Emma paused. "I miss you Ben, especially today. Christmas breakfast didn't seem the same without you popping your head in the inn."

"And somehow, you still managed to get me my favorite coffee cake."

"That was Dev's idea. I only talked him through it."

"Well, it was a great idea and it was nice of you to help. Made me think of home. And of you."

"I'm glad you still consider Eastport your home. I wondered."

"Philly is fine. It's been good to me, obviously, but Eastport will always be home." There was a moment of silence between the two. "Emma, I, uh…"

"Sorry, Ben, just a second." Ben could hear someone speaking frantically to Emma. "I have to go. Something's wrong in the kitchen and we have an enormous crowd coming today. Give Dev a hug for me will you? I'll talk to you later. Merry Christmas."

"Merry Christmas."

Ben stared at the phone for a moment. Once again, you can't find the words. Good job, lunkhead. He looked at his watch. "Dev! Time to go, buddy."

Dev came down the stairs and smiled at Ben. "So?"

"So what? It's time to get going."

"Did you tell her?"

"Who? Emma? Yes, I thanked her for the coffee cake and the computer."

Dev gave his father a slow shake of the head and sighed heavily.

"Let's go. People will be waiting."

Ben and Dev walked to the homeless shelter on Broad Street, the same shelter Ben saw Dev exit months ago. Dev suggested instead of exchanging numerous gifts to each other for Christmas, he and his father should do something for someone else. During his days of living in the park, Dev would visit the shelter on occasion to take a shower or to have a meal, so they decided to help serve Christmas dinner to the residents.

Ben watched his normally shy son talking with adults and children at the shelter with as much ease as if he were talking with Chase.

He speaks their language.

At the end of the day, as they were walking home, Ben said, "What you did today, Dev, you made those people feel really special. How'd you do that?"

"I talked to them. That's all. People like it when you talk to them. And when you listen."

"That's good advice."

"You should try it with Miss Emma."

Ben gave Dev a side-eyed glance, but he knew his son was right.

CHAPTER 34

Spring Break

Jennifer met Ben and Dev at the front door when they arrived at her home. "Oh my goodness, what? Have you grown a foot since December, Dev?"

"Hi, Aunt Jen. Uncle Bill." Dev greeted his aunt with a hug and waved to his uncle, who was coming in from the deck.

"I don't think it's a foot, but he has grown. I understand what Angela means now about not being able to keep her son in pants that fit," Ben said.

"Da-ad."

"Ah, there it is. The whine. I am a true father now." Ben placed his hand on his chest as if posing for a statue.

Phil and Elsie were waiting for them in the living room, and after hugs and kisses were given all around, they settled in for a family chat.

Ben watched as Dev shared the latest happenings in

school, about the young writer's club he joined, and about how track season had started. As Phil shared a story of when he ran track back in the day, Ben excused himself, and went to the kitchen for a drink. Jennifer followed him.

"Hey, big brother, let me do that for you," Jennifer said. "What would you like?"

"A cup of hot tea would be great. Thanks, Jen."

"Dev sure has changed since we first met. Listen to him in there chatting away. He hardly spoke two words the first time he visited. He's doing great, thanks to you."

"Hm-mm." Ben said as he stared out the window.

"Ben?"

"What?" Ben turned to Jennifer. "Sorry, I wasn't paying attention."

"What's going on with you? You're a million miles away. Are you all right?"

"Nothing. Nothing's going on. I'm fine." Ben gave Jennifer a half a smile.

"Ugh, what is it with men? You are not fine. You haven't been fine for months. Every time I talk to you, I can tell something's wrong. So please, stop with the 'I'm fine' and fess up. What's going on?"

Ben took a deep breath, then blew it out in a puff. "I think I'm a moron."

"Well, that's mostly true, so what's the problem?"

Ben smirked at his sister. "Thanks for the boost."

"Do you want a boost, or do you want the truth?" She raised her eyebrows at him. "Why are you a moron? This time?"

"I can't talk to you about this." Ben turned away from her.

"Come here." Jennifer went to Ben, reached up and placed her hands on both sides of his face. She pulled his head down so she could look him in the eye. "You'd better talk to me or I'm going to tell Ma and Pop who really started the fire behind the shed."

"You wouldn't."

"Oh, wouldn't I?"

"Fine." Ben pulled away from his sister. "It's Emma."

"Emma? Good, now we're getting somewhere. Yes, I agree. You are a moron."

Ben rubbed his face with his hands. "You're not making this easy."

"Okay, how's this? You like her. She likes you. She's not going to do anything about it though, because she's a classy woman. She's not going to chase after you, Ben. She's waiting for you to make a move, but you're too . . . moronic, to do it." Jennifer crossed her arms. "Do I overstate the case?"

"I guess not. At least on my end." Ben stuffed his hands in his pockets.

Jennifer took him by the arm. "Here, sit." She sat him at the breakfast table and massaged his shoulders. "I'm sorry for picking on you, big brother. Listen, it's understandable. You haven't exactly been lucky in love, but that doesn't mean love isn't meant for you. Maybe this is the time."

"But Jen, how can I take the chance? I have Dev to think about now. He's already attached to Emma. They're good friends. He calls her at least once a week. That's more than I do. She even helped him make a coffee cake for me on Christmas day. Walked him through the whole process over the phone.

"You know her. She's amazing, one of the best people I know. We've been friends forever, but how can I date her, or anybody else for that matter? What if it doesn't work out? Dev has already lost so much. I can't do that to him."

"So you'll spend the rest of your life by yourself, is that it? Do you think Dev would want that for you?"

"No, I don't," Dev said, standing in the kitchen's doorway. "Is that why you haven't called Miss Emma? You're worried about me?"

Ben stared at Dev.

"Aunt Jen, can I talk to my dad? Alone?"

"Sure. Maybe you can get somewhere with him." Jennifer patted Ben on the shoulder and left for the living room, kissing Dev's head on the way. Dev sat across from his father and waited.

Ben finished his tea then stared at the empty cup. "When I was in high school, I wanted to be a rock star. Had it all planned out. I'd start a band, we'd play some local gigs. I'd go on to college and learn about music. I'd form another band with better musicians, then we'd make it big. Tour around the country, maybe around the world."

"What happened?"

"I kept hitting dead-ends. I started a band, but we only played a few dances and pool parties. Then the band broke up. I applied for a couple of music schools my junior year, but got turned down by all of them. I auditioned for some other bands, but got rejected there, too."

"Is that how you ended up being a cop?"

"Sort of. See, your grandpa, he's a wise man. After watching me go down dead-end street after dead-end street, he sat me down one day and said, 'Ben, a dead-end street is a good place to turn around.'"

"I don't get it."

"I didn't either, not at first anyway. And your grandpa is not one for explaining. He wanted me to think about it, so I did. He was right. Every street I took to have a music career ended in a dead-end. I was going nowhere. There had to be another road for me, but what?

"That's when I realized at no time did I ask God what He wanted me to do, what He wanted for my life. I said I believed in Him, that I trusted Him. I asked Him to help me all the time, but I didn't with this. It seems so obvious now—*that* should have been my starting point. I should have been asking, 'What would *You* like me to do, God?' So, I did. I started asking that question, then a funny thing happened."

"What?"

"First, I realized I wasn't as talented as I thought I was. That was a kick in the pants. Sure, I could carry a tune and play a little guitar, but honestly, I was no Stephen Tyler or Eric Clapton."

"Who?"

"Never mind. My point is, I was an okay musician, but not a great one. And I was never going to be great because that's not where my heart was. I kept trying to deny the truth. I liked music, but I *loved* law enforcement. I read magazine articles and books about it all the time. I'd hang out and listen to my dad and my uncles talk about their work. Even my favorite TV shows were cop shows."

"So why didn't you want to be a cop?"

"Because almost all the men in my family were cops, and I didn't want to do what everyone else did. It seemed like the easy way out."

"Doesn't seem easy to me."

"Well, you're right. It wasn't. And that was the other problem." Ben paused. "I was afraid."

"You? Afraid? I didn't think you were afraid of anything."

"Well, I was. I was afraid of disappointing everyone. If I

tried to be a cop and failed? Well, it felt like I'd be letting the entire family down."

"And now you're afraid of letting me down."

Ben took a breath and gave Dev a slow nod. Dev stood, then went over and wrapped his arms around his father's neck and rested his head on his shoulder.

"Have you asked God about Miss Emma?"

"As a matter of fact, I have not."

Dev stood up straight and looked Ben in the eye. "What's that saying of Grandpa's?"

"Pray on it," Ben said.

"Yeah, that. Maybe you should try that."

Ben smiled. "Out of the mouths of babes . . ."

"I am not a babe."

"Knucklehead."

Dev laughed and mussed Ben's hair.

That evening, after dinner, Ben went for a walk by the lake. He stood on the shoreline, staring at the constellations, then went to Jennifer's shed, removed his kayak, and set out. He dipped his paddle into the water, pulling himself to the middle of the lake. Once there, he closed his eyes and listened to the loons calling to each other.

Dev's right. They do have a plaintive cry.

Their muted love song pierced Ben's heart, almost bringing him to tears. He paddled forward. Praying, he poured out to God all that was troubling him. As he did, a verse of scripture came to mind. *Be still and know that I am God.* Ben pulled up his paddle and laid it across his kayak.

Inside the house, Dev watched from the patio door. Jennifer came up behind him and put her arm around him. "Don't worry, he's going to be fine. This is what he does to refocus himself and listen to God. It's a good thing."

"Aunt Jen, Dad's always worried about me. He wants to do things to make me happy, but I want him to be happy, too."

"I know you do. And he will be. He just needs to find his way, and we'll help him, right?"

Dev nodded and leaned his head against his aunt as they watched his father wrestle with himself and with God.

CHAPTER 35

The Green-Eyed Monster

The following morning, Ben left Dev with his parents and went to Eastport. He intended to go directly to the Sunrise Inn, but instead, found himself standing outside of the WaCo Diner.

Might as well grab a cup of coffee since I'm here. He went in and sat at the counter.

"Sheriff, good to see you this morning." Judy, the head waitress, said.

The sound of men's voices filled the diner as the front door opened. "I'm telling you, Chummy. I would have clocked him right there if he yapped another second. That guy gets under my skin."

"Now Paulie, that's no way to talk about Rev. Biggs." The two men burst into laughter.

"Up to your usual antics, I hear," Ben said to the men.

"Ben! Hey, how you doin'?" Chummy said.

"Fine. I'm fine. Sounds like *you're* being the peacekeeper now. Who you wanting to clock, Paulie?"

Paulie grunted and took a seat.

"Eh, it's the usual–bureaucrats," Chummy said and took the stool beside Ben.

After an hour of coffee, blueberry muffins, and stories of happenings in Eastport, some of which were true, Chummy stood. "Well, I best be heading out. Got a big job over in Perry today. Those pipes aren't gonna fix themselves. Good catchin' up with you, Ben."

"Nice seeing you, Chummy. You too, Paulie," Ben said as he stood and shook Paulie's hand. "Guess I should be going, Judy."

"You have a good day, Ben," Judy said as she wiped the counter.

Ben went outside and while he should have turned left to head to the inn, he turned right instead. He crossed Water Street and went into Wadsworth Hardware. He roamed the aisles, then after chatting with the clerk, he ventured back outside. He walked past The Commons and the fishing pier. He greeted the Fisherman statue, and Nerida, the Eastport bronze mermaid, then paused to watch a Coast Guard ship exit the Breakwater pier into the bay.

Before he knew it, he was standing in front of Todd

House, a classic New England cape that sits on Todd's Head, the easternmost point of Eastport.

"What am I doing here?" He looked out at the bay, then turned around, and headed back into town, this time directly to the Sunrise Inn. When he arrived, he stared at the door, took a steadying breath, then entered.

Emma stood behind the front desk, helping guests. She noticed him and smiled as she continued to point out areas of interest to the family in front of her. Ben could feel his face flush. He pulled at the neck of his shirt.

Take a seat before you make a fool of yourself.

He sat in one of the overstuffed chairs by the fireplace. While he waited for Emma to be free, he studied her. She possessed a calm confidence that radiated through her smile. Her words were expressed with a softness and tone unusual for native Mainers, revealing her true roots lie somewhere closer to the Midwest. Some may have considered her winsome face ordinary, but to Ben, she was as ordinary as a snow moon suspended over Boyden Lake. For the first time, he noticed her eyes were blue, not the sapphire blue of Dev's, more spring sky blue, clear, and full of life. Why hadn't he seen them before?

Emma finished with her guests and walked over to Ben. "Well, this is a surprise."

He stood to greet her. "Emma, you have blue eyes."

Emma laughed. "Why, yes. Yes, I do. I also have brown

hair, and pink fingernails." She showed Ben her manicured hands.

"Sorry, I'm not with it today." Ben tucked his shaking hands in his pockets.

"Afternoon, Emma," the UPS man called as he entered the lobby pushing a handcart laden with packages.

"Hi, Karl." Emma greeted him with a smile.

"Got a lot of boxes for you today. Need you to sign." He wheeled the cart to the front desk.

"Be right back, Ben," she said with a pat on Ben's arm, which sent an electric charge down his spine. Emma went over to the front desk and signed Karl's pad.

"Would you like me to put all this somewhere? I can roll 'em wherever you need 'em, no problem." Karl smiled at Emma in a way that made the hair on the back of Ben's neck stand at attention.

"That'd be nice, thanks."

Is she blushing?

"Would you mind taking them to my office?"

"Anything for you," Karl said with a wink. Emma smiled, and lowered her head, then turned to her office, holding the door open for Karl.

She is definitely blushing.

Ben's heart pounded in his chest and reverberated to his ears. He stood transfixed, listening to Emma and Karl chatting and laughing in her office.

Sounds like they're having a good time in there. What's so funny? If I was still sheriff, I'd give ol' Karl a ticket for unlawful entry. Or vagrancy. Or theft. Maybe I should just clock him one when he comes out.

"Have a great day, Emma. See ya tomorrow, I hope," Karl said with yet another wink as he exited Emma's office, dragging his handcart behind him.

The man absolutely needs a good clocking.

Emma returned to Ben with a smile, and seemingly to him, a spring in her step.

"Who's that?" Ben said, pointing with his chin toward Karl.

"Oh, him? That's Karl. He's the new delivery guy. Started right after Christmas. He got transferred up here after Charlie retired. Nice guy. He's been living in Perry but wants to move to Eastport. He likes the town."

"Hmph," was all Ben could bring himself to say.

"Are you all right? You look upset."

"You seem to know an awful lot about *Karl*." Ben almost choked on the man's name.

Emma tilted her head at Ben. "Yes. He stops by almost every day with packages for the inn."

"For the inn . . ." Ben glared at Karl through the lobby window, his jaw tight. He watched as Karl pulled away in his truck.

"Ben," Emma smiled a slow smile. "I do believe you're jealous."

"What? Me?" Ben said, giving his attention back to Emma.

"And I believe, that's a good thing," Emma whispered.

"Well, I have to go."

"Go? But you just got here."

"Yeah, I uh, I just came to say hi. I'll see you later."

Faster than a Maine summer, Ben was outside, standing alone on the sidewalk wondering what had come over him.

It took another day, but Ben found the courage to go back to the inn to see Emma. He went first thing in the morning, not wanting to take the chance someone else may arrive and capture her attention. Or her smile.

When Emma came out of her office, she found Ben standing in the lobby, staring at the front desk.

"You look like you need some coffee. Come with me." Emma took Ben's arm and led him to the west wing.

"Have a seat. I'd offer you decaf, but I think you need regular and a shot of espresso, maybe?"

"Regular's fine, thanks." Ben sat at the small table in the

breakfast nook and glanced around the living area. It reminded him of Emma, relaxed, peaceful, beautiful without pretense. "Em, did you change things in here? The place looks different."

"Same as it's always been." She came in with a coffeepot. "Except, I put some fresh hydrangeas on the table. I love those. They don't require much arranging and the florist had some exceptional blue ones yesterday."

"They match your eyes. They are beautiful." Ben glanced up at Emma.

Emma stood still for a moment. "Ben Hudson," Emma lowered her chin and looked into Ben's eyes. "Are you flirting with me?"

Ben looked down at the floor, understanding now why Dev did that so much. "Perhaps." He looked up at Emma. "Would it bother you if I was?"

Emma placed a coffee mug in front of him and whispered, "Maybe. Just a tad." She poured coffee into his mug and took a seat in the chair across from him.

"Have dinner with me tonight," Ben said.

"Sorry, can't. I have a date."

"Karl," he growled to himself.

"What's that?"

"Ah, nothing. A date, huh. Well, good for you." He took a swig of coffee, and kept swigging, even though it felt as if he were pouring hot lava into his gullet.

"Are you all right?" Emma asked. "That coffee's awfully hot."

Ben placed the mug down, then with a cough and as much casualness as he could muster, he said, "I'm fine. Good coffee." He twirled the mug on the table. "So, who's the date with? Anybody I know?"

"Oh, he's new in town. A real charmer, very handsome."

"Mr. UPS?" He couldn't help himself.

"Who?"

"Mr. UPS guy. I saw him here yesterday. He was smiling at you. A lot. You were smiling too. Guess he's handsome, if you like toothy grins."

"Well, Karl is attractive, I suppose, but this guy's much more handsome. He's got sandy blonde hair and blue eyes the color of sea glass." Emma sipped her coffee and Ben shifted in his seat. "He's a little young. And maybe a little short, about four-foot nine I'd guess, but I don't let that bother me."

"Dev."

"Yes, Dev." Emma smiled. "He called this morning to see if I would have dinner with him tonight. He wanted to ask you if you'd like to come along, but he didn't know where you'd gone. He said he was sure you'd say yes, but he wanted to be the one to invite me, so . . ." Emma sipped from her cup again. "I love that boy."

"And he loves you. I can see I have competition."

"Oh really? I didn't know you were in the race," Emma

said with a slight tilt of the head.

"Ouch." Ben rubbed his hands on his knees.

Emma sipped from her cup again, then placed it on the saucer. She looked at Ben for a moment. The smile disappeared from her face. "Is that why you're here? You think I may be seeing someone?"

Ben became fascinated with his coffee mug.

"I haven't had a proper phone call from you in weeks and the first time I saw you in months was yesterday, just for a minute before you dashed out of here like the place was on fire."

Her voice was calm, but Ben could sense the hurt behind her words.

"How long have you been here . . . in Maine?"

Ben looked up at Emma, his face guilt-ridden.

Emma nodded. "Today you show up here, unannounced, flirting with me. Worried I may be dating someone else, when I don't remember ever dating you."

Ben could see Emma's breath increasing as she furrowed her brow and folded her hands in front of her. "Ben, I am not some child's plaything you can pick up and place down whenever it suits you. I have too much self-worth for that. You and I, we've been friends, the best of friends, for a very long time, and you mean the world to me. You know that. And I promise you, no matter what, you will always have my friendship. Always. But I will not be played with." Emma's chin trembled.

Could I be any more of a lunkhead? How could I hurt her like that? You don't deserve this woman's time, or her–He shook his head at himself, then looked at Emma. "I'm very sorry, Emma. I'm sorry I've made you feel that way."

Ben could see Emma doing her best not to give in to the tears fighting their way to the surface.

"I know I don't deserve it, but could you possibly forgive me? And would you allow me to join you and Dev for dinner?"

Emma stared at Ben for a moment, then said softly, "Of course. I can't disappoint those blue eyes." She stood. "I need to get back to work."

Ben stood with her and reached for her hand as she walked by. "Em, really, I'm very sorry."

Her eyes still reflected her disappointment with him. "I know. I know you are. I need to go." She squeezed his hand, then went back to the inn.

CHAPTER 36

Forgiven

Determined to make things right with Emma, Ben stopped by the florist on his way back to Jennifer's. He visited the shop in Perry, not in Eastport, just to be safe. He wasn't sure what he needed to be safe from, but it seemed like a good idea at the time. The Perry florist didn't have any hydrangeas, so he settled for a bouquet of light pink Gerbera daisies. They reminded him of the blush on Emma's cheek when he complimented her.

Hours later, he knocked on Emma's door in the west wing. When she answered, he didn't say a word, but held out the bouquet of daisies. Emma smiled at the flowers, accepted them, a blush returning to her cheeks. She turned and went inside, Ben followed. After placing the flowers in a vase, she stared at them for a moment, touching the delicate petals.

"Forgive me?" Ben said.

"Forgiven, always. But thanks for asking. And thank you for these, they're lovely."

"Well, I would say something like 'not as lovely as you', but I don't want you to think me insincere."

"Of all the words I could put on you, insincere is the very last one."

They picked up Dev on their way to Lubec for dinner. Ben was relieved Emma was so willing to forgive him. Still, he was on edge and thankful Dev was with them. His son made the perfect buffer between Ben and his feelings.

Once they were seated in the restaurant, Dev told Emma about his recent adventures around his Aunt Jen's house—how he saw a porcupine out for a morning stroll, and eagles flying over the lake. He even saw a mother moose and her baby coming to the edge of the lake to sample the marsh grasses. Dev got so excited telling the tale he stood as he demonstrated the chomping of the grasses by the mother moose.

"It was awesome, Miss Emma," Dev said, grinning as he sat back down. "I never saw moose before. They're huge!"

"Yes, they are. Rather frightening if you meet one on the road at night. I don't recommend it."

"Dad, do you think we could bring Miss Emma to Aunt Jen's one day? Maybe we'd see the mama moose again."

"That's a great idea. I'm sure Aunt Jen would love to see Emma, too."

"Miss Emma?"

"We'll see what we can work out. I know you'll be returning to Philadelphia soon, so we'll see." She smiled at him, then looked at Ben.

At the end of the evening, Ben left Dev in the rental car as he walked Emma back to the inn. "Thanks for coming tonight, and for giving me a second chance. I hope you don't regret doing that."

"I don't. We all deserve a second chance. I had a good time. It's a rarity for me to have dinner someplace other than my own establishment. I kinda feel guilty, like I'm cheating."

"Well, don't feel too guilty." Ben took her hand. "I'd like to do this again. Any chance we could have a repeat performance tomorrow night? Maybe just you and me?"

"No, I can't."

"I see." Ben let go of her hand.

"It's not that I don't want to." Emma took Ben's hand again. "I have a big event here tomorrow night. It's all hands on deck, so I can't leave."

"Got it. How about Thursday? Wait, I can't do that. My brother Oliver's coming up and we're having dinner together with my folks. How about Friday?"

"I couldn't do Thursday anyway and Friday is the first night of the holiday weekend, that's a no go."

"Saturday?"

Emma shook her head no. "Easter Egg hunt on the back lawn, then a banquet in the hall. And Sunday's Easter. There's a brunch here and I'm sure you're going to be swamped with family things. I'm sorry, Ben."

"There must be some way." Ben paused to think. "Would you consider coming to church with us Easter morning and any chance you could sneak away for brunch with my family? I know you should be here, but maybe just for a couple hours?"

Emma looked at Ben and sighed. He could see the wheels turning in her head. She's pretty when she's thinking. Heck, she's pretty all the time.

"It would mean a lot if you would." He tucked a bit of stray hair behind her ear, then traced the side of her face with his finger. He took both her hands. "Dev and I are leaving first thing Monday morning. This may be our last chance to see each other for a while."

"Well, everything is planned out for the brunch, and I have the full staff working. I suppose I could slip away for a few hours, if you're sure it'd be fine with your family."

"It will be, I promise."

"Okay, Easter it is." Emma's eyes softened, and she smiled at Ben.

"Easter." Ben cupped her face in his hands and kissed her gently on the lips. His heart soared. He looked into her eyes. "Our first kiss."

Emma smiled and caressed Ben's cheek. "But not our last."

He pulled her close and kissed her again. He took her hand, kissed her palm, then closed his fingers around hers. "I'll see you Sunday."

"See you Sunday."

CHAPTER 37

Easter

Dev stirred and got himself out of bed at the break of day. He showered and dressed before anyone even considered turning their alarm clocks off, a habit he developed for holidays and special occasions. He waited in Ryan's room, and as he did, he pulled out his spiral notebook and began writing.

"How'd I know you'd be dressed already?" Ben asked as he entered the room an hour later.

Dev grinned.

"Happy Easter, buddy. I have a little something for you." Ben handed him a thin rectangular box.

"An Easter present?"

"Just a little one. Go ahead, open it."

Dev opened the box and revealed a new necktie.

"I thought you'd like to have one of your own, a new one."

"This is great, thanks." Dev stared at the tie in the box.

"You don't seem too enthusiastic about it. It's okay if you don't like it."

"No, I-I like it. It's just . . . well, I was gonna wear the tie Miss Emma gave me. You know, the one that was Harry's? I thought she'd like it 'cause it was his and because she said it matched my eyes."

"You know, that's a great idea. Emma would love that. Let's save this one for another time."

"Really? You don't mind?"

"I think I should mind because I understand you're my competition when it comes to Emma."

Dev blushed, then went to his duffle bag, and pulled out Harry's tie.

"C'mere, knucklehead, let me tie that for you."

"Can you teach me? I wanna learn how to do it myself."

"You're growing up too fast for me." Ben turned his son toward the mirror and knelt behind him. "All right, step one . . ."

Following a light breakfast, Ben and Dev left to pick up Emma for church. Dev looked his father up and down as they pulled out of the driveway.

"You're lookin' pretty good today, Dad."

"Well, thank you, son. You're lookin' pretty good yourself."

"Be sure to tell Miss Emma she looks nice. Girls like that."

"The Love Guru returns."

"I mean it. Girls like it when you tell them stuff like that."

"And how do you know what girls like?"

Dev blushed.

"I see. What's her name?"

The blush in Dev's cheeks grew deeper. "Madeline, but that's not how I know." Dev picked up his tie and stared at it for a moment. "I know 'cause of my mom. She said it was important to notice things about people, and it was especially important to say something if what you noticed was nice. She said if it wasn't nice, I should keep my mouth shut."

"That's good advice."

"Yeah, and she was right. I noticed Madeline had a new hairband, and I told her I liked the color. She smiled at me and that made my stomach feel funny."

Ben laughed. "Yep, women can do that to you."

"Does Miss Emma do that to you?"

"Ah, look at the time. Hope we can find a parking spot, so we're not late."

Dev rolled his eyes at his father.

Ben pulled into the inn's lot and spied a spot. "Great, there's one. You stay here. I'll be back in a minute."

"Say something nice!" Dev said as Ben exited the car.

Ben walked at a brisk pace to the inn, shaking out his hands. He stood outside the entrance, took a few deep breaths, stretched his neck from side to side, then pulled the door open.

Emma stood in the lobby, chatting with a guest. Her back was to him, but when the door closed, she turned her head. Seeing Ben, she smiled.

My stomach feels funny.

"Thanks so much for coming and I hope you have a pleasant stay," Emma said to her guests. They thanked her, then went on their way.

I don't think she's ever looked more beautiful. How have I missed seeing who she is all these years? It's a mystery.

The mystery deepened as he watched Emma walk toward him. A pattern of tiny blue forget-me-nots dotted the white dress she wore that fit every curve of her body, as if it were custom made for her. Her hair fell in soft waves against her shoulders and bounced gently as she walked. He drew in a quick breath, his heart pounding in his chest.

"Good morning. Happy Easter." Emma gave him a kiss on the cheek.

"Yeah, good happy morning to you, too."

"Are you all right?" Emma said with a laugh.

"Why's everybody keep asking me that?" He took Emma's hand. "You look beautiful."

"Why thank you. It's nice of you to say." Emma said with a dip of her head.

"I mean it, Emma." He squeezed her hand. "You're beautiful, really." Emma gazed into his eyes, then looked away with a smile.

She's blushing.

"Shall we?" Ben extended his arm to her. She nodded, then put hers through his and walked with him out the door. Dev stood by the car, waiting. As they approached, he opened the car door.

"Morning, Miss Emma. Happy Easter!"

"Good morning, Dev. Happy Easter to you, too."

"I like your dress. The flowers are the same color as my tie."

"I had a feeling you'd be wearing that tie, so I wore this. I thought we could match." Emma got into the car.

Dev raised his eyebrows at Ben as he closed the door.

"Knucklehead," Ben said.

Pots of purple hyacinths, multi-colored tulips, and Easter lilies welcomed the congregants to the church with a splash of color and the aroma of spring. Ben found his parents already seated in a pew along with Jennifer and Bill. They were all eager to see Emma, someone they'd known for years, but hadn't seen often enough. Just after they said their hellos, the service began.

Following a welcoming prayer, and a song by an

energetic though slightly off-key soloist, students from the youth group entered the sanctuary from the rear shouting, "Hosanna to the King of Kings!". They marched down the center aisle waving palm branches. A high school student playing Jesus followed them riding a real donkey. Ben looked over at his son who was mesmerized by the scene.

The students acted out the story of the final week of Jesus's life with the last supper, Jesus praying in the garden, his capture, and the trial by Pontius Pilate. After Pilate washed his hands, the stage and the sanctuary darkened as a cross was raised, and Jesus placed upon it. The scene was backlit, and all that could be viewed was the shadowy figure of Jesus hanging on the cross. Dev leaned into Ben.

A student read from scripture: *"It was now about the sixth hour, and there was darkness over the whole land until the ninth hour, while the sun's light failed. And the curtain of the temple was torn in two. Then Jesus, calling out with a loud voice, said, 'Father, into your hands I commit my spirit!' And having said this, He breathed his last. Now when the centurion saw what had taken place, he praised God, saying, 'Truly, this was the son of God!'"*

Dev leaned closer to Ben, his brow furrowed and his breathing heavy. Ben whispered, "You okay?"

Dev whispered back, "Why'd they do that to him? Why didn't he fight back? Or run or something? Where'd all his friends go?"

"It's gonna be okay. Keep watching."

He doesn't know. He doesn't know the whole story of Jesus. Why didn't I realize that? Until he was with me, he's only been to church with his mom at Christmas. The only Jesus he knows is the baby who was born in a manger.

Dev reached for Ben's hand and gripped it. The skit continued with Jesus being removed from the cross and laid in a cardboard tomb, his mother weeping by it as the disciples scattered. Dev wiped away his own tear.

The sanctuary remained in darkness, and all was quiet. A small child, lit by a flashlight, walked across the front holding a poster with a large "1" written on it, followed by another child with a "2", then a third with a "3". The lights grew brighter in the church. Two girls went to the tomb and stood next to the boy soldiers who were guarding it. Without warning, they shook as if experiencing a great earthquake and the boys fell on the floor in response. The girls fell to their knees and looked at the tomb.

The "stone" had been rolled away and an angel came out from the tomb and said, *"Do not be afraid, for I know that you seek Jesus who was crucified. He is not here for He is risen, as He said. Come, see the place where the Lord lay. And go quickly and tell His disciples that He is risen from the dead!"*

Then all the students gathered in the front of the church

and shouted, "He is risen!"

The congregation answered, "He is risen indeed!"

Dev looked up at Ben with tears in his eyes. "He's alive?"

"Yes, He is. He's very much alive." Dev breathed a sigh of relief and before he could wipe his eyes on his sleeve, Ben handed him a handkerchief. "Use this, bud."

Dev smiled and took the handkerchief.

Following the service, as they made their way to the car, Ben said, "Dev, why don't you sit up front with us?"

Dev slid into the front seat between Ben and Emma.

"That was a lovely service," Emma said as they left the church parking lot. "The youth group did a great job."

"So, that's what happened to Jesus when he grew up?" Dev asked. "The people were so mean to him. I didn't like that."

"No, they weren't very nice, but that's what happened," Emma said.

"Why'd he have to die like that? I don't get it. Even the guard guy said he was the Son of God."

"It's hard to understand how you could love someone so much you'd be willing to die for them. But that's how much Jesus loves us." Ben patted Dev on the leg. "Do you remember when you and Chase broke the window in the Mongelli's house?"

"Yeah, when Chase hit that home run. We thought it was awesome until Mrs. Mongelli got home."

"Right, and then what happened?"

"She made us pay to fix it. We had to do all kinds of chores to earn the money to pay her back for what it cost."

"How would you have felt if Emma came and paid for the window instead?"

"I would've thought it was awesome," Dev said, smiling at Emma.

"But what if it cost her all the money she had?"

"I wouldn't want her to do it then."

"What if she insisted? What if she said she loved you so much she wanted to pay the price for you? And then she did."

"I'd be grateful. And I'd be happy she loved me that much to do it, but I'd be sad she had to."

"Well, that's what Jesus did for us. When we do things that are wrong, like when we lie or lose our tempers or talk bad about someone, all those things, they're called 'sin'. And when we sin, there's a price to pay. Jesus loves us so much He wanted to pay the price for us. That's why He died. But you saw the story, it didn't end there, did it?"

"No, he got alive again."

Ben and Emma smiled. "Yes, He did. He got alive again," Ben said.

"Miss Emma, when you told me about Harry being in heaven. Is this what you meant about believing in God?"

"Yes. To believe in God means you believe He loves you

enough to come to this earth, to live here, to teach us, then to die for us, and finally, to get alive again. That's what I believe."

"I do too," Dev said with a nod. Emma put her arm around Dev, and he nestled himself into her for the rest of the trip.

Once at Jennifer's house, Dev took Emma out on the deck and showed her where he saw the moose, the eagle, and the porcupine. Ben watched them from the kitchen.

Emma seems enchanted by his stories. I feel the same way . . . and not just about him.

At brunch, Dev made sure Emma sat between him and Ben. The ensuing conversation was a free-for-all with speakers and topics changing at breakneck speed. Emma was up to the task, navigating through the maelstrom of discussion with the confidence of a seasoned ship's captain. She was neither intimidated nor intimidating but fit right in with the family mix as if she'd been a Hudson herself.

When it came time for clean-up, Emma stood to help Jennifer, but Ben intervened. "Nope, you're our guest. Why don't you go have a chat with my parents? Dev and I will take care of this. Right, partner?"

"What happened to people helping people?" Emma said.

"Not on holidays," Ben said with a wink.

"Right, Dad. Miss Emma, this way." Dev took Emma by the hand and led her into the living room and left her to chat with Phil and Elsie.

In the meantime, Ben started clearing the dishes and taking them into the kitchen where Jennifer was waiting. With each load he brought in, she grinned at him.

"Not a word, little sister." Ben gave Jennifer a side-eyed look.

"Did I say anything?"

"You didn't have to. Your thoughts are practically shouting at me."

Jennifer continued grinning at her brother, and every so often she'd suck in her lips to swallow any words that wanted to escape.

"Ben," Emma appeared in the kitchen, her face stark white, her body trembling. "Fire . . . at the inn."

He took her hand. "Let's go."

CHAPTER 38

Firestorm

Ben rushed Emma back to Eastport, ignoring speed limits and double yellow lines. He had no siren, nor flashing red lights. His horn and headlights had to suffice. They arrived in Eastport in seven minutes, half the normal travel time. Ben sped down Washington Street, made a right on High Street, then a quick left on Key Street. When they arrived at Water Street, a barrier had been put up. Fire trucks, police cars, and an ambulance were parked chockablock down the street.

Emma whispered, "An ambulance. Oh, God, please."

Ben pulled the car over and added to the number of other vehicles left abandoned on the street. He squeezed Emma's hand. "You ready?" Emma nodded and exited the car. She and Ben weaved themselves in and out of parked emergency vehicles and bystanders. When they got to the inn, they were met with another police barricade.

Firefighters, like red ants whose hill had been disturbed, ran back and forth from truck to inn, laying hose lines, gathering equipment, and shuttling people. Emma stood motionless until Ben took her by the hand. "Come with me."

They went to the barricade and crossed over it.

"Hey, get back behind there! This is dangerous," an officer shouted.

"Hank, it's Ben. What's happened?"

The officer approached Ben and Emma. "Sorry, didn't see it was you, Ben. Emma, glad you're here. I need to get you to the fire chief. He's got questions." Emma followed Hank with Ben by her side.

"Chief, Emma Martin's here."

"Emma, sorry about all this. I need to know—is there anything in the inn that could cause an explosion? Propane, fuel, anything like that?"

"Yes. You know we're on propane for cooking and heating."

"Right, we know about that, and that's taken care of. Anything else?"

"Yes, we have small propane canisters for catering. We store those in the shed outside of the kitchen area."

"Any other flammable things stored inside?"

"No, nothing. What's happening, Jeff?"

"We're not sure yet, but it looks like it started in the kitchen. I think we've about got it under control. We got a 911 call about forty-five minutes ago and the guys have been working hard."

"My staff, my guests?"

"Everyone's out. Everyone's safe. Your guests are being shuttled over to the high school."

Emma breathed a sigh of relief as the tears flowed. "Oh, thank God. Thank God."

The chief nodded to Ben. "Take her aside, will you, Ben? I'll talk to you when I can, Emma."

Ben put his arm around Emma and led her beside one of the fire trucks. Emma's body trembled and Ben wasn't sure if it was from the damp weather or from the emotion of seeing a place she loved in flames. He took off his suit jacket, wrapped it around her shoulders, and held her close. She rested her head on his shoulder as she stood in silence watching flames pour out of one side of the building that had been her workplace and her home for thirty-five years. The place where she raised her children, and laughed and danced with her husband, the place where she cared for him in his last days.

"I shouldn't have left. I shouldn't have left." Emma whispered as her tears flowed.

Amid the bedlam, Iris and Frank tracked down Emma and found her by the fire engine with Ben. They persuaded her to stay with them for the night. It was well after midnight before she was willing to leave the inn and well after one in the morning before Ben was willing to leave her.

After a few hours sleep and a few bites of breakfast, Iris walked Emma back to the inn. Fog shrouded the bay, its mist stretched out like fingers, entwining themselves around the inn, gripping it in a somber haze. Emma and Iris stood across the street, stared at the scene for a few moments, then moved forward into the inn.

Ben arrived shortly afterward. When he saw Emma, she took his breath away again, but for a different reason. She stood dazed in the lobby, pale, all color, all life it seemed, drained from her face. Her sky-blue eyes were now red-rimmed and swollen. A look of anguish replaced her ever-present smile. As she stared at her surroundings, she wrapped her arms around her body, as if she were afraid she'd shatter if she let go.

The lobby, once neat and tidy, had been transformed into something from a black and white horror flick where one was sure an unnatural apparition would appear at any moment. Ben watched Emma walk through the lobby, void of any emotion as she picked up water-soaked literature, crushed flowers, and overturned chairs.

She went to the fireplace and looked up at the portrait of Harry, covered in soot. She fixed her eyes on it, then crumpled into a ball, sobbing. Ben and Iris went to her and wrapped her in a cocoon of consoling arms and empathetic kisses.

When the last of her morning's tears were spent, Emma stood. She took Iris's and Ben's hands and looked at the portrait of Harry.

"Though He slay me, I will hope in Him." She took a deep breath, looked around the room and let go of their hands. "I need to get to work."

The fire chief came through the door. "Emma, I thought you'd be here already."

"Chief Miller, how are you?" She went to him, her hand extended. "How is everyone? Thank you for everything you did last night. You saved the inn."

The chief grasped her hand in both of his. "Everyone's fine, Emma. I wanted to stop by and let you know what we've found out so far. We've still got some investigating to do, but I think we understand what happened. We talked to your chef, and it seems some cooking oil ignited, and the flames got into the kitchen's ductwork and exhaust system. That caused the fire to spread throughout the kitchen quickly, but what saved the day was the sprinkler system you had installed a few years back. It did what it was supposed to do and helped prevent the fire from spreading throughout the rest of the inn."

"I disagree. What saved the day was you and your firefighters. I'm forever grateful." Emma managed a small smile.

"I know you've got a lot of water damage, and the kitchen, well, I'm sorry to say you no longer have a kitchen, but other than that, the inn is intact. It's gonna take a lot of work, but you can bring it back."

"Thanks, Jeff. I'll get right on that." Emma said, her voice trembling.

"You won't have to do this alone, Emma. You know this, in Eastport, we take care of our own."

"Miss Emma!" Emma turned. Eddie came into the water-logged inn, a shovel and broom thrown over his shoulder. He dropped both and ran to her. He wrapped her in his arms.

"I'm here to help. We'll get this place cleaned up in no time, you'll see." Emma held Eddie's face in her hands as she cried and nodded.

"Don't cry, Miss Emma. It's gonna be okay. We'll fix it. Right Sheriff?" With tears in his own eyes, Eddie looked over at Ben.

"Yes, we will. You can count on it, on us," Ben assured her.

"Well, this is a mess. But I seen worse." Mary stood in the doorway, surveying the lobby. She turned her head this way and that, making tsk-tsk noises with her tongue. She walked to

Emma and surveyed her as well.

"You look about as I supposed." She went to the front desk and examined the damage behind the counter. "Ayuh, it's stoved up all right."

She went back to Emma, who hadn't moved a muscle since Mary arrived. "Now, I bet you're wonderin' how you're gonna fix all this." Mary took Emma's hand. "I'm here to tell you—one bit at a time. That's how.

"Just so's you know, last night I took care of the people they shuttled to the high school. You were busy here, so I didn't think you'd mind. They're all set up in other places in the area and they're all just fine. I checked in with them this morning. And I've started calling people. People with reservations, people who booked the banquet hall. I should have it all wrapped up by the end of the day." Mary patted Emma's hand.

"How? The computer. It's, it's non-functional. How are you calling people? How do you know who to call?" Emma asked.

"Emma, you know I don't fancy that computer. Nuisance, if you ask me. I do that to satisfy you. Everything I need to know is in the computer in my head." Mary pointed to her temple. "And that's not a mess. At least not yet." A small smile escaped her lips.

"Emma, excuse me. I'm going to have to ask you and everyone else to leave now," Chief Miller said. "We've got to finish our investigation. Once that's done, your insurance people will want to get in here, and then the hard work can start. In the meantime, why don't you all take a walk over to the diner."

"Good idea, Chief," Ben said. "I think we all could use some coffee. Come on, Emma, Iris. Eddie, you come too. Mary?"

"No, I've got phone calls to make." She walked up to Emma and took her hand again. "Emma, don't you worry. We'll fix this place up and make it right out straight again."

Emma nodded and squeezed Mary's hand, unable to speak.

"Go on, now." Mary patted her hand.

Ben put his arm around Emma and led her through the lobby as Iris and Eddie followed. He stopped, then turned back and went to Mary. They stared at each other for a moment, then Ben bent down and kissed Mary on the forehead. She looked up at him, her jaw set, but a glisten in her eyes. He whispered, "She's in good hands with you. Thank you."

Mary gave him a single nod.

The sun made quick work of the morning fog and while its rays shimmered and danced on the bay, the pungent stench of burnt wood and oil lingered in the air.

The group arrived at the diner and Ben held the door for Emma and the rest of the party to enter. Once inside, Emma stood motionless. The room was packed with shopkeepers, businesspeople, and gallery owners from all of Eastport.

"Emma," Chummy, the plumber, stood and approached her. "It's a terrible thing that's happened, just terrible. But we want you to know, you don't have to face this alone. We stand with you. Whatever you need, however we can help, we're here for you. We've been talking, and as soon as you get the all-clear, we've got a clean-up crew ready to go to get you through the first stage, then we'll see what needs to be done next. You and the inn are an important part of this town. You're always taking care of the community. Now it's our turn to take care of you."

Emma looked at the faces of friends in the crowd, shaking her head. Judy, the head waitress, came and took her hand. "It's gonna be okay."

Emma nodded and gave her a hug as her tears flowed once again. One by one, the others came and hugged Emma, conveying their love for her and pledging their help.

"We've got your back."

"We'll get you through this."

"You're gonna be fine."

"We'll do this together."

Judy put her arm around Emma's shoulder. "You come sit over here now." She led Emma outside and put up the umbrella at one of the tables on the deck. "Get you some fresh air and sunshine. Just keep breathing, honey. I'll get you a coffee or would you prefer tea?"

"Hot tea would be nice, thank you," Emma managed to say.

Iris sat on one side of Emma and Ben on the other. Eddie sat across, looking like a puppy in need of his mother.

"Eddie, don't you worry. It's gonna be fine. With friends like you and everyone else here, it's gonna be fine," Emma said.

"You bet, Miss Emma. We won't let you down."

"I know you won't."

"Eddie, could you do me a favor?" Ben asked, standing, and pulling Eddie aside. He whispered something to him, Eddie nodded, then took off like a shot.

"What was that?" Emma asked as Eddie left.

"You'll see." Ben sat again and took Emma's hand.

Iris took her other hand. "Now, I'm going to explain what's going to happen next. And you, my dear, are not allowed to argue, though I don't believe you have the energy to do so. You're going to move in with me and Frank until it's safe for you to go back to the inn. I will not have you roaming the streets like a, well, you're staying with us."

"Thank you. You're right, I don't have the energy to argue. But are you sure it's all right with Frank?"

"Absolutely. He suggested it before I did. He stayed

behind this morning to rearrange some space. You'll have the whole second floor to yourself.

"Now, once you're allowed to go back to the inn, we'll concentrate on your living space. Hopefully, it will only need a good cleaning."

"Shouldn't we focus on the inn first?"

"Absolutely not. Emma, you're going to need a place where you can close the door and relax. This is going to take a while. Now, if you want to live with me and Frank for the next six months . . ."

"We'll work on the west wing first," Emma said with a smile.

"Miss Emma." Emma turned to see Dev coming through the doorway with Eddie. He walked to her and took both her hands in his. "I'm sorry this happened to you. You helped me. Now it's my turn to help you. That's how it works." He held her hands to his chest. "Anytime you wanna talk, you call me and if you wanna call and just be quiet, I'll be quiet with you."

Emma pulled him in, and hugged him, her body shaking as the tears fell.

"I love you, Miss Emma."

Emma looked at Dev, then Iris, Eddie, and Ben. "How am I so blessed with so many wonderful people in my life? I woke up this morning so sad, grief-stricken really, and now, all I feel is grateful."

CHAPTER 39

Up from the Ashes

Ben wrapped his arm around Emma. "I wish I could fix this for you." They sat together on a bench on the walkway overlooking the bay.

"This helps," Emma said, leaning into him. "Thanks for taking me out for dinner. You and Dev are good medicine."

"Well, about that. We were supposed to be back in Philly today, but—"

"Oh, I forgot. How could I forget?" Emma sat up.

"You've had a few things on your mind."

"But Dev has school. Oh, I'm so sorry I've kept you here. You're leaving tomorrow then?"

"No, I'm not, but Dev is. I've got him booked on a flight out of Bangor in the morning and the Mongellis will meet him in Philly. They'll keep him for the week, so I can stay here with you."

"No, no. You need to go. You need to be with your son."

"Dev's gonna be fine. I'm not so sure about you. I'm staying."

"I don't know what to say, except thank you."

"You don't have to say a thing." Ben caressed her hair, then wrapped his arms around her and kissed her.

"Yes, I understand. Thank you." Emma hung up the phone, pressed her lips together and rapped her fingers on the table of the booth at the WaCo Diner.

"Bad news?" Ben asked.

"Not exactly. It's just, everything's going to take so long. I've got a meeting in two days with my public adjuster and the insurance adjuster, then there's getting the report from the fire department, then finding a contractor, cleaning people . . ."

Ben took her hands and kissed them. "You can do this. You can."

"Really? I'm not so sure. It's pretty overwhelming."

"Emma, I know you can. You've done a lot of hard things in your life. This is just one more. Remember you're not alone. I'm standing with you and so is all of Eastport."

"Right. Just keep reminding me."

"Anytime." Ben squeezed her hands.

"You're going to have to stand with me from a distance, though. I can't believe the week's gone already."

"I know. I'm sorry, Em. I wish I could stay. You know, I could stretch things out for a few more days."

"No. You need to get back to Dev. And a few more days won't really help. This is going to be months and months. And you're right, I've got the whole town behind me. Everywhere I go, people tell me that. I'll be fine. Iris and Frank are here. And you know Iris, she'll keep me sane."

"Still, wish I could stay." He kissed her hands again.

"It makes me happy to hear you say that." Emma took a breath and sat back. "Iris and I talked last night. About you."

"Me?"

"Yes. With everything that's been happening, I haven't had a chance to tell her about you and I . . . well, that there's been a change in our relationship."

"I see." Ben took a deep breath. "That must have been awkward for you. I'm sorry."

"Actually, it wasn't awkward at all. You know what she said?"

"I have no idea."

"She said she wondered why we hadn't gotten together years ago."

Ben smiled. "I've wondered that a few times myself recently. So, she's fine with it?"

"More than fine. She's very happy for us. And I'm glad she knows."

"Me too."

"I heard from Mary last night."

"Now there's a bull in a china shop. She'll get things done, Emma. She reminds me of Angela, only with more attitude, if that's possible. Can't believe I'm starting to like that little gnome, but don't tell her I said so."

"She won't admit it, but she's starting to like you too."

"I think we've come to an unspoken understanding, and I'm glad you have her."

"Well, she's amazing and I love you both so much."

What did she just say?

"More coffee?" the waitress asked.

"Yes, please." Emma slid her cup over. "Mary's already contacted all our future guests and everyone who reserved the banquet hall. I was so worried. A wedding reception was scheduled for June. There's a rental place for those enormous tents–they offered to rent them to me for half the usual price. The wedding couple, that's what they want to do. Mary said we could rent the kitchen equipment and do everything outside, so we'll have some income from all that. Mostly, I wanted the bride to have a good day in the place she wanted to be. So, what do you think?"

"Uh, great. That's great." Ben took a sip of coffee. I have

no idea what you just said, but I hope it was great.

"That's what I thought too. Maybe from there we can do some other outdoor events over the summer. We still have the patio."

Outdoor events. Got it. "That's a fantastic idea, outdoor events. See, you're doing it, Em. One step at a time, you're doing it."

She is amazingly resilient. I'm so proud of her. But she didn't say what I think she said a minute ago. Did she? *She loves me?*

CHAPTER 40

Return to Eastport

"Em, I'm sorry I can't be there in person."

"It's okay. Iris and Frank, Eddie, Mary, and dozens of people from town are taking good care of me."

"Still, I should be there."

Ben returned to Philadelphia and the end of the school year rush threatened to bury him under a mountain of science projects, research papers, sports tournaments, and concerts. April ended as quickly as it begun, and before Ben could blink an eye, May was on him, trying to break all land-speed records getting to June.

During these months of chaotic activity, Ben spoke with Emma daily, listening to her, encouraging her, and praying with her. Even so, it was difficult for him to reconcile being so far away.

"I talked to Jen yesterday and she said the place is

coming along," Ben said over the phone to Emma one evening in early May.

"We're making terrific progress. I had a nice surprise today. My kids got a group call together and let me know they're all coming up. They've arranged everything and they're each going to be here for a week! Christopher will be here on Friday."

"Chris is coming? Sorry I'll miss him."

"He wanted to see you too. They all do, but they understand. The other kids will follow Chris' week, so for a month, this mama hen is going to be surrounded by her chicks!"

"I'm glad you'll have family around. I'm sure that'll help."

"Yes. And your family has been a big help too. I think there's been at least two Hudsons here every weekend."

That should be me. I should be there with her. But maybe it is better I'm here. Maybe.

"Heads up!" JJ passed the basketball to Ben, hitting him squarely in the stomach.

Ben grimaced.

"Hey, what's with you?" JJ said.

"Eh, got stuff on my mind." Ben passed the ball back to JJ. "My realtor called last night, and my tenant gave notice. She said the house is going to need some attention before it can be rented again."

JJ took a shot at the rim. "Okay, so what's the problem? Can't she hire someone for you?"

"Yeah, she can, but if I do the work myself, I could save a lot of money. As an extra benefit, I'd be available to help Emma with the inn."

"Sounds like a good idea."

"Maybe, but to be any real help to Emma, I think I'd need to spend the whole summer in Eastport. Can I do that? What about Dev? Can I take him away from Philly for the entire summer? Is that fair to him? He'd have to give up a summer course on writing. And what about Chase? Is it right to separate the two of them? You were right, JJ, this parenting stuff ain't easy."

JJ grinned at his friend. "You're gonna make yourself crazy if you keep this up. The answer's simple."

"Okay, what is it then?"

"Ask Dev. That's the only way you're gonna know how he feels. Let him tell you what he wants to do, then go from there. You're still the parent and you get to make the decision, but at least you'll know how he feels about it. And knowing Dev, he'll probably surprise you."

"Are you kidding? The whole summer?" Dev said, his blue eyes shining.

"Yes, the whole summer. There's a lot to do in the house, and if I do it myself, I can save a lot of money, but it'll take a while. Plus, I thought I could help Emma with the inn."

"I can help, too!"

"Glad to hear it. I was counting on you."

"And I can help Eddie with landscaping. He said he'd hire me, if I wanted to work when I was there."

"Well, let's not get too carried away. You're only eleven and there are laws about child labor. You don't want to get me arrested, do you?"

"Not yet," Dev said with a grin. "Okay, but I can help you, right? And Miss Emma?"

"Absolutely, and I'll even give you a raise in your allowance. You sure you don't mind going? I know you'll miss hanging out with Chase, and I'm sorry, but you'll miss the writing course, too."

"Maybe Miss Iris will help me with writing. And Chase . . . do you think he could come visit?"

"Sure he can. Maybe we can convince the whole Mongelli tribe to come."

Dev jumped up. "Okay, I'll go pack."

"What's with you and packing so soon for every trip? We've got two weeks before we can leave. You have to finish school, remember?"

"I know. But I want to get organized, so I don't forget anything. Maine..." Dev muttered to himself as he headed up the stairs to his room. Ben could hear something about kayaking, moose, and eagles... and Emma.

The day after school let out, Ben and Dev were on the road again to Eastport. As they had the summer before, they overnighted in Portsmouth, New Hampshire, then spent the next night in Bangor for a visit with Oliver and Vanessa. The following day they went straight to Ben's home.

Ben opened the door and stood in the center of his living room. *Has it really been over a year since I left this place? Thought I was leaving forever. Feels weird being back. House looks the same, but something's not right.*

He did an inventory of the downstairs. *Definitely needs work. Rooms need painting, should replace the rugs. Hardwood floors could use some maintenance too. And the kitchen looks the worse for wear. Not sure a summer's going to be enough.*

Dev walked into the house, carrying his bags. He dropped them against the wall and walked in a circle. "So this is it, huh? This is where you lived?"

"This is it. Home, sweet home. Not much, but I liked it."

"I think it's great."

Ben grinned at the enthusiasm of his son.

"Where's my room gonna be?" Dev picked up his bags.

"Top of the stairs, to your right, just like home."

Dev ran up the stairs. A moment later he yelled down, "Dad, I can see the bay from my window!"

Glad he's excited. That's a relief.

Dev flew down the stairs and fell into Ben. "This is gonna be a wicked awesome summer!"

Ben caught his son. "Whoa, partner! Be careful. Wicked awesome, huh? You're sounding like a Downeaster already."

Dev grinned.

Ben walked to the front door and looked out. "Would you mind hanging out here on your own for a while? I thought I'd take a walk."

"Going to the inn to see Miss Emma?"

Ben turned to Dev. "Mebbe."

"It's okay. I want to see her too, but I'll wait my turn. You go first. You know, age before beauty."

"Oh, your chore list just got longer, mister. I'll be back soon. Don't blow up the house." Ben went out the front door, and Dev followed.

"Hey, Dad, be sure to say something nice!"

"Yes, Guru."

Ben wasn't sure what he'd find once he got there, but the

sound of hammers and the smell of freshly cut wood as he approached his destination were encouraging. He arrived at the inn and stood across the street to take in the full view.

When he stood in this very spot in April, the day he left to return to Philadelphia, gray ash covered the formerly white inn like a worn-out woolen blanket. The left side of the roof collapsed in on itself, revealing charred beams and blackened wood. The damaged beams and wood were gone now, a sturdy structure took their place. The newly installed roof hugged the building in a protective embrace.

That is an amazing amount of work done for this short time.

Ben crossed the street and stepped into the lobby. At first, he found it eerily quiet, then as if someone threw a power switch, he could hear sounds of a circular saw and hammering. He assumed it was coming from the kitchen area where the bulk of the work needed to be done. Most of the damage to the lobby had been cosmetic. The tables and chairs were gone. The front desk and the curved staircase, architectural features the inn was famous for, were spared any permanent damage, but looked like they needed restoration. Ben went to the fireplace.

"Lookin' good, Harry." He smiled at the portrait hanging above the mantle, freshly cleaned. "And, hey, I hope you're okay with me and–"

"Sheriff." Mary walked out of Emma's office.

"Mary."

"Office." Mary pointed her head toward Emma's office. Ben gave Mary a nod and walked behind the front desk.

"Got any room in the inn for a weary traveler?" Ben said as he popped his head around the corner of Emma's door.

"Ben?" Emma's eyes welled up.

"Em? I'm sorry. I didn't mean to upset you." Ben went to her and knelt by her side. She looked at him, unable to speak. She reached out and held his face.

"It's me. I'm here. I didn't mean to make you cry. I never want to make you cry." He kissed her on the cheek, tasting the saltiness of her tears, then made his way to her lips.

When they parted, Emma smiled and caught her breath. "Oh my, you sure know how to surprise a girl."

"You okay?" He gently stroked her hair.

"Yes, it's just . . . It's been so long since you've popped your head around the corner like that I forgot how much I missed it."

She stood up, and Ben stood with her. She embraced him, resting her head on his chest.

I forgot how much I missed having her in my arms. And how well she fits there. He breathed her in, and the sensation made his head spin. He combed his fingers through her hair, tilted her head up, and kissed her again.

"Emma, I've missed you."

"Good. I'm not alone then. I've missed you, too." Emma wrapped her arms around Ben's neck and stroked the back of his hair. "Why didn't you tell me you were coming?"

"I wanted it to be a surprise. I thought maybe it would cheer you up. I'm sorry, it seemed to have the opposite effect."

"Oh, no, it didn't. I thought I was imagining you. I'm so glad you're here." She rested her head on his chest again. "So, what brought you back?"

"Besides you? My tenant moved out and there's some work that needs to be done at the house before it can be rented again."

Emma looked up at him. "So, you're here to arrange that?"

"Actually, it's all arranged. Dev and I are going to do it."

"Dev? He's with you? Where?"

"He's at the house. He's anxious to see you."

"Oh, and I'm anxious to see him. I've missed that boy."

"Well, you two will have plenty of time to spend together. We'll be here all summer."

"The entire summer?" Emma's eyes lit up like fireflies on a summer's night.

"Yes, the entire summer. There's a lot of work to be done on the house, but more importantly, we want to help you. Whatever you need us to do. We're yours. So, what can I do?"

"Well, you can start by kissing me again," she said with a

blush to her cheek. "I've missed you so."

Ben pulled her close, and kissed her neck, inhaling a delicate scent of flowers combined with the unmistakable fragrance of vanilla, as if she'd spent the morning baking a floral cake. He studied her eyes and Emma looked at him in return as if she were trying to memorize every line and feature of his face. Ben tipped her chin with his hand and pressed his lips into hers. Emma wrapped her arms around his neck and returned his kiss.

"Sheriff Ben, is that you?" Eddie burst into Emma's office.

Ben released Emma and spun toward to Eddie. "Eddie, how you doin', my man?"

"I'm great. Miss Emma, I finished up the banquet room. I'm gonna head out, if that's okay with you."

"That's fine, Eddie. I'll talk to you later. Thank you," Emma said, her face flushed.

"I gotta go, but hope I'll see you around, Sheriff Ben. Dev with you?"

"Yeah, he is."

"I'd like to check on my little brother sometime, if that's all right."

"He'd love that. We're staying at my house for the summer, so you come on over whenever."

"Okay, sounds good. Gotta go. Talk to you later."

Ben turned back to Emma. "I should go too. I left Dev to

his own devices, which means all the bathrooms will be spotless by the time I get back. Say, maybe I should stay longer."

Emma laughed and pushed Ben toward the door of her office. "I think it's best you go." Then wrapping her arm in his, she said, "But don't stay away long."

Ben's heart skipped a beat, and he kissed her again. "How about dinner tonight? I'll grab some takeout and you can catch us up."

"Sounds wonderful."

"I'll pick you up at five. See you then." He kissed her on the bridge of her nose and reluctantly left the inn.

"Miss Emma!" Dev rushed to Emma and threw his arms around her as she walked in the door of Ben's home.

"Dev, it's so good to see you. I've missed you!" Emma returned Dev's hug.

"I missed you too. Here, come sit here." Dev took Emma by the hand and led her to the dining room. He pulled out a chair for her.

Over dinner, Emma shared all that had taken place over the past few months. "You wouldn't believe it. I can hardly believe it myself, and I've been witness to it every day. Ever since the fire, and I mean literally, every day someone has stopped by or called or emailed me with offers of material, and workmen, and well, whatever else I've needed. It's been amazing. And not just people from Eastport and Perry. Word got around somehow, and I've had offers of help from people in Machias, and Calais, Lubec, and even Canada!

"And here's the best part—I knew it was time to do some renovations, but I've been putting it off. I didn't have the heart to make some necessary changes, but now, well, I guess I don't have a choice."

"That doesn't sound like the best part," Dev said.

"I guess it's not, but what *is* the best part is Harry and I always saved for future needs, and we had a special fund for renovations, so I've got a nice sum put aside. In all the chaos, I forgot about it. So, besides the money I'll receive from insurance, I've also got money to cover expenses for the time we're closed. Enough to keep paying Mary and the rest of the staff. They don't have to go looking elsewhere for work and I won't lose them. They've all come in almost every day, helping to do whatever. You should see Joseph, who, by the way, doesn't mind me calling him Joey while we're going through construction. Who knew he was great with a hammer?"

"That's awesome, Em. I'm sure it's a relief to see things progressing so well," Ben said.

"It is. Even the art museum people and some of the gallery owners have offered their help. There's someone who specializes in the restoration of furniture, and he's going to come and redo the front desk and the staircase. He said he'll have them looking good as new. And someone else already cleaned and restored Harry's portrait. Don't know if you noticed it."

"I did. He looks great. He looks like he's pleased with how everything's coming along."

"I hope so. This was his dream, you know. I'm just the caretaker."

"Not anymore, Em. This is your dream now."

Emma smiled and nodded.

"What can we do? We wanna help too," Dev said.

Emma took Dev and Ben's hands. "You two can do something for me no one else can do."

"What's that?" Dev asked.

"You're doing it right now." Emma squeezed their hands, then let go, and wiped away a tear. Dev got up from his seat and hugged Emma. She held him and allowed more tears to flow.

"It's gonna be okay, Miss Emma. It's gonna be okay. We're here now. We'll carry you."

CHAPTER 41

Summertime

What time is it? Two in the morning? Why in the world am I awake? Ben rolled over. After a moment, he sat up with a start.

"I'm forgetting something . . . what though?" He got out of bed and went downstairs. Doors are locked. Windows are closed. It's nothing. Go back to bed. Probably just a weird dream. But why do I feel like there's something I need to take care of?

He went back upstairs, laid down on the bed and listened to the Cherry Island foghorn sounding its rhythmic tune before finally returning to sleep.

As Emma handled contractors at the inn, Ben and Dev got busy in his home. Dev couldn't wait for "Demo Day" when he and Ben would take down the wall between the kitchen and the dining room.

"Too bad Chase isn't here. He would have loved knockin' down a wall," Dev said.

"Probably would have been hard to get him to stop there," Ben laughed.

"Dev, I was thinking. The Fourth of July is almost here, and we've gotten a lot done on the house. I think we should take a few days off for Old Home Week."

"What's that?"

"It's how Eastport celebrates Independence Day. It starts with Canada Day on the first and keeps going for the rest of the week. There's a lot to do, you'll love it."

"Maybe Miss Emma could take some time off too."

"We think alike, young *padawan*. Let's go ask her." Ben and Dev walked to the inn and found Emma in the lobby.

"Emma, we think it's time you had some fun," Ben said.

"Yeah, Miss Emma. Dad's been telling me about Old Home Week. Do you think you could stop working on the inn for a few days? We could do stuff together, the three of us."

"I don't know, there's so much to do here," Emma said. She walked behind the front desk and pulled out a box from underneath the counter. "I really shouldn't leave." She took a book from the counter and placed it in the box. She picked up another book.

Dev joined her behind the desk. "Please?"

"Em, you've been working hard. It's time to take a break." Ben went behind the desk and took the book from her hand and placed it in the box. "The inn will be fine, and we'll be close by. Nothing will happen."

Emma surveyed the lobby, looked at Ben, then at Dev. "You Hudson men are difficult to say no to."

"So . . .," Ben said, taking her hand.

"Say yes, Miss Emma." Dev took her other hand.

Emma smiled. "I guess a few days off wouldn't hurt. And you're right, it's time we had some fun. So, yes. Yes!"

That night over dinner, Emma and Ben shared more stories about Old Home Week.

"Why do they call it Old Home Week?" Dev asked.

"Well, this is a time when families come back to Eastport for get-togethers and class reunions, so basically, everyone's returning to their 'old home'," Emma said. "There's all sorts of events throughout the week. It's a lot of fun."

"You think the town is busy now? Just wait. By the Fourth, everyone's packed in like sardines," Ben said.

"We'll have to go to the library for the frisbee and limbo contests. You can do those, Dev," Emma said.

"Oh, and don't forget the strawberry shortcake there on the third. And the blueberry pancake breakfast at the airport," Ben said licking his lips.

"And you like dogs, Dev. There's a pet show where people dress up their pets, mostly dogs. It's pretty funny," Emma said.

"Then there's the fireman's muster," Ben said.

"What's fireman's mustard? Do they sell that at Raye's Mustard Shop? Is it spicy?" Dev asked.

Emma laughed. "No, it's not mustard, it's *muster*. Muster means coming together, like for a battle. The fireman's muster is a competition between different fire companies in the area. The Navy sailors even join in."

"Navy sailors?" Dev said.

"Yes. That's my favorite part of the week," Ben said. "Seeing a naval ship come into port. It's an impressive sight and they've been doing it for decades. The sailors join in a lot of the events around town, and they even march in the parade on the Fourth."

"They're very handsome in their dress whites," Emma said. Ben tilted his head at her, and she gave him a playful wink.

"Then of course, there's the annual codfish relay race," Ben said.

"A codfish race? They race codfish?" Dev eyed Ben. "You know, Dad, your stories need to get better. Maybe you should get Mr. Mongelli to give you some lessons."

A Good Place to Turn Around

"I'm serious. There's a codfish race. It's a relay race. Been going for years. People form teams and they race carrying a codfish."

"That's crazy!" Dev laughed. "I wanna do it."

"You'll need to make a team," Emma said.

"Can we be a team, Dad?"

"Uh, I guess so. I mean, why not? I've watched these races for years. It might be fun to be in one for a change. We need four people though."

"Well, there would be you and me . . . and Miss Emma?"

"No, thank you. I'm happy to cook a cod, but I will not be racing with one. I've seen those things by the end of the race. Ewww."

"Okay . . . I bet Eddie would do it. And maybe his dad. We could be a father-son team! I'm gonna call him." Dev got up from the table.

"You do that," Ben said.

"Oh, this is going to be fun," Emma said, squeezing Ben's hand.

Ben, Emma, and Dev made the most of Old Home Week, joining in the many activities spread throughout Eastport. On the day of the codfish race, for the first time in thirty-three years, Ben found himself in the middle of it, instead of on the sidelines cheering and working crowd control. The father-son team placed a respectable third, but for Ben, it might as well have been first.

On the Fourth, after a day of flag-raising, parades, and barbequing, Emma, Ben, and Dev prepared for fireworks over the bay. The trio put a blanket out on the back lawn of the inn, and as the fireworks lit up the sky, Dev laid his head on Emma's lap. She stroked his hair, and in no time, he was sound asleep. She looked over at Ben in disbelief.

"He does that sometimes," Ben whispered and patted his son on the back, then leaned over and kissed Emma.

Ben made great progress on his house throughout July, with Emma offering her design help. He admired her sense of style, and she brought out Dev's artistic side as they picked out colors, textures, and patterns together. Dev and Ben, in turn, helped Emma at the inn with smaller projects, particularly focusing on Emma's west wing. During the second week of July, they helped move Emma back into the inn and, to celebrate, Dev brought her a special gift.

"Miss Emma, this is for you. I've been working on it for a while." Dev handed Emma a box wrapped in pink paper, with a blue hydrangea for a bow.

"I hate to open this. It's so beautiful."

"Oh, you're gonna want to open it," Ben said with a grin.

A Good Place to Turn Around

Emma smiled at Dev, and removed the hydrangea, then slowly unwrapped the box. She lifted the lid, then let out a gasp as she held her hand to her mouth. Her hands shook, and tears flowed, as she lifted a framed pencil sketch of the inn prior to the fire, signed and dated by the artist, Dev.

Dev went to her and held her hand. Ben sat beside her and wrapped his arm around her. "It'll be like this again, but until then, Dev wanted you to have this to remember."

Emma wiped her eyes, then kissed Dev on the forehead, still unable to speak. Dev smiled and nodded. "I love you, too."

By the end of the month, Ben's house no longer looked old and tired, and it no longer felt empty. His home had a new lease on life, and Ben wanted to feel the same way about himself, but didn't. For months, he had been carrying with him a sense of foreboding.

It started innocently enough, waking once in the middle of the night when he and Dev first arrived in Eastport for the summer. Over the next few weeks, these midnight wake-up calls became more frequent and unlike the usual bad dreams or nightmares, in the light of day, the feelings they aroused remained. Thoughts of impending doom rattled around in his mind, distracting him like too much change in his pocket, something too noisy and too heavy to ignore. He shared these feelings with no one, not even Emma.

"Emma, everything all right? You sound flustered." Ben said, answering Emma's call late one evening.

"Everything's great! It's more than great! I just got off the phone with the contractor. He says they're a month ahead of schedule! Can you believe it? An entire month. He said the help he's gotten from the community and from all of us has put him way ahead and under budget. He's sure he'll be finished and handing me the keys by the end of August. Isn't that incredible?"

"Fantastic! I'm so happy for you. You've done an amazing job, Em."

"Wish I could take credit, but you know as well as I, this had very little to do with me, and everything to do with God and His provision and with everyone else in the community, and especially you and Dev."

"Well, I still think you're amazing." Ben gripped the phone. "Em, I–."

"Yes?"

"I, uh, I can't wait to see you. Breakfast tomorrow?"

"Breakfast would be great. See you in the morning. 'Night."

"G'night." Ben hung up the phone and sat up in his chair.

Why is it so hard for me to tell Emma how I feel about her? Why won't the words come?

CHAPTER 42

Moonlight and Mayhem

There was a time when Ben enjoyed August. The long summer days and kayaking on Boyden Lake spoke peace and harmony into his soul. Not so this year. This year August represented separation, and longing, and anything but peace.

"Dad, I wanna invite Miss Emma over for dinner on our last night here."

"I was thinking the same thing. Maybe we should go out somewhere though."

"No, I wanna make dinner for us. I'll make it special, I promise."

"No explosions of flour? We won't have that kind of time for clean up."

Dev smiled. "No explosions of flour, cross my heart."

"All right, knucklehead, the kitchen is yours."

"I think it's sweet of Dev to make dinner for the three of us," Emma said as Ben walked her to his place.

"He's really excited about it," Ben said. "He insisted I leave the house this morning and I was instructed not to come home at all until it was time. I got a very stern warning not to cheat and come home early."

"What did you do all day?"

"Mostly I stayed at the station house, spent a little time at the diner, then I walked around town."

"You could have come to the inn."

"I know. I didn't want to bother you."

"Since when are you a bother?"

Ben looked down.

"Never mind. I understand." Emma squeezed his hand.

They reached Ben's house and when they stepped inside, they stood frozen in the foyer. Soft music, glowing candles, and twinkle lights strung about the living room greeted them. The dining room table was set for three with fine china and crystal glasses. A savory aroma wafted from the kitchen to the dining room, to the senses of two adults who could not fathom how an eleven-year-old boy could create something so captivating.

Dev came out of the kitchen, wearing a white shirt, navy pants, and Harry's tie. He went to Emma and brought out a single red rose from behind his back, handing it to her with a smile. He offered her his arm and said, "This way, please."

A Good Place to Turn Around

Emma took Dev's arm, and he escorted her and Ben to the dining room. He indicated Ben should sit at the head of the table, then he pulled out the chair at the foot of the table for Emma. She sat with a look that said she didn't know whether to laugh or to cry.

"One moment, please," Dev said, then disappeared into the kitchen. He returned with two bottles, a red cabernet and sparkling apple cider. He placed them by Ben's plate and said, "Would you do the honors, Dad?" He handed him a bottle opener. Ben nodded, unable to speak, and poured wine for Emma and himself, and a glass of sparkling cider for Dev.

Dev exited and returned three times, once bringing in a serving bowl of spaghetti, once a tureen of red clam sauce and last, a basket of Italian bread. When he was satisfied everything was placed as it should be, he sat down and smiled at Emma, then at his father. He folded his hands and bowed his head. They followed suit.

"God, thank you for this meal and for the friends that helped me make it. Thank you for Eastport and that Dad and I could spend the whole summer here. Thank you for fixing the inn and thank you for Dad and for Miss Emma. I love them both. Amen."

Emma lifted her napkin to her eyes. Even Ben had to whisk away a tear.

"Dev, what you've done here, this is really special. Thank

you," Ben said. He stood up and went to his son and kissed him on the head.

"Miss Emma, you okay?"

Emma smiled through her tears. "Yes. Dev, your father's right, this is very special. I'll carry this night with me for a very long time. Thank you."

Dev went to Emma and wrapped his arms around her neck, then kissed her on the cheek, bringing on another round of tears.

She took a sip of wine. "I promised myself I wasn't going to cry my way through the entire evening, so let's be happy. We're together now, let's concentrate on that."

"Right," Ben said. "Looks like you worked hard, son. Let's enjoy it."

The spaghetti and sauce were passed around and once everyone was served, Dev watched as Ben and Emma took their first taste.

"This sauce is wonderful. You are an amazing chef." Emma said after her first bite.

"She's right, bud. This is great. How'd you know how to do all this?"

"Well, the spaghetti was easy. I helped my mom make it lots of times. Don't tell Mrs. Mongelli, but I bought the sauce," he whispered. "She offered to help me, but it sounded too complicated, so I went to that fancy restaurant in town and told them what I needed. They were super nice. They said they don't usually sell just the sauce, but since it was for you, Miss Emma, they sold it to me special."

"That was generous of them." Emma said.

"But what about the rest? We don't have any china, or twinkle lights, or candles. And how did you get wine? I'm not gonna get arrested, am I?" Ben narrowed his eyes at Dev.

Dev laughed. "Not this time."

"So where did it all come from?" Ben said.

"You won't believe me if I tell you."

"Try me," Ben said.

Dev looked at Ben with a grin, then he looked at Emma. "Eddie . . . and Miss Mary."

"Eddie?" Emma said.

"And Mary?" Ben finished.

"Mm-hmm. I told them what I wanted to do, and they helped. Eddie said he was good with twinkle lights, and his mom had lots of candles. Miss Mary helped with the china, and the glasses, and the tablecloth, and the wine. She showed me how to set everything right."

"The gnome . . . has china?" That brought a laugh to Emma and to Dev.

"That was very kind of them both. I'll be sure to thank them tomorrow," Emma said.

"Send them my thanks too, would you?"

"Of course, but I'll leave out the gnome part." Emma said with a wink to Ben.

Though they tried to keep the mood light, none of the three could ignore the fact that in the morning, they would be parted. And none of the three knew for how long. But all three sensed the pain separation would bring. By dessert, their hearts were so heavy it was impossible to pretend otherwise.

Without a word, Dev got up and cleared the uneaten dessert from the table. He came back to the room and stood before Emma with tears in his eyes. Emma leaned over and drew Dev into her arms. He clung to her as he had that terrible night on the patio of the inn. With one last hug, Emma whispered to Dev, "I love you. Be good. Watch after your father." She stood, wiped her tears, then went out the front door with Ben.

Ben took Emma's hand as they began a wordless walk back to the inn. They reached their destination, but instead of going to the entryway, Ben turned and took the path by the bay. Emma made no sound or motion of objection and instead, entwined her fingers with Ben's.

They walked the full length of the path, then turned back. A quiet bench underneath a lamplight called to them. Ben looked at Emma, nodded to the bench and she nodded in return. They sat, Ben put his arm around her, and she nestled her head against his shoulder. Sea rose bushes lined the pathway and their sweet scent of comfort was carried to the couple on a soft evening breeze. Even the tide seemed to understand the solemnity of the moment, rocking the buoy in the harbor with waves so gentle its bell could scarcely be heard.

"I'm sorry, Em." Ben broke the silence.

"Sorry? Sorry for what?"

"Sorry we have to leave. Sorry summer is so short. Sorry Philadelphia is so far away."

"Yes, me too." She leaned into him. "Wish we could stay like this." Ben held Emma but he looked away.

I know what I should be saying. I just can't say it.

The foghorn from Cherry Island lighthouse sounded across the bay. Its call sent a shudder down Ben's spine. *It's like the whole bay is in mourning. Or sitting in judgment of me. And I can't blame it. I'd judge me too.*

Emma picked up Ben's hand and examined it. "You know, this is one of my favorite features of yours."

"These old beat-up hands?"

"Mm-hmm. They're workingman's hands. They're not afraid to get in there and do what needs to be done. They're strong, and yet, they can be so gentle. And when they're wrapped around me, I feel safe, like I'm home." She kissed his hands, then looked up at him. "I love you, Ben."

He froze. Darkness seized him. Then a searing light, an image of Claire, his first love, passed by in a whirlwind. Their first kiss. Dates on the lake. His proposal. Her back as she left him.

Years of loneliness swept by in a moment. Then a cat in a tree. Iris. That red hair. Love. Another proposal. Acceptance, then heartbreak.

He felt sick.

The images stopped. He was back on the bench, staring at the bay. He pulled away from Emma.

"Ben, are you all right? What's happening?"

"Yeah, yeah. I'm fine." He stood up and paced, his breath increased in tempo.

"You don't look all right." Emma approached him and he stepped back.

"Ah, I think I should take you home now. I need to get back. Dev's waiting. We've got an early day tomorrow." Ben's heart was pounding in his ears. He took Emma by the hand and walked her quickly back to the inn. When they got to the front door, he stopped.

"Do you want to come in for a minute? Have a drink of water or something?"

"No. I-uh, I should go. Emma, this summer . . ." Ben looked up at the night sky. "Goodbye." He kissed her on the cheek, then turned and ran, leaving her standing alone.

CHAPTER 43

A Good Place to Turn Around

When he got home, Ben checked on Dev. Already in bed. Sound asleep. Good. He went to the kitchen, circling it like a caged animal. He rubbed his forehead, then stared at his shaking hands.

What is wrong with me? Drink of water, yeah.

He took out a cup from the cabinet. It slipped from his hand, dropped to the floor, and exploded sending shards of glass sliding from the kitchen to the dining room. He pounded the sink. He wanted to scream, but instead, he flew out the back door and slammed it behind him.

He patrolled the yard, mumbling to himself. Every deep-seated emotion he pushed down for years, every fearful midnight thought he had surfaced like the rip current that pulled Dev out to sea. He was drowning on dry land, gasping for air, reaching out for hands that refused to come in rescue.

He stopped. His eyes darkened. His entire body shook with pent-up fury as he looked up at heaven with contempt.

"It wasn't enough I had to lose Claire. And then lose Iris. But now this? This? You give me a summer with this incredible woman I've known practically my whole stinking life, and never knew . . ." Ben clenched his teeth together.

"And now. *She loves me.*" He beat his fist on his chest. "*Me!* What a joke! And what do I do?" He laughed a sardonic laugh. "I leave. Once more, I leave the woman I—" Ben turned and pounded his fist into a tree, bloodying his knuckles.

"I can't even say it. Not to her. Not to You." He pressed the palms of his hands into his forehead.

"What is the point? What in the world are You trying to teach me? Is this a test to see how much I can take? Well, this is it. I've had enough. I surrender. You win." Ben stood still, his face twisted in anger, rage still coursing through his veins.

"I get it. I'm not meant to have the love of a good woman. I get it! What was I thinking? That Emma would love me enough to leave Eastport? Emma can't leave here. She's part of its make-up, it's part of her. She could no more leave here to be with me than Dev could leave Philadelphia. And how could I ask him to leave there? It's all he knows. It's where the only family he ever had, and still has, is. Chase, the Mongellis, they're his home. I couldn't ask him to leave them.

"It's enough I have Dev. That should be enough. And if

it's a choice between his happiness and mine, I'm picking his every time. *Every time!*" Ben circled the yard. "I'm going back to Philly. That's the end of it. I'll say goodbye to Emma. She'll hate me. She'll have every right to. And I'll never come back here. Ever. And one more thing—I will never make this mistake again. It's too late for me. You've shown me that. Thanks a lot."

Ben stood alone in the center of his yard. His body still shaking, hot tears stinging his eyes. He wiped his face, then stormed back to the house.

Dev was in the kitchen, sweeping up the broken glass. "I heard something break. I got it." Ben nodded at his son, afraid to speak for fear of what he might say.

"Dad, your hand."

Ben looked down at his bloody knuckles. He scowled. "It's fine. Go to bed."

Ben went upstairs, rinsed off his hand and wrapped it in a towel. He lay on his bed and fell asleep fully clothed.

Morning came too soon, and Ben rolled out of bed. Couldn't even bother to get undressed? Too much trouble for you? Well, you're good at that. Avoiding trouble.

He saw his Bible on the nightstand. Not today. I have nothing to say to You. And I don't want to hear what You have to say to me.

He threw water on his face, washed the dried blood off his hand, bandaged it, then went downstairs. Already up, Dev poured a bowl of cereal for himself and one for Ben.

Ben tipped his chin at Dev, still unwilling to speak. He ate half the bowl of cereal, then threw the rest in the trash. Dev watched his father as he finished his breakfast, then did the dishes as Ben remained stewing in silence at the table. When the dishes were done, Ben said, "Let's get the truck packed. It's time to go."

Ben went upstairs to his room. He picked up the last of his clothes, jammed them into his duffle bag and zipped it up. As he picked up the bag, the zipper separated, and his clothes erupted onto the floor. "Great."

He heaved a heavy sigh, picked up his clothes and stuffed them back in the duffle. He managed to get the bag to zip, but while carrying it down the stairs, the zipper separated again, and the contents spilled out. He slipped on them and fell down the last four steps.

"For cryin' out loud." Ben grabbed his clothes and shoved them in the duffle bag. "Stay closed this time, or it's the trash heap for you."

"Who you talkin' to?" Dev asked as he came into the living room with his own duffle bag.

"My duffle," Ben snapped.

"Huh?"

Ben glared at Dev. "You have all your stuff together?"

"Yes, all except my books."

"Well, get them and put them in the truck. We have to go, Dev." He checked the zipper on his duffle.

"Okay." Dev stared at his father.

"Now!"

Dev shuddered then rushed out of the room.

Ben put the last of his things in the truck, then went through the house, gathering the trash and making sure lights were turned off. He took his keys off the keyholder in the kitchen and they slipped from his hand. He bent over to pick them up. As he stood, he banged his head on a cabinet door that had come open. He slammed the door causing one hinge to come loose.

"Stupid—"

Dev walked into the kitchen and saw his father rubbing his head. "You okay?"

"I'm fine. Is your stuff in the truck?"

"Yes."

"All of it? Cause we're not coming back here."

"Yes, it's all there."

"Good. Let's quit playing around and get outta here."

Dev hustled to the truck and got inside. Ben opened the driver side door and caught his pants pocket on the handle, ripping a two-inch gash in his pants. He slammed his fist on the truck.

"Son of a—"

Just as he was about to use language he'd almost forgotten he knew, he saw Dev through the windshield. The boy stared at him with the look of a son who did not recognize his father.

What are you doing? You're scaring him.

Ben closed his eyes and took a few deep breaths. He walked over to Dev's side of the truck and opened the door. "Son, I owe you an apology. I'm sorry."

"It's okay, Dad."

"No. No, it's not okay. I've had a rough morning and I've been taking it out on you. You don't deserve that, and I'm very sorry. Really. Please forgive me."

"I forgive you. We all have bad days. This is a hard one. For me, too." Dev hugged his father.

"I don't know what I'd do without you, buddy." Ben wrapped his arms around his son, and swallowed his tears and the bitterness that went with them. "You're so much more than I deserve."

Ben returned to the driver's seat, put the truck in gear, and made his way out of Eastport. As they reached the town line, he pulled over just as he did a year ago. He looked back and found it hard to believe his heart was even heavier this year. He returned to his seat, and headed south, grateful his truck knew the way.

This being the end of summer, construction crews were

A Good Place to Turn Around

in a race with the weather to complete road improvement projects. A never-ending maze of orange and white construction barrels slowed traffic and quickened tempers along the highway.

"We've been at this for over two hours, and we haven't even gotten to Bangor." Ben stared at the line of cars on the highway. "I've had enough." He exited off Route Nine.

"I'm sure I can figure out a back way that's faster than this," Ben said.

Dev nodded in agreement.

Ben made the first right he could, but it was not a thru-street. It was a dead-end that fed into a bowling alley.

"Great."

He made a U-turn and got back on the main highway then made the next right. This road was a loop road around an apartment complex.

"Fantastic." He banged his hand on the wheel.

Back to the main highway once more. Ben made a third attempt, and this time, the road seemed to travel in the direction he wanted, but a mile later, he was once again staring at a dead-end. Ben stopped the truck and turned off the engine.

"This isn't right," Ben said.

"Yup. There's no more road here," Dev said looking around.

"I don't mean that," Ben said softly.

"Dad . . . are you okay?"

"Yes. Why does everyone—?" Ben stopped mid-sentence and looked at his son. "Actually, no. No, I'm not okay."

"What's wrong?"

How can I tell him what's wrong? I hardly know myself.

"Dad?"

Ben took a deep breath. "You know, before I adopted you, I was worried. I was worried I wouldn't be a good enough father for you. I was worried I'd mess things up. I told Emma and you know what she said?"

"Something good, I bet."

Ben smiled. "Yes, you're right. It was something good. She said you didn't need a perfect dad, you needed an honest one."

"So, you gonna be honest with me? You gonna tell me why you're so angry today?"

Ben paused. "I was angry at God. As a matter of fact, we had a fight last night, although it was pretty one-sided. He let me have my say, though."

"Is that how you got a bloody hand? You punched God?"

"No, I'm not that stupid. But I am embarrassed to say I yelled at Him."

"Why? Why'd you do that?"

"Maybe because I am stupid after all." Ben sighed. "And frustrated. And angry at myself . . . and scared."

"Scared? Why?"

"Because . . ." Ben clenched his jaw.

Dev scooted closer to Ben. "Because we're going back to Philadelphia and leaving Miss Emma behind, and you love her. You're scared to say it, but you love her. I know you do. I can tell.

"'Loving someone is the best and scariest thing in the world.' That's what my mom used to say. I asked her why it was scary, and she said, 'Because if the person doesn't love you back, it can leave a hole in your heart.'

"You're afraid to get another hole, so you didn't tell Miss Emma you love her, and you yelled at God instead."

Ben sighed. "That's about the size of it." *About time I admit it.*

Dev nodded. "I guess you need to pent then."

"I need to what?" Ben asked with a tilt of his head.

"*Pent.* You know, like Pastor Steve always says. When we do something wrong like yell at God, we need to pent."

"I think you mean 'repent', son."

"Did you do it once already?"

"No."

"Then how can you *re*-pent if you haven't pented yet?"

Ben smiled. "Repent is a word all its own. It means you're so sorry about something you've done, something that doesn't please God, that you alter your behavior. You change your mind, turn around, and go in another direction, so you don't do that behavior again."

A slow smile crept across Dev's face. He raised his eyebrows and pointed his head toward the road that led to nowhere.

Ben followed his son's gaze. He nodded, then closed his eyes and bowed his head. Dev closed his eyes too and whispered a prayer for his father.

A moment later, Ben opened his eyes. A peacefulness he hadn't felt in years washed over his body, and air returned to his lungs. He had been rescued from drowning after all. Father and son sat in stillness together, each thinking and continuing to pray silent prayers.

Minutes passed then Ben got out and paced in front of the truck. Dev watched, then joined him outside.

"Dev, what would you think if we went back to Eastport? For good? I know it'd be a sacrifice to leave your family–Chase and the rest of the Mongellis, but what would you say about starting a new life there?"

"I'd say–you're my family." He looked at the road. "And a dead-end street's a good place to turn around."

Ben tousled Dev's hair. "Go get buckled." Ben started the engine, spun the truck around, and headed back to Eastport.

He drove directly to the inn. When they arrived, Ben left Dev in the truck and ran to the entrance. He stared at the door for a moment, trying to corral the wild herd of emotions inside him. He took a deep breath, whispered, "Help me, Jesus," then opened the door.

His heart stopped when he saw Emma. She was near the fireplace, her back to him, straightening the magazines on the coffee table. Humming, she went from table to table, patting a flower here, tucking a chair in there, moving from place to place making sure her new world was just as it should be. There was a softness about her. The quiet calm returned.

She *is* enchanting.

Emma stopped what she was doing and looked up. "Ben? What are you doing here? You left hours ago. Is everything all right? Where's Dev?"

"He's, uh, he's in the truck," he pointed with his thumb. "And no, everything's not all right."

"What's wrong? You seemed so odd last night. I've been worried."

"I know. I'm sorry. I was a bit out of sorts. Can you . . . will you forgive me?"

"Of course. But why are you back here? You should have been near Portland by now."

"I realized I left something behind. Something important." He walked toward her.

"Oh, I'm sorry. What was it?" Emma said, as she stepped around a table.

"You."

She stood still. The slightest quiver came to her chin. Ben walked toward her, not taking his eyes from hers. When he reached her, he caressed her cheek with the back of his hand. "Em."

"Emma!" Karl, the UPS man, called out as he entered the lobby.

"Wait!" Ben held his hand up to Karl, keeping his eyes fixed on Emma. "Just wait. I will not be interrupted. Not this time."

Karl nodded and stood fast.

Ben took Emma's hands in his, in awe of how small and soft they were against his own. He kissed them. "You told me last summer love was staring me square in the face and if I turned away from it, I'd regret it for the rest of my life." He pressed her hands. "Well, I'm not turning away. I love you, Emma. I can't imagine going another day, much less another hour, without telling you . . . without asking you . . ." Ben looked down.

Emma squeezed Ben's hands and whispered, "Go ahead, it'll be okay. I promise."

Seeing the reflection of love in Emma's eyes, Ben smiled. He bent down on one knee and looked up at her. Holding her right hand, he asked, "Emma Elizabeth Martin, will you please marry me?"

Emma held Ben's cheek. "Of course, I will. Of course.

A Good Place to Turn Around

Ben, I love you so very much."

Ben let out a relieved sigh, stood, then slipped his arms around her waist, pulling her close. "And I love you. So very much." He tilted his head down to meet Emma's, their eyes locked, then he pressed his lips into hers. In all his life, he never imagined he could experience the joy he felt in this moment as he kissed the woman he loved and who loved him back.

They separated just as Dev came running through the door of the inn. Spotting him by the fireplace with Emma, Dev yelled, "Dad, you found her! Did you ask her?"

Ben smiled at Emma. "Yeah, I did."

"What'd she say?"

Emma giggled. Ben crooked his head at Dev, "C'mere, knucklehead." Dev ran over to the two of them. "Why don't you ask her yourself?"

Dev looked up at Emma, his sapphire eyes glowing. He took her hand in his. "Miss Emma, will you marry my dad?"

Emma smiled. "Yes, I most certainly will."

Dev beamed at Emma. With tears in her eyes, Emma kissed him on the forehead. "I love you, Dev."

Through his own tears, Dev said, "I love you too, Miss—Mom."

About the Author

After spending one decade in the business world, then two more as an educator, Marilyn K Blair has left technical writing and the classroom behind to explore the world of fiction. When not writing, Marilyn enjoys her roles of wife, mother, enthusiastic Philadelphia sports fan, and devoted woman of faith. An avid RV-er along with her husband, Jim, Maine has become their favorite place to visit since honeymooning there almost forty years ago. She is a lifelong resident of Pennsylvania and currently resides in the beautiful farm country of Lancaster County.

For discussion questions, bonus chapters, photos,
and information about
the Eastport Series,
as well as other stories and devotions
visit www.kidspitpub.com.

Support your favorite authors – Tell a friend, spread the word, and leave a review.

Contact Marilyn K Blair at KidSpitPub@gmail.com

Made in the USA
Middletown, DE
08 September 2024